For Dad and Gabrielle

In memory of Fiona, and James

THE YEAR MY HAIR FELL OUT

BY

Bob Blunt

RBG

Copyright © 2014 Bob Blunt

Bob Blunt has asserted his right under the Copyright, Designs and Patents Act 1988 to be identified as the author of this work.

This book is sold subject to the condition that it shall not, by way of trade or otherwise, be lent, resold, hired out, or otherwise circulated without the publisher and author's prior consent in any form other than that in which it was originally printed and published, and in the case of reprographic production, in accordance with the terms of licenses issued by the Copyright Licensing Agency.

This is a work of faction – part fiction and part fact. Hence, the author would like to make it known that characters, events and places are the product of his imagination, but some may well be connected to what might have actually happened.

ISBN: 978-0-9925577-0-6

Typeset in Sina Nova (Hoftype), Jura (Tenbytwenty), Arca (Pintassilgo Prints) and OCR A Std (Linotype)

Typesetting, design and illustration by Ru Brown Graphic
www.rubrown.com

Author's photo by Christ Hampson, 2006

The paper used in this book is natural, renewable, recyclable and made from wood grown in forests managed under the environmental regulations of the country it was produced in.

Printed and bound in China by Our Man south of Beijing.

Acknowledgments

Thank you to Gabrielle Luoni for her never ending patience, hard work and belief in this project. I am also indebted to Ru Brown for his dedicated artwork and professional contributions, as well as Angela McKenna for her editing assistance. Also a big thank you goes out to local Australian poet and literary man Brian Purcell (Renaissance Manuscripts) for his constructive criticism and editing work. Brian you inspired me to pursue this to the bitter end when I could have easily given up. Thanks to our printers, also to Lulu Mao and Zhang Lang Fang. and those people who helped promote and launch this – The Beijinger, The Bookworm (Beijing), Korean and Australian outlets. Last of all I cannot forget the very people that I met on the way in South Korea; those that enriched my experience there – the country, fellow teachers, students, the food and of course the ducks!

PROLOGUE
late March 2004

It's barely daylight and two mallard ducks are helplessly banging their beaks against a patch of frozen ice on the Han River in downtown Seoul. As they jostle and taunt each other, their body language indicates a conversation that's best construed as vulgar. In bird talk it's as if they are telling each other to get fucked.

'Get out of my way. I was here first,' says the younger duck.
'Fuck you kiddo. This is South Korea you numbskull. Haven't you heard of filial piety? You need to show some respect,' the older duck replies.
'Fuck that shit man. It's not a cultural inquisition. I am here for the food and this isn't fish.'
'What do you mean?'
'I want that down there.'
'What down there?'
'The body, you idiot.'
'What the fuck are you talking about?'
'Look I saw a scrap here yesterday. There were these two guys in suits going hammer and tongs at each other.'
'Yeah, I am listening,'
'Well, it was ugly man. It was so vicious that I couldn't watch it anymore. I had to bail.'
'So what makes you so sure that there's a body here?'
'Sure? For fuck sakes old man, look around would you. There's blood – open your eyes for goodness sake!'
'Um yeah, so there is.'
Hacking his way through a less forgiving hole, the older duck soon confirms the younger duck's suspicions. It's as if he has won the lottery as

he duck dives and bobs freely, parading his catch; a collection of savaged body parts – first an arm, then a hand, and finally a black size 12 shoe.

'Fucking yum apart from the leather shit. I have to say you were right. Some cunt was really angry. I reckon this was a stabbing for sure. Anyway I am going down to feast on some more before anyone else comes.'

Sensing the commotion, other birds turn up and soon the river is lit in a feeding frenzy.

Welcome to ice fishing - a popular pastime on South Korea's foreboding pulse, one of its main rivers stretching all the way from North Korea. Migratory birds of all kinds whether they are ducks, eagles, swans, and herons are often here in winter, joining humans for signs of fresh meat. However recent cleanses and pollution problems have meant scanty trawls of small fish. Thus this morning it is little surprise that this raucous chorus of noise has the bird community agape. The last time any birds were truly excited was a few years back when a high flying business executive topped himself in a suicide jump off a bridge upstream from here. The reason – he'd lost face because his business had financially crashed.

1

WHAT THE *&ˆ%$#?
Seoul late February 2003

Yikes! This was definitely not in the grand master plan. It is morning peak hour, and I am in the front seat of a big shiny black van that's banked up on a traffic island on the periphery of town. We're on our way from the airport, and to my left is the driver who for some unknown reason reckons it's time for a nap.

He's blissfully snoring, this sweaty smoke stink of a man in his mid-forties, while I am wondering what the fuck I have gotten myself into – an Australian in his mid-thirties here to teach English, jetlagged, half asleep, and terrified, preparing for an entirely different existence.

Outside, the cold Korean winter air has quickly frozen the window panes of the car and there are traces of grey washy sleet on the road, with sheets of white snow on the surrounding mountains. The sky is a sharp blue colour, and apart from the countless streams of cars passing by, and the endless rows of large apartment buildings from here to Africa, there is little to capture the imagination. Seoul is yet another monster Asian city that heaves; an almost sleepless metropolis, well over the ten million mark, far more populated than my hometown Sydney, which I have just left – maybe for good.

We're heading to some place called Chuncheon, which on a good day is a three to four hour drive from Incheon International Airport. The internet has told me that it's a fairly laid back place, a resort town that feeds part of the Han River.

Half awake, I rub my eyes and try to get my head around the new surroundings. I prod the driver, his eyes squinting, half sunken into what can only be comically described as a pie-faced shape of a head. He snores happily wearing clothes that reek of a chain smoker, the nicotine emanating from his pores. From the stench I'm assuming he hasn't had a shower for a bit, whilst his ruddy red nose and face reflects the product of some kind of strong liquor, maybe *soju* which I'd been reading about on the plane.

Stirring him again, it is of little surprise that the burly man is almost fuming as he'd only just non-verbally informed me that we must sleep. Still, I can't stop scratching my head thinking what, how and why the fuck would anyone even think that now is the right time for a nap? Here in the middle of a busy Seoul expressway?

Earlier it was he and a middle-aged lady who had greeted me at the airport. They threw a placard in my face to capture my attention. It read 'MR. DON' in bold lettering with a drawing of a kangaroo in its right corner. The lady excitedly hoisted a yellow flag as I arrived. Straight away, it dawned on me that here I was in an Asian country I knew very little about, and that the first people I met were the types turned on by kangaroos, koalas, and maybe in time, Holden cars.

Now on the freeway I have little choice but to do what most Koreans practice when traffic and tiredness are an issue. Following the locals on the buses, I try to get some shut-eye, the warmth of the air conditioner brushing against me as I attempt to rest a mind that's meandering back to where I have left and forward to where I am going.

Frustrated I make a gesture with my hands but the driver mutters something in Korean, which I assume means either 'I don't understand?' or 'What the fuck are you talking about precious white boy?'

Damn bloody language, if only we could share some. If only that lady had stayed with us. After all she was doing all the pointing and controlling when they'd picked me up.

'So, what's your name then? What can I call you?' I asked her.

'I am Chae,' she replied. 'Please take a seat in our car boy.'

'It's nice to meet you, Mrs. Chae. My recruiter in Sydney told me many nice things about you.'

'Look, I speak little English and he no English!'

'Don't worry, me speak no Korean either.'

'Look boy, we go to car now ok, we go car!'

It was only when we later arrived at a large apartment complex that I felt that something was a little askew.

'Goodbye Don, I have to go up there now,' Chae said, pointing to the sky. 'You see boy I live in one of these new blocks.'

But Mrs. Chae I don't quite understand? I was told I would be collected by two people and they would drive me to Chuncheon. It says this on a piece of paper I have here. Look!'

'Mr. Don, I promise that you will be ok. You now have your driver and he is your boss. He is also your new friend. He is Mr. Lee, a good man, so please don't worry. If you have problem then here is my name card.'

However my efforts were too late. The car windows were automatically shut before I had a chance to tell her my confusion. Like it or not, I was with my new mate Mr. Lee, heading out of the capital towards our destination.

Awaking from our little cat nap, we plod along an endless expressway until we see a sign that says we're only an hour from our destination. It's only here that we are privy to any half-decent scenery. On both sides of me are mountains capped with snow, but what is really intriguing are the different kinds of birds that are chopping up a storm on frozen sections of the river. Looking happy and industrious, they are tapping their beaks against glassy crevices of ice, in the hope of finally piercing a hole and finding some fish to eat. And by their enormous presence and noise, I reckon that they are onto something.

Noticing my curiosity, the driver gives me a big warm smile, gesturing the action of fishing and banging with a hammer in the hope of a feed. I reckon that Mr. Lee has probably done some of this in his time.

I use sign language with him to indicate how beautiful the surrounds are now compared to Seoul's expressways and buildings. We both share a nervous laugh and it seems that even with our language barriers we can still get along. In fact Mr. Lee doesn't seem like such a bad bloke. Sure he looks worn and weathered, but you can see from the lines on his face that he has some character. He looks like someone who has really lived through his own share of good and bad.

Gaining some confidence, he shouts, 'Here this maybe beautiful, but Chuncheon where we go not beautiful! Chuncheon is work!'

In the backdrop the river fades, and soon we are surrounded by the Chuncheon Dam which means we are close. The large amount of water supply and varying hill slopes indicates that there's some nature to be had so I am happy. Maybe my grand master plan would finally take some semblance – a job away from the city, not cooped up in those endless apartments in and around the capital.

As we enter the western side of town, Lee stops the car in front of some shops before happily informing me that we have arrived, 'Bags now, bags we go.'

We walk to a nearby building taking a lift upstairs to Global World. It's a big office, with two levels. The classrooms are upstairs, whilst on the first floor there's an office and an internet access area. Mr. Lee calls someone to come and collect me. It is Kevin, my new flat mate and fellow teaching colleague.

2

WHY THEN?

I knew two things about South Korea before I arrived in early 2003. One, that it was a divided nation due to a war in the 1950s, and two because it had put on some major sporting events – first the Seoul Olympics in 1988, then the 2002 Soccer World Cup which was co-held with Japan.

Through school and up until now, I had never befriended any Koreans. Part of this was because I'd grown up in a fairly standard Anglo-Saxon 1970s suburban environment. Most of the people around me could barely distinguish a Korean from a Japanese or Chinese person. The majority of Anglos in Sydney's west weren't that bothered by the differences either, preferring to lump all oriental people into one basket - Asian, slope head, power point, those weirdoes who eat rice instead of bread, or the kind who'd rather spend time in a library than play cricket or rugby league with us white-bread boys.

However we suburbanites were content to eat Asian food, even if it wasn't the most authentic. It was pretty good grub to have on the weekend as a substitute for your mum's Sunday roast. Most of us lived in a comfort zone which we'd hardly admit to or talk about until we either got out of there or went to university and "grew up", so to speak. Even in my college years, I remember meeting a girl from Mackay in northern Queensland, who boasted how much she liked Chinese food and how that was her badge for being politically correct. That was in the early 90s, when being multi-cultural meant you were deemed smarter and supposedly more open-minded than your average "dumb ignorant" Anglo Aussie folk.

Essentially, life in suburbia was mostly spurred on by competitive sports, outdoor barbeques, a taste for the 'good life', and schoolyard taunts. This kind of life took on a uniformly singular shape - a bland vacuum, with little room for difference, quite different to the growing and diverse suburban Sydney environs decades on.

Throughout the 1980s and 90s, most of my peers had tried their hand overseas, working in the UK, America or Europe. If any opted to teach English as a second language, they most likely chose cash-fuelled nations like Japan, somewhere in the Middle East, or a European city like Prague or Barcelona. South Korea was definitely the unknown and it wasn't quite on the map. There was no real benchmark to judge it by, and if anything that was a good enough reason to attract me. The very idea of somewhere new meant one could be potentially surprised by it. And what better place to reinvent the wheel of life after a shitty last few years.

Yes, by the end of 2002, I was in a rut, a deep dark hole, beset by two life changing events in 2000. I had lost the two women closest to me within the space of three weeks. I had cut ties with my best friend and supposed "life" partner, and then I experienced the death of my mother. Although the former hadn't died, for me it was as if she had.

It was a bleak time and for the most I couldn't see an out. As much as I tried to lift myself out of it I mostly saw darkness wherever I looked. For a year or so I tried to digest it experiencing the stages of shock, acceptance, rage, denial, and depression. I avoided seeing her because I couldn't bare it - I was fearful, too scared of bumping into her with someone new, so instead I opted to lay low and nurture new things.

Obviously this wasn't easy to do, but at the time it was my way of grieving, and protecting who I was then. In the last year of our relationship things had slowly crumbled like a once-loved favourite novel that had been left out in a shed, exposed to the elements, lost and never to be returned. We both tried to find it, but the search had taken us further from each other. When we broke up we were no longer on the same page, not even in the same book, and the book itself, with all the loving moments we'd written on its pages had well and truly vanished. And then on the very day we decided to close that book, there was a call from my Dad telling me to come out and visit because there was something wrong with Mum.

A few days later Mum was transported to a large hospital in Sydney's west, only to find out that her reflux was actually a heart attack. Three weeks later she had passed away.

And it was a day I will never forget – because just like my beginning, we also spent an end together. The two of us in a hospital room, me holding her hand right to the last seconds. I had never experienced any kind of death before and it sure gave me a sense of empowerment that nothing had quite ever given me. Feeling her pulse, listening and monitoring it as it clocked down, it then suddenly stopped – it was like a kid turning off a light switch. On, off, on, off! Except this time the switch wouldn't go back and everything had suddenly changed.

Sure, the break up and my Mum's death were the catalysts or the vehicles for my life to take a new route. I know it may sound clichéd but those events definitely made me question my own mortality - where I was and my happiness. I'd always aligned myself with the theory that when you die, you don't take material or wealth with you to the grave or fire. Call me serious, unsettled, ants-in-my-pants, or whatever, it is a take on life that is not for everyone. However, I can say that it provided me with a fresh way of living and eking out an existence, accepted by many, held in disdain by some and envied by others.

I moved south to Melbourne in 2002, a year before coming to Korea, because I'd always wanted to, and now I could. There I did an internationally recognized teaching qualification called a CELTA (Cambridge English Language Teaching to Adults) which would set me up with a ticket for travelling and teaching English around the world. It was this very certificate that would later change the course of my life. After all, I already had a communications degree, which was partial in a vocational sense, but on another scale it was simply fodder for dinner parties and open conversations.

I had tried my hand at journalism which was all stars at first, only to find it competitive, macho, self-serving and less satisfying as time went on. Having a by-line, I got to write a little for the papers but my desire for travel had distracted me. Plus, there were better things to do in life than serve some apprenticeship to opinionated journalists who lived to write to a deadline. Those guys were mostly moody and cranky, the types with the audacity to belittle you, before they'd send you downstairs to grab some oily Malay noodle dish and a sugar-laced coke. All of this was done in the name of their own power because they didn't have to do such things – that was the rookie's job.

After returning to Sydney in the summer of 2003, I saw an advertisement in the employment pages of the Saturday paper which read, 'Teacher of English wanted, university degree required, some teaching experience preferred.' I hastily answered the ad, asking a thousand questions. I got the interview, signed some documents, and was given a free return air ticket to South Korea. It all seemed too easy to find your university degree, answer a small ad in the city paper, make a phone call, then arrange a visa, but that's what happened. Within a moment one could be away in a foreign country, soaking up a different culture.

After all people from all over the world had been doing this for years and for different reasons; most in need of change, some wanting new things, some running away from something, some seeking employment, or others hitting their 40s and 50s with grown up kids wanting to try something new. Then, of course there are those steeped in debt with the knowledge that working for a few years as a cash cow might fix everything.

A lot of people view this expatriate lifestyle as a stopgap for a better job later on, or as a travel experience. For some it can also be construed as a huge career gamble, because there are companies out there who don't take these kinds of jobs seriously. I recall a friend of mine returning to Canada after ten years teaching in a respected university in Korea, where she had worked tirelessly organizing and arranging everything - only to be told that it had little value for working in the supposed real world. One prospective employee said, 'Well my niece is doing that kind of thing now for her gap year, and soon she will return and find a real job!' And another said, 'I did that in my twenties, when I was finding myself!'

As for me in 2003 I didn't really give a fuck what other people thought, and to be honest it wasn't the lure of the dollar that interested me. I was thirty-seven and I'd never had or wanted any so called "direction" in life. To be able to jump into another place, somewhere new and somewhere unknown was most attractive.

I was ready.

3

KEVIN

Kevin is a Korean American, in his thirties, who has recently returned home in the hope of finding a better job. He has lived most of his life in Chicago Illinois, and like many Korean Americans, who return to their home roots after many years away, he has been exposed to a completely different culture and land. People like him in South Korea are better known as *gyopos*, not an endearing term by any stretch – Americanized Koreans who return home to the democratic south to try and make good, competing with the locals for jobs and hard-earned *won*, the Korean currency. This can attract some resentment with some South Koreans referring to them as bananas - yellow on the outside and white on the inside.

At the apartment after barely a minute of meeting him, he sidles up to me and in an almost speech-like manner says, 'Look I am not here because Chuncheon is a cool place ok, because it's not – it's backward here mate trust me. Most of the people here were originally farmers. Seoul is hip man and the people there have style. Here they still have old political announcements on loud speakers. They're peasants trying to be capitalists but they don't know anything about money least how to behave with it.'

He then begrudgingly tells me about his work situation, that he doesn't have any real intention to stay around for long, and that he will move back to Seoul as soon as he can, because there he knows he can be treated well.

'Listen mate, I mean Don I don't meant to disappoint you but you're in the wrong fucking place. Even the girls in Seoul are classier man. They are savvy bitches and a white boy like you would have a field day there. Here they all wanna speak English as well but as much as they want to they just can't. It's really pathetic.'

I am guessing that for Kevin a better life means more money and more possessions. However, his diatribe so far is baffling and confusing. I mean why the fuck is he telling me how I should stage my existence when he barely knows me?

'Another thing you have to remember while you're here is to always check your guard. The people aren't what they seem, particularly the ones that run the schools. Trust me there are shitty schools all over the country.'

'What do you mean?' I ask.

'Look if I was you I'd get the fuck out.'

'What?'

Answering his phone, he stalls for a minute and says, 'Hang on a second I have to answer my bitch.'

Before I'd left Sydney, I'd read about the odd notorious Korean/English institutions - private schools, that would hire a white face from another country, send them on a plane with a free air ticket, and once they got there trick them with lies and misleading information. Some stories implicated that certain bosses would fail to pay employees, or even hold them to contracts written in their own language, thus negating the English version the foreign teacher had signed.

Kevin gets off the phone and continues his tirade, 'Man, listen you've got to be careful. For all the bad gigs, there are a few that will work out. Look it isn't such a bad place otherwise I wouldn't be still here. But as you can guess I am particularly emphatic about my passions. My goal is to fight the ills of this society, these lies, this corruption, so that South Korea can become a better place.'

I am ambivalent towards this guy but I have little choice. Sure, he's not the kind of person I'd hang out with at home but right now I know no one, so I need to give him some time.

He shows me around our apartment which is big and spacious, filled with furniture, a microwave (no stove), three bedrooms, a courtyard, and enough sunlight to stop it from being relatively drab or clinical. I then agree to go down town with him later but first I need a nap.

It's mid-afternoon and I am a little groggy and disheveled. The dogs across the road have been keeping me half awake, as have the vendors with their loudspeakers, which is quite a contrast from the streets back home. After all Koreans like to be heard and who can blame them? The population exceeds forty-six million people, all in a small space of land that fits more than fifty times into Australia.

In the bathroom, I can see a face in a foreign land, with dilated pupils, jet lagged and needing rest but at the same time shell shocked - this newbie expat who is trying to come to grips with a new situation, with that helpless feeling of 'what the fuck have I done!'

Walking into the kitchen in a jet lag stupor I spot some sachets of instant coffee.

'Have as much as you like mate,' Kevin says. 'You can buy them for three hundred *won* a cup. People live on them but the stuff is shit really. Yet what can one do when there's no Starbucks in this little tin pot of a town? We don't have anything fancy here as far as coffee goes or anything else for that matter. You better get used to it mate.'

Out of the blue, he tells me that he's felt rather lonely in the last month or so, since moving here. I take another look around the place, and sensing the cold and dankness I can't blame him. Before him, a Canadian woman called Mona had lived here. She'd left a bunch of stuff behind, the most prominent being three goldfish who struggle to swim in an oversized dirty fish tank next to the big television.

For all its size, the apartment has a dark and noticeable sweet musty smell. It's a waft not helped by the landlady who lives downstairs - an elderly Korean woman, an *ajuma*, who prepares batches of pickled cabbage day and night which I learn is *kimchi*, a Korean icon that accompanies most dishes. Koreans swear by it - this pickled cabbage that can supposedly boost immune systems and fight off illness due to its garlic/ginger/chilli properties.

Over coffee I begin to dig a little into Kevin's past life in the States, learning that he once studied theology at a university in Chicago.

'After college I came here essentially to pay off my debt. Aside from the army, that's what brings a lot of us Americans here.'

'So you can make it work?' I ask.

'I never said you couldn't. Look dude you'll find three types of foreigners here - *gyopos* like me, guys in the US military and English teachers like you.'

'So how do you feel about the military?' I ask.

'I think they are ok but not everyone will agree with me. They are basically sent here on a tour of duty to protect the south from the north.'

'And us teachers?'

'Well we are mostly here with the one sole priority to make money, and recover debt, or if you're a man to land a Korean girlfriend. You have heard of the term yellow fever haven't you?'

Kevin quickly confirms to me that it means an attraction to an Asian girl. He likens it to an almost insatiable lust for something exotic, a need some people have to satisfy the unknown, or an experiment for those who aren't too good at landing girlfriends back home.

'Like I said before you'll find out about this fever. Who knows, you may get it sooner than you think mate. Just be careful, because amongst some of the student communities there will be university students or even housewives who are bound to be white stalkers. And man, who can really blame them. I'd want to get the fuck out of here if I was a Korean girl. The way their husbands and boyfriends treat them is sad man. Those guys are always having affairs with other women. It's just the done thing and society accepts it no question.'

He is almost preaching at me. Noticing my shock and slight disbelief at his last few blanket statements, Kevin then half smiles and says, 'C'mon mate, what do you think all those hotels were on the way out from Seoul? Didn't you see them? And what about the van that he picked you up him? Did you notice the black tinted windows? '

'Sure, I didn't come down in the last shower mate,' I reply.

'Ok maybe you didn't, but mind you, you need to know that the women are also starting to have their own affairs now. White chicks do what white guys do plus yellows do the same Don,' he says almost playfully.

'What are you going on about? I am lost,' I ask.

'White chicks come here and they want fun also. Plus Korean men like what they see. They are good fodder for the professors, the local doctors, dentist and businessman who want to have trophy fucks. Get my drift.'

'Yes I do now. But what do you mean by the local women?'

'They do it too. They are starting to do exactly what their naughty husbands are doing. I've even done a few.'

I shudder, remembering the many right-minded friends I had just said my goodbyes to, as I listen to this theology major who is happy to pontificate and stumble through a series of gross generalizations.

Hitting the streets we approach the downtown area which is *Myong Dong*, the central part of Chuncheon city. I cannot stop noticing the masses of people around, most either shopping or lazing about by the side of the road. We quickly enter an underground mall that spans for what seems like a kilometer, with shops selling anything from oversized underwear to cheap pirated DVD/CD copies of Radiohead and Mission Impossible.

When we return outside Kevin is happy to maintain his social commentary, this time shouting obscenities at the local drivers, "Fuck! What the fuck are you doing? Damn, you motherfucker you brushed my arm.'

After a tirade of abuse, he turns his rant towards me, 'See what I mean, here's some selfish cunt who thinks he has the right to the road. But that's what they do here. Pedestrians like us are second rate. I mean you would get killed for honking a horn like that in Chicago. Plus he hit me! The stupid idiot! Fuck him!'

He yells out verbal abuse in Korean at the driver who doesn't budge. This theology major isn't shy in telling the locals how he feels. He then looks at me and shouts again, 'You see these fucking guys are stuck in the dark ages and they don't care. Like I said Don, life in Seoul is where it is at in Korea. They have more style and they don't need to try. The thing is that here they want to be in touch with America but it's bullshit man. People in Seoul show off their assets and have bravado man. They get away with it, but some of the ones here are just clueless peasants.'

Avoiding any real confrontation, we then arrive in the centre of town before turning into another alleyway that's lined with chicken restaurants. The local delicacy is Chuncheon *dak-galbi* which is famous all over the peninsula. Word out on the street is that this the best place to find it.

Doting middle-aged waitresses adorn us in red and white checked aprons whilst chicken doused in fiery chilli paste is cooked in front of us. It's not until the first piece of spicy chicken hits my tongue that I lunge for my beer, a mid strength Hite to tone down the taste.

Plucking up the courage I say, 'Kevin we need to talk. I am a bit worried about something you earlier alluded to. You see before I took this job I did a lot of my own research. I'd heard stories about places, you know bad stories, and I don't want the same thing to happen to me.'

Kevin gives me a baffled look, 'Are you that naive man? You can do as much homework as you like but in this country there's always the possibility that you will be working for a crook. Sadly our company Global World doesn't have a great track record.'

'I know, I'm not stupid, but I gathered that those kind of things happened in another part of the country. Wasn't that down south? I mean, the person who got me the job here knows her shit man. She wouldn't just send me to a dodgy school. I mean she is responsible for camps in this province. Surely she has a reputation to uphold?'

'Do you want to know why Mona the last chick left?'

'How the hell would I know?'

'Well, the real reason was that our *soju*-head-of-a-boss, the one that drove you from the airport today, refused to pay her out.'

I start choking on the spicy chook whilst my head starts to throb from Kevin's voice which by this point is relentless.

He starts again, 'So now why in the world would he want to replace one foreign teacher with another, when they still had trouble reaching the last teacher's three monthly payments? Let me tell you something. Our boss was originally a driver for one of their chains down south and because of his hard work he was offered a managerial role for the Chuncheon office. That's how things work here.'

I am in shock. Who really were those two people who came to the airport? Again I listen attentively.

'For fuck sake Don, the guy can't even speak English, so how can he deal effectively with his teachers. Plus if his sole work experience is driving, no one can imagine that he could have any managerial skills, now could they? But Don my new friend, what you have to remember is that this is South Korea, and here they do things differently to what we are used to in our own countries. Private businesses here are littered with these ageing men who could never get ahead in their twenties and thirties. Now they are trying to make money be it with little or next to no acumen.'

It's as if Kevin has had this bottled up inside him for some time and now he can really let it rip.

He continues, 'In Korea Don, if you have the cash, or have married into a rich family, you will always have truckloads of power. Money means you can do anything, whether it be getting that black fuck truck with tinted windows, purchasing a business on credit, or hiring young graduates at a cheap cost. Now this kind of cunt we have, well he sits in a big black chair happily looking down on this small town. He is rubbing his hands with glee as he makes a quick buck that he will spend on god knows what. All at the expense of us so that is why he is a cunt! And Don you know what? It has to stop!'

'That sounds terrible Kevin. I can't imagine what it is like,' I reply with some sympathy.

'Look, I am not saying this to scare you. I just want you to listen to what I have to say because everyone else is passive and it shits me. I have not been paid in months, and there are others. First it was the office staff, then the Japanese teachers didn't get paid, and now it's the rest of us foreign teachers. You might as well call us all volunteers. It disgusts me!'

Kevin then stares directly into my eyes and tells me not to expect my first salary on time, and that I would be better off looking at another country, like Japan, for real work, 'They are honest there I have heard, but sadly that is not always the case here in Korea.'

I'm spitting chips at such news. It's not the best kind of start, but what I have to remember this is all coming from Kevin, someone who could have different interests at heart. However the negative stereotypes are of concern. He seems a real head fuck. I mean who knows what to really think? Maybe he sees me as a competitor? Plus, I don't want to judge things too quickly either. Maybe it's best to breathe now, observe, try and listen to other people, before making some kind of concrete decision to go or not. After all I didn't travel all this way just to turn back home or go to a new country – I've only just got off the plane.

On the walk back to the apartment Kevin shows me Daphne's place, another colleague who comes from New Zealand. He is quick to tell me that she is looking forward to meeting me tomorrow night when she gets back from her hiking weekend in Seoul. I'm thinking the same, as Kiwis and Australians are often the best mates overseas, particularly when they don't have a sporting field or a ditch in between them.

READING BETWEEN THE LINES

If Japan was the lure for so many foreigners to relocate and teach English in the 1980s and 90s, then South Korea was definitely carrying the flag into the new millennium and beyond. The bubble that burst in Japan in the 1990s resulted in a downward economic crisis, with many foreigners pursuing other alternatives to ply their teaching trade. Many Japanese gave up on learning English and the belief that it would provide them with a better job and economic success was quickly dispelled in troubled times.

South Korea on the other hand, apart from its own national economic crisis in 1997, was on an upward spiral. This meant there was an insatiable demand for learning English, particularly of the communicative teaching method with the preference being to learn via teachers who came from native-speaking backgrounds. So, if you were from the USA, Canada, the UK, the Antipodes or South Africa, you could be pretty much guaranteed work. Most South Koreans believe that English is the answer for a country seen by many as being too long in the background, often caught in the fire, literally, between the much bigger China, and the more tech-savvy Japan.

The sheer lure for hard cold cash, money for jam some have called it continues to transport native-speaking English teachers to South Korea. A lot of them choose to relocate in search of a relatively comfortable anonymous life, with the main drive to make money fast – to save more than they ever could back at home, and / or to recover large sums of college and tax debt. I am probably one of all three.

While living in Sydney and Melbourne, I had never saved much money. I was often in debt taking loans from the government, only to find that years later they had accrued healthy sums of interest. My disdain for dealing with paperwork has always been a huge block for me. The whole regime of boss, order, ego, rewards, and people climbing up trees for better status had exhausted me.

Daphne, on the other hand, represented another kind of foreigner living and working abroad. Hailing from Wellington, by the time she'd arrived in South Korea, she was in her early fifties. She had her own story, a mother with kids, married for a good part of her life, meeting her husband when she was in her late teens. Like so many of her generation, they stuck together through the good and the bad, then got to a crossroad and bang, suddenly change was inevitable as both found they were in a relationship that had reached an end.

As I tentatively ask her about the rumors that the business is failing, she is quick to launch into a tirade of anger a little like Kevin. She also can't believe that they would have the balls to provide a return air fare to recruit a new teacher all the way from Australia, given their current financial situation.

'Man, you don't want to know. Mona, a good mate of mine got totally screwed. Anyway she'll be back from her holiday in Vietnam soon. I really hope this time she gets into the ring with that dumb boss of ours.'

'That bad is he?' I ask nervously.

'Look,' says Daphne, 'I haven't been paid for February and I am pissed. The writing is on the wall here, and Don I have to say that I am not surprised. Let me offer you a stern warning - it's not just Global World. It's the same for a lot of these private businesses. The contract means shit in Korea. It means absolute dog shit. There are places that don't care about foreigners. Some of us are hired to be performing seals by these businesses. There's not a lot of goodwill I am sorry to say and I must say many places are just plain shoddy. On the other hand, university jobs are a little different. I reckon you should get out before things turn to shit – what I mean is that this is fucking dire to excuse my French.'

The next morning I make my way cautiously down the iced steps of our apartment. I can still sense the overriding waft of freshly made *kimchi* from my landlady's flat, and the barking dogs. Five minutes later I am at the office being greeted by one of the office workers.

'Hi teacher, I am So-Hee, I am a native of here and I am your secretary. Please welcome Mr. Don Laridis, to your first Global World English class. Can you please sign this paper and then take the door to the right. And Mr. Don you will need to do this every day that you come in to teach.'

I smile and sign before quickly noticing that up close our secretary has soft doll like features, some tarnished by the odd bump and crack, which are most likely from some hard-earned cosmetic surgery. She graciously nods and bows adding, 'Our lovely country Korea students are looking forward to meeting you. Also I must say that Mr. Don I am sorry for my English, for it is a little poor.'

I can't help noticing her gracefulness. Here is a twenty something woman doing her job for the company, giving me utmost respect, and making my first experience at least cordial.

As I pass the front counter I notice the head honcho, Mr. Lee. He is standing in his office smoking a cigarette and pondering.

He doesn't notice me and it's only just before I enter the door of my classroom, that I hear his voice barking at So-Hee with army like instructions, 'So-Hee quickly to the room now. So-Hee, *ba-li, ba-li*,' meaning come quickly in Korean.

I can't imagine a male boss shouting at a high-powered suited up female back at home. I grimace, move ahead, and open the door to my new class.

There are six students, and they all give me an almost raucous reception. After the clapping they attentively sit down, all hushed and modest as fuck, while I stand embarrassed and elated, preparing my first words; 'Hello Korea. It's so nice to meet you!'

In an almost copybook like manner they reply, 'Hello teacher. It's nice to meet you too!'

I reply 'How are you?'

The students reply knowingly, 'Fine thank you and you?'

I then tell the class my name, and not long later they ask me where I am from. Most are familiar with the two big Australian icons, the Sydney Opera House and the Harbor Bridge. And of course the kangaroo and koala, most believing that they live in our backyards. They are however horrified to learn that people could even consider eating a cute bouncing marsupial even after I tell them that they are herbivores, and that their meat is considered to be of high quality consumption. I can't help thinking how this is quite ironic given that I am in a country where some are proud to breed dogs for eating.

Wanting to know a little about my students, I ask them all to stand up and introduce themselves. This is systematically done in rapid-fire rote learnt fashion.

One young boy who looks like he plucks his eyebrows; and has probably spent more time than he needs to playing with hair gel trying to get that Beckham 90s look, replies eagerly, 'My name is Hyun Seok, but you can call me Beckham. I am a native citizen of here so welcome to my hometown. Of course sir, I like Manchester United, and my hobby is playing computer games.'

A girl called Jin-Hyun then introduces herself, 'Teacher I am just twenty-one years old and I know I am a little fat, which is why I don't have a boyfriend. I am a huge fan of Mariah Carey, and teacher I do know of Australia your country. I love your actress. I think maybe she is Nee Cold Kiddo Man.'

I try my best to hold back any laughter. By the time I have gone around the circle it has dawned on me that most of class one, who I will see at 6:30 every morning, five days a week, aren't overly confident with their oral English skills.

Daphne mentioned that the local teachers basically train them by parroting words, then asking them to recite the vocabulary ad nauseam. There doesn't seem much to go on as far as conversation goes so it is going to be my challenge to try and change that.

The second class at 8 a.m. is small with just two students, one the boss of the local Korean Air branch, Mr. Park, while the other student is his willing and able and willing secretary So Hyun. They both make it clear to me that they are there to only learn Business English.

'In Korea we believe teacher, that if we can possess the tool of English it will help us in gaining a promotion as well as prestige. We are a strong country as you know. Last year we had the World Cup. Please don't forget this teacher,' says Mr. Park.

'I won't, I promise. In fact I know very little about your country,' I reply.

'No one did before last year. Most just knew we were divided from the north. People still don't take us seriously,' he adds. 'Anyway let's not be negative. Please take this,' he says as he hands over his name card.

'Why thank you Mr. Park.'

'Mr. Don, I hope you never forget me when you ever need my help, or someone to play with. I am always here and I know a lot of people.'

So Hyun passes it to me on his behalf and I quickly glance at it, remembering that in my travel book it said that one of the customs here is to pause and take a second look at name cards, just long enough to be considered polite. The rule is not to grab it and scrunch it up in your pocket, and more often than not it is important to bow in return as a form of respect.

South Korea is a country full of social graces, airs and customs which I'm not quite used to back home. In Australia, a thirty-seven year old generally speaks to an eighty year old man like his mate, sometimes taking the piss out of him in that larrikin Australian manner. Respect here is far less obvious and hidden. Here bowing is probably the first and foremost custom, stemming from the Confucius principles of having respect for your elders.

Before leaving, Mr. Park enthusiastically adds that we should go to dinner soon, 'I will treat you to some delicious Korean food, and we drink together, ok!'

Even though I feel that this is a little forced of him, I know that in the long term Mr. Park could work out to be a good contact. He looks immaculate in his pin-striped company suit and slicked jet black hair. Like me he also has a penchant for golf, informing me that in Korea it isn't cheap for a round. The average cost is about 100 US dollars or more. This makes sense given the lack of land mass and the seething numbers of people here.

'Great Mr. Don, we can go and play some day. I treat golf like my English. It's something I really want to make perfect.'

At Park's side sits So Hyun, who's saying very little, just smiling and nodding her head every time her boss speaks. I can't help thinking that she probably lights his cigarettes and shines his shoes when the occasion is right, and god knows what else. Within such subservience, there is a glittering sparkle in her eyes – almost like a calm halo. She possesses the same kind of gracefulness that So-Hee had earlier shown; contained but believable.

In the first class, one of my students, Jeong Hwa had mentioned that her dream was to be an air hostess. In Korea this is a position of status and glamour for many a university student, yet back in Australia an airline attendant was probably cool back in the 1970s when I was growing up. These days it doesn't seem as cool anymore.

However ironically for So Hyun, landing a job working for Korean Air, is the start of a career of kowtowing, long office hours, liquid lunches with her bosses, cosmetic renewal, and being paid only after and never before her boss. Either way she is content, humble, and selfless in her approach which is admirable. Pleased to finish, Mr. Park slaps me heavily on the shoulder and offers some reassurance for a good job done.

'Mr. Don from Australia, I look forward to being your friend, and I am expecting that we will eat, drink and play golf together!'

I'm happy knowing that things have gone smoothly so far on the first day on the job. I can see Mr. Park and So Hyun outside talking to Mr. Lee and just through their body language it appears that they are praising me for my class.

As he leaves the building, Mr. Park gives me a big wave, while So Hyun graciously bows. On the stairwell I meet a parade of well-heeled Korean woman, aged maybe in their late 20s. They all smile and giggle, covering their mouths with their hands as they excuse themselves on their way up the stairs. It's my next class - the housewives.

Bumping into Daphne outside she asks me how the day is treating me. She's happy enough, a contrast from last night when she was busy complaining about the business.

She says, 'You know, I am sorry Don that I was angry last night. It's not fair on you particularly since you have only just started here so I want to say sorry. It's just that the last few weeks have really been getting to me. I am going to ask Mr. Lee very soon when we will get paid next. Sure, I have money to survive for now, and the students are lovely, but it just isn't fair. I can't take the lack of payment thing too much longer.'

'And fair enough Daphne. You have every right as an employee. Don't get me wrong either, I understand. I just need to sort my own surroundings out. I didn't travel here to be a volunteer either you know.'

'Don I want you to remember that in Korea what seems to be on the surface is not always what it really is. These people are champions at using their face as a shield. It's a culture propped up by so many social graces that you will feel wanted and respected, but a lot of the time there is an underlying message. Simply speaking, Don, please mate, whatever happens, just take care hey,'

Before the bell, two more new teachers introduce themselves to me. At first I mistake them for Korean students, so I'm kind of embarrassed when they introduce themselves to me as Yoko and Yuri from Japan. Kevin mentioned yesterday that there were two Japanese teachers who hadn't been paid for quite some time. They also graciously bow and shake my hand, smiling and giggling while constantly apologizing for their little English.

There is much to be said about the cultural similarities of Korea and Japan. Recently an increasing number of Japanese people have found the lifestyle in South Korea to their liking too, and one of the big reasons has been the South Korean TV drama series Winter Sonata which was a huge hit in Japan in 2002. Despite Yuri and Yoko's smiles and enthusiasm, I can't imagine that they could have ever envisaged that life here could possibly turn into a pile of shit far deeper than what could happen in any TV drama.

All four of us go back upstairs ready for our final class of the morning. Ahead, the Japanese teachers pass Mr. Lee's office, bowing to him, despite their penniless situation.

It is then that Daphne points out that, 'What you have to remember is that some people from this part of the world don't question so much like we do in the west. They're not so upfront. Basically if the shit hits the fan they tend to endure it much more than some of us hot-headed westerners. So you cannot really imagine what they are feeling deep down.'

She then looks me directly in the eyes, and whispers four words that for a moment rock my world, 'four months no pay.'

When I approach the next class the students are already in a state of delirium. It's the very same dozen women that I had passed on the stairs who welcome me with big smiles and giggles. I ask them what is so funny but they are all speechless, most of them again covering their mouths with their hands in embarrassment. We get through some formalities, realizing that they are mostly housewives who want to practice their English in their spare time.

Out of the blue Hyun-Ju tells me how cute I am, and how much she likes my laugh, 'You seem so happy Mr. Don. We love you when you show us your laugh. You must do it again for us Mr. Don. Please do it?'

'Sorry but I'm not your personal robot. I am your teacher I believe.'

Another student Eun-Ju who is not a housewife, but a recent university graduate adds, 'I want to say dear teacher that you have a cute face, and interesting eyelashes too, but you have one misfortune.'

'And what might that be Eun-Ju?' I ask.

'Well your hair is slowly getting lost, and teacher you have to watch it because you are a little fat.'

I immediately stop her as I am not sure how I am supposed to handle such a comment. Sure my weight is one part of me, but it seems that Eun-Ju has a different perspective on the word fat. In the most polite way possible I try to tell her that.

'The word fat back home in Australia sometimes means that you are putting someone down.'

'I don't quite get what you mean by down?' she replies.

'Ok, let's say that you came to my hometown Sydney, and you told someone that they were fat. There's a good chance you might get a broken nose or a fat lip!'

'Oh, I think our culture different Mr. Don.'

'Ok, Eun-Ju. I think it's time that we move on then.'

During a short break I quickly ask Daphne about it, knowing that she has had much more experience here than me.

'Don't let it worry you too much, mate. Mona our last teacher from Canada was always subjected to this too. What we foreigners have to remember is that the word fat here has a host of different connotations compared to back home. Simply speaking they don't perceive the term the same way we do. For a lot of them, if a person is a little fat, it's probably got something to do with how much money you have and that you can afford to eat that much food.'

Still, I am not so won over and it has obviously struck a nerve. For one, I can't help thinking that the use of the word also implies that I need to do more exercise, or it's a slight on how lazy I am, or even how much I don't like sport, or maybe how much I like my food and beer. My own paranoia goes as far as thinking that the student perceives me as having a poor diet, that I eat too fast, and that I cannot control my eating habits. I know that in some ways she could well be right, but it's a comment that I find hard to let go.

Resuming after the short break, I reiterate to the class that fat is a negative term in this classroom, and is one that should be avoided.

'Sorry to get so angry before, but this is a cultural difference I think. I just want to remind you that if you're meeting a foreigner for the first time it is better not to use this word. Where I come from it is best not to describe someone so openly by their build. Even thin people don't like to be reminded of their lack of shape. You might be talking to someone who is sick or doesn't like eating. These are considered to be personal comments.'

The class is hushed for a moment, particularly Eun-Ju who wasn't meaning to offend. They are shocked by my forcefulness and emotion, but it doesn't last long. A minute later the cultural inquisition starts yet again with a barrage of questions generally perceived to be quite the norm in this part of the world. I am thinking I bet that the first one will be about age, the next about marriage, then children, then weight, et cetera. Am I right? Yes, believe it or not that is what follows. These questions, considered to be culturally inappropriate in the west upon first meeting, are considered differently here in Korea. For example, as far as language is concerned, age has a lot to do with the Confucian values of respect and social status. The older you are the more respect the more you respect you have and in some places the deeper the bow. Chuncheon is very much a town with a long history, based a lot on Confucian morals of discipline, respect and knowledge.

Hyun Sook, who is married, tells me that the teacher is like a parent in Korea, 'Mr. Don we want to get to know you. We all need to feel comfortable so please Mr. Don our questions aren't meant to hurt.'

'Sure, but you also have to understand that for me the teacher, it's a question of cultural difference. I mean, if you Koreans are so much into respect let's not be so forward. After all it's our first lesson.'

I then tell them that I am a hundred years old, that I was married, but it finished because my wife slept around, and that we never had children because we couldn't as I was shooting blanks. I also tell them that an English teacher earns so much money, that half the time they don't know what to do with it. They like my sense of humor, even if they cannot fully comprehend me. They are intrigued that someone from where they would perceive to be a dream-like country, could possibly leave everything to come miles away, to the other side of the world and teach English to a bunch of strangers. They want to know why, and they won't stop. They are curious, and it almost seems that aside from cultural formalities, they are a culture that's not into wasting time. When class ends I let them out of the room, shaking their hands individually and wishing them all a nice day.

On my way out I can't help but notice Daphne is sitting in Mr. Lee's office looking somewhat distressed. Instead of caring and listening to her, he is content to sit, smile, smoke, and only half take in the conversation that Kevin is translating back to him. Daphne's face on the other hand is a fierce red shouting 'why, why not's' at him with gestures that would gain responses from most people. However they're falling on deaf ears and it seems the more Kevin tries to calm her down the more fed up Daphne gets.

I bump into the two of them as they come out and both are somewhat dejected by the lack of response they received. Later at a noodle restaurant across the road Daphne almost cries in frustration as she bangs her fist on our table, explaining to me that the pay for February and March is going to be late.

Kevin knows the drill and is embarrassed. He says very little. He also hasn't been paid and feels stuck in the middle of everything – one as he is Korean and is culturally never supposed to question his boss and the other because he can see and can empathize with Daphne's current rage.

'C'mon guys we need to hold on to some trust. I know that this may seem very hard for the two of you, and man it does suck, but I can't see why he would fork out money for a new teacher like you Don and not find a way to pay us as well. Daphne you have to be patient when you are in his office talking about money. You need to calm down and re-think how you can deal with the situation. Getting angry will get you nowhere in Korea.'

Daphne looks directly at me, 'You know what gets me is that when we are talking money with him, he just stands there, puffing away and smiling!'

5

A DAY IN THE LIFE

Kim A-reum is an eighteen year old Korean teenager growing up in a society where a perfect education record is often the key to making it in life. It's all about being a someone, having prestige and being savvy. Her parents are Seoul people that have made it good, thanks to the car manufacturing boom of the late 1980s. Her dad is top dog for one of the many Hyundai Motor branches in Seoul while her mum is a local hair salon owner. She rarely sees either of them.

A typical day for her mirrors the life of a senior high school student, which is best perceived as a daily struggle immersed in study with little time to eat. She has constant headaches, complains of tiredness, and spends most of her time in a classroom or in a cram school van.

Up at 6 a.m. she leaves home an hour later, arriving at school half an hour early to review last night's homework. Then when the bell goes at 8:50 a.m., she is expected to be saddled up in her chair for the first of her six classes that will take her through to 3:30 p.m. At 5:30 p.m. she has what is called compulsory study time, where a teacher walks around a classroom making sure that each student is reviewing everything they have learnt that day. For dinner these very same teenagers race downtown to a cheap takeaway Korean for instant noodles, or if they can afford it some western KFC or Burger King.

Fast food does a big trade here, hence the rising levels of obesity in some young Korean kids. When dinner is over the students are back at it, returning to school for more study, even until nine or ten at night, before heading home for some more homework. The Korean university entrance examination, which she will sit this year, is infamous not only for its toughness and competition, but also in some cases for bribery and cheating. Some candidates even commit suicide because the stress is too much.

Mothers and fathers will often visit temples on the day of the exams to pray for the success of their child.

Hence, it is of little surprise that Kim A-reum is somewhat delirious and tired when she walks into my first evening class. She is one of two students enrolled in this class. Her classmate is Park Min-seok, a middle school student who is absent.

'You sure you want class? You look exhausted,' I comment.

'Tired? I'm always tired but teacher trust me I'm one of the lucky ones. My parents pay for this; just so I can avoid school and doing homework.'

'Why?'

'I came here because I can learn from you. You're a foreigner and I think you guys are cool.'

Attending cram schools at night helps ease her study burden. After my class, she will head to a math cram school, another institute *hagwon* class, which fortunately is on the seventh floor of this building. Then at 9:30 p.m. she will be whisked back home in a mini-van.

'In Korea teacher let me tell you one thing. Kids like me have no choice but to study. We go to school seven days a week when we are in our high school years. Middle school kids go six days a week, while elementary school kids only have to attend five days a week and that sadly is the Korean education system.'

'You ought to study in Australia. It's a lot easier.'

'Man, if I had the chance I wouldn't be here. Mr. Don, remember we don't want to be peasants anymore. We want to succeed. I want to go to Seoul University where my father went, and after that my dream is to study abroad in the States at Yale. After that, I want to be married at around twenty-seven to a man who will love me dearly, and give me one or maybe two children. At least we can do that here. I have heard that in China you can only have one!'

Her English ability borders on being potentially bilingual. She tells me how she spent some of her junior high school years in Boston, and even though she hated being away from her Korean friends and her family, the experience was good for her because her English rapidly improved. Her enthusiasm to learn makes it an easy one-on-one lesson for me. Although, she might be tired and delirious, her ability to converse freely is far more advanced than any of the other students I have met today.

She opens up saying that she loves talking to me. It's like she feels happier in her second language because she can speak in ways that she can't otherwise. It's as if she has removed herself temporarily from the society that she was born into.

When the 7:50 p.m. bell goes, she stands up and bows gracefully to me as a way of saying thanks for our first lesson. She then leaves reluctantly for her math cram class.

By the time the last class of the day comes around, I have a renewed kind of energy. This isn't a bad thing either, because on my attendance sheet I can see the names and ages of at least 20 students. The majority of them are from the three surrounding universities, as well as some office workers.

Many of the next class are students that have come from other parts of the country to study here and most of them are particularly savvy. Lee Ji-hyun for example is a twenty-five year old art graduate from a Seoul university. She has returned to Chuncheon, to pursue further study in the hope of opening an art gallery one day. She is keen to learn more English from a foreigner, because like A-reum, she feels happier speaking in her second language than her native one.

'I love English and when I lived with an Australian family, we ate vegemite on toast for breakfast, had Sunday roasts, and we even drank beer all night. I was able to play, I mean hang out in a place like Cairns and make friends with backpackers from all over the world.'

'Did you go to Sydney? I am from there.'

'So why you come here then? How can you come from such a beautiful place to Chuncheon?' she asks.

'Well Chuncheon doesn't look that bad,' I reply before adding, 'I came here to teach English to people like you and to have a new adventure.'

'I got to go to Sydney for three days, and I saw the Rocks, the Harbour Bridge, and your beautiful beaches, Bondi and Manly. Your country is beautiful I think. So for that reason I envy you.'

Ji-hyun is cool and chic. She looks very much like an artist, and thinks like one. She is open and I can see on first meeting that there could be more interesting chatter even outside of class.

Mari is another student who seems switched on. She is twenty-seven years old, and has recently got engaged to be married in the fall. Upon hearing this, her peers all clap and wish her well. Getting married by the age of twenty-seven seems to be the norm for modern day female Koreans. Mari modestly accepts the praise of her classmates.

'At twenty-five most ladies in Korea who haven't got a boyfriend, are considered to be dead. Thanks to the help of my parents, I have recently found Mr. Right, a young businessman from Seoul,' she explains.

'You are so lucky,' says Ji-hyun. 'I never have such luck. Anyway I want to marry a foreigner. It makes more sense really.'

I ask, 'It must have been hard for you Mari?'

'It was boring sometimes. I mean, every Sunday for six months I had to take the train into Seoul and meet different guys for coffee. I couldn't stand it a lot of the time. They would smoke in front of me and tell me how badly they wanted to find a wife. It took me such a long a time to meet the right one. Of course my face didn't help.'

'What do you mean your face? 'I ask.

'Well, the guys that didn't like me would smoke directly in my face and laugh at my acne and call me pizza face. Oh, it was so terrible.'

'Well, I'm glad you have found someone good to marry. Let's clap again for Mari everyone,' exclaims Ji-hyun.

I leave the class happily knowing that I will see my students again tomorrow for some new stories and laughter. Harking back to my last job at home, I can't remember ever having such a feeling. I always seemed to be dealing with my boss's own indifferences and erratic moods, but here it is a world away and I am pretty much my own leader. I can set the mood of the class, and not rely on being told what to do or be criticized by someone else.

6

AN OVERSEAS BUS STOP

On Friday, Daphne mentions to me in passing that she is feeling like a beer tonight and invites me to join her. My classes are running smoothly and the students seem interested, particularly Hyun Seok, one of the boys from my early morning class.

He tells me that he finds it hard to engage with a foreigner on the street because he simply doesn't know what to say to them, 'I have no idea teacher. My mind fails me and it's so awful.'

'It's normal, don't be so hard on yourself,' I reply.

'A lot of the time people just run away from me. It destroys my confidence. Teacher, my English is so poor that I can't find the right words to say. Please what can I do? I'd love to come out with you. I need to practice my oral English.'

'We all need to practice our language skills but you also have to be aware of the time you see people. You have to remember that it's not that foreigners don't want to engage with you. You need to know how to read the situation, like when it's a good time to talk. People have a right to relax my friend and that sometimes means they need to be left alone.'

Hyun Seok is a college boy and is very much an English keener - a sponge for language and desperate to put his learning into practice. I can't help feeling for students like him who actually have the balls to want to engage with the language they are learning.

Daphne doesn't mix with students outside class. She's been an English teacher for some time now, teaching mixed classes back home, in middle and high schools in China, and now mostly adults in South Korea. Her view is that students are not our responsibility; that we are there only to teach them inside the classroom and that once class is over it's our job to separate our personal lives from them.

'It may sound a little callous and cold, but once I leave these classrooms I don't want to spoon-feed students in my downtime. It might be boring or safe, but I warn you Don, never tell your students where you are going after class. These students of ours are very immature.'

Catching a cab we head to the back gate of the central university which is lit up with neon lights and cheap eats.

Daphne then informs me of the bar situation, 'Basically it is either Jacks or Hells Bells. That is it as far as bars go for western expats – the teachers and military hang out at both, and sometimes you will find some of our students, so like I said be warned because tonight is a Friday so the bars will be packed.'

We arrive at Jacks first, a large horseshoe shaped bar which is served by about a dozen university students, all in khaki clad uniform, and all on a minimum wage of 2,000 *won* an hour which is less than two Australian dollars. The waitresses are dolled up to the eyes in makeup, and are serving giant mugs of beer that seem almost as tall as they are. The customers are a diverse bunch of your Friday night regulars mixed in with university students. In the background there is some bad American rap, and we can both sense that the US military presence is near.

'Can't help thinking how cheesy this is,' I tell Daphne.

'Well we're not in downtown Melbourne or Sydney,' she quickly replies.

We find a table that is near a Korean birthday celebration. The birthday girl is caked in cream as her guests are happily plied with drinks. They look like lightweights who are probably on their first and only beer. They all stand taking turns to skull, most of their faces alit with that red Asian glow that stems from genetic makeup. Some of the girls take shots of *soju*, most trying hard not to vomit. It isn't that different to student culture back home, although gathering by the games that they are playing, and their ability to consume, the maturity levels do differ. They notice us and call out but we project a disinterested response. So Daphne grabs my hand and we quickly find a nearby table away from their view.

Sitting near us are two foreigners, so I take the opportunity to introduce myself, 'Hi, I'm Don from Sydney, Australia. It's nice to meet you two guys.'

'Mike from Manitoba.'

'Mike from Arizona.'

'Ah, the two Mikes eh, well that makes things easy.'

'Don't push it buddy. He's American and I am Canadian,' confirms Manitoba Mike.

'Just call me Arizona Mike. That'll do.'

'What do you guys do here?' I ask.

'There's only two things people do here bud and we don't do the military,' says Manitoba Mike.

'No, fucking way,' replies Arizona Mike.

'You're teachers like me then.'

When they hear that I am working for Global World they look at me knowingly. It's obvious that word has quickly gotten around, and sensing my slight discomfort, Manitoba Mike in a rather loud booming voice asks, 'So what's up Don?'

'What me? Nothing's up mate! I am fine,' I respond defensively.

Both laugh out loud, as it seems I have missed the joke.

'I was just asking how you are Don?'

'Please take no offence Don. We are great ones for using 'what's up' when we meet someone for the first time.'

'Ah, I should have known better with all those dumb rap songs and that bad basketball lingo. Sorry mate I thought you meant that something was wrong.'

'We read you Don. We have a lot of that crap in Phoenix where I come from as well. That's why I am here except my gripe is that I wish people would take me a little more seriously from time to time.'

'What do you mean? I don't get it?' I ask.

'Well, I've got yellow skin but I wasn't born here. The students here pay big money to go to English academies and they strictly want teachers that are white and native-speaking.'

'Do you know a guy called Kevin from Chicago?' I ask.

'Yes, we all know Kevin and I'd watch out for him if we were you,' he replies.

'What do you mean?'

'Well, I'll let you be the judge on that Don. Better to keep my mouth shut on that one.'

The bar starts to fill slowly and it's not long before more teachers arrive, the next being some Brits.

Daphne introduces them as Jack and Carol from England and Gordon from Scotland.

'We have heard about you Don. I hope everything's ok,' says Carol.

'Sure, why wouldn't it be? And guess what, we're here to have some drinks, so sit down and grab one.'

Carol and Jack remind me of two academics who have a leaning to post punk. They were most likely raised on The Jam and the Damned, who are probably around my age. Gordon looks like their brash son, straight out of high school with an early 80s new romantic styled hair cut. He works for a private academy teaching kids.

Jack informs me that a university job is the best sought gig in town - no split shifts, four contact hours a day, ten week vacations, all paid summer and winter, 'It's a great job Don. A bit restrictive and all, but who cares. We get the same holidays as professors back home and our students are great, as you probably already know.'

'So how long have you been doing it for Jack?' I ask.

'About three years now. When we got here we were in an academy so we know what that is like.'

'It's a lottery ticket that's for sure,' says Carol.

Both proceed to tell me how they'd met in their university days in Norfolk, and that they got married last year, after being together for eleven years. They seem interesting – Jack with that British humor which I have come to love over the years, and Carol who has a great shrieking laugh on her. We hit it off immediately, and although they know about my situation we make a decision not to talk about work.

'There is nothing more boring than a bunch of expats going on and on about their jobs,' Jack says.

'Hear, hear. We're here to drink,' I reply.

A few tables away, the much younger Mikes are joined by Gordon. The three of them seem quite happy to practice their Korean with the bar staff, who are lapping up their attention.

One of the things about teaching abroad is that age isn't such a big deal. This kind of work attracts people from all walks of life at different stages of their lives. Gordon has only just finished a degree in archaeology in Edinburgh, but because he can't find a job, he has come to Korea to chase good money and have some post-college fun.

Not long later his girlfriend, Mi-ra, walks in and proceeds to plant herself on his lap. They converse in Korean as her English isn't up to scratch. Gordon makes a real effort to speak in her local tongue. He tells me later that if I want to pull a local it's all about getting their number and sending them text messages.

'If you can show them that you have a little handle on the local tongue, and then extend part of your wage with a meal and a movie you're then on the way to doing ok,' he advises.

'Sounds interesting,' I reply, only half interested.

He then adds, 'Mate, if she asks you back to her folk's house then you know it's serious. And if she is happy to go to a DVD room well then she is asking for a little more than a rose.'

Gordon is all stars, cocky, young, and upfront - a boy out of university here for a good time, if not a long time. He tells me that he is happy teaching kids, and that his boss looks after him like only his mother would.

'She always pays me on time and I can say that after one year now I'm saving more than a thousand US dollars a month. What kind of cunt my age can do that in the UK? And I'm from a little border town with a degree in a subject no one really gives two hoots about. Teaching in Korea is an out for me mate. I can live it up in my early twenties in an exotic location.

Two more local teachers join in from the late shift, both thirsty and hanging out for a beer. One is David, a Cambridge graduate with a posh accent and a double barreled surname.

'I'm David Harold Marvin Worthwood from Chelthnam in the UK,' he says firmly shaking my hand. 'I take it you are the new boy then?'

'Yeah, I guess so. I'm Don from Australia.'

'I went to Australia once. It was fucking great mate. We had a few barbeques and we watched the cricket.'

'He's trying to take the piss mate. Don't take him seriously,' interrupts his friend.

'Australian I am guessing?' I ask.

'Yeah, I'm Justin, good to meet you,'

'Sydney?'

'Actually Brisbane, but I last lived in Sydney. Let me grab you a beer Don.'

Noticing Gordon with Mi-ra, David is quick to tell me that he hasn't been having any luck with Korean girls, 'I am a little older than Gordon you see, which is probably why Gordon gets the digs. I had a bird but she was more into learning English than anything else. I'll be heading off soon anyway. There's always more fish in the sea, isn't that right Don?'

'Yeah, I guess so David. You said you were heading off?' I ask.

'Give it another six months I reckon and then I will leave for Japan. It's funkier than this place. I mean look where we are on a Friday night, listening to fucking Tupac and Eminem. Japan has the real shit - Shonan Knife, 5, 6, 7, 8's and The Boredoms. They are cool over there, but here all the fashion is dictated by basketball and baggy pants. The yanks have ruined the culture here.'

I can see that David is your true diehard indie nerd. He looks like he is in a rut, not really knowing what he wants to do next. It's a conundrum some post university graduates find themselves in when they are abroad. I remember the sheer amount of backpackers marking the Sydney beaches of Bronte and Coogee, sunning their bodies without any fear of skin cancer, while working in market research centers and English bucket schools. They were lured by the warmth and sun and who could blame them? After all they are people who travel the globe in search of something, constantly craving, moving from one place to another, but never really settling. The problem is that when some of them do hit thirty, they sometimes wonder that maybe they have wasted time.

Thankfully Justin the Australian is more like Carol or Jim as far as ideas on the world and his dress sense. For one, he is wearing a white t-shirt with 'I am not an American' written in Korean on the front. In black bold letters it reads *'Mi Guk Saram ahn im nida!'* He knows that this cops a response wherever he goes, but he doesn't care. He is of the opinion that South Korea doesn't need an America to help fight its squabbles.

Both he and I instantly click. He reminds me of a guy called Brett that I used to do community radio with in Sydney in the mid 1980s. We'd hang out a lot, go to lots of gigs, smoke pot, drink till sunrise, and were both political and reckless.

'So where did you get the t-shirt from then?' I ask.

Justin replies, 'There's a shop down in Seoul. They have been making them by the truck load ever since that yank tank steamrolled two local school girls last year. Some people are finally getting sick of those army guys who come here on tour. A few of them are real idiots, so I guess this is my way of not being identified as one. Not bad hey mate.'

'Good on you. About time people stuck up for stuff,' I reply.

'The way I see it is that President Roh Moo Hyun is making things better. He wants to have dialogue with the North and this has meant slowly cutting ties with the west. I don't want to talk about it too much but I guess you can label me as a Canadian who puts a maple leaf on his backpack to tell the world he is not American, or a Kiwi that wears an All Black jersey to say that he isn't Australian. Plus some of the older locals here think that every white face is American. They're often saying Happy Thanksgiving to me when I don't even know the first thing about it.'

It's getting close to eleven and the place is starting to fill up. Daphne, Carol and Jack all say their goodbyes, but a few of us including me are keen to stay out. Along with David the three of us each chug on a pint of Cass before downing a vodka red bull and heading to the other expat bar Hells Bells, which is just across the road.

This bar is intimate and more to my liking. Justin is obviously chummy with the owner John who quickly takes a shine to me.

'What style of music Don? Take your pick mate. I've got a bunch of stuff here thanks to Justin and David. I am also familiar with some of the Aussie underground stuff.'

'Where do I start? These days I am listening to a lot of Radiohead, some Nick Cave, early Sonic Youth, and early Nirvana,' I reply.

'Well these days Don I am digging the Celibate Rifles, Mogwai, and Augie March.'

'Fuck that's great man. We have similar taste yeah?'

'Yeah mate we do. So, I think it's time for me to get you a drink Korean style.'

John quickly puts three shots of tequila under our noses. David then tells me that this is a normal thing for new people in town, particularly at Hells Bells.

'If John likes your music tastes he will welcome you like royalty, so please don't knock him back otherwise he will get offended,' he warns. 'Trust me mate, it's a cultural thing. Korean style can get really gregarious as the night goes on. It's not uncommon to be out with the locals and then visit five to six different bars in a night, eating side dishes and trying out different types of alcohol.'

'They seem be quite different in so many ways.'

'Welcome to Korea mate,' he replies sarcastically. 'That's right I forgot you just got here. You're green and all, I should have remembered.'

'It's no big deal mate,' I reply.

'One thing Don to remember is that some of the people here can be straight up, even emotional when they drink – they say it how it is. Sure they are less likely to do it when they are in a classroom, or at the office, but it's some of these very same Koreans who share cigarettes and secrets in bars, and ply each other with shots of any spirit on offer.'

We down our drinks, then move to the lounge to listen to some more of the owner's catalogue. Close by are a trio of done-up-to-the-nines western women, one of whom accosts Justin with a warm welcoming smile. The same one looks at me knowingly, before Justin confirms that I'm the Australian who has just arrived at Global World. The said person introduces herself as Fiona from Toronto, her eyes lighting up like the others before, as she also already knows about my so-called plight. She then embraces me with a huge first time hug, and straight away starts apologizing, feeling sorry for the mess that I have arrived into.

'My good friend Mona worked there before you. Man those guys really sucked. They didn't pay her, the pricks! She is pissed still and I don't blame her. She'll be here in a few days so you can meet her, but be warned because she's a real firebrand when she is unhappy. She has a temper on her. The two of us were senior high school friends in London near Toronto. I just hope you will be ok bud.'

She squashes me with her second hug. Fiona's laced with lipstick and an overly pungent deodorant which forces me to nip out to the wash room. On my way I meet her friends Janine and Kelly, who seem kind of ditzy. They stand, pout, blow gum and raise their eyebrows. Both are wearing black boots that stretch up to the top of their thighs.

I ask them what they are doing here and they reply that they can't get a job back in Toronto so they have come to Korea to pay off debt.

'What do most Canadians do when they come to Korea? We don't work for the army so we teach. Most of us have a shitload of university debt to pay off and there isn't the work back home,' says Janine.

'Plus Don, I had a ball at university and I want to continue that kind of life style of all care and no responsibility. C'mon mate you know what I mean?' adds Kelly.

'Yeah I guess I do, or at least you obviously do,' I reply.

Kelly whispers into me ear, telling me that she has a hankering for a tall Irish guy at the bar called Padraigh, 'That's him over there. I need you to come with me. He's a great guy and I think you'll want to be his friend,' Kelly adds.

By this stage I am well liquored up on tequila and a few beers, so I'm happy to meet anyone. She takes me firmly by one hand, but soon enough it is obvious that he has little interest in her.

After all Padraigh is busy chatting up a young student. Eavesdropping, I find out that he graduated last year from Dublin University, and that he loves Joyce and Keats, so we share common interests.

Tapping him on the shoulder, I ask him, 'Sorry to interrupt but I take it you're a mover and shaker here?'

'I don't know what you're talking about. By the way who are you?' he asks.

'I'm Don from Australia. And you?'

'Padraigh but just call me Paddy.'

'Where are you working Paddy? I'm guessing the university?'

'Yeah, I am working with Carol and Jack at the university up here. Ah, now I know. You are the Australian who was with them earlier tonight? Anyways, we four should get together sometime as we are arranging a James Joyce night in celebration of the great author. We'd love your help if you can spare it Don?'

'Sure, I'm up for anything.'

'Yeah he certainly is,' adds Kelly.

It's past midnight and the tall Irishman is holding up well on the orange juice. Kelly on the other hand has had way too many shots. She grabs my hand firmly and we return to the sofa, where Justin seems entangled in Janine's attention. A deflated Kelly grabs me by my jean buckle, pulling me onto her lap as she falls onto the sofa.

Meanwhile David the English guy with the double barreled name is trying his best with a Japanese girl at the bar whispering bad Japanese at her. She manages to politely fob him off with subtle aplomb. When John spins 'Lust for Life' by Iggy Pop, suddenly everyone is up and jumping around. He then follows it with 'Touch Me I'm Sick' from Mudhoney, and then Nirvana's cover version of Bowie's 'The Man Who Sold the World.' Soon it feels like I'm back at home, but it's barely a few days since I left Sydney.

Between songs I notice that Gordon has arrived with two new faces both in their early twenties who are as green to this caper as he is. They greet me with high fives, as if they have bumped into a long lost friend.

They introduce themselves as Bruce from Auckland and Daniel from Wellington. Both are happy to meet someone from their part of the world, and are quick to buy a few drinks in celebration. Bruce and Daniel have Korean girls on their arms, though they basically ignore them while we talk about rugby, cricket, the underarm fiasco, weather, vegemite and the Flying Nun record label.

It's around 3am and I am encouraged by Justin and the others to get my dancing shoes down to Brain Bar, 'It isn't anywhere as cool as here but it's worth a laugh as they play very bad rap. It's where the American GI's hang out when they have escaped their curfew. They're all hungry for local female companions. We teachers usually create a bit of havoc but it is all fun and games mate,' says Justin.

Two blocks away you can hear the horrible rap sounds of Eminem pulsating from Brain Bar and when we arrive there's a long line. It's obvious that most are GI's waiting to get in, their buzz haircuts and solid pectoral physiques being a dead giveaway. In front of us are two of Justin's mates, Hooch and Frank. Both are from the deep southern part of the states, Alabama and Louisiana. I ask Hooch how long he has been here.

'Well, my Aussie pal, I arrived on this tour of duty only a few months ago. Before that I was in Berlin for a few years, which was cool. In a few months I hope to be in Iraq.'

'Yeah man, we go wherever our government needs us. It's our duty to do a tour Don. If we weren't doing this we'd be in a local penitentiary back home,' adds Frank. 'I was always on the wrong side of the law before the army asked me to join up. I thank them and the Lord for where my life is now.'

Inside the bar I notice a skinny cool Korean guy who has a Japanese style haircut, wearing tight blue jeans, and a black Ramones T shirt. It's the latter that raises my attention, given my long term interest in this band from New York. I approach him and I boast about how I first saw them play in Australia in 1993 in Sydney, and how I can't believe that he's wearing their t-shirt.

He looks at me in disbelief before telling me, 'I bought this shirt in a market here in Chuncheon. I liked the design but this is the first time I've heard that they were a band.'

I look at Hooch who is still behind me and I ask if he knew of this band back in the states, but he is clueless as well.

'It's all Tom Petty and Springsteen where I am from. Bands with that look back in the south are just considered underground - you know gay shit.'

Around me the number of military buzz cuts and dressed up cosmetic Barbie doll locals is nauseating and I quickly feel like I'm in a bad movie. The rap continues to echo up the stairs and out onto the streets. Inside a mob of army guys all wearing chains and baseball caps patrol the dance floor. Justin was dead right. This is definitely a place to go and observe the hilarity of life, not one for conversation and like-minded tunes.

The barman introduces himself as Jim. He tells me that he has just finished working as an art lecturer at the nearby university, and that Brain Bar is his new business. He started it with his new Canadian wife who is now talking to Fiona, Kelly and Janine who I'd just met at Hells Bells.

'You're an Aussie right? I am Jim's wife Raelene. The girls here, my mates from Toronto have been talking about you sugar.'

'Have they now? And what have they been saying?' I ask.

'I don't kiss and tell. Now are you done?'

'What do you mean am I done?'

'I said are you done?'

'No. I just got here.'

'It's a joke silly. We crazy Canadians like to have a laugh at our down under mates. I was asking you if you were Don?'

'Yes, I am Don.'

'Get it?'

'Ah, I do now.'

'Don, let me fix you up with a drink. You must try one of my famous cocktails called Raelene's Love. It's got just about every spirit on the planet in it.'

Justin notices what I am up to and shouts, 'If you drink that shit mate you will be feeling it tomorrow. I had one six months ago and I couldn't face the outside world for two days.'

'I've had heavier shit and survived mate.'

'Well Don, you want to try one or what?' asks Raelene.

'Yeah, fuck it. Give it to me man.'

After downing a few, the rest of the night becomes a blur, though somehow I manage to get home.

7

LOST AND LONELY

She has a look in her eyes that says things aren't quite right. She's been over here for a while now and admits that she is tiring of the place, her work, and her constant searching for a place to be in life. I don't quite know her well enough to express any real advice that might help. I want to say something but I feel that it isn't my place to.

It's Carol, the very same bubbly Brit that I met last night at Jacks, the like-minded one, with that great laugh and a zest for life. We are standing outside a main walking mall where we have bumped into each other. It is a particularly cold snowy Saturday afternoon and we're both a little hungover after last night.

'I got so fucked up after you left Carol. All I can remember was this bar from a bad movie then snow on the steps to my apartment. I had a few drinks at Brain Bar that really did me in. I should have listened to Justin because they literally destroyed me. He was right in front of me saying don't do it.'

'Don't worry Don. I've done the same thing many a time and regretted it. Once is ok mate so don't beat yourself up, but if you do it again and again you're hiding something I reckon. When I first got here, I was meeting strangers, getting drunk to the early hours and ending up at Brain Bar just people watching. It's a good lifestyle but Jack and I don't go as hard as we used to. After all we have just hit forty.'

'I'll soon be there as well. Club Forty is nearing.'

'If you're smart Don, there's no reason why you can't get ahead in this part of the world,' Carol says. 'If we had stayed in Britain, the rate we were going, we would've both ended up tearing our hair out. You can't buy a place in England unless you are super rich. Here we work less hours, so there is time to do the other things we want to do. We can actually afford to go out and socialize on the weekends and no one is telling us how to live.'

'Doesn't sound that bad to me,' I reply.

'You have a lot of freedom here Don. There's no one standing over your shoulder saying get married, take out a mortgage, get on with your life, be a someone. But then sometimes that's not enough. That's my quandary now. What to do next?'

Carol starts to get more personable with me, and soon both of us open up about our past, 'He is my soul mate Don. I can't describe it. It's like we fit, we were made for each other. He makes me laugh and we have this great cerebral connection which I have never had with anyone else. Do you know what I mean?'

I nervously nod back at her, my stomach a little sickened as I gesture with a half shrug. Without really saying anything I let out, 'Yes sure, Carol, I do know what you mean.'

Under her arm is a folder of leaflets that give voice to the comfort woman of Korea. She half notices me looking at them with interest.

'Do you know about the comfort women Don? I wrote my thesis on them back at home before Jack and I came here. They were forced into sexual slavery and prostitution by the Japanese military in World War II. Some came from other countries like China, Thailand, Vietnam and even Japan, but the majority came from here. This is one of the sticking points from the Japanese occupation of Korea from 1910 to 1945 and I can see why a lot of the Koreans resent them. The Japanese government won't apologize for their actions so we need to protest.'

'You seem really passionate about it. Justin is also politically active which is great.'

'He sometimes helps me. For over a year now a group of us go to Seoul for all night vigils. Abused Korean woman from the occupation period sometimes come along and speak. It's a solidarity action that is starting to hopefully get some voice. I won't stop Don until it stops. It's the reason I am here, more so than the teaching.'

'You don't like your classes that much?'

'They are pretty run-of-the-mill really. The students respect you, but they have little energy most times. It seems that it's all been soaked up by their own teachers. So when they see us, the native teacher can sometimes become a bit of a novelty and a chance to tune out.'

'Thank god they have people like us then. The education system does sound tough,' I reply.

'Look, I'm not meaning to put you off or anything, but that's how it is, particularly for me at the moment. Jack is much luckier as his classes are far more interesting. He teaches the postgraduates from time to time. He's free to teach them about the origins of punk music in the UK and they love it. For me it is just big over populated freshman classes and a boring textbook.'

As the snow starts to fall heavily we take refuge under a shop front that is pumping out some bad rap. Realizing it is time to say goodbye, I tell Carol how good it has been to talk.

'It's been tough these last few days you know. I guess it is like that for everyone when they arrive in a new place. But you two seem to be doing fine I reckon. You've reignited my desire at least to get out and try new things.'

'Korea is an interesting place Don. Please don't get me wrong. There are so many good things here I swear. That's the conundrum isn't it? I guess there comes a time when you have to think what next? That's life my friend,' she adds.

I walk away from Carol determined to embrace new things starting with the local street market. I look at food and medicine I know nothing about while watching the locals interact.

LOCAL BATH HOUSE

There's a knock on the door. It's the electrician guy and he's shouting but I have no idea what it's about. Kevin comes out of his room hearing the ruckus so I leave them to it. I can hear both of them engaging in a slanging match that takes forever. Without alcohol, it seems some of these locals have a habit of talking in circles before getting to the point. Kevin is years younger than the other man so his official place is to kowtow. It's a style of communicating that I am not quite used to.

Kevin bows and almost kisses this man's feet, pleading, begging, in an over the top apologetic manner. I suspect that the man wants payment for a bill, and that Kevin is doing his best to cover up the mess.

When the man leaves, Kevin confirms my suspicions saying, 'Well, our electricity bill hasn't been paid for three months. We have only the minimum amount left on our meter, and pretty soon we won't have anything unless it is paid for within the next day. If you check our contracts they say the company will pay all electricity and utility costs on a monthly basis.'

'That's not good,' I respond, not really knowing what to say.

'Of course it is not good! Our fucking boss is way behind with payments. Sooner or later our television will also be on the blink. We don't have much power and being late February, you and I are going to suffer my friend. It's still a good month or two before the cold snap is over.'

'That's serious,' I reply.

'Yes, of course it is fucking serious and you know what Don? This is the last straw for me. I suggest you start going to the bath houses. There are a ton of them in this neighborhood so you better become familiar with them.'

He then slams his bedroom door. It's obvious that Kevin is on the brink of shutting down completely. Again I think what kind of hell have I walked into?

I'm familiar with Korean bath houses as in Sydney there are two that I know of, one being in Kings Cross, Sydney's infamous red light area. Here in South Korea they are as ubiquitous as pubs back home. You can find them on most street corners.

When I knock on Kevin's door I ask him where exactly one is and he points to a large sauna that is close to our apartment. I ask him what it's like but he just looks at me dumbfounded waving his hands as if he is unable to talk.

I get up very early the next morning to experience the bath house before my first class. A young boy greets me at the door. He points to my shoes, gesturing that I should take them off first before I go inside. He then gives me a key for a locker which he straps onto my wrist. As I enter, the place feels like a palace. There is a barber, a masseuse, five different spas, three saunas and a big swimming pool. It is teeming with people, and it doesn't take long before I am naked with the throng of bathers. Unfortunately though, I quickly become the source of attention, at least it feels that way. I can hear some people saying things like *wae-guk* a term for foreigner. It's almost as if I have the fear after a bout of drinking. I am scared and I have second thoughts about being here. However it is too late. I think fuck it so I try the green tea spa, the barley rice spa, and then the sauna, before finally the icy pool to cool off. It all seems weird, somewhat surreal, and I alternate between feeling shit scared while at times I feel like a proud swan that's just happy to relax and wile away the time.

In one room I can see people sleeping, while in another people line up for haircuts and pedicures. The place is open twenty-four hours, so Koreans from all walks of life come here to rest and bathe.

One man looks at me knowingly. He makes a gesture with his hands as if he is driving a car, smiling and laughing loudly. I have absolutely no idea who he is and when I ask him how he knows me he has no idea what I am saying. I guess he could be the guy who took me home in a cab from Brain Bar early on Saturday morning. Sensing this, I nervously laugh back at him, mockingly swaying my drunken behavior and realize that I am right. It was him.

I still have a little of the fear so I quickly change and exit as fast as possible only to slip on some sleet on the outside footpath on my way to class. My grey trousers are soon stained with dirt and ice, yet this clumsy moment of panic seems all in vain. As I reach the top of the stairs, the classrooms are pitch-black and empty except for one of the Japanese teachers who has made it inside.

It's Yuri, and she has her head faced down on the desk with her hands stretched out in front of her. She looks like she is in prayer so I do my best not to disturb her. What's strange is the absence of Kevin, Daphne, So-Hee, Yoko, and Mr. Lee. There's not a soul to be seen and the mustiness makes it feel like a morgue. The walls are damp and there's a lot of mould. It looks like a cleaner hasn't been here for months.

I try to photocopy notes for my lesson but the copier is jammed. As I attempt to fix it, Yuri senses my presence and she lifts her head off the desk, then bows to me with a customary *ohayo guzai mas* in Japanese as a way of saying good morning. She doesn't appear to have a lot of English, but between us we make the odd gestures, both agreeing that it's very quiet this morning. I ask her of Yoko's whereabouts.

'Maybe Yoko has gone back to Kobe. Just me here alone but me alright, I promise. Why are you here anyway? No one ever comes to the first class. Even So-Hee our secretary won't be here until 9 o'clock.'

'My class is supposed to start at 6:30. Are you sure you are ok?'

'Just tired you know. In Korea and Japan we hard work really. We always work a long day. This gives us a lot of stress. We need to relax ourselves. Yoko work very long hours, and even Friday she was here for a long time, maybe 11 p.m. That man Lee, bad man, very lazy, so bad. He sit down in that big chair, smoking, while he still not give me or Yoko money. I come early because of internet, that's all. I can talk boyfriend.'

Yuri's family lives in Hiratsuka, a small suburb in the outskirts of Yokohama, an hour and half out of Tokyo. She has a lovely soft and attractive demeanor. Like Carol, I can sense her loneliness and isolation.

'One friend Yoko, you know her, and now she go Kobe. I have some Korean friend. They sometimes help me. I like Korea because in Japan I can't stand the pressure. Here some people think me Korean. I will learn the language. I like language. English is too hard for me.'

'Your English is fine Yuri.'

'Are you sure? My English Don-san is very poor. But let me tell secret. I was an English major at university in Osaka. I once work hard at English, but you know English in Japan these days isn't as important as before. Japanese people want to learn other languages like Korean or Chinese. If we learn different languages I think that is good for business, and as you know it's a global world.'

Yuri seems humble and modest. She reminds me of someone who works herself to death as if it's her duty to, just like some of the foreign students that go to Australia to study English. The kind who coop themselves up in Fisher Library at Sydney University doing it for their parents and aiming to succeed so that one day they can give back.

Yuri's virtues come from a sense of duty that seems remote these days from my own upbringing. Although my father relocated to Australia on a ten pound boat, to pave the way for his mother and brothers, I at least see myself from a different stock. Growing up I didn't experience the same kind of pressure that she is going through.

9

CLASS BEGINS

When Daphne and Kevin arrive they aren't surprised that no students have shown yet.

'So I take it you found the bath house then Don?' Kevin asks.

'Yeah I certainly did. Thanks for the tip but you could have mentioned that I didn't need to rush. Yuri told me that no one ever comes to the first classes on a Monday.'

'Are you ok Don? You look a little testy,' asks Daphne

'Yeah I am ok. I've just had a long morning that's all. For one, our shower had fuck all water and the electrician who visited yesterday was a real prick. I had to take a visit to a blooming bath house, which was an experience to say the least. People were looking at me as if I was some monkey in a zoo.'

'Get used to it. You're a foreigner mate,' shouts Kevin.

'Fuck you Kevin; now is not the time,' I reply.

'I was only joking Don. You don't have to be so serious mate.'

'Yeah get used to it Don. We all do,' advises Daphne. 'After all this is Korea, it isn't Sydney or Wellington. If I was you I would get your students' phone numbers for the early morning classes, and ask them if they are going to show or not. Or get them to call you. I sometimes have to text them the night before. It's just one of those things.'

'But we shouldn't have to be following them up,' I retort.

'No we shouldn't but here things are different. Look, just enjoy the fact that you can get more sleep.'

'Do you have the same problems with your shower?' I ask.

'No, but I must admit with the two of you it is a lot harder. Mona always used a lot of water despite the fact that we were always reminding her that she wasn't in Toronto. Also, her highness is arriving today from Vietnam so expect fireworks and shouting matches!'

'More drama, just what I like,' I reply sarcastically.

Soon Mr. Park and So Hyun arrive for my class and outside I notice the company van leaving to collect its next batch of Global World students. It's a Monday so it makes sense to talk about our weekend, but here in Korea discussing this has a different kind of meaning. Most Asian people aren't so interested in what others do on the weekend. For some it is considered weird, as weekends are deemed private. At least this is what my Korean Air man, Mr. Park thinks.

'Mr. Don, you have to remember that we Ancients are very different to you English people. This comes across in our language. Don, do you know Confucius? He is why we are Korean. We Ancients don't need to ask people how they are feeling or what they did on the weekend like you Australians might. We don't say things like, hey mate how's it going? In Korean we say *bap isseo*? That translates to have you eaten yet? Sometimes, we might say *odi kayo* which translates to where are you going? This is part of our old tradition, Mr. Don.'

'But Mr. Park it seems a little weird for me. The weekend is just a way of shooting the breeze that's all. It is like small talk.'

'I know what you mean Don, but you have to remember we haven't always been a rich country. My parents had to escape to the south to get away from those damn communists. We once had a farm outside of Seoul, which my parents worked really hard for. Hence the saying goes, to ask someone if they have eaten yet, is a form of politeness, a way of asking about their well being. Rice means a lot to Korean people. I think you will find that is the way for most Ancient countries.'

I love these interesting insights. As a language teacher I know that I must respect difference. I need to be culturally sensitive towards my students, however I must also claim my place as a teacher. It's a relief that both Mr. Park and So Hyun are happy to hear my honesty with regards to this.

'In western countries asking someone about their weekend is normal, and if you were to live in say Australia you'd be expected to do the same, It's just like that old saying 'when in Rome do as the Romans do.' In some ways it comes across as a more direct language. That's why we often use WH questions to start a conversation. I it's our way of getting information from the person you are talking to. For you it may sound a little rude and upfront to use why in a conversation but for us it's very much part of our culture. So, I ask you both politely to take off your Korean clothes while you're in my English class and put on your English ones.'

'Sure, we can do that Mr. Don, just for you our Australian mate,' Mr. Park replies.

The two of them are both eager to learn about Australian culture and although they may not agree with me, they realize that if their oral English is going to get anywhere they need to respect difference. I start to tell them a story.

'In Australia I knew this student studying English whom I will never forget, because she always had a go. Some Australians really believe that idea - to have a go at something. It shows that you are willing to try and to dive in; to embrace what you are learning. What you two have to remember is it isn't always about being perfectly correct. You need to learn to be cool with your second language. Trust me, you need to change out of your clothes and dress in a new outfit – an English one.'

Mr. Park then says, 'It's ok Mr. Don Teacher. So Hyun and I want to understand the way you talk, and why you do these kinds of things, and so on. We can get to know you and we can be friends. I told my wife about you Mr. Don and she wants to meet you. Tomorrow night you must come over and we can have a meal, then we can go out. Please don't disappoint us Mr. Don.'

'Thanks Mr. Park,' I reply only half noticing his offer.

I then check the clock and realize that time has passed and that we're almost done. To finish, I ask So Hyun about her weekend.

She passively replies, 'I didn't do very much teacher. I had a fight with my mother because she wants me to marry but it isn't that easy Mr. Don. Look at me, I am twenty-seven and life here is very hard for me. My mother often tells me, "So Hyun you must marry now. You marry man and you look after your father and me." So Mr. Don when you ask me, what did I do on my weekend? You know what I did? I stayed inside and cried whole time. That was my horrible weekend!'

'I am sorry to hear that your weekend was bad. I hope you can meet someone, I really do.'

'Thanks dear teacher. We have really loved your lesson today and we look forward to our next one.'

My next class is the friendly flirtatious housewives. Hyun-Ju, one of the more talkative students, walks into class and says; 'Mr. Don! I must say you look very nice today - so cute and well gloomed.'

The other dozen students all giggle and cover their mouths again, before sitting down and bowing their heads. They are a happy bunch of people that basically use this class as an opportune social time to take them away from the stresses of family expectations. For some women here it is a custom to live with the in-laws once you're married, and it is expected that money be distributed to either sides of the extended family. This isn't always easy, and the truth is that a lot of late-twenties early-thirties housewives are simply bursting boilers. It's like their marriages include not just themselves, but also both sets of parents as well as their reputations and names.

Lee Seon Na for example, was married just a year ago at the age of twenty-seven. She enjoys coming along to a class like this while her husband's mother takes her newborn for a stroll around their large apartment complex. She lives about five minutes away and is a local girl who's proud of her roots and family. Her husband Lee Jeong-Il works in the nearby town of Gapyeong as a food trader and due to his countless business trips away, the two don't share much time together.

'When my husband comes back from his business trips we often go for a drive around the lake, or take a picnic to Gangcheon where our baby can enjoy the afternoon sunshine. Here is a picture Mr. Don of my son and my husband. Isn't he beautiful? I'd like you dear teacher to one day come and spend some time with us together. Maybe you can teach my son English. We'd love you to visit my home.'

I smile warmly back, thanking her for the invitation. Again I can't help wondering where to draw a line at such generosity. People here seem so inviting and this can be particularly hard for me as I don't quite know the protocol of refusing without hurting anyone. I express my gratitude through thanking her. Soon the whole class smiles warmly in unison as if they're all inviting me to their homes.

10

BITCHING

It's mid-afternoon and I am enjoying a rest between shifts but that doesn't last long as I hear a voice down below in Daphne's room. Bleary-eyed I peep through the blinds. I am guessing it is Mona as Daphne warned, and that she has returned for one last fleeting chance to get paid before she goes back to Canada forever.

Eavesdropping, I hear her say, 'Ok I will go down to my bank now and check this shit out. I can't imagine that he has put anything in, but to hell with it, I need to check this out. For the last few weeks this hasn't been on my mind. Man, it was so nice to lie on a beach in Vietnam with all this Korean stuff behind me. But fuck it, we are going to try Daphne. We are both going to give this a shot. We have to give it a go! Way to go ok?'

Kevin wakes up annoyed that his sleep has been broken too, 'Fucking hell, I knew it. The blown-out Canuk-of-a-whale has returned from paradise to fucked-up Korea in the hope that she will get some spoils. But I tell you what man, the way she goes about things, she has fuck-all chance. Look at that ugly brute, would you? She just parades herself around the joint with her loud fucking voice. I mean, I have friends in the Bronx and they have big voices like hers, but they know when it's time to shut their trap.'

'She must be quite the teacher?' I ask.

'Apparently she was. I bet she knows that we are probably up here trying to get some rest, but she doesn't give a fuck. It's all about her and what she can get. It's that typical me, me, me thing! I mean, man, it is mid-afternoon for crying out loud, and what about poor innocent Daphne? I wonder if she has had any say in this brute coming around and venting at her, yet again.'

Splashing my face, I then make my way to the internet café a few doors down to check emails. Upstairs the PC room is wall-to-wall with middle school students who are most likely wagging their afternoon cram-schools. The noise is deafening as they play at their PC stations, urging each other on, shouting and spitting into ashtrays, whilst consuming sugar laced fizzy drinks. Some of the older kids are smoking, but what I find funny is that when they see me they react apologetically by hiding their smokes as a sign of respect for their elders.

Protocol in some parts of Korea says that it's best to not smoke in front of those who are older than you and if you do, to always ask first as a form of politeness. It's a similar behavior when drinking with an older crowd; the young ones will turn their face to hide their drink.

When I later venture to the office to prepare for the evening lessons, I can sense from the bottom of the stairs that something is wrong. I can hear a screaming match between Mona, Kevin and the head honcho, with my flat mate playing the reluctant mediator.

Mona can understand some of what Lee is saying to Kevin – things like 'No' or 'I am sorry but we don't have your money yet, please understand us.' This only fuels her anger as she shouts back at Lee.

'How the fuck can you sleep at night? You are a big dumb fuck. Do you think you can go and screw us teachers around and spend all our hard-earned money on your fucking gambling and drinking habits? We don't do that in our countries. We honor contracts and we expect to be paid. Plus stop staring at me with that smile on your face. It makes me sick!'

For Kevin like it was with Daphne earlier it's definitely a big juggling act. Mr. Lee does not care about Mona's problems. She senses this and ends up storming out of his office shouting a big "fuck you" to his face.

Nearly tripping, about half way down the stairs she lunges into me, 'Oh, I am sorry. Oh, are you the new boy from Australia? So this is you?'

'Yes this is me. I'm Don from Sydney, Australia. It's nice to meet you. I take it you are Mona then?'

Totally ignoring me she shouts back up the stairwell, 'Jesus Christ Korean man, you won't pay me, you won't pay Daphne, even Kevin, the Japanese girls, or your own people. And then you have the fucking gall to go and pay an air-fare for this hobo to come all the way to Korea. Are you out of your mind? Fuck you all. This isn't the last you'll hear of me.'

She quickly runs out of the building refusing to have any dialogue with me. At this point my high school student Kim A-reum follows me up the stairs looking confused and a little scared.

'Teacher, Mona just ran passed me and looked really angry.'

'I know I also saw her. Look, I am sorry A-reum, but this is not a good time. I'll talk to you later.'

'It's ok Mr. Don. I might be young but I do have an idea of what's going on in there. I just wanted to tell you that Mona really is a great teacher but I can tell that today she's is a little angry. When she worked here she was always concerned about us Mr. Don and we learnt a lot from her. I don't know exactly why she's angry now. You know Korean businessmen are sometimes bad and all they care about is power.'

'You know too much don't you A-reum?'

'I know because my mother and father have the same problems. Some of us Koreans have no idea about how to look after our workers. That's the problem with my country! We have too much respect for age here and we carry that on at work, when sometimes you also have to give some respect back. Everyone deserves respect Mr. Don you know. It has to be a two way thing. You are my teacher and we don't want to lose you.'

'That's kind of you A-reum.'

'Please Mr. Don I want you to believe me that we all love your teaching. You know, ever since this new guy came up from the south, our Global World has started having some serious problems. I can feel it. There is something wrong around here,' she says.

'Are there any solutions?' I ask.

'I will talk to my mother and father about this problem, I promise. Anyway Teacher Don let's go to our classroom. Today is a special day because you will meet Park Min-seok.'

She takes my hand and squeezes it tightly.

Park Min-seok has a reputation for being a troublesome child that spends most of his time wagging academy classes because of a computer addiction. His love for computer games starts from 3:30 in the afternoon until the late evening. He has become part of the Korean latch-key brigade. These are children who wear a key around their neck 24/7, who help themselves at home to the family fridge, and are able to get money from their parents seemingly at will. Park Min-seok's family has a maid, so little is expected of him. He pretty much has the license to do whatever he wants.

Arriving five minutes late he appears happy to see me, 'It's great to meet you again Mr. Don. My name is Park Min-seok and I go to the same school as Kim A-reum. As you know I met you earlier today when I saw you at the PC room. I was with my elementary school friend. We like to play computer games and Star Craft is my favorite. I have been playing it for years. Do you like play computer games Mr. Don?'

'All I can remember from the computer room was smoke and kids spitting into cans of coke. I am sorry young man but I don't remember meeting you.'

'I remember you Mr. Don. You didn't look very happy with us kids.'

'That's because at your age I was more into sport than computer games and smoking. Too much of that will kill you kid. I may have played space invaders as a high school student but that was years ago and if I got caught my mum would get angry. So, you shouldn't spend all your time in these PC rooms. Didn't your parents tell you that study and health are your first priorities?'

'I know what you are saying teacher but my Mum and Dad are always out anyway, so I don't like being at home. I'm boring there because Mr. Don what can I do? So we play computer games. You can understand can't you?'

'Not really,' I reply.

Min-seok likes to show off his English and I can tell straight away that he's a perfect complement for A-reum, only without the same experiences. He has a go, and provided he can stay away from PC rooms he might well excel at English and do his parents proud. However like some kids his age he does have a problem prioritizing between work and play. Computer addiction is rife in Korean culture with PC rooms everywhere. For many it has become a sign of status, with a lot of kids begging their parents to get them the best and newest computer software.

A-reum tells us both about an article she read on the internet where a fourteen year old boy in Seoul managed to send himself into paralysis after spending a record twenty plus hours online.

'Also Mr. Don, I heard that in China if you develop this habit, the police will come and take you away from your home and put you into a program to relieve your addiction. Every coin has two sides Mr. Don, and this unfortunately is one of the dark sides for us Koreans.'

'So Min-seok do you have any way out of this?' I ask.

'I don't know teacher. I think we have to study but you remember Korea was a poor country once and we like our technologies. The problem is our school. We are told not to play computers, not to have fun. We are told to just study and do homework, but I feel boring! That's why I sometimes like coming to this Global World school. We can have fun, learn English, and you know Mr. Don, English is very important in today Korea,' he adds.

I put my head down for a moment thinking how many times I have been told this before he starts again, 'We want to be like America one day. We want to be successful and be a nation that everyone can know and learn about. But our day school just has no idea. We are stuck in the old days and the teachers won't change with the times.'

'So computer games are a way out? Do you know what that stuff is doing to your eyes and your body? Ever wondered why so many kids have glasses these days?' I ask.

'I think Min-seok has a point Mr. Don. I think that if we can get English in our schools earlier then we can have a chance to meet cool people like you and Mona. That's what Korea needs if we want to be cool with the rest of the world. We need to learn from people, see what other people do in this world. That's why I don't mind Japanese people because we can learn from them too. If we don't learn, we will end up like our other family in the North - we will be shut away from the rest of the world. In business and in pleasure I think we must welcome our foreign friends.'

For the last class the topic is food. This generates a lot of discussion, particularly when it comes to different cultural cuisines and what they can offer.

Mari says, 'Our culture is defined by our food whereas yours Mr. Don isn't.'

'I don't think you can really say that. I mean in the east and the west we both like to eat exotic food, don't we?' I question.

I start to add more but I notice that some of the students seem a little distracted so I ask if everything is ok.

'Sorry teacher but we are a little tired,' yawns Mari.

'We can always change the topic guys?'

'Mr. Don, we all like your class. It's valuable to everyone here. It's just that a lot of us are either tired from our own work or MT.'

'What do you mean by MT?'

'It's Membership Training,' says Seok-hyun, one of the freshman students.

'It is our obligation Mr. Don. We students must go MT because we can have a chance to play with other students. We can for example, play with girls, play games, drink the beer and *soju*, get drunk, before most of us throw up. Each university had it on the weekend. It's fun Mr. Don. We would like you to come to MT next time ok? We promise to speak English too with you, kind teacher Mr. Don.'

I half-smile knowing that in reality it will be a test of endurance.

At the end of the class, a group of four girls invite me along to their own MT, which has nothing to do with a university group. It's for their local church and they feel that after meeting me that I could do with some of God's loving.

One of them Hyun-Ju quietly whispers in my ear that she saw on my way home last Saturday.

'I said hello to you teacher, but you didn't meet me. You were drunken Mr. Don. I don't think you need to do that while you are here. You need to look after yourself otherwise you will hurt yourself. God gives you back love which you need, not hangover. He does that for all of us. Come next weekend Mr. Don and we can sing and play together and be funny!'

My first reaction is to shun the idea completely. Instead I smile and nod, deflecting the idea, telling them that I'm too tired, and that I need to go home quickly to get some rest.

On my way I bump into Daphne and Mona who are about to go for a beer at Jacks but I am not really up for it.

'C'mon, you cannot be that tired. Don't worry too much. Plus, remember the job really is a piece of cake. You could go out every night and you'd still be able to function in this kind of job. Trust me, we will go now and have a few quiet jars. Most likely some of the other teachers in town will be out too. Don't let the schedule beat you Don.'

'Yes, please come. I'm sorry you had to see that shit before. We'd be happy for you to join us,' says Mona.

'Ok then I'll come,' I reply.

For a week night there are quite a few people out. When we arrive Arizona Mike, Manitoba Mike, and Justin are all perched at the bar having shots. They join our table with most of the focus on Mona's return.

Justin turns to me and quietly asks about the other night, 'So then how was Raelene's love potion? Did it hit the spot mate?'

'I don't remember much do I? I had a few in fact and then I think I got a taxi ride home. There was snow on the footpath. That's about all

I can remember mate,' I reply. 'The funny thing is one of my Christian students was having a go at me tonight because she reckons she saw me swaying about near the university on her way to church. Also, a guy at the bath house was taking a dig at me. It's as if the whole town knows about it.'

'Mate, it goes with the territory. Without drinking and the presence of other expats, this would be a pretty dull town. That's what has kept me here man. I was going to go back after my first year here, but I have to admit that there was little to go back for. All of my mates are in Sydney, but the bummer there is that my wife is around. She got caught up in some money crap, as did I. Please don't tell anyone about it. We broke up not long before I came over here. I needed an out. The bitch is living with my best mate somewhere on the North Shore. Can you believe it?'

'You don't have to talk about it mate if you don't want to.'

'But I am aren't I? Mate I don't need that kind of thing to go back to. Particularly, now I am here trying to get on with my life, starting afresh. You know what I mean don't you? Plus, who wants to pay the rent in post-Olympic Sydney town?' Justin questions. 'That place really shits me man. It's so overrated. I can earn more here, not pay rent, and be somewhere completely different. That's the buzz man. You will learn it too, the longer you stay.'

I then tell Justin about my own break up. After all I like him and we seem like-minded. He has a sense of humor, and unlike a lot of other males I know, he can speak his mind. He tells you how he feels and I dig that because he can open up about what's going on back in Sydney. It's like we feel each other's pain and we that have this kind of empathy for each other. While ignoring the others, we hang out with John listening to the new Radiohead album. John loves the band and he even named the bar across the road Cleep bar.

'You know the song 'I'm a Cleep don't you guys?' he asks.

'Sure we do,' Justin responds, trying not to laugh at John's pronunciation knowing that it isn't good form.

John pulls out his acoustic guitar and strums a few chords of the same song, singing 'I am a Cleep' over and over again, grinning from ear to ear.

We don't dare to tell him that the title is wrong.

I then tell Justin that I can sing a bit and ask him if he can play, 'Yeah, a little bit. I sang in a band back in the mid-80s. We did a few Joy Division and Bauhaus covers but we never quite made it out of the lounge room. In fact I have an acoustic at my apartment so you should come around and we can have a jam? John's always hitting me up to play here.'

'That sounds great to me.'

'Cool. Come over man and we can have a smoke and do some covers, not Hotel California of course – some more obscure and quality tunes.'

From afar, we notice Gordon, who is looking pretty glum so we both go over to console him.

'What's wrong man? Don't tell me, not fucking Korean girl trouble again? Are they fucking with your head again man?' Justin asks.

'Man, this time I swear will be the last time. Her fucking parents are here in town. She got the shits big time because I said I wouldn't come over to see mummy and daddy this weekend. Whenever I don't budge mate she just goes crazy. It's all because of the pressure that's coming from her parents.'

'Yeah, but you got to understand mate that a lot of these Korean girls are straight out of a Cinderella book. The first few months are a dream for some of us white guys, but then out of the blue, they start putting the same pressure on you that their parents put on them. I bet the most important secret she conceals is the one about your sleeping arrangements. You have to take your hat off to her that at least she's admitting that you are her actual boyfriend. Most wouldn't even dare to go there,' Justin says.

'Is it that bad?' I ask.

'Sure, not for all of course, but some families do want to keep the one blood thing. And can you blame them?' Justin asks. 'I mean, they have been in the middle of Japan and China for so long after all. They have always been at their beck and call, colonized and told what to do, how to speak et cetera.'

'And Mi-ra is just another one you think?' asks Gordon.

'I didn't say that. In my eyes she is really cool mate. Believe me my friend, so many Korean girls are vapid and naïve but not all of them. We can't generalize for fuck's sake. I mean, you are on to a good thing. She is a German major after all.'

Daphne and Arizona Mike chat away while Mona and John get closer at the bar. Word has it that they had a thing going before she went to Vietnam. David, the other barman has brought out a tray of customary tequila shots which are brought out in repeat sets for the next hour. It's getting late for a Monday and 'Tequila Sunrise' from Urge Overkill is playing but none of us are giving a fuck about what we have to do tomorrow. We're all living in the now so I follow suit, and nip around to a local shop, ordering my first pack of Korean cigarettes.

'*Tambae chu-sae-you*, or cigarettes please,' I say hesitantly as I practice a learnt phrase from Gordon.

A man with ruddy features smiles at my request and I am chuffed that I can be understood. The language is tough but if I can survive with small learnt phrases that will do me.

Despite the lateness the lane is packed with groups of university students, openly holding hands and hugging as they take photos of each other in the snow. I bump into a group of them and some ask me to pose with them. Soon I start to feel like I am in an Axl Rose MTV shoot so I quickly return to the bar, where I find both Justin and Gordon hammered. The girls by this stage have gone back home as it has just gone midnight. My class is in six and a half hours but that's only if the students decide to show up. Justin tells me not to worry and after the morning I had yesterday I agree with him.

11

EIGHTEEN

Fuck translates in Korean to eighteen *ship pal*, and probably isn't a great word in a language full of social airs and indirect communication. However, this morning I am not feeling too sharp as my judgment is a little out. I have awoken with a terrible hangover and deservedly so. I see Kevin and tell him that I can't be bothered teaching the 6:30 a.m. class even if they are there.

He agrees, but suddenly my own guilt takes over. I freshly shave and change and with all the right smells of face wash, soap and oil, I do my best to mask the smelly alcohol grump of a teacher that is well and truly growling inside me. In a way that's what I like about teaching. It's like performing because you have no other choice. You have to get up in front of your audience, conduct, facilitate, orchestrate, educate – and most of all show them a good time. The performing white monkey is ready for the task.

Not surprisingly the class hasn't shown. Its 6:45 in the morning and I'm seriously thinking of going back to bed. Queasy and unwell, I reek of tequila sweats and my eyes feel like I have been through a bout of punishment in a boxing ring.

Kevin then tells me to go across the road to try a Korean meal called *hae-jung-guk* which some Koreans believe is a cure for a hangover.

'You westerners always like to eat greasy food after you drink. It only makes you fatter, so you better get some soup into you. Remember, Korean girls don't like fat men Don, and you should really watch yourself now you are in your late thirties!'

Two Korean guys who are close by are quick to agree with Kevin.

'Sorry, but I don't think I have met you two,' I say.

'It's nice to meet you Don. I am Jason from Chicago.'

'I'm Zac and like Jason I have also spent some time in the States,'

'What did you both do there?' I ask.

'I did some fashion trade work on the east coast,' Zac replies.

'I was a golf journalist. Actually I still freelance,' Jason says.

Jason is wearing a while polo shirt and a woolen vest, whilst Zac has a tweed suit on.

'Gidday mate,' Zac smiles using a firm handshake.

'Likewise buddy. It's good to have an Aussie here with us,' Jason adds.

Both Kevin and I look at each other, a little shell shocked as to why Mr. Lee would hire two more cronies. Kevin then ushers them into Mr. Lee's room for a talk, whilst I find some breakfast across the road.

As I walk into the restaurant, the head woman, the *ajuma*, smiles at me as I ask politely for *hae jung gook*.

Within seconds she brings over a huge bowl of stringy soup with some meat broth. She watches me intently as I take a sip as the steam seeps through my nostrils and brows. I smile back at her and we have a good giggle. Her gold filling shines in the morning sunlight, her large round face beaming. It seems sweat is like gold for some Koreans, given the sheer amount of saunas and soups around.

I pass over my cash and depart happily, indicating to her that I will definitely be back. She pampers me like any kind Korean *ajuma* in restaurants might do, straightening my tie before I head back to work, treating me like her own son. This has got to be one of the nicest things about being abroad. A smile is worth a million.

As I'm busy pondering the passive and the active for the next lesson, my Korean Air business guy Mr. Park walks nonchalantly into the classroom without his able ally So-hyun. Instead he's armed with a bunch of travel brochures.

'What have you got there with you?' I ask.

'Well, Mr. Don, what I have here is our first holiday together. You and I are both going to go to the Philippines sometime soon. We need to do this and trust me it'll be a vacation you'll never forget.'

'Vacation, what do you mean? I only just got here, plus where is So-hyun?' I ask.

'She won't be joining me today, and please do not worry about having time off. You're a man Don, and a man needs some fun from time to time. We will go together and have some real fun my friend. There are women in every port in this island paradise.'

'Your wife will also come?'

'No, it will be just us two. In fact I was calling your bluff Mr. Don. That's what you say in English isn't it? I was pulling the wool over your eyes. Something like that, right?'

'That's right Mr. Park.'

'Don, you are my special English teacher and new good foreign friend. You remind me of a freshman at university, just like a baby in pyjamas who has just arrived in our country. Let me tell you that there are a lot of things that you foreigners don't know about. I can help explain such things to you Don, so please trust me.'

'But aren't you married?'

'Yes, I am married and my wife is like all the other Korean housewives. These days we don't really live together. I only get to see her and my child once a month because my company wants me to stay here. What that means is I am married to the job first. It's the same for a lot of Korean businessmen. Sure, I'd like to see more of her and my child, but these days I think it'd be best to say we had love,' he confides.

'So it's more a marriage of convenience? Or is it more like a business relationship? I don't quite get it, Mr. Park? Can you explain it a little more? I mean only if you want to,' I ask.

'Ok, Mr. Don one more time. But first let me tell you another one of our Korean rules. We are a busy society and we work hard every day to feed our children. We sacrifice love and passion Mr. Don because we believe we can get rich quickly. So I am a businessman which means I have needs. My company expects me to not only work but to also go out for regular dinners with clients and then go to a karaoke room or nori bang as we call it, where we sing and play with young girls.'

'So, does this mean you and these young girls, you play, um, you mean hang out don't you?'

'Yes, right on Mr. Don! You hit it on the head my smart great new foreign teacher and friend. You're smarter than you look but let's not finish just there. There's one more thing I need to tell you to complete this little Korean jigsaw puzzle.'

'Shoot then.'

'It's not just us males Mr. Don. Some of our wives are just as bad! They are going away on weekends too. They take bus trips down south and stay in hotels to meet those Korean men who don't want to go to singing rooms. This has been happening here for a while now. So teacher can you now understand these rules?'

I get the message but I don't want to go any further. I then ask him to turn to the passive/active section of the text and he obeys my instructions, knowing that he can talk to me about the Philippines trip another time. All I can do for now is to get on with the text and brush his requests aside. He sits attentively with a wide grin on his face while I get the chalk out.

When the class finishes he walks up to me, proudly shaking my hand. He then whispers into my ear, 'Please don't worry kind teacher, you need to trust me and remember that this is Korea not America. We do things differently here, and we are happy that you have come all this way to see us and get to know our country.'

As I follow him out of the classroom I notice that the two new *gyopo* employees, Zac and Jason have their eyes glued to a big 1970s colour TV in the school's waiting room.

'What's happening? Is everything ok?' I ask.

'Gidday mate! My buddy Jason and I here are watching the CNN report. Take a seat man,' Zac replies.

'Well guys it looks like America is going to fuck up those Muslim cunts, excuse my French. It's our revenge for 9/11 and it's about fucking time!' says Jason.

'Way to go Uncle Sam! Way to fucking go!' echoes Zac.

On the TV are flashes of a bombed Baghdad. Sure what happened in New York nearly two years back wasn't good form, but it seems now that the US have broken UN protocol and are doing what Bush promised he would – smoking out weapons of mass destruction in an attempt to remove Saddam Hussein. Beside me the two *gyopos* are almost partying with their arms around each other singing chants of 'America, God Bless America' whilst other students flock to the television to watch the news. Both Yuri and I find the noise too hard to bare so we leave the waiting room and return to our classrooms gob-smacked by their passion. Noticing our lack of interest and disgust, Zac walks into my room looking almost worried.

'What's up man? Aren't you happy man that your America, I mean our USA, is going to make this place a better world?'

'What do you mean a better world? You think this kind of bombing of innocent citizens is going to make it a better place just because the same thing happened two years ago in New York? Is this the way the world should communicate? And what do you mean by our America?'

'Man, you are so serious. I thought all you Australians were supposed to be laid back man. C'mon it's important that the west shows their strength to the rest of the world, particularly those Muslims. Otherwise without them we'd still be living in the dark ages under dictators like Il-Sung and Mao!'

'So showing your might means basically bombing the shit out of a place without permission and without any real proof? I don't get it Zac, and plus this has nothing to do with being laid back!'

'Sure a lot of war and bombings don't make any sense but 9/11 has to be avenged. It just has to be and we shouldn't question that. You have to understand Aussie that what those Muslims did was wrong.'

Jason comes in and adds, 'My adopted country bled so badly that day.'

'And what's all this got to do with South Korea?' I ask.

'This has got everything to do with us. I hope my president also thinks the same way as me.'

Jason explains. 'The Yanks are our long term friends and we can never forget what they did for us in the Korean War. They helped us to defend Seoul at a time when we had been forced so far south. If it wasn't for them we'd be lucky to own any part of this land. The fucking commies would have had us and we'd be like all our northern neighbours now, living in darkness.'

For the second time today I am receiving my 'this is Korea' speech.

'Listen closely Don. The help that the Americans give us to this day is paramount in ensuring that some of us Koreans can have a peaceful life here. We have to defend ourselves and without them we would be fucked. In our second year of university we have to go to the military and we have to be trained to fight in an emergency. It's the hardest part of a man's life, but essentially it is a big part of what makes us men today,' Jason continues.

'What do you mean? Please help me understand this a little more. Where I am from we have choice. So here you are saying it's mandatory?' I reply.

'Of course it is. Every male goes to the military, even our best soccer players, our actors and our businessmen. We have to serve for a whole two whole years.'

'And what's that like Jason?' I ask almost sarcastically.

'Well, it's just something we have to do,' he replies.

'Don, if you're looking at me as an example you better look away. I hated my two years in the army but I had to endure it, 'explains Zac. 'It destroyed my relationship with an old girlfriend and for most of it I was too scrawny and not strong like my peers. We were teased by our seniors. People that didn't hack it would suicide. One day a friend of mine lost his mind and shot seven of the soldiers who wouldn't stop teasing him. He killed them all and then himself. So, in a nutshell it wasn't a good time.'

12

M*A*S*H

Back at the apartment I'm more than content to wile the night away in front of the television, even if it's a hard task avoiding news of Baghdad.

Kevin, on the other hand, is out teaching some private lessons to a council businessman and just as I grab a Hite to relax and wash down dinner my cell rings.

'Hey mate, it's Justin. Want to come around and have a jam tonight? I thought we can make some of our own noise eh?'

'You're right, it is noisy out there. Good reason for me to stay in and rest I think,' I reply.

'You're not going to be able to sleep for a while mate. People are out partying all hours. What with the blockhead American GI's around. They have their heads in their pants with this news on Iraq. They're chomping at the bit. It's Operation Desert Storm all over again,' says Justin, taking the piss out of an American GI accent.

'You should put your t-shirt on mate and go and join them?' I joke.

'I've got it on right now. At least there's some cynicism in the house eh.'

'Any news about it back home?' I ask.

'Yeah, in Sydney they're expecting nearly a million on the bridge this weekend as part of an anti-war rally. Fuck how I wish that I could be there now chanting slogans. It makes me sick seeing all these buzz cuts parading around here.'

'Yeah, you're dead right mate.'

'You know, I was on my way home tonight keeping to myself, and about a hundred meters away from me there were a bunch of soldiers eating barbeque and chanting, "We're going to Iraq, we're going to Iraq, and we're going to get Saddam." It made me sick.'

'They didn't ask us teachers what we thought did they? You should have seen some of the *gyopos* at work. They were in hog heaven over the news.'

'Yeah but those gyopos mate, they think differently to us.'

'So I'm beginning to realize,' I reply.

'Essentially teachers here mean shit mate. Most of us are pacifists, but the worst thing here you know is that we're all seen as Americans. Please rock on over tonight. I could do with the company.'

I accept Justin's offer and on the way over in the cab I think about life and how cool it would be to be a musical duo in a foreign land, belting out covers in small bars. When I get to the apartment address I realize the enormity of the building with its security cameras and high rise accommodation.

Opening the door Justin says, 'Check out the scenery mate. The only eyesore is the army base. See that chopper there? That's one of the many that fly over town. In fact they aren't supposed to at this time of the day. Typical of them but I guess they're just showing off their power and basking in their so-called Christian morals of safety and reputation, once again!'

He then shows me his recently acquired acoustic twelve-string. On the ground are a bunch of chords and lyrics that he wants us to get to know.

'Mate, I have some You Am I, Hunters and Collectors, and even U2 if you're interested. My idea is that we give them some more obscure covers and throw in some old expat favorites. We can go to town on this one. It's 'Throw Your Arms Around Me,' that old Hunters cover. I reckon it's a genuine Australian love song.'

'Yeah, I could probably wing that. I remember some old dude singing it when I was on holidays in Koh Samui in Thailand once. It's easy to play right?' I ask.

'It's a three chord wonder mate. "I will comfort you at night time and I will raise you from your sleep. I will kiss you in four places as I go running along your street." Such great lyrics – a true Australian love song in times of war and trouble. We can stick it up those buzz boys and give them something else to think about,' Justin laughs loudly.

'You really don't like them do you?'

'It's not that I hate them all mate. Please don't get me wrong. I mean, look at Hooch and Frank who you met at Brain the other night. They're not nasty people per se. They're right when they say they'd be in prison without the military. But is that a good enough reason? Firearms aren't going to save the world Don, now are they?' Justin asks.

We both muck around with a few song ideas while sinking some beer. Justin then rolls up a long joint for us to share, and not long after we move to the patio outside. When I start to make a move to go back to my apartment, I sense that he is a little disappointed.

'What are you going back to mate? I mean we both have classes in the morning so fuck it. How about we go to Hells Bells and tell John about our jam tonight. He'd love to see us I'm sure,' Justin excitedly adds.

'But won't the place be full of buzz heads?'

'Not now. Most of them should be back in camp. C'mon mate we'll just have the one. I know what you mean. I also had a terrible hangover today.'

When we get to Hells Bells it seems curfew is later because it's crammed full of soldiers.

'At least by midnight most of them will be gone?' I say.

'Man, look at them would you? They are like a pack of dogs ready to unleash themselves on someone.'

'I can see that. Sometimes I can't believe that I'm living in an army town.'

'Essentially they are all army towns here mate. They are all over the peninsula.'

'What do John and David think of them?' I ask.

'They don't have time to make any comment. They are business for the bar and they spend big. However, they are less likely to bring out the tequila shots for them. I think they are worried that if they did, it would only take one loose cannon to get wound up.'

Noticing Hooch and Frank, we have no choice but to join them.

'Hey what's up? Good to see you Aussie fellows. Frank and I here have just been shooting shit for hours. I guess you have heard the news eh? We two might get a chance to shoot some AK47 in Iraq man!' Hooch bellows at the top of his voice.

'Way to go guys, way to go,' is the chant from most people at the bar. It's cheesy corny stuff, but we both sense it is better to not make any personal comments so we don't upset anyone. Soon, the military police walk in and within seconds the place clears. Hooch and Frank leave so we take to the bar to share our music news with John.

'You guys are great man. I am so happy that you have had a jam. Justin has been hanging out to play in my bar and now you're here Don that's great,' John says.

'You must be feeling better now it's gone quiet then?' I ask.

'Yes and no. They are good for business but they can get very rowdy from time to time. Shall we have a shot for future good times then? And I don't mean war.'

'Sure, we can do that can't we Don?' Justin adds.

'Of course,' I reply, knowing that I could be setting myself up for another drink fest.

Just as we're lining up our shots a senior looking man walks into the bar. Still feeling a little stoned from our jam we have problems answering his quick fire questions.

'What's happening here tonight you two? I couldn't help noticing you both, particularly the top you are wearing my friend? What's the meaning behind that?'

'As an Australian I wear it a lot. It's a bit like that Canadian/ American thing. You should know about that? We need to make those distinctions sometimes sir.'

We try to ignore him, and as we begin to have our shots he interrupts again and says who he is,

'My name is Chester, and I'm proudly out of North Carolina. And Aussie I take it that your shirt has nothing to do with not wanting to be from my country – correct?'

'Like I said it's just a shirt and to be honest I don't need to feel that my identity is American when it obviously isn't. After all, we all come from somewhere.'

'Now I have been studying Korean for years and this reads, "I am not an American!" Praise the good lord, but I am sorry because I am deeply offended by it!'

'Like he said Chester, it isn't meant to offend anyone,' I reply.

'But it is an offence. You're basically cleaning your hands of what we represent, which is freedom and democracy. Without any of that the world wouldn't be what we live in today my friend.'

'That's arbitrary and you know it,' replies Justin.

After some silence, John aptly decides to play Jimi Hendrix's version of 'Star Spangled Banner' cranking up the decibels. Chester quickly downs his beer, holding his head high before making his way out of the bar.

13

NOTHING IS 100%

Bleary eyed and half-asleep I make my way to the office to the 6:30 a.m. class but yet again no one shows. I'm only half way out of the classroom when Mr. Lee walks up to me somewhat pissed off that I am about to go.

'Where you go? What you do?' he says in a barking voice.

'There is no one here. No student here today boss. I'm going to have some *hae-jung-guk*. Maybe you can come with me?'

'You drink again? That's why you want our soup? You think I don't know what you do at night? Ok, we go soup now and then we go Japan! I take you to airport then you go Osaka ok. You must go Osaka today and come back tonight. You get your visa today or we have passport problem. And don't worry I pay airfare,' he informs me.

'But today I am teaching and you said nothing to me about Osaka. Christ that's another country. And just in one day? Surely you could give me some notice,' I say in a low voice.

'We have no time. We must go. We must get visa stamp. We have soup now and then go. We go.'

The *ajuma* is again happy to see me and knows exactly what I have come for. Laughing she says, '*Ojae pam, meakju, soju?*' (Last night you have beer, soju?)

'Um it was *meakju* and *soju*, auntie.'

Lee gives me a hearty pat on the back as if he is praising my limited Korean. The *ajuma* then prepares the soup in barely a minute. Lee is in a hurry and like most of the locals he ploughs through his food like a thoroughbred so I can't keep up with him.

'*Ba-li ba-li* quickly,' he says.

In no time we are in his van and with Lee driving like a maniac it takes around an hour to reach the outskirts of Seoul. This means we're roughly two and bit hours away from the airport terminal.

'What time is my plane?' I ask him.

'You know, no English,' he shouts back.

I point to my watch and then make an aeroplane gesture by flapping my arms.

'Ok I know. We go faster. Hang on to your seat!' Lee shouts.

He puts the foot down accelerating only to stall in the Seoul peak-hour traffic. Ahead of us cars are ambling at a snail pace into the big smoke - some honking at each other, impatient, and not so polite. Soon a large white Pajero van makes a bee line for us.

Lee shouts out, 'Mother fucker – *arsh* (shit) you *ship pal* (fuck) you motherfucker!'

A man then gets out of his car to let Lee know that he was only playing a game. Lee then jumps out of the van and both their shrieking laughter and animation catches the attention of the traffic around them. Soon other cars start honking their horns in celebration of the two drivers. One would get the impression that they have both known each other for years. When Lee jumps back into the van after one more lingering hug, I ask him if he knew the guy in the white van.

Lee replies happily, 'Yes, he my *chinggu* - my school friend.'

Taking the airport expressway, Lee continues to swerve and dodge traffic not giving a fuck about anyone else. He's what I call a road anarchist with the every man for himself driver mentality. It seems that in some cases the bigger the car you own the more prestige and power you have on the road. For some there's a real disregard of the road rules, at least between the tollgates. You pay your money to the toll and the rest is pretty much open slather while you're on the highways.

By the time Lee drops me at the international terminal, he cautiously reminds, 'Just one day ok? Meaning you come back tonight to here. If you don't, you pay the Japan hotel ok?'

Looking at my watch I reckon I have missed the check in time.

'No English, no English! Just hurry and go now,' Lee shouts as he gives me the tickets before heading off.

But inside it's too late. The plane is boarding and I have missed the check in. I have two options – the midday flight or the same plane tomorrow morning. Either way I will have to stay a night.

In a panic I ask, 'Can't you race me through to my flight? Please, if it's boarding now. We still have time surely?'

'Sorry sir. I cannot take you there now. You are supposed to be here three hours before your flight leaves. It is international after all. How about we book you onto the midday flight instead? It's only two hours from now and I can fit you in no problem.'

'Ok then but my boss won't be happy,' I confirm.

While I am waiting I notice the headline from the English newspaper, *The Korean Herald*. In bold letters it reads 'Americans strive to make Iraq pay.' The airport security here is tight. Each customer is being checked, while some are asked to take their shoes off to ensure that they aren't concealing anything dangerous.

'No bottles from outside. No bottles sir,' shouts one of the attendants.

The first thing I notice is the lack of Koreans on the plane. The flight is loaded with business people and tourists from Japan. Their body manner and even fashion sense is a dead giveaway. They seem less pushy and aren't as anxious unlike some neighbors as comments of "you sit", "no you sit", "thank you", "excuse me", "are you ok?" bounce around the walls.

The power of the yen is a contributing factor to the amount of Japanese people on board. Many flock to Seoul for a day or two just because they can, particularly because the cost of living in Japan is so high.

Just before the hostess announces that the passengers need to make sure their seats are in an upright position, two young backpacker types board the plane. They both have an air of coolness about them as they take their seats. I try to get one's attention but he isn't interested.

The colour of the winter sky is blue and sharp when the plane leaves. It's only a short flight, maybe an hour and a half, so it seems like no time has passed when the plane lands, much to the happiness of the passengers who clap loudly in appreciation.

'Welcome to Japan, welcome to our country,' the flight attendants say as we exit the plane and like some Koreans they also cover their mouths and giggle.

Through customs I then take the city bound express train to Osaka on the orange line. I bump into the two backpackers, but it's bleeding obvious that they want nothing to do with me.

'Hey there, are you two off to the visa office? Is it this way?' I ask. 'It's ok I don't mean to bother you or anything.'

'Yeah, we're off there, and yeah you are going the right way,' the tall blonde American guy replies.

'Ah, are you Americans? In the army hey like every other one in Korea?' I jokingly ask to piss them off a little.

'Actually we're teachers and we've got to go because we're in a real hurry mate,' says his friend.

Before I get a chance to ask if it is ok for me to tag along with them they're gone. They have made their message clear, such is the 'hands off' code for people abroad who like to avoid others. Not that I care. These guys are probably more intent on hanging out in Korean bars, picking up Korean girls, learning the language, and trying to be as un-western as possible. And fair enough too, but if that's their trip I don't need to be told. It's not as if I was asking them for their life story.

What their antics do though is remind me of a German I met once in Thailand who went on about how he thought all Australians and New Zealanders seemed extra friendly and interested in others. He had an opinion on every nation. In his eyes Americans were mainly loud mouths and full of themselves, whilst most Brits were sarcastic, funny but a little cold. Canadians on the other hand were a little noisy and said 'eh' and 'like' a lot, whilst Israelis were horny, loud and obnoxiously cool. Generalisations do abound in expatriate life.

As the train races and speeds into town, I put on my disc-man and listen to Silver Ray, an instrumental act from Melbourne. It's as if their music fits; the sky, the air, and the low density housing. Although it's a seething mass, Japan's second biggest city seems shiny and hip, much like the cities of Melbourne and Amsterdam.

Getting a taxi is also fairly straightforward. A cream-coloured sedan greets you with an electric opening door. I show the address to the driver, who bows his head knowingly murmuring, *Hai hai*. (Yes, Yes).

There's a long line at the immigration office so I wait patiently for my turn. Ahead I notice the two American teachers. They stand over the small Japanese assistant yelling at her hoping that they can quickly get their visas done.

'We are in a hurry miss. We want to get back to Seoul tonight. Please help us,' they shout, almost overtaking the room with their loud voices.

'Sorry but we cannot do this for you. Maybe you have to stay in Osaka tonight. I am incredibly sorry sir but you will need to stay here,' she replies.

'But our boss said it wouldn't be a problem. I mean why all this red tape? We were told it could happen almost straight away,' the smaller paunchier one asks politely.

'I am sorry sir. It seems that your boss gave you the wrong information. I apologize but we can't do this for you. You have to wait like everyone else,' she replies.

The tall blonde guy bangs his fist down on the counter shouting at the assistant. Embarrassed, his friend walks out of the line and not long later they both pass me in a fit of anger, letting me know that it'll take two days.

'Sorry happy Aussie but you're going to have to wait an extra day here. You are going to have to suck it up man!'

I chuckle to myself, not too worried as I give the assistant all my paperwork before heading to a nearby Holiday Inn.

Although I have to fork out 150 AUD for the night, I am not that fussed. I'm only too happy to soak up a city like this before heading back to Seoul. Armed with my disc-man I take to the streets like a kid on candy, or even a drug addict, totally enthralled by the town and what it has to offer. It's this part of travel that I love and for me it's quite therapeutic - being somewhere alien, listening to music, watching people on the street going about their everyday business. It's what reminds me of my earlier backpacker times in my twenties, visiting the streets of South East Asia soaking up the smells and the smiling faces. What I particularly love about Asia is the way some people smile. Osaka isn't exactly like those places. It is different with its hipster feel of wealth and technological development and leaves the transport systems of my own home town lagging far behind.

Up ahead, I notice lots of neon lights promoting sex shows and strip clubs. Some tattooed Japanese men stand outside of them with their arms folded, watching like hawks as people pass by.

'Fucky fucky show. Come see! Very good time here for you my friend,' a larger built goateed man shouts.

I avoid him and instead notice a place advertising *udon* noodles and tempura fish. I walk inside the small cafe, otherwise known as an *izakaya* and I am soon descended upon by six members of staff. They all try to take my coat off and get me to sit down and I gratefully oblige. I look at the menu and find a picture I like of battered seafood *tempura* with rice. Soon I'm led into another room of more tables and waitresses who look like maids. They are wearing very short white dresses and seem happy to see me.

'Konbanwa! Good evening! Please come in and welcome to our new chain of special Japanese restaurants. These places of fine dining and fun are new to Japan - one of our country's very fine new inventions,' says one maid.

The rest of the maids cover their mouths whilst trying not to giggle too loudly. A rather voluptuous maid leans over me showing the menu and I point at the seafood and she takes down my order.

'Why, thank you master! At your service and should your require my help please don't hesitate to ask,' she says as she straightens my shirt.

'We have many games here to play. Would you like to play the cleaning game where one of us spills food on you and we clean it up in a sexy way?' another maid asks.

'Or how about some ear cleaning?' says the next maid.

After a barrage of these rapid-fire questions, I quickly reply that I just want some food.

While I'm waiting I notice a flyer on the table advertising this very street as being full of themed restaurants. This is a maid restaurant whilst next door is the Vampire Café and behind that is a Christian one. The former one specializes in an interior which is steeped in red blood with drapes of heavy velvet and coffins that are covered in candle wax, skulls and crosses. Most of the meals are themed but food isn't really the important focus. The Christian place on the other hand is gothic and a little on the macabre side, which would probably raise the eyes of most god-fearing shareholders. I eat quickly resisting the temptations made by the maids to engage in some food frolicking and cleaning.

14

ABANDON SHIP

On the four hour bus ride from the airport I notice the ducks again when we come to a roundabout. They are busy at work on a frozen part of the Han River. Gazing out the window, I can see thousands of them almost helplessly bashing their beaks into frozen chunks of ice. At times it is like watching paint dry; this repetitive sound which echoes their efforts. At the same time it is also eerie and surreal. Then within a second a loud chorus of screeches and squawks are heard before the engine of the bus resumes its journey.

I decide to take a good look at my new paperwork and my freshly stamped passport. I notice that the terms of my visa have an employment status for twelve months and that is bound to the contract I have signed. It says 'under no circumstances is the holder allowed to work elsewhere in the contracted period other than for who they are assigned employment to.'

The demand for private tutoring means that a lot of teachers don't care much for the visa terms. After all, most teachers are either forced to take on other work because of the dodgy schools that employ them, or simply because they are hungry for money and have substantial debt back home. Also in South Korea the belief of most English teachers is that the contract reads one way in your home country and another when you arrive. Hence I need to remember that what I'd signed with the recruiter back in Sydney was probably a different document to the one that Chae and Lee had presented me. Either way I now have the gold E-visa (employment) in my passport which I am pretty sure will count for something if shit did hit the fan at Global World.

When I arrive at work, I see Jason and notice that So-Hee is upset and sobbing.

She tells me her news, 'I am so sorry Mr. Don. My English is very poor but I must tell you our Lee, he has left Chuncheon and no one is sure where he has gone.'

'I don't understand. You mean he has cleared out? Gone?' I ask.

'Cleared out? Um, yes I am sorry Mr. Don; yes he has gone from here. Yesterday he take you to the plane. Then he go. Maybe south down to Busan. We are not sure. He left nothing here.'

'So-Hee, have you told Kevin and the other teachers?'

'Kevin and Daphne maybe they know, but you know Mr. Don that Mona and he had a big fight. Maybe Lee scared now. I just don't know! Our problem is there is no money and this Global World here maybe no longer.'

Jason interrupts us and tries to explain the new situation, 'Hey mate, sorry to bother you but how did you get on in Osaka?'

'It was fine Jason. I had to stay an extra day but it wasn't the worse thing,' I reply.

'That's ok. We heard that the boss dropped you at the airport. Can you believe it? He has upped and left the place after hiring us two guys. He simply cleaned out all his belongings yesterday. What was he thinking?'

'It does sound pretty strange to me, though it isn't too much of a shock to tell you the truth. Talk to most people and they will tell you that he was up to his eyeballs in debt and the very fact that he hired all three of us never made much sense. Surely he did a lot of it on credit?' I ask.

'Everything is done here on credit. He probably had a bunch of accounts, kept a few safe, while the others were ransacked through his own usage. Man the guy needs a swift kick in the balls,' shouts Zac.

Kevin can hear us talking and happily joins in the anti-boss tirade.

'Yep he is a cunt no doubt about it. I mean, like I have said many times before, how can he sleep at night with all this going on around him? You told Don your news yet Jason?'

'No I haven't but I will now. Don, I am going to be the caretaker here for a while. We need to get this place back into shape. I have done some management back in the States for a golf magazine. We're in a mess here and it will take some time to get out of it, but I think we can survive so please trust me,' insists Jason.

'Yeah man! I know that we can. Fighting is the best way,' interrupts Zac. 'I don't want to be the laughing stock of my country. After all, I'm originally from this little humdinger of a town and I am not working for any dodgy English school.'

'Who said you aren't now?' questions Kevin.

'We will see,' Zac replies.

Daphne and Mona arrive, and when they hear that Lee's missing they too are angry.

'He's a cheeky cunt excuse my language. He really is a weak human being. I tell him the truth and he runs away down to wherever because he can't face up to his demons. Damn him!' shouts Mona, as she bangs her fist on a table, yet again.

'Calm down would you. There's not a lot we can do about it for now,' adds Jason. 'We have to hang in there.'

'How many times have we been told to say nothing and just get along with it?' questions Daphne. 'Sorry, but I am not even really sure who you are? For fuck sake is does get a little tiring all this bullshit. I mean, why do we have to be so polite?'

'Because it is custom that we don't over react,' explains Jason.

'Fuck that. It's just some man-made rule for crying out loud! Sorry but that man has ripped the whole bleeding company off and a good part of this town. Plus our customers are hurting because of this! The morale of the staff here is at an all time low and you're saying we have to hang in there and be calm? I don't quite get it.'

'Sorry, and by the way I am Jason. I know that we have met before. You're Daphne right? And you must be Mona? Look, I really do understand both of your feelings. I know what it is like to be in a foreign place and to be ripped off. If you want to know the truth I had an awful experience as an apprentice journalist back in the States.'

'This kind of thing would never happen back there. What are you talking about?' challenges Mona.

'Well sadly the fucked up thing was that it did. My boss, an American, took us all to town. He got us the best tickets to the premier golf events on the tour, but he fell short didn't he? He failed to pay us for our last three months so the company went bust.'

'So fucking what!' Mona interrupts.

'Look Mona, I know you're going tomorrow and this might mean shit to you but we can visit the office and lodge an application before you go. I can't promise you anything but we can try.'

'Ok. I will go with you tomorrow,' Mona replies half-heartedly.

'But one more thing before you leave now is that I think as employees of Global World we should all go out tonight. We need to let off some steam and laugh a little. After your last class this evening, I want all of you to come and try and forget this mess for a bit. We can all take a taxi to the other side of town where I know a great *galbi* restaurant. After that, I am sure you foreigners know some fun bars that you can introduce Zac and me to.'

'Oh, yes we certainly do,' I add.

15

BOOZE

The *galbi* meat place is classy. It's an establishment where every customer is fawned over as waitresses are quick to take your coats off and escort you to a big table. Deep bows are exhibited as a mark of respect to the customer. On the walls there are portraits of South Korean leaders, each with their own story. The one that captures my attention is an old portrait of the nation's famous leader from the 1970s, Park Chung Hee, who was assassinated.

'That guy made a huge mark in our political history so much so that they made films about him,' explains Zac. 'We had an industrial revolution when he was our president. He made the country what it is today, though I have to say that in doing so he was a ruthless pig. You could call him a power-monger-of-an-asshole, but that'd probably be treason for some. We don't forget him. Guys like Jason and I were brought up on his legacy.'

'Yeah,' adds Jason, 'He instilled this rigid army militaristic feeling into Korean education and if you didn't follow his rules you would be strictly dealt with. That's why some Korean parents these days believe that it is their right to be harsh, even ruthless with their children. His belief was that education wasn't about having fun which is different to you western people, am I right Don?'

'Yes and no I would say but I am no real expert,' I respond.

'This guy believed that the only way to succeed was to get the highest score possible, at any cost. It goes back to our rice and poverty days,' explains Jason.

'What do you mean by that?' I ask.

'Well I am not so sure about Australia, but here we had it tough - particularly our parents. I mean, can you imagine eating only a bowl of rice a day and maybe some watered-down porridge for breakfast? Such were the living conditions back then. We just didn't have the money that you developed countries have always been blessed with.'

'I disagree with you there. In New Zealand, money didn't grow on trees for my ancestors either. There were hard times and people struggled. We had to work really hard to get where we are today and we still do. I mean you have to remember it takes years for countries to develop. I think you need to read some more history books you guys,' Daphne points out. 'Otherwise we will make gross generalizations and that isn't right.'

I then add, 'Daphne is right I reckon. After all, development has to start from somewhere, though what happened to our indigenous people was cruel too. But it doesn't mean you have to fuck someone over in the process either.'

'Are you talking about the Maoris and the Aboriginals?' asks Jason.

Both Daphne and I retreat for a little, knowing that what happened to our indigenous people was completely fucked up. Jason knows he now has us in a corner and continues his monologue on the former leader.

'Ok, my friends, I guess you can see what I am getting at. I am trying to explain to you that without great asshole leaders like this man, we may not be the country we are today. He is one great asshole and I mean that in the most positive and negative way. His daughter will be President one day - you watch. Anyway, I don't want to talk politics anymore because we are here to have some fun and let off some steam. So I say let's order and eat, but first we will drink a toast to our team and then we can dine on the best succulent *galbi* in town.'

Jason will take centre stage tonight seeing he is the oldest here aside from Daphne. He will order, initiate the toasting and control everything. In Korean culture the boss gets all privileges at the table and is always the master of ceremonies. We are expected to follow him and not even eat before him.

Four bottles of the finest *soju* arrive and each member of the table stands for a toast. I stand excitedly and instead of waiting for the others I fill my glass before Jason tells me to wait my turn. Having spent some time in the States, he can understand that I mightn't know protocol, so in a back-handed joking kind of way he tells me not to offend him. Together we shout *kom-bae* or cheers and starting from him we go around the table and do our best to each down the *soju* in one shot. But it doesn't stop there. Jason gestures to the waitresses to refill our glasses. I can hardly control my giddiness, taking to my chair like an amateur, whilst Mona's face turns a bright shade of pink.

Two mini-barbecues are set up on the table and it is Zac and Jason who cut the meat into bite size pieces using scissors, while an endless supply of green lettuce leaves and small bowls of garlic and bean paste are brought to our table. Kevin whispers to me to take some water to nullify the *soju* so that I won't feel too sick on an empty stomach. The small grills are then heated and the indoor barbecue begins. For an hour or so we feast on succulent supplies of meat which we cook and roll up into lettuce.

For a meat lover this is a real treat – a classy Korean restaurant with some locals who know what they're doing. The last course is a bean paste soup that is piping hot and served with barley rice on the side. Dessert then arrives in the shape of a plum drink which is sweet and refreshing. When we finish up we're more than ready for some heavy drinking by the university gate.

First we stop at Jacks which is surprisingly quiet for a Friday night. The only people there are the two Mikes and my Australian mate Justin, who seems preoccupied with a girl that looks in her early twenties.

'Yeah mate I will come over and talk to you a bit later. Got my hands full and I am not sure how this is going to play out,' Justin says while taking a break from her.

'It's more than ok mate. We are on a work thing anyway. Good luck then,' I respond before all of us opt for a big table near the front window.

It isn't long before we all feel a little embarrassed by Jason who continues to dominate the talking and the ordering. He isn't ready to shut up either or let anyone else share ideas.

'Ok, since we're having such a great night folks, let's try and up it a notch or two. I can tell that my buddy Zac and the rest of you could do with some extra shots. After all, it puts hairs on your chest, and us Koreans could do with a little more of them,' he shouts.

The rest of the table half smile at his comments knowing that we have to suck it up for now. We are all hoping that some of our own friends will show up and rescue us. As we stand for another group shot, Jack and Carol arrive for some drinking and socializing. Daphne and Mona call them both over but Zac interrupts, reminding them that tonight they're part of a work function so it's best they respect that.

'It's not that I don't like your friends. It's just that tonight we have to stay together,' Jason adds.

'But these people are our good friends, trust me. They work at the local university here. Can't they at least sit next to us? After all it's a free world isn't it, Zac?'

'Ok' Zac says reluctantly.

Carol and Jack settle in before they are joined by David, who straight away can tell we are engaged in work shenanigans.

'Typical Korean style I can tell. They don't know the meaning of sipping,' David says, referring to how pissed we all seem.

An inebriated looking Gordon then arrives and orders his own *soju* beer chaser so we all follow suit. Jason interrupts again asking all of us to play a drinking game.

'Ok guys this is a great game called The Titanic. The idea is to float your shot glass in the beer and make sure it keeps floating. So you take a sip, then the next person sips and so on. The person that's sipping when the glass sinks must skull all that's left. It's not that easy but I think we can all have some fun with it.'

A booming voice at a nearby table interrupts proceedings, 'That sounds like a great game man. Do you mind if I join you dudes?'

Jason adds, 'My friend we don't really know you but can I ask you, where do you come from in the States? That's a familiar accent if I have ever heard one buddy.'

'I am from New Jersey. You might know it? It's a place called Newark you know and it's famous for an airport. Most people call it the armpit of America.'

'Yeah I know that place,' boasts Jason.

'Anyway, can I fucking sit down with you guys? You know, I just arrived in town and all the military folk are staying at home tonight.'

'Sure, what's your name?' Jason asks.

'It's Matt.'

'What brought you over here Matt?' Zac asks.

'I just got to Korea. I was a marine in Africa for a bit. Do you remember that movie 'Black Hawk Down'? You could say I was almost in it.'

'The one with the apaches and shit?' asks Jason.

'Yeah that was me. I also took a posting to Germany. After that I thought what the hell am I going to do with my life, so I went back home to Jersey and decided to study engineering. And now I have a job as a contractor for the military.'

'So you're not a soldier then?' I ask.

'Hell no! I will never be a fucking soldier again. I get paid well for what I do now. Finally I can work on the lasers for the helicopters. It's interesting stuff and I don't have to go to the front line and shoot guns - which suits me fine,' he adds.

'But in some ways you are still in the front line anyway - don't you think? You're pressing buttons after all? You're just as responsible mate.' interrupts Justin who has now finished with his date.

'Look, I don't even know you, and I think you need to think about what you're saying. Sure there are weapons involved in war but these terrorists that we are up against are able to hide in the most secluded of places. Like our good President has said on CNN over and over again - we must do our best to smoke them out of their holes or we're never going to get rid of this scum.'

'What a load of rubbish,' Justin concurs. 'There's no proof in the pudding my friend.'

'What's got up your ass mate?' Matt asks. 'We're here for a drink for fuck sake, not a political discussion man.'

I whisper in Justin's ear telling him not to worry. At this stage he is fuming so he goes outside for a cigarette. As he leaves I ask him if he is ok and he tells me that the date went all pear shaped and the last thing he needed was some guy telling him about his leaders wishes.

In the background the drinking game is getting noisy so when David asks me about my work situation, we decide to go to another table to chat and have a cigarette. I then quietly tell him about the visa situation and today's new news.

'I am not in a good place at the moment mate. I don't know what to do. The best thing is I now have my E-visa, so I might be ok if any shit goes down. But to tell you the truth I am not that comfortable talking about it right now.'

'You followed me over to the table mate.'

'Yeah I know. I am just a little tired of talking the same shit about how fucked up my job is, and how people always ask me why did you come here, and why don't you just go home. It's boring.

'I think I can help you. I know someone that will take some pressure off you. His name is Mr. Lee and he recruits people on the quiet for jobs out of town. You can earn a packet I promise for not that much work,' David confides.

'Mr. Lee? Shit, my boss has the same name. Even that stinks,' I respond.

'It's a common name for fuck sake.'

'So why should I meet this one? I can barely trust them mate. I mean really, what is this Mr. Lee going to do?' I question.

'Trust me. At least give it a go. On Monday I want you to go down to the LG supermarket in the downtown. I'll set it up for you. I won't be there but I'll make sure he is. I met him there last Monday. He actually hangs out in the area just to meet people like us. You have to try. It might just take the pressure off.'

'Ok, I will try then,' I reply. 'Thanks for your help David.'

Winding down after a few goes at the Titanic, most of the work party are ready to go back home. It is only Zac and Jason who are still keen to tie one on so David and I join them for a song or two at a *norae bang* karaoke room before heading home.

16

A MEETING OF MONEY

The work party on Friday evening took its toll. Saturday was a complete write-off and by Sunday I had little time for anything except day-to-day chores. Gordon called and tried to get me out to kick a soccer ball but I chose to stick around home instead. After all I had other things on my mind, particularly this other Mr. Lee who I had to meet tomorrow morning outside LG supermarket, a new franchise on the other side of town.

LG is the epitome of the brands it sells, i.e. Nike and Adidas - the rich mainstream, the popular and the new money brigade. So for many of the forty-seven million South Koreans it's the place to be seen. People don't just shop at LG; they flock there mostly on weekends, crowding the aisles to see what products they have on offer. Kitchen appliances, children's toys, oversized underwear and housing appliances populate the racks, while in the basement there seems to be large endless aisles of food, stocking frozen, fresh, green and even live stuff.

The next day when I head on down there I feel blown away by its enormity, so I linger outside for a cigarette but just as I am about to finish I am tapped on the shoulder by a suited middle-aged man with a soft voice.

'They are bad for you but I guess you know that? I used to smoke for donkey's years and drink. My doctor told me to give them up so I did. Haven't had one for ten years now and guess what?' he asks.

'What?' I ask.

'I have just turned fifty! It's a milestone for us Koreans you know. My liver is functional and my hair, unlike you my friend isn't falling out. I play ping pong every day and my weight is normal. I am your opposite my friend.'

'Look mate I am not waiting here to be criticized. Who the hell are you?' I ask.

'You're the kangaroo guy right?' he asks.

'Um, yeah I guess you could say that. I am a skip if that is what you mean? Do you know what that means?' I add.

'Well Skippy was the name of the bush kangaroo wasn't he?'

'Wow, you are smart,' I reply.

'By the way, Don I am Lee and David my good British friend has mentioned that you need to see me. It's good to meet you,' he says shaking my hand firmly.

'Likewise Mr. Lee,' I respond.

'Don, let's not talk here. I know a café down the road where we can go. Can you see that van? We're going to drive five minutes down the road. I can even treat you to a coffee if you like mate?'

'A coffee would be good.'

The café is called English Corner, another small chain that has been set up to promote the joy of learning English and speaking to potential foreign native speakers. It has also become a bit of a pick-up place for English keeners and teachers.

Lee tells me how he knows the owner here and how he often brings people for a coffee and a chat when he wants to do business. Upon entering I notice that Arizona Mike is here talking to a middle-aged business woman.

'I thought about hiring him once but the parents of the kids weren't interested when they saw his photo. He looks too much like us. They want a pure native speaker. You do know what I mean don't you Skippy?' Lee says.

'Yes, I can see what you mean, but I don't think one should discriminate on the basis of colour. He is probably a much better teacher than I am plus he's had more experience. I talked to him the other night and he seems really professional but he's annoyed that people don't take him that seriously because of his skin colour.'

'Yes, but that doesn't mean anything here my friend. Half the time it is more about how good you look than how well you can teach,' Lee explains.

We order coffee before Lee gets down to business, opening his shiny black bag and preparing a notepad and pen.

'So Mr. Don, I heard from David that you are in some trouble? I am aware of Global World and its financial problems. The whole town knows and it won't be long before that place is closed. He is a bad guy that Lee and he has annoyed so many people. I doubt he will return Don because that my friend is the Korean way.'

'What do you mean the Korean way?' I ask.

'When things go bad some people here don't want to show their face so they run. He is aware that people know of his *soju* and gambling habits. He has run out of friends in this town so his next choice will be to leave. We can only hope that the police or someone will finally get him. Man I would love to see him gone.'

'I am confused. What will happen to him? Hopefully they will lock him up?'

'You would think so but you can never tell. After all this is South Korea where things aren't so cut and dry,' he warns. 'Don, what you badly need now is some money so I want to introduce you to a small country school that is absolutely hanging out for a teacher like you, and particularly one that comes from Australia. It's not rocket science my friend. You just need to teach the basics – A to z, Simple Simon, The Hokey Pokey. You know them?'

'Yeah I get it.'

'Trust me Mr. Don. We can even go and see them today if you like?'

'Ok, let's go. I could do with getting out of this town for a little bit.'

'Don't worry, the school is only half an hour away, and you will also see some countryside. I love going to this place Mr. Don and you will too. I can fix you up by driving you there for a bit, but once you become comfortable you'll need to get your own way there,' Lee adds.

As we drive out of town we do a bit of small talk such as family and jobs etc. In fairly good English he tells me he is married and that he has his own business.

'So what kind of business do you run?' I ask.

'English of course. And guess what Skippy? We have six classes a day and we have two native English speaking teachers.'

He then tells me that his main dough comes from Korean elementary public schools, which are now taking on conversational English from Grade 3 as part of the national curriculum.

'You see I am well known around this region. I find teachers for these schools. I am a middle man,' he says.

'Another business guy hey? I hope you're better than the guy who I am working for.' I reply.

'Look mate, I am here to help you. It works two ways ok? Trust me you won't be disappointed.'

'I am all ears.'

By the time we arrive, the school is getting ready for lunch. It is real country living - lots of chooks crammed around miniature old houses with basic amenities. The South Korean flag flutters outside as the loudspeakers request the students' attention for lunch. It has the feeling of a bygone era - it's as if communism has never really left this village.

Kids openly stare at me in the corridors pointing and screaming, '*Wae-guk* ha-ha *wae-guk* ha-ha – look at the foreigner!'

I smile back and point, saying, 'Korean ha-ha, Korean ha-ha' and the kids run away giggling, with the girls covering their mouths, just like the housewives back at Global World.

Lee takes me into the principal's office and I wait patiently in a chair while they chat. The headmaster, Mr. Park greets me and offers a cigarette which I have little choice but to accept. We can barely communicate, but he seems impressed, smiling back at me while nervously laughing.

In broken English he mutters, 'Tomorrow ok, tomorrow?'

I reply, 'Ok!'

I can see that Mr. Lee is chuffed, rubbing his hands, aware that he has probably sealed another transaction. I shake hands with both of them as a gesture for their support and although we haven't talked money yet I have a feeling that this will be ok. What I also have to remember is that in Korean culture the protocol is that money comes last in any conversation about business. Hence it is only on our way back that he tells me that I will be working two afternoons a week for a healthy sum.

17

EXIT DOOR

When I arrive back I notice that Mona is waiting to grab a taxi to the bus station.

'Hey, there, it's good to see you Mona. I guess you're happy to be getting out of here?' I ask.

'Well there isn't much you can do about it is there?' she responds. 'You better get out of here too otherwise you will be left swimming in this shithole.'

'I get your drift Mona. How did you get on with the money you're owed?' I ask.

'Well, that's another fucking story. That-know-it-all Jason and I went to the Labor Office today and all they could say was that it's going to be hard to get any money back, particularly if I leave the country. But hey I'm not going to hang here in this godforsaken place and wait forever am I?'

'Look Mona. I am sorry and if there is anything we can do we will try. I met a good Mr. Lee today and he has hooked me up with this great job at a country school not far from here. They are real village kids and all.'

'Is that the guy that preys on whiteys when they go shopping at LG?'

'Yeah, that's him. He's such a nice man and I reckon I can trust this one. He's the good Mr. Lee in my books.'

'Well, trust me mate he isn't what he seems. Don't believe a word that any of these people say, and if you decide to believe anyone, do make sure your ass is covered. I have seen it happen too many fucking times. Anyway my taxi is here so I better go. Good luck Aussie even if this place is shit.'

As the cab approaches, I offer to help with her heavy bags. I try to give her a hug but she doesn't want anything of it, only half-heartedly meeting my gesture.

The next morning is my first day at the elementary school so I decide to suit up for it. As I open my apartment door, Mr. Lee is most impressed.

'Well, well you foreigners really are a mixed bag. I mean my teachers always come to school in casual wear. They are always scruffy? I think that's the word isn't it?'

'That's it. Your English is good Mr. Lee,' I reply.

'I swear that Broderick the boy who works for me wouldn't know what a suit is. He's a little scruffy, and I don't like it. One should always make a good first impression in this country my friend. After all it is paramount to make people notice you. I think we should always dress as if we are going to church. The more immaculate you are the better is my belief.'

'I cannot promise to do it all the time, but I will try my best,' I reply.

Knowing that today should be a relatively easy task, I am also aware that it could also sap my energy. Teaching kids isn't an easy task, and it's true that most foreign teachers prefer adults, where conversation is a little more stimulating and not as draining. However the money in Korea is with teaching kids, with many a private and public school branching out to accommodate new interests that have been invested in English education.

As we arrive a dozen or so kids run to greet me. They crowd around me latching onto my ankles, some attempting to jump into my arms. Whilst Chuncheon probably sees a hundred foreigners at most, villages like Sangcheon are lucky to see one.

At the door we meet the principal Mr. Park, who smiles approvingly at my suit.

'Look nice and very handsome.'

'*Gam sa ham ni da!*' I reply in my best Korean to say thanks.

'Your Korean is very good as well Don. Please come inside as the children are excited to meet you.'

Mr. Park speaks more English than I realised. He is a proud man, most likely in his mid-fifties and like a lot of Korean men his vintage, he does a good job keeping his hair and stopping it from graying.

When we enter the dining room about a hundred or so children stand and welcome me. An older lady in the corner of the room strikes some keys on an old rusty piano and everyone places their right hand firmly on to their hearts as a form of respect for their national anthem. They all then bow to a photo of the current leader, President Roh Moo Hyun, before the principal publicly welcomes me.

'We all want to say that we are very grateful for you being here. Thanks so much and we expect to learn very much English from you.'

I smile and reply that I will do my best to help them. My job is to come here twice a week to teach two combined classes grades three/ four, and five/ six. I haven't taught kids before so I am quite clueless about my role and this is obvious when I walk into my first class with Park and Lee who are beside me. The children are running around shouting in excitement. I must say I feel somewhat intimidated.

Park tells me to calm down, 'Don't worry Mr. Don. Think of yourself as an old pro and they will all love you. Look, this is what I like to do,' he says while grabbing a stick and slamming it down on the desks.

Like a pack of dogs the students wilt to his attention. He then grins widely, hollering at them in Korean, whilst I look nervously at my new class from the side of the room, 'You can start now Mr. Don but you need to come to the centre like me.'

'Hello! My name is Don and I am your new teacher. Everyone together say Don!'

This falls on deaf ears so Park then translates to the students.

'Don. Don. Don,' the students repeat three times.

Sensing the struggle to motivate them, Park suggests a new method, 'I know one thing that you can say to them. Ask them how they are, and you are bound to get a response.'

'How are you?' I ask.

Immediately they respond, 'Fine, thank you and you?'

'I am fine too,' I reply.

'What is your name?' a student asks.

'My name is Don.'

Mimicking me they hang onto my words. Not long after Park and Lee leave, the real litmus test starts. The book has a very basic introduction of pictures, cut outs, and short stories to arouse young minds. Sensing quiet and boredom, I try again to initiate, saying, 'I am Don. What is my name?' I ask one of the girls up the front.

'Don, Don, Don, one two three,' she replies.

'No it is Don. Just Don,' I repeat.

She then starts to cry as the rest of the students bang their fists on the table saying my name over and over again. Some laugh and giggle until like Mr. Park, I am forced to get the stick and forcefully bang it on the table. I apologize but they have no idea what I am saying.

In the end I resort to teaching them body parts. I even draw a person on the blackboard in white chalk - a face, some hair, eyes, shoulders, mouth, legs and shoes, much to the their amusement. One student points at me and laughs, doing his best King Kong gorilla impersonation, as he blows up his cheeks and stomach. Soon all the students have left their chairs and are now dancing around the classroom acting like King Kong. They are obviously amused by my size and hairy features, with some of them touching and laughing at the hair on my arms. Again I am forced to use the ruler but this time the same girl starts to cry and heads towards the door. I follow her out, but there is little I can do.

It's chaos. Other students start to run amok, throwing their books and pencils around the room.

Noticing Lee in the corridor I shout out for his help, 'It seems that they don't really want to listen to me. Sir, I don't know what to do? Can you help please?'

'You have to make them want to listen. You need to be strict with them. That is the only way that these kids are going to learn, my friend.'

He helps by talking sternly to them and banging the ruler on some of their desks as a way to let them know who is boss. The room is hushed and luckily he decides to stay to the end, showing me some new tricks to get their attention. He likes my drawing of the human body and through modelling and some drilling the students acquire new words. Later they are able to rattle off a number of body parts which impresses us both.

After the class finishes Park returns to see how it went.

'How was it?' the principal asks.

'Ok I guess,' I reply, 'But if it wasn't for Mr. Lee here I don't know what I would have done.'

'You were good Mr. Don. Please don't ever say that you weren't. You're a good teacher and we both know that. Now have your coffee and get ready for the next class. They're waiting for you in the other room,' Lee orders.

I quickly down some more instant coffee before I am introduced to the new students who are somewhat more docile than the last. Park starts by conversing a little with them in English and I can immediately see that they are more confident than the first class.

'This is your new English teacher Don, and I want you to all help him. He has just been teaching our younger kids and it wasn't easy for him, so please be nice ok?'

'Of course we will. Welcome dear teacher,' they all reply.

I draw a picture of Australia on the blackboard and a house to indicate where my home is as Park leaves me to it.

'Where is this? What is the name of this country?' I ask, pointing to the map.

There is a hush around the classroom before one student politely replies by saying, 'Kangaroo? Kangaroo country isn't it? Sorry teacher, but I don't know the name. It's very hard word for us.

'It is Australia. Ok everyone please say it – Australia,' I lead.

They reply 'Au slay lia!'

From my small experience it seems that a lot of Korean students have a liquid consonant problem of differentiating between 'l' and 'r'.

'Right light, right light, light right, right light,' I repeat, as the class tries to copy my accent. 'Ok that's much better. Just remember it is an l not an r. Ok and here is my home. Does anyone know it?' I ask.

'Sydney' all the students shout.

'And where are the kangaroos? Where do they live?'

'Not in Sydney! You can find them all over Australia but not in the big cities,' a young girl in pigtails smiles.

'Fantastic. I mean very good. And what is your name?' I ask.

'My name is Jeong Son-A and I am fifth grade student at Sangcheon Elementary School. My English name is Janet and my favorite colour is green and I like to play badminton and help my mother cooking. That's it - I am done now,' she finishes, reeling off her profile.

'Well done Janet. Ok today all of you are going to tell me your names. I need to know who you are and you can also tell me your hobbies and age. I want you to practice writing it down. First write down your name for me on a piece of paper and put it in front of your desk.'

'I guess you want our English name sir?' asks a larger boy up the back.

'If you have one that would be good but it's really no big deal.

'Now you're confusing me. Just call me Sang-hoon. I don't need any stupid English name,' he answers.

The rest of the students mock the larger boy and as he sighs heavily they all laugh back at him. The students quickly write their names down before I ask them to introduce themselves just as Janet did.

The larger boy Sang-hoon prepares his introduction which draws the loudest response, 'My name is Sang-hoon and I am a fat fifth grade boy and I go to Sangcheon Elementary School. I like pizza and hamburger. My father is a policeman and my mother is a cook. I love to eat very much and I know I am fat but that's ok. That's all.'

The class is in another fit of laughter. Stopping them I ask them all to take turns with the rest of the introductions. At 3 p.m. a loud siren indicates that classes are over for the day.

Driving back home Mr. Lee passes me my first white envelope and in it is a healthy sum of money to cover my first month of teaching. I am so excited knowing that at least for now I don't have to worry about spending more of my savings.

However returning to the apartment I notice Kevin is in a bad mood, 'What's wrong mate? You're pissed off again it seems?'

'Today is pay day and we aren't getting anything. Daphne is fuming and I suggest you be careful when you see her.'

'But we knew we wouldn't be getting paid. I mean the guy has run away. What else can we do?'

'Are you kidding man? The parents are still paying fees aren't they? We just need to get our hands on some of it or soon we'll all be out on the street. I mean either that or we will be heading to Seoul for work. That's three months now for me,' he shouts. 'Three fucking months, excuse my French.'

'It's ok. I actually got hold of money today so if you need I can lend you some?'

'It's ok mate. Thanks for offering but I still have enough stashed away. It's not like I've maxed my credit card limit quite yet. Where did you get it anyway?'

'Mr. Lee, I mean the good Lee gave it to me. I did my first day out at the elementary school and he paid me upfront. I couldn't believe it, given the kind of crap we have been putting up with here. Makes me wonder whether I should just go and work for him full time.'

'Well mate don't go spending it too quickly, ok?' he warns. 'And I recommend that you don't tell Jason about your private work for now. He probably won't care, but you have to remember that we're not supposed to be doing privates. Employers can use it against you if you piss them off.'

'It's ok Kevin I hear you, and I won't mention it. Just remember mate if you need a loan I am here to help. After all, you did help me when I first arrived and I really do appreciate that.'

On my way to the office I pass Daphne who's in her apartment. Like Kevin she is also pissed off.

'Can you believe it? Another month and it looks like I'm not going to get my severance now either,' she informs me. 'That new guy Jason, I reckon he is a little dodgy. He told me that I need to sacrifice some things in my life, and that it would be better if I held on for a few more weeks and to not think about it. What I don't get is that there are still students here so where is their money going?'

'Your guess is as good as mine. Kevin was just telling me the same thing.

But yeah that sucks as I know you are on your way out and you need to be paid. What are you going to do?'

'Most likely give up my severance. There is nothing I really can do. I'll be lucky to get February and March as well. I have to head back to New Zealand in two weeks so time is running out for me. Better still, what are you going to do Don?'

'Well I am ok for now. I am thinking of other options but I am not sure what they are quite yet. Anyway I better run as I have to go and check my email before classes start tonight.'

'Thanks for popping in and seeing me Don. I really appreciate it.'

After the evening classes, Mari and Ji-hyun pick up on my despondence and ask what is bugging me.

'As you are probably aware things are not so great at the moment. It doesn't look like the boss Mr. Lee is coming back. He was last seen driving me to the airport and has since disappeared. That was nearly a week ago, so you can imagine how we are all feeling?'

'I hate Korean businessman. They are cowards! How can they do this?' Ji-hyun replies banging her fist on the desk.

'I know. I have only been here a few weeks and I just can't understand why. I mean we have the students but where is the money?' I ask.

'He has spent it on himself. He is a low-lying dog and if I could see him right now I would pull his eyes out from that ugly round Korean head of his. I am so mad!'

'Calm down Ji-hyun as we can't afford to be too angry. We just have to find ways to change this feeling,' Mari replies.

'But what about Mr. Don? What are you going to do? You have to live or will you go back to *Hoju*, I mean Australia? I know what I would do,' Ji-hyun says.

'I will stay here and fight. I didn't come all this way just to turn back now.'

'Let me take you to Seoul some time. I want to show you around our great capital. Ok?'

'Sure I'd be into that. How about we go on Sunday?'

'That is fine with me.'

'And Mr. Don, don't forget me as well. I want you to come to my wedding,' says Mari.

'Now that would be great Mari. I've always wanted to go to a Korean wedding.'

'Ok it's a deal. You can come to my wedding and this weekend you can go to Seoul with Ji-hyun.'

18

DRINKS AT CLEEP

Tonight I am meeting Matt the American and British David. The plan is to follow the usual route of a few at Jacks then some at Hells Bells. However on arrival both are packed so we try Cleep instead. We notice that the bar has little to do with Radiohead - the only noticeable thing being a huge poster of Thom Yorke that greets us at the front door.

The barman is a burly lad wearing an NFL jersey and a ridiculous oversized NY black baseball cap, 'Hey dudes what up? Can I get you anything?' he asks.

'A beer mate,' I reply.

'Sure coming right up. By the way are you from the army?'

'No, certainly not,' I reply.

'What about your friends then? You don't look like army guys to me.'

'Well I have a bit to do with the army, but the other guys are teachers. So grab us beer would you. Make it three Coronas ok?' says Matt.

'Like I said that's cool brother, coming up in a minute. Just sit down guys and put your feet up. Jacks and Hells Bells always get the crowds so why not come here to Cleep eh? And by the way boys, the owner made a mistake with the name of this place so don't laugh!'

'Yes, we wondered what was going on there? Radiohead and their famous song 'Cleep.' There's a bit of Konglish for you hey?' remarks David.

'Maybe Konglish it is teacher. Are you some English guy with a well-to-do accent?'

'I am from England my friend. I'm from a village an hour or so west of London.'

'And what about you other friend?' he asks, pointing to me.

'Does it matter?' asks Matt. 'Where's our beer for fuck's sake?'

'I'm just trying to strike up a conversation with you dudes,' says the barman.

'Mate, look we just want to relax and like you said put our feet up. So can we just have our fucking beers please?' Matt adds.

'Ok dude. I got it.'

I then add, 'And if you really want to know where I am from then it is Sydney, which you'll find on the east coast of Australia. Maybe you know it from some geography text book you read when you were at school. Or because it is now an Olympic city.'

'Yeah just like our Seoul. Of course I know it. Here are your drinks gentlemen. Please sit down and relax yourself here at our Cleep bar.'

We manage to fob off the barman's attention as he sings along to Eminem. Matt is a huge Tupac fan and it isn't long before he tires of the bar's music choice.

'While you are there brother how about you spin some Tupac for us?'

'Sure my man, it is coming up next,' replies the barman, shaking his hands around in his best hip hop imitation.

Cleep has a surreal feel about it and is quite small compared to the other bars. It's not long before Matt's booming voice can be heard over the sounds of even Tupac as he launches into a spiel about why he came to Korea.

'I have an ace job you know. Guys I'll probably only have to work until I am fifty and then I can retire easily on the package I will get,' he explains. 'The way I see it is that they give you so much shit - some of it good and some bad, but all jobs are like that. The bottom line is that you work hard and the army will reward you.'

'But don't you ever feel like ethically you are doing the wrong thing?' I ask. 'I am not having a go at you mate, but there's enough guns and warfare around to blow the whole planet up. Is that a good thing? The world doesn't need or want more nuclear problems does it, Matt?'

'Maybe you are right Aussie. But I am more into it for what I can get later on. I want to have a family and I want to build my future. Plus I am an engineer and a good one,' he explains. 'If I can help detect strange and harmful activity in say North Korea, aren't I helping the greater cause of mankind? I mean have you heard of the atrocities that idiot is doing up there?'

'Do shed some light on it, Matt,' I ask.

'Well I was only looking at the satellites today. The border is just a few hours from here and if you cross it you will find that the people have no power and no food,' he explains. 'What isn't fair is that fat fuck Kim Jong Il is feeding off his own people's needs whilst having his own personal harem. The media goes on about Gaddafi and Mugabe, but this guy up the road takes the cake.'

'Ok let's not talk politics guys,' David interrupts. "We're here to have a few beers, and chill. In fact I wanted to ask what you two are planning to do tomorrow.'

'I really haven't thought about it,' says Matt.

'Me neither. All I ever do after a big night is just sleep a lot, eat crap food and regret how much I drank,' I reply.

'I know what we could do. Matt, you said you have a van, so how about we go for a drive somewhere?' suggests David. 'There are some really cool mountains just north east of here towards the ocean. In fact we could head towards a coastal town called Sokcho. It will take about two to three hours and I hear that they have great seafood there. It is a famous place and it is supposed to be really neat.'

'I don't mind,' replies Matt.

'That sounds great guys. How about we head over to Hells Bells now and have a shot or three then we can hatch a plan?' I ask.

After a few shots courtesy of John and the bar, the three of us stumble to our homes.

The next morning none of us are feeling so good so we agree that the best cure is some brunch.

'How about we grab some KFC, hey? Before we hit the road? It's the real shit man because it soaks up the crap from the night before,' says David.

'I'm out. I'd rather have some soup, something liquid,' I add. 'That KFC crap rots your insides man. You should know better, but then again you do come from the country of greasy spoons, so that goes without saying.'

'I'll join you David. Kentucky rocks!' says Matt. 'We made the stuff after all and you have to think of the bigger picture buddy. We're all hung-over here so I know what a horse wants and that sure isn't any soup from some shitty market.'

Just as David and Matt head into KFC I bump into A-reum my student, who is with a rather striking lady in brown high leather boots. I am totally bowled over by her as she is one of the most attractive women I have ever seen and I immediately feel somewhat tongue-tied.

'Teacher what are you doing here? Were they your friends? Why don't you go inside and get some yummy chicken with them?' asks A-reum.

'Yes they are my friends and I don't want any um chicken um A-reum. They're going to um, get um, some um food.'

'What's wrong teacher? You seem a little strange. Are you ok?' asks A-reum.

'Sure A-reum I am fine. I just need to go and grab some um o-deng tang, you know some um fish ball um soup. We are going to Sokcho today so we're um in a hurry um.'

'Sokcho? Oh, how nice. By the way your Korean is very good. How long have you been in Korea?' the attractive lady asks.

'Not long. I got here um a few weeks or so ago. I am A-reum's, um English teacher, at um Global World, aren't I, um A-reum?'

'Yes he is Mum. This is Mr. Don from Australia and Mr. Don this is my mother. I am sorry I didn't introduce you first.'

'*Bang geop sum nida*. It's a pleasure to meet you.'

'Yes, it is nice to meet you too Mr. Don. A-reum has told me many sweet things about you. You are from Australia I believe? You really must come over some time and I can cook you some *o-deng tang* if you like? I can cook many things Mr. Don,' the mother offers.

'Um what can I um say?' I reply.

'Surely you can. What about Sunday night?' the mother asks.

'That's um fine with me. I am going to Seoul that day but I'll make sure I am back by the latter part of the afternoon. I can um always contact A-reum if there are um any problems.'

'Yes, um Mr. Don you can,' the mother cheekily adds, winking at me.

'Ok Mum, we better go now and do some shopping. Have a great Sunday Mr. Don and um catch you soon. Have fun.'

I immediately run off to the market and grab my soup, slurping it down like a native. Later in the van we talk about the amount of alcohol that was consumed last night.

'Was it three or four shots that we had?' asks David

'I don't know man. I didn't count. All I know is that after Cleep, John at Hells Bells was plying us with a bunch of tequila and whiskey shots so we were pretty loaded,' Matt replies. 'They sure know how to drink in this country don't they? A buddy of mine told me that some of them go all night and end up in church the next day reeking of the stuff.'

'And we don't know how to drink? That's calling the kettle black don't you reckon Matt? David replies.

'Yeah, you could say it's a voracious appetite for the drink. I have only been here less than a month and from what I can see is that drinking is par for the course. Plus, they smoke like chimneys. My clothes have stunk of late.'

'Like I said it is normal. And who really gives a fuck?' David adds, trying to end the conversation.

Matt then tells us to jump in the van as it's time to head to the hills. Unsure of directions we take a basic north east direction out of town following exit routes until we see a sign that points us towards Mount Seoraksan; the most famous of the South Korean mountains due to its interesting rock cliff faces and sheer viewpoints.

For a while the drive seems quite rigorous with an exceedingly large amount of hairpin bends that test our dry, hung-over mouths.

'Sorry guys but due to the small amount of space that we have in the front of this van there's little I can do about these bends. You're just going to have to wear it unfortunately,' says Matt.

'It's cool mate. I have been on similar trips out in the Australian bush. The bends might not be as bad as these, but the sheer stretch of road and heat can really play with your mind.'

'England just doesn't compare unless you go far north. Where I come from it's all rolling countryside,' says David.

Just as we get some respite from some downhill stretches, up ahead we notice a sign to the left that says there's a five hundred meter tunnel and that entry is strictly forbidden.

'It's one of those tunnels the north attempted to build so that they could invade the south. They are cheeky those people,' Matt explains.

'Hey, do you mind if I get out and take a nature stop? All this excitement is getting to me and I can feel a real stir from last night, if you know what I mean,' I ask.

'Don, we don't need to know about your visits to the crapper mate. What is it about Australians and their need to tell you every finite detail? Do you ever notice that Matt?' asks David.

'Not really. You should know though shouldn't you? I mean aren't they most of your nation's offspring?' Matt asks.

'Yeah the convict kind, well some of them are at least,' David adds.

'Fuck off would you David, and what would you know anyway? You are just a plum rich English boy with a barreled name for fuck sakes,' I retort.

'No need to get personal mate. I was only joking cobber,' David replies, again taking the piss.

We stop the truck at a nearby resting place and are greeted by a pregnant dog that's tied to a pole.

'Hey, get a load of this. Real Korean dog soup! This is what some of the people here eat when they want some virility,' David says. 'No shit man! Jack and I were once walking around a lake and an old guy wanted us to drink dog soup with him so he showed us the breed and we ran for miles.'

'So there's little wonder she's pissed off with us then. I've heard horror stories of how particular breeds are beaten before they are cooked in a soup. Anyway, we don't treat a lot of our own livestock that well either, particularly the way we force feed them,' I respond.

Just as we are leaving, a young boy on a bike approaches, 'Ni hao! I am from China and I go Sockcho today. I training for long bike race,' he says.

'Well good luck buddy. I hope you have a great time. I guess you don't need a lift then?' asks Matt.

'Me no English. Me Chinese! China you know? Goodbye,' he adds.

Pedaling off he turns around and smiles at us and we give him an almighty cheer for his efforts. We keep to the road passing him once more unable to imagine what he is going through, given the terrain he is cycling on. Soon we hit Highway 46 with signs leading to the National Park that will eventually take us to the sea. More traffic looms as we approach the park, mostly vehicles with Seoul number plates. The mountain isn't a place for the faint-hearted hiker though, and I am not that confident of doing any climbing in this state.

'Sorry guys but I have dreadful vertigo, so there's no way you will ever catch me on any of those craggy cliff faces even if we have some rope.'

David grins, 'That's ok mate. None of us are feeling the best and we don't plan to do any real hiking today. However, I think we should all climb that cliff for the view. I have heard it is really special.'

'Come on you pussies. I used to be a marine. It isn't too hard to climb. Plus Don, once you get there you will be amazed by the scenery mate. A buddy of mine went last weekend and he raved about how spectacular it was,' says Matt.

'Well you two can find out for yourselves. I think I'd rather be back at the nature stop with the pregnant dog than on some cliff face,' I reply.

'Ok then, how about we drive up a bit, and then we can walk to the base of it. Or if that doesn't work then just David and I can take a look?'

'Like I said I'd rather not. You guys just go ahead,' I reply.

'We're only kidding man. I mean if you don't want to do it that's cool - I read you,' Matt adds.

While I wait for the others I notice a tour group pointing excitedly towards the east, confirming that Sokcho isn't too far.

Soon Matt and David arrive back and Matt sighs, saying, 'Ah it was beautiful up there.'

'Too right, you would have loved the view. Would have reminded you of back home mate I reckon,' David says.

When we finally get to Sokcho we notice signs to the fish market beside the pier. On our approach we pass a group of women in black tight wetsuits and goggles. They all laugh at us, particularly Matt who does his best to engage with them.

'If they are going to stare then they have to at least acknowledge us. That's my way of thinking,' Matt explains.

The market is buzzing with noisy vendors competing to sell all kinds of seafood including live octopus and squid which are being packed into plastic containers or buckets overflowing with water. Not even Matt's booming American voice can top the hustle and bustle of this place. Sellers shout through loudspeakers fighting to get the attention of customers.

An elderly lady grabs David by the arm and gestures him to eat some of her live squid from a bucket. She covers her hand over her mouth but he shakes his head in response. She then puts three fingers up and tells him a price.

'She's giving you a price mate,' I say.

Sensing his deliberation, she then makes hand gestures at Matt, but he nods his head firmly, finally shrugging her off despite her continued barking in his ear with her loudspeaker.

'Fuck man all this noise and chaos is getting me hungry,' Matt says. 'I just need to sit and relax, plus that KFC is wearing off now as well. I reckon we should grab a table over there near the pier. At least we can have a view while we eat. What do you think?'

'That sounds like a great idea.' David responds.

A waiter then comes over to order from us, while we stumble on words to describe what we want.

'You have been here longer than all of us David so you can have the honors of ordering mate,' I tell him.

'Ok waiter, we will have three sea *gae* fish head soups,' he says while motioning fish and head and soup in three gestures much to everyone's amusement. 'And we'll have three beers as well,' he adds.

'We're going to eat fish heads?' Matt dubiously asks.

'Trust me Matt. It's delicious. It's the head of a fish in this warm bowl of soup with chilli and they give you rice as a base. It rocks.'

To our side is a table of local fisherman who look as though they have just knocked off work. They're laughing raucously as one of them proudly shows his prize, a massive squid that's panicking in a bucket of water. As they eat their prawns whilst drinking the local beer, Matt gets their attention by pointing at the squid and giving a thumbs up.

'*Mi guk? Mi guk saram?*' one asks Matt, a polite way of asking if you are American or not.

'I am *mi-guk*. Me *mi-guk*,' Matt replies proudly.

This draws huge shrieks of laughter from the men and soon enough we are asked to sit with them. They order a few large bottles of *soju* and not long later shots start to fill the table. Rather than declining and hurting anyone's feelings, we follow protocol.

It's only when our fish head soup arrives that we are able to get some respite from the *soju* shots. After all it is lunch time and we only expected a few beers and some soup. Red faced, we enjoy our huge bowls of piping-hot soup.

'I don't know about you guys but I am off my chops,' says Matt. "That fire water is potent man.'

'Yeah it sure is,' adds David. 'You have to be careful how much you have and I reckon we have had enough. It was lucky that the soup arrived otherwise we'd be under the table now. I mean look at them. I reckon they could drink that stuff all day.'

We walk along the pier which is about a two hundred meter or so stretch of well-worn plank heading out to what is known as the East Sea. Somewhere in the distance is probably Japan whilst directly north is North Korea.

'Yep, the dictator and his family live in that compound area somewhere north of here,' says Matt. 'He is probably salivating on imported seafood bisque at the moment while his own people are frantically finding something to eat. It sucks man.'

'Yeah, I once heard that people would dig fresh bodies from the ground and eat them because they were so famished,' says David.' You hear lots of weird stuff. And what about those gulag camps? I mean if you didn't agree with the party and their rules you would be sent to a reform place – not only you but your whole family as well.'

'I doubt that any of the propaganda you get on North Korea is going to be positive is it?' I add. 'I mean there are, what, twenty-four million people living there? Who's to say that they aren't happy with the life they lead? Maybe that's all they know?'

'There's no freedom Don. It's the world's biggest prison camp,' replies Matt.' They can't get the internet like us and most of them have absolutely no idea what is going on with the rest of the world. They believe that their leaders and army are doing the right thing. Does that sound like happiness to you?'

'Ok Matt. I read you but who really knows? Are we really experts on life there and how they feel about it?' I reply.

'Look guys, how about we drop it, and head back to the van. My head is still spinning from the shots we had before and I wouldn't mind leaving. There is nothing much else to see here,' says David.

It's only 3 p.m. but because of the fog the street lights are on. Just as we start to head back to Chuncheon, Matt almost runs over the same group of fishing ladies that we encountered when we first arrived. They are a proud bunch of silver haired toothless ladies who fish the seas using traditional methods and without any real diving equipment.

'Watch it man, we nearly hit them,' I shout.

'You don't want to hurt their kind mate. They are priceless as far as the seas go,' says David. 'They are unique man. I saw a documentary on National Geographic about them. Their diving is fearless compared to the modern shit we use. And guess what, it's a method that has been working for years. The simpler the better really does work.'

'Don't stress David, it's all ok,' Matt adds, before saying, 'Guys, it's time to go. Let's leave the twilight zone.'

19

A DAY OUT

Ji-hyun and I are about to catch the 6 a.m. train to Seoul and to my surprise there's already a long restless queue of people outside the ticket office.

'Is this normal? Why do people have to push?' I ask.

'It's just what we Koreans do. It's not like Australia where you seem to have time for everything. We need to be organized and we rely on trains more than you guys do.'

'It's a population thing I guess?' I ask.

'Everything is about the population - there are forty-seven million people here Mr. Don. Australia has what, twenty? And unlike here your country is massive. Is that the right word?'

'Yeah, yeah I get what you're saying.'

At the front of the train about fifty students arrive making themselves heard with their valiant efforts to sing 'Come As You Are' by Nirvana. They look like my evening class, except most of them are wearing cardigans and flannelette shirts, and not your typical baseball garb.

'Look at those idiots,' exclaims Ji-hyun.

'Why do you think that? I think they are rather cool,' I respond, surprised by her manner.

'Cool? They are a bunch of students who simply have no idea about life. They don't care about their own people. I can't wait for the day they have to go the army. That will make men out of them.'

'Ah yes the army. I remember my two colleagues telling me about their military days. It sounds awful the way some people treated. We don't have that kind of thing in Australia as you probably know.'

'Well every male has to go because without it how do you think are we going to fight the North should they decide to bomb us? Think about that one Mr. Don?'

'Well I am not as stupid as I look. And don't forget I am your teacher after all.'

'Sorry Mr. Teacher Don but today I have women's problems. I am sorry sir - my apology for this kind of talking. It is just that there is more to here than meets the eye. We need our army like the fish needs water. I am sure you can understand this.'

'Ji-hyun you're forgiven. Let's enjoy the ride and I want to say that I am really excited about going by train to Seoul. I hear that the Chuncheon to Seoul line is considered to be one of the most romantic train travel routes in your great country,' I say, sensing her frustrations.

'Yes! You're right my teacher,' she enthusiastically replies. 'That's also why there are so many young male and female university students here.'

Up ahead I notice a graceful older looking man instructing passengers to sit down as they board the train.

'Check out the way that guy is bowing to us. A rail attendant from Sydney would never show that kind of respect.'

'He's our train conductor Mr. Don. Each carriage has two.'

'Wow, I can see that. Look at the other one, how elegant looking she is. She is almost picture perfect; such beautiful soft skin and those white gloves.'

Up ahead the young students light their cigarettes and aggressively strum their guitar strings. They are happy singing the song embracing the lyrics 'Come as you are, as you were, as a friend, as a friend, as an old enemy.'

I stand up and clap alone but Ji-hyun isn't impressed. Instead she stands up and shouts, 'Turn it down would you!'

The students are quickly embarrassed and retreat to games of cards.

'They will get off soon and have their MT. You watch, in five minutes it will be silent here I promise Teacher Don,' says Ji-hyun

'Silence in Korea? What do you mean?' I ask.

'We'll be at Gangchon in less than five minutes. There you will see thousands of Korean teenagers wearing either Backstreet Boys or Nirvana t-shirts. You'd swear that's the only music that these people know - the girls are sissy-like and the boys are weak as piss. I know I studied art but deep down I always wanted to be in the army. That's why I don't like the kids of today.'

'That's a bit hard isn't it?'

'No army yet Mr. Don. They are what we call freshman students. Look at them - they have no idea. One shot of alcohol and they are falling on the floor.'

'So weren't you like that once?'

'As you know I like art but because I come from a small village outside of Chuncheon my family always had to work really hard for everything. I would say most of these kids are from rich families that can afford to send their kids to private universities. It's a different cup of tea, Mr. Don.'

'Well, how did a village girl like you make it all the way to Cairns then?'

'I got a scholarship to James Cook University in Townsville, but the campus I went to was in Cairns. Look here is my sketchbook - these are the kind of things I like to draw.'

Her sketch book is full of drawings mainly portraits of people and her family that could well reveal her soft and graceful side.

'I want to go back to Cairns someday Mr. Don. Maybe you can help me with my English more? I just need to get a higher score for my IELTS test. Now I have a grade 5.5 for speaking but I need a 6.5.'

'I'll be honest. I can only try to help but my situation at Global World isn't easy at the moment as you know.'

'Yes I understand. Maybe you can teach me in your spare time? Also, my sister has a baby daughter, a toddler, just a year and six months, and she wants lessons. Everyone wants to speak English here Mr. Don.'

'Let's talk about that another time. Look ahead of us. Is that Gangchon?'

'Yeah this is it. Please relax now dear teacher and enjoy the scenery.'

The train hugs the Han River for another good hour or so taking in some of the scenes that I can remember from my first day; the ducks, the different birds, and the people who are all ice fishing.

'I love this ice fishing stuff. You'd never see it in Australia,' I comment.

'You don't know about this?' Ji-hyun asks.

'You should know. Our rivers are never frozen. I mean, this is kind of strange for me but in a good way. I have seen this about three times now and I must say there is something weird and exciting about the way those birds keep banging their beaks against the ice. They must be tough creatures don't you think?'

'It's normal and you know what, they are actually good at it. They catch more fish than the locals ever do. I'd say they are more patient than us.'

'Don't the locals get annoyed by that?'

'Sure they do. More than you could ever imagine teacher.'

'What's that supposed to mean?' I ask.

'I am kidding. How would I know about what birds and fishermen get up to,' she responds, almost taking the piss out of my interest.

We both nap a little before we hit the junction of urban Seoul in the north east part of the city. It is here that modern Korean emerges - apartments and shopping malls.

'Not long now Teacher Don. Say goodbye to beautiful Korea and hello to ugly Seoul,' she jokes.

'I like your humour Ji-hyun. Thanks for bringing me. Maybe we should kip a little more.'

'Kip? I don't know what you mean?'

'We call it a short sleep - a nap.'

'Oh yes but sorry there is no more time. Now that we're here in Seoul we need to get off at the next station. However I must warn you to be careful.'

'Ok, I am with you. Don't worry about me.'

'I will grab your hand so we can walk together ok?'

'Are you sure? But people might imagine things and get angry?'

'Yeah, they might but Don I will deal with that.'

'It's ok. We aren't in class.'

'Anyway, just watch me Don. I'm a village girl remember?'

Ji-hyun tells me she is an old hand and has guided foreigners around Seoul before. She says that it is Korean courtesy to hold hands when taking visitors through busy places. As we pass through a bustling market, a group of old men give us disapproving looks which we ignore. Further ahead we arrive at a red light street with women plying their trade from what looks like old barber shop saloons.

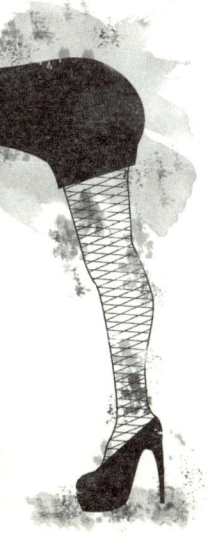

'Hello Mr. would you like to come and have some real fun?' a working girl asks.

'No, he's not interested,' says Ji-hyun.

'Fuck you. What would you know, you dumb student,' the working girl replies.

It's nine in the morning, and the worker looks as though she's still up from last night. She's caked in make-up and isn't wearing much aside from a tight-fitting camisole, fishnet stockings and high heels.

Ji-hyun, now angry, stands up to her telling her to sod it, and pushes her onto the barber chair.

'Don't talk to me like that, you whore.'

'Get fucked. You get the fuck out of our area,' the working girl replies as she attempts to grab Ji-hyun by the throat.

'Fuck you bitch,' Ji-hyun exclaims pushing her to the ground. 'C'mon Mr. Don we better go fast or no good people will come. Let's rush before someone arrives.'

I tell her how strong she is and what a great soldier she would make.

'I am sorry kind teacher but I hate these kinds of people as they are not what our country is about. Today is typical of here - a noisy train ride, some beautiful scenery, then there's this ugliness. I swear one of these days I am going to do an exhibition about it – Ugly Korea and Beautiful Korea.'

We quickly enter the subway which is full of people rushing to various destinations. Cheongyangni station is a major crossing point for the suburbs and is on the number one line that heads straight into the centre of town.

'Hold my hand and hold onto your bag. Don't trust anyone and don't look at their faces,' warns Ji-hyun.

'Ok. Did anyone tell you that you worry too much?' I ask her.

'Look, I have seen people beaten up on a subway so don't laugh. You need to be serious here.'

Cramped into a carriage we make our way to Jong-gak, which is the main drop-off point for the older and more traditional part of Seoul. People continue to stare at us as the crowds build. Nearby I can see a man smiling and imitating sexual gestures at both of us.

'See that man. He is looking at us strangely,' I tell Ji-hyun.

'Don't look at him, just ignore him,' she replies.

'What do you think he wants?'

'It is hard for me to say in English Mr. Don. He wants me. Remember the red light area? He probably thinks that I work there.'

'But you hardly look like a sex worker.'

'It doesn't matter. I am with you so he probably thinks I am.'

'Does this kind of thing often happen on the trains? I mean do men always have a go at women in broad daylight?'

'Yes sometimes they do. Sorry, I don't have the right words to explain what I want to say. It is not normal behavior and in my opinion I strongly believe we need to follow our neighbors Japan. They have their own trains for women, did you know that teacher?'

'What do you mean? A women only train?'

'No, sorry I mean a women only area.'

'You mean a carriage just for women?'

'Yes, you are right as always Mr. Don. I hope that will happen in Seoul one day.'

Grabbing my hand tightly, we walk through another crowd, and then up an escalator that leads us outside to an wide open street.

'That's better. That was crazy in there.'

'It was, but that's life in Seoul my Teacher Don. It just goes to show that Chuncheon is really a country town.' she says.

We then notice a group of protestors across the road in a small park. Loudspeakers are urging people to join them, whilst on the other side of the road there are about three hundred armed policemen dressed in combat gear, ready to pounce if things get out of hand.

Ji-hyun grabs my arm again, pulling me the opposite way.

'What are you doing? You don't need to treat me like a kid.' I tell her.

'Mr. Don this is my country and you don't need to go there.'

'But it is interesting, isn't it?'

'Can't you see all the policeman waiting to stop these people?'

'But it seems all fine to me. What is going on anyway? What are they saying in Korean?'

'I don't know a hundred percent but they are angry with our government so it is better we stay away.'

I notice a placard in English that reads 'Protect Migrant Workers Rights!' Escaping Ji-hyun's clutches, I make a bee-line towards the sign only to realise that the person holding it is Justin my Australian friend.

'I didn't know you were involved in this mate,' I say, as I give him a hearty embrace.

'Yeah mate of course I am. Plus this has been a serious problem of late. It is time we teachers and laborers stop exploitation,' Justin says. 'There are laws that are needed to stop this rot. As you know there are too many clueless cunts around here acting as bosses. We need to make some noise so that people who come here in the future aren't also fucked over.'

'I should come down for the next meeting.'

'It's easy mate. I was planning to tell you but I didn't want to bother you yet. In Seoul people meet here every weekend.'

'Ok mate. Look I better go. Good to see you and although I'd love to stay, I can't. I have my crazy student with me and she won't stop babying me. I'm like twenty years older than her and she's treating me like a kid.'

'That's very Korean when people show you around. You've got to just roll with it. Lap it up.'

Walking towards us Ji-hyun barks, 'C'mon Mr. Don we have to go. I want to show you some of our old Seoul - let's go quickly.'

'Alright, alright I am coming. I've just been talking to my friend Justin. He lives in Chuncheon and he's also from Australia.'

She ignores Justin who tries to give her a leaflet and instead grabs my hand warning me to be careful of such protests.

'It's not like Australia teacher. The Korean police here are known to be horrible when they want to be. I mean look at those shields and helmets. They mean real business so we better go somewhere quiet. Let's go towards the big bell and then I will take you to our number two protected site, the national pagoda in Tapgol Park. It's just up the road from the bell.'

'I must say I like all these parks. By the way, what are all the old men doing milling around and smoking?'

'They are just hanging out and talking about the old days. That's quite common here. I mean, don't you have that sort of thing in Sydney?'

'Sure we do but I don't think we use our parks like you guys do. After all we have so many beaches.'

'Yes, you have many beaches Don. There are so many beautiful things about Australia, yet you are here?'

'Yes, I am here and I am ok with that,' I reply.

'For me the evening time was the hardest in Cairns, because everyone would go home and stay inside. People in Korea like to be on the streets enjoying themselves, but in Cairns you're supposed to be in a pub or relaxing in your home. We Asians get so boring because we're used to being out enjoying ourselves.'

'Maybe it's a cultural difference.'

'Look Mr. Don. This is Bosingak Pavilion. We ring the bell here every New Year.'

'That must be romantic for some I guess?'

'It was for me once,' she replies quietly.

'Ji-hyun, what's wrong? Are you ok?' I ask, noticing her frown.

'I am ok Mr. Don. I am sorry but this place makes me sad.'

'But isn't it a place where people are usually happy? I mean on New Year's Eve wouldn't people come here to enjoy themselves?'

'Yes of course they do but this is where I broke up with my boyfriend earlier this year.'

'I'm sorry to hear that.'

'No I am sorry my dear teacher. It is really hard for me as I miss him so much. He is going to stay in the army forever, and he doesn't want to have me anymore as his girlfriend. It is complicated because I want to go back to Australia as well.'

'It's ok. You don't have to be sorry. I understand you.'

'What about you? Don't you have someone?'

'I did but it is complicated as well. Why don't we just go and look at the other place you mentioned? The pagoda sounds good.'

Walking further south we arrive at Tapgol Park, which is packed with locals. Today being the first of March, it's a public holiday which explains the crowds. Here was also the site of the first reading of the Proclamation of Independence in 1919. Older citizens hand out flyers to people which Ji-hyun translates as a celebration of Korean freedom. People embrace each other and beat drums. Ji-hyun then urges me to go to a different part of the park where the large pagoda is.

Admiring the pagoda which is encased in glass she tells me that it's the second oldest relic in South Korea, 'Look how beautiful it is. Did you know that an Irish man organized this whole garden and the park as a symbol for old Buddha? Also, can you see the turtle base and its head? It's all cut from marble and I think it's so elaborate. Don't you think so too, Mr. Don?'

'Sure it is nice to look at. You really know your information so I must say that I am very impressed. Where did you learn about these things, and how can you say them so well in English?'

'It is my duty dear teacher. As you know, I used to be a guide and part of the registration exam was to really know about your own history. This is rare today as a lot of young people don't seem to care about it. Ok, let's now go to Insa-dong because if you like history and culture, you will love this street.'

'Ok, I'm all yours.'

'Let me introduce you to one of the most traditional streets in Seoul. This is Insa-dong, and here you can find paintings, street food, art and all kinds of traditional souvenirs to make your stay a more memorable one. In the Joseon Dynasty this place was where artists came to study. Some products even trace back to the Three Kingdom Period. Did you know this, teacher?'

'Sorry Ji-hyun, I don't mean to be rude but can you stop talking like a robot. I only got half of what you just said.'

'What do you mean teacher?'

'What I mean is you don't need to race through it all. How is anyone going to understand what you're saying when you talk at them like a wind-up doll?'

'Oh, I am sorry Mr. Don dear teacher, but that is the way I have been trained to speak. I'm a national guide remember and here is my card to prove it.'

'I'm not saying you aren't a good guide. I just think when you're describing an area you need to take a breath and remember who you are talking to. No one wants to be talked at. Remember people need to digest what they are looking at.'

'Oh, I am sorry dear teacher. I didn't know you would be so upset by this.'

She loses face from my comments, and for a moment turns her head the other way.

Before I get a chance to apologize, a small girl with a squeaky voice taps me on the shoulder and says, 'Hello dear foreigner, we would like to ask you some questions. Please help us get a good grade sir because our teacher said the more foreigners we find the better our scores will be. Please help me. I know you can, dear sir.'

'Sure, why not?'

'Thank you kind man for your five minutes time,' she responds happily.

However, five minutes soon turns in to ten, and before long I'm surrounded by at least ten students asking for my help. I look around for Ji-hyun, but it seems that she has disappeared. Up ahead I spot her talking to a monk who's showing her some Buddhist carvings. Sensing a chance for a getaway, I tell the kids that I have to go to the toilet and that I'm not feeling well. I head to Ji-hyun's side but she ignores me. She's happily ensconced in a conversation with him.

I try to apologise but she's still pissed off, 'Look I'm sorry, Ji-hyun. I realise that what I said to you wasn't fair. Can I make it up to you somehow? How about I buy you some lunch?' I ask.

'Excuse me sir I am talking to my friend here so please show more respect. After all I am the one showing you around today.'

Embarrassed I wait for the conversation to end before I politely ask her again if I can buy her some lunch.

'Yes of course you can. It's your duty to.'

'It's my duty is it? I didn't know I had to pay you as such? You were the one who asked me here after all.'

'Teacher, this is common courtesy. After all, I might be your student but I am also your guide and I don't come for free.'

'So stop calling me Teacher then. Anyway, what would you like for lunch?' I ask.

'How about eating Burger King? I haven't eaten that since I was last here with my ex-boyfriend. Can we Mr. Don?'

'Ok, but promise not to get too emotional with me?'

'I won't I promise.'

'Ok, just this time we can have Burger King, but in the future I'd rather have Korean food. After all if you are a guide you need to show me some traditional food as well as the sights.'

'Isn't that what all you foreigners love eating? You like greasy food I can tell.'

'Not all foreigners eat Burger King. C'mon you have to remember that there are people from all over the world where we live and there's more to life than some hamburger with fries. You should know having lived in Australia before.'

'Yeah, I know I was just joking. Anyway follow me, and remember you're buying.'

Over our set meals, Ji-hyun prods me a little, taking some time to ask me some personal questions, 'Tell me Mr. Don, why did you come here to our country? I sometimes can't really understand you foreigners. I mean, you come here and teach English and then most of you get sick of it, so you go back home and find real jobs. Or some of you stay on and marry a Korean girl and have a family.'

'The way I see it is that everyone is different and we all have things we want to do with our lives. I have only just arrived so I don't really know what is going to happen to me. What I do know is that I feel lucky that English is my first language. I wouldn't be able to travel the globe if I didn't have it.'

'You are extremely lucky my teacher. I truly envy you Mr. Don.'

'Like I said Ji-hyun, everyone is different, and for better or worse it's all about the choices we make. There are times when my heart feels crushed and I can't for the life of me imagine why I ended up doing something like this.'

'So, why then?' she asks.

'Well, I don't want to be back at home in some boring job, or some relationship of duty. This is not where I want to be, at least for now.'

'You are right, we are all different.'

Walking through some small confined streets, I get an idea of what traditional life in Seoul was once like.

Ji-hyun aware of not speaking too fast tells me slowly that most of this area is for the Buddhist community in Seoul and that this is the home of one of Seoul's oldest temples, Jogyesa.

'That sounds interesting. Can I ask you what you were talking to the monk earlier about?'

'We were just talking about how many people were out today and how noisy it was.'

'I'd love to meet some monks. I remember in Thailand seeing so many and I always thought how cool and noble they looked.'

'Cool? They are just wise and old. Don't you think that God or Jesus are a lot more interesting?'

'You are on your own there Ji-hyun. I am not really that religious but if I had to choose I would probably pick a monk.'

'You're quite strange Mr. Don. The cross is by far the most modern religion these days.'

'But don't you think it's nice to see and feel the difference here? I mean all these streets are so well-kept and historical. This is what I want to see when I come to a new country. Why aren't there more places like this?'

'It's because they are the past. No one really lives like that anymore. I mean some people in China might, but us Ancients, we sometimes want to be young and energetic.

'You are joking right? This is your heritage, your tradition. How can you think like that? Plus you are not Ancients, you are Asians!'

'I am kind of kidding Mr. Don. But after all I am only twenty-five you know. Anyway, today I am your guide so check out this street if you like old stuff.'

On the street elderly women are dressed in balloon-like dresses which Ji-hyun explains are a traditional dress called *hanbok*. They smile at me.

'*Annyong Haseyo*! Hello. *Pan-gap-seum-nida!* Nice to meet you,' I say happily.

They laugh loudly but respectfully at my vain attempts to speak Korean.

A silver-haired toothless man smiles at me and says, '*Mi-guk saram im ni da*? (Are you American?)'

'No, no. I am not. I am from *Hoju* - you know? I am from Australia!'

'Ah, Australia yes I know yes. Korean War, kangaroo and Holden car - thank you, thank you,' he replies in broken English.

Aware of the time, Ji-hyun politely tells me that it's time to go. We leave the alleyway and then notice a big blue dome ahead of us.

'That's an interesting sight. It looks like a spaceship. What is it?' I ask.

'That is where our leader lives. It is called the Blue House or *Cheong Wa Dae* in Korean. The gated area of the whole park is probably the richest property in all of Seoul.'

'Can you go in there?'

'You can, but we don't have time today. I am so sorry.'

Beyond Insa-dong is one of the greener and more manicured parts of the old city. In recent years, Seoul has been developing not just in terms of skyscrapers. It has also been attentive to its environmental infrastructure, and the maintenance of its old palaces and museums.

We soon arrive at another gate where more nationalists are waving Korean flags and shouting independence slogans.

'Now Mr. Don, not too many questions because we haven't got so much time to waste, alright?'

'It's ok. I get what they are doing.'

We enter the gate to the palace and I tell her how beautiful it is.'

'This is called Unhyeongung Palace and it is famous in Korean history not only because it dates back to the fourteenth century, but also because it symbolizes the Japanese occupation of our land. A lot of these buildings had to be restored because the Japanese destroyed them,' she explains, again in a slower speed. 'We are still angry about this, and that is why all those old nationalist men were shouting and waving flags. Fucking Japan, sorry Mr. Don but they did so many bad things to us.'

We then enter some halls that capture the historical element of the centre of Seoul, with each area displaying the regency and opulence of the Dynasty era.

'The Japanese took over this place and some of their generals used our women for their own pleasure,' she explains.

'Ah yes, the comfort women I have heard about. In fact a friend of mine in Chuncheon is doing some research on it.'

'Sorry dear teacher but we should really go now. I am feeling a little sick telling these stories. I think we have had enough history for today don't you? We have one more place which is the market where you can buy whatever you like.'

'It's ok. I don't really need anything.'

'But you have to buy something Mr. Don.'

'No I don't - I'll buy only if I want to. I don't need any souvenirs. I've only been here less than a month. It's not like I am going back home yet.'

'Oh, I'll take you to the traditional market today and if something takes your fancy don't be shy, ok.'

Namdaeaemun is one of the best traditional markets in Seoul. Harking back to the fourteenth century, it is very active in selling grains, meat, and vegetables, as well as antiques and more modern products. Cars aren't allowed inside this bustling area, so most goods are transported either by cart or hand.

'This place is also packed. Are there any quiet places here?' I ask.

'Look Mr. Don we are in Seoul after all. There's a lot of stuff here and it's cheap if you bargain. What about this jacket or these shoes? They usually have western sizes for you guys. I'll even help you to get a real good price.'

'It's ok Ji-hyun. Like I said, I don't want or need anything. Remember I am only looking.'

'But you would look really handsome in this jacket. Please try.'

'Sorry, but for the last time, I really don't want anything. Actually I'd like to go now and head to our train as I don't want to be late for dinner.'

'Ok I understand. You win today Mr. Don, but next time you must bring some money with you.'

20

HELEN'S RECIPE

A-reum is almost jumping out of her skin to see me when the train stops. 'Mr. Don, I can't believe it. You are here and you are coming to my place. It is so good to see you,' she hollers from the enclosure.

'I feel honored to visit you A-reum. Where's your Mum?'

'She's parked across the road.'

Taking my hand and grabbing it tightly, she's almost skipping with excitement while I'm exhausted from the journey to Seoul. I am immediately whisked into her Mum's black Range Rover.

'Nice to meet you again Don,' says A-reum's mother as she slams on her breaks at a stop sign.

'Yeah, it's great to see you again Mrs. Kim. Thanks for coming to the station and collecting me.'

'It's my pleasure,' she turns to me and smiles. 'By the way Mr. Don, you can call me Hye-ran, or Helen which is my English name. I was given it from my dear American friend Charlie, because he said it would be easier to pronounce for you foreign people.'

'No problem then Helen.'

'Mum will now take us to our new apartment. It's about ten minutes from here so it is really convenient,' A-reum says.

'Yes, my husband and I bought it last month so please excuse the mess. We are still preparing.'

The apartment is part of a new estate and although it's not completely finished it has most mod cons, as a well as a spacious car park down below.

'Well Don we have a sports centre so if you ever want to come and exercise do let us know. As you can see there is a lot of land around here. My husband is teaching me to play golf and there is talk we will have a driving range here soon.'

'It's pretty neat isn't it Mr Don? Wait until you see our apartment,' adds A-reum.

The apartment complex is half-occupied, mostly by new rich types who have come to Chuncheon from Seoul to make money from business. A-reum's Dad is in Seoul most of the time while her mum has a successful hair salon business in the middle of Chuncheon.

'You have to work hard to be successful in Korea. I have been lucky Don because my dreams often feature pigs, and in Korea that means you will be wealthy. It is like a good luck charm in our culture.'

'That's interesting – where I am from we often think of pigs as a negative sign. Anyway, I must say that you have a lovely place here. The view really is amazing.'

'Yes, it is. Teacher Don, look outside you can see the lake and the mountains. It really is beautiful here. My Mum and I say that we have the keys to the city.'

'I can see what you mean, A-reum.'

'Ok you two, it's time for dinner,' says Helen. 'Please come inside, and A-reum you can help me set the table while our guest relaxes with a drink. Mr. Don, I'd like you to try some of this fine Korean *soju*. This bottle here is top class and because my husband is hardly ever here, I'd like you to try it with me tonight.'

'How sweet of you Helen to offer me the drink of your country but I probably shouldn't. I have classes tomorrow,' I reply.

Helen looks almost disappointed with me.

'Your husband looks like a nice man. This photo of the three of you is really lovely.'

'Yes it was taken last year at *Chuseok* when all the Korean families get together. We were in Seoul, weren't we A-reum?'

'Yes, we were at my grandparent's house. That's them in the other photo on top of the piano.'

'They look great,' I say.

'Yes they are only in their late fifties after all,' replies Helen. 'They're not too old and they look after their bodies very well. Old people in Korea don't end up in nursing homes Don. What about your parents? Don't you miss them?'

'Sure I do,' I reply feeling a little uncomfortable with the conversation.

'What's wrong Don?' asks Helen.

'I just have my Dad now. He's in his seventies but you wouldn't know it looking at him.'

'Seventy! Wow, that is quite old in Korean culture. You look like a baby Don. You can't be fifty surely?'

There's a weird tension in the room as A-reum helps her mother. I notice that Helen places the bottle of *soju* on the table.

The first serving is *gimbap*, California rolls and miso soy bean soup. Like most home dinners, everything is fresh, and typical of Korea, not to mention the abundance of side dishes and the obligatory *kimchi*.

'I take it you love *kimchi* Mr. Don, but it may be too spicy for you?' asks Helen.

'I don't mind it. In fact, I have had it before in Sydney. There is a suburb called Strathfield which has many Korean people, so you can always get *kimchi* there. I hear a lot of Koreans travel with it when they are abroad?'

'Yes, we do travel with it, although I prefer not to. In Rome do as the Romans do? That's right isn't it my new teacher?'

'Yes, I guess so Helen,' I reply, a little half-heartedly, hoping that tonight won't into turn into a long English lesson.

'So do you know Strathfield?'

'Of course I do. I have some family friends in Eastwood.'

'That's not far from there.'

The mood has altered again, so Helen offers me a glass of *soju*, 'It's much better with some food Mr. Don. You should never drink it when you have nothing on your tummy or is it your stomach in English - sorry I am not sure? Please try some with me,' she asks, brushing my arm suggestively in the process.

'Ok you win this time. But only a small amount ok?'

'Sure - I didn't say we would drink the whole bottle,' she replies. 'You should have met my American friend Charlie. He could really drink and he would often go out with my husband and me for a dinner and chatting.'

'That's lovely Helen, but I don't see myself as a big *soju* drinker.'

'Really Mr. Don I don't believe you. I mean you have a big stomach and that means you can and drink. I've heard about you Australians,' she replies.

'Look I didn't come here to be abused!'

'Sorry Mr. Don I was just kidding you know.'

'Ok I forgive you Helen,' I reply.

We then have one each before helping ourselves to the food on the table.

'We have a knife and fork if you need,' she offers while pressing my arm again flirtatiously.

'No, I want to practice with my chopsticks if that is ok? After all, I am in Korea and I think it is polite to do that.'

'Like Mum said before, in Rome do as the Romans do,' interjects A-reum. 'Isn't that right Mummy? Mr. Don, we were in Rome last year and Mum and Dad often told me that it was more polite to be like everyone else.'

'Yes, I guess your parents were right A-reum. The big problem with me and chopsticks is I don't have a good handle on them quite yet. I was brought up with knives and forks.'

'But surely you would know by now Don that chopsticks are used by every Asian person in your hometown Sydney?' asks Helen.

'Sure they are, but most of us western people use our traditional method. Anyway, I think I am getting better the more I practice.'

'Your chopsticks are great Don. I know your Korean is also good. A-reum told me that you are good at it.'

'Not really. I need to practice more that's all. If I can use chopsticks and speak some Korean, who knows where I'll be in ten years - I might be an expert!'

'Yes, let's have another drink to that,' Helen offers.

'Ok one more but remember I have to teach tomorrow. Plus A-reum is one of my evening students so I don't want to waste her time.'

'You won't. Trust me Don – just shut up and drink,' she says almost forcing me this time to put my lips to the glass.

'Not bad Helen. It's a nice drop.'

'Ok my dear daughter, I'd like you to get the main dish now from the kitchen. Don we are now going to eat some fish from the Korean sea.'

We both look at each other and giggle. A few more glasses of this stuff and our limbs will be most likely drop off. Helen winks at me but as I lean forward to catch her expression, she draws back sensing A-reum who has now arrived with some squid and vegetables covered in red spicy sauce.

Pointing at the food, Helen warns me, 'I really hope it isn't too hot for you. This is one of our favorite dishes – spicy squid and vegetables and purple Korean rice.'

'No, no it looks amazing!' I reply.

'Ok, enjoy your meal everyone,' shouts A-reum.

It is spicy and hot. Soon enough I have a smile on my face welcoming more shots. A-reum picks up on our emerging drunkenness and immediately stands up before saying goodnight. I also half stand, telling them both that I should go home soon as it's getting late. After all I have a 6:30 a.m. class.

'Don't worry Mr. Don, I will drive you back home, or I can arrange for a driver to come and collect you. You need to sit down for a little longer so you can rest. You must let the drink properly digest. You're drunk right now.'

'That's why I better go Helen. Sorry it has been lovely and all.'

'Wait my friend. I'll call a driver to come and collect you in thirty minutes ok? You need to rest first.'

'Ok thirty minutes then. Um, thank you Helen.'

She makes the call while I admire the night view from the balcony.

'What a lovely place you have up here,' I tell her.

'My husband and I have worked hard for this. Maybe you can do the same one day Don when you make some money here?'

'Money, what is that? The way Global World is going I will soon be out of a job and who knows what will happen?'

'My husband and I can help you Mr. Don. Don't worry for now. Just enjoy the time we have here with each other.'

She leans closer towards me asking for a hug. I gently put an arm around her, but it's awkward as I don't really know how to handle her.

'Sorry Helen, but I really must go,' I say, as I slowly release myself from her.

'But we have another twenty-five minutes and the driver won't know. Please another hug and a cuddle Mr. Don. You are so cute you know.'

'Helen, you are married, and you are the mother of my student.'

'It doesn't matter. No one but us can know Mr. Don.'

'No, this is wrong and I won't do this sorry.'

'Don't worry Don. Nobody needs to know. Just please kiss me and be quiet,' she begs, almost forcing her body upon me.

I try to push her away but she won't have a bar of it. She starts to force her lips on me and as the *soju* takes over I soon succumb to her strong wishes. We collapse onto the sofa embracing, fondling and kissing until I hear the sound of the bathroom door. I then hold myself back from her and realise how much I am shaking. My head is fuzzy but at the same time I'm intrigued. Should I break away now and flee? Or should I let it roll and enjoy the moment? But what if A-reum comes back into the room? What about her husband in Seoul?'

'Helen, I think I heard something. Maybe it was the driver? Maybe it was your daughter? Look this isn't a good idea. We can't do this again!'

'Yes, we can Don, we can. My husband is doing this all the time in Seoul. We can keep it as a secret Mr. Don. Don't worry! Nobody needs to know. Remember, we can help you to stay here and enjoy your new life in Korea.'

'That's the bell, I'm sure of it. I can't do this Helen. I have to go,' I tell her tucking my shirt into my trousers so that there aren't any signs of play.

She takes me to the door and lunges at me yet again with another hug and a tongue kiss.

'Quick, the driver won't come up unless I tell him to. Let's fuck on the sofa. C'mon Don, I am begging you now,' she offers.

'You're not listening to me Helen. Look contact me, or something, I really have to go.'

Through the intercom she hears the driver speaking. Winking at me as I leave, she reminds me of the fun that we have had tonight.

'It was a lovely dinner Helen. Thanks again – I need to go home and rest before class tomorrow.'

'Yes it was Mr. Don. Goodbye and see you again.'

21

TEXTING

```
Good morning darling Donald. Ha-ha! I looked up
Don and it told me Donald. I hope you had a sexy
sleep young man, love Helen xxxx
```

I can't help but grin a little. If last night is any indication, Helen's persistence may not die that easily. A second later another message appears.

```
May we meet again soon? I need to see you Mr.
Donald, my Australian man.
```

I ignore her messages and instead get ready for work but am forced to take another sauna due to the lack of hot water in the apartment. When I arrive back Kevin is propped up on the couch, and it's obvious that he got in late too.

'Well, well,' he says. 'What has royalty brought this morning? So you have been to the bath house again young man?'

'Mate, if you cared to turn the tap off properly, I could have had a normal shower like anyone else. Plus, you ate all the breakfast stuff.'

'I'm sorry Don. I had a hard night mate. This bitch was all over me at the club and she wouldn't let me go.'

'You are kidding aren't you? I don't want to hear any excuses. Just stop apologizing and get with the program. It's about fucking time you bought some groceries. We have nothing, just this instant noodle shit, and that lingering *kimchi* smell from downstairs.'

'Well, we have no groceries because some cunt won't pay us any money,'

'That's bullshit. You can use that excuse all day if you like, but it won't work on me. You didn't have to go out last night and bar it up with your bitches then did you?' I ask. 'I mean, I'd rather eat than listen to your conquests any day Kevin. Get your fucking act together would you?'

'What are you talking about? I don't have to do anything. As far as I am concerned I am over teaching these students.'

Slamming the door behind me I notice Daphne also leaving her apartment so we walk together to class.

'What's up?' she asks.

'I'm ok, it's nothing. I'm just a little pissed off with Kevin. He never contributes. All we have in our kitchen cupboards at the moment are instant noodles and a few tubs of peanut butter that Mona left behind.'

'Don, sharing isn't fun, and you can imagine what it would be like at my age. One of the first things I made sure of when I arrived was that I wasn't living with anyone. I'm just too old for that caper.'

'Well, that's funny because I was told that I'd also be having a one bedroom apartment all to myself, but it seems I had no say in it. Instead I have ended up with this Korean American who is nothing but a contradiction-of-a-bible basher and a sex-crazed addict. I guess you can't pick your types.'

'No, you can't. Maybe you can have my apartment when I leave? After all I will be gone in a fortnight.'

'Shit I didn't realise it was so soon. I am going to miss you Daphne and so are the students. It will be really different without you.'

'Whatever you do Don, if you don't get your money you have to inform people about this company. Find a local with some influence. This kind of thing shouldn't be happening and it's our job as internationalists to let people know about it,' she explains.

'But how can the word get out?' I ask.

'We have to spread the word, paste things on the internet, and let new teachers know why schools like this continue to be blacklisted in Korea.'

As class starts my phone vibrates with yet another message.

```
Why not contact me Donald. I wait for you and I
miss you. Please write me - love Helen.

I am in class today. Sorry but I cannot talk at
the moment. D

Don, that is ok. I will call you today when I
know you are free.
```

The weird thing is I kind of like the attention she is giving me. For the last two years I haven't cared for anyone, let alone myself. Instead I have been playing to a short-lived tune of quick impersonal meet-ups and flings. I have been emotionally devoid of attachment, so this situation with Helen isn't so unfamiliar. In some ways it should be easy and manageable. Why not just be and have some fun for the moment? But there's a lot to lose particularly with A-reum as my student and her being married.

When I get to the classroom, the Korean Air man Mr. Park is waiting attentively for me. I wonder what he would think of last night and the shenanigans with a married woman.

'Don my good teacher and new friend! What's up buddy?'

'I am fine Mr. Park. It's good to see you. Where's So Hyun this morning?'

'She had things to attend to. Better still, I told her not come. Today, I want to have a real man's meeting with you. I have some good news about our trip to the Philippines. I hope you haven't forgotten teacher!'

'Um, no I haven't sir. I remember you talking about it when we last met.'

'Good, because you and I will go there the weekend after next, ok?'

'Let me check my diary as I might be busy then.'

'Ok check it now as we have time!'

'Sorry Mr. Park but I can't because I left it at home. How about I email you later today? Then I can let you know if it is ok? After all we're in a lesson now.'

'Ok, later today will be fine. I will be waiting for your reply. Plus, Mr. Don, you won't be disappointed with my plan. It involves lots of different girls, beaches, casinos, and of course drinking. Can you handle it?'

'Like I said, I'd better check my diary first.'

In an attempt to soften things, I praise him for his kindness for asking me to go on a trip even though I'm not interested. Most of his ideas are pretty sordid. Basically he is planning a sex romp through the islands. The weird thing is why me? Why would he want his new teacher to come with him?

'Today Mr. Don I thought we could look at some of my photos from my last trip to the islands where I had such a good time. I love these islands very much you know.'

Taking a deep breath, I reply, 'That's good Mr. Park. Let's have a look then.'

He excitedly shows me his photo album, 'Isn't she sexy Mr. Don? How about this one? I had both of them one evening in Cebu. All these Korean couples were getting married on the island, while I was having the two of them in my penthouse. Man, they were great. They'd do anything you want - I mean anything.'

'Is that so Mr. Park?' I ask.

'Oh and we can also play golf while we are there. Isn't that great dear teacher? Golf, sex and booze! What else does a man want?'

'Ok, I want you to tell me some other things about the islands. Like, for example, where did you go and what did you like about it. Tell me a little about the food as well.'

'It was only Cebu as we didn't have time for anywhere else. Plus, our airline flies directly there. We ancients can only go on short holidays. This is very short as we are busy - we have no time. We are businessmen after all Mr. Don so please understand.'

'I get you Mr. Park. Well done by the way. Your English is improving every day.'

He is chuffed by my comments about his English. It is the perfect compliment for a Korean businessman. 'You really know what to say don't you Mr. Don. You know that my English is very important to me and the future of my company. I so hope you can join me on this trip. I will treat you to the best time any man would want on an island. Just trust me.'

'Ok, Mr. Park, it has been lovely seeing you today. Keep up your good work and I will email you later today,' I add in a more professional tone.

Shaking my hands firmly, he smiles like an excited child.

'Talk to you later and have a nice day won't you,' he adds as he leaves the classroom.

Jason then enters the room asking me what that was all about.

'Look he just likes to tell me lots of things,' I reply. 'You know too many things.'

'Consider yourself lucky. That man has a lot of influence.'

'I am not sure. I get the impression he is like a lot of businessmen that have too much money.

'Just remain aware Don that these guys will get you involved in their drinking and dinners. Then there will be the singing room activities and the hostesses. This will all mean huge bills on credit. That's how some of them live and I'd say that Mr. Park, as much as the nice and influential guy he seems, he is already living that life.'

'Does that explain why he wants me to go to the islands with him for a holiday?'

'Absolutely it does. And take my advice, make sure you don't go. It's a recipe for disaster and if you need an out just tell him I need you here as the company is undergoing some restructuring. That will definitely keep him quiet.'

'Thanks Jason, I didn't want to go anyway. The problem with a lot of these Korean invitations is that they make you feel bad if you have doubts. I have never been good at being decisive.'

'Well if that's the case my friend, you better start - otherwise this country will do your head in. There are so many formalities and rules that one can be easily led astray and before you know it, you become indebted to others. Don't let this happen to you mate. I take it you're smarter than that. And watch his type as well - they're not always as real as they seem,' he adds, pointing to the housewife group who are approaching.

'Mr. Don, you smell a little strange today. Are you ok? Have you been out drinking with Korean man?' asks Eun-Ju, one of the senior housewives.

'Not at all, why do you think that? I am a good man,' I say sheepishly.

'I know you are a good man but I think you have been drinking last night. We Korean wives aren't stupid you know.'

'Look, if you really need to know, I had dinner with a family last night and it was lovely. They also asked me to drink some traditional wine and I couldn't say no to that.'

'Of course we understand - and you're right. It is better to not say no. If someone asks you to do something in Korea that means you should,' she warns. 'After all we are only trying to be friendly. Just be careful with some businessmen, because sometimes they are really bad guys. Often they just like to have foreign friends to show off.'

This could well be the reason why Mr. Park is so keen for me to join him in the Philippines, I think to myself. I begin to wonder whether real friendships can actually exist with your students, let alone flings with their mothers. Before class starts, another text message arrives from Helen. This time she informs me that A-reum isn't so well and won't be attending class today. I reply:

```
Ok thanks for letting me know that. Have a nice
evening Helen and tell A-reum I hope she feels bet-
ter soon.
```

A second later she responds;

```
She will be OK. How about you though? My young Aus-
tralian friend - would you like a massage tonight?
```

> I can come and meet you if you like? I can drive over. I know where you live by the way so you don't need to tell me how to get there. You are sexy my Australia friend. Please don't disappoint me Donald.

After class finishes Helen asks me to call her to explain myself, 'Where were you? Why didn't you call me? I have been waiting for a whole two hours for you! You can't do this kind of thing to a Korean woman?'

'Um, Helen could you please listen for just a moment.'

'No I won't listen to you Don. You are not a sexy Australian man anymore. You are another bad man, just like my husband.'

'I beg your pardon? Helen, listen to what you're saying. I don't understand what you mean.'

'You let me down Don. You didn't call me back. How can I forgive you for this?'

'Well you could give me a chance to explain.'

'That's not true and you know it,' she replies, now sobbing uncontrollably.

'Helen, I was at work! I turn my phone off during class. Look I am sorry that I didn't reach you but my students always come first. I can't be busy taking phone calls or receiving messages while teaching.'

'Yes you can. Our teachers always have their phones on just in case there is an emergency. Tonight I needed you!'

'What do you mean?'

'I needed to talk to you about A-reum. She needs to work hard on her high school work, which means she has no time for Global World. She will study and pass her exams. Mr. Donald I am sorry but this is the way so please understand me.'

'Ok, that's a pity. She is a great student.'

'Please don't be angry with me Mr. Don. She will come back when she can, but now there are more important things on her mind.'

'But she likes my class....'

'I know that but she can't come right now. The university entrance examination is the most important thing in a teenager's life in Korea. Trust me, parents even go to a temple and pray for their child when they sit these exams. She cannot afford to fail this one. My husband and I want her to go to Seoul University, just like any other Korean parent would.'

'Ok, thanks for letting me know. I will inform my boss that she may not be around for a while.'

'And Mr. Don it was good talking to you again. I always like to practice my oral English you know. And if you ever need me to cut that terrible hair of yours let me know. It is thinning and it looks stupid. You would be better off having an army hair cut. You need a buzz cut as we say.'

'What and then look like Bart Simpson?'

'Who is that?'

'Never mind, it doesn't matter. Ok Helen thanks for your compliments. I have to go now so goodbye, and please say hello to your daughter from me.'

22

THE CANE

Arriving at the country school I am again welcomed by yet another enthusiastic star greeting. A bunch of Grade 3 students see me approaching and run up to me diving at my legs. Inside the staff seems a little distressed.

'Why didn't you join us for lunch today?' asks Mr. Zhang, the vice principal.

'I had a few things I had to do back in town. Sorry about that, maybe next time I can come and eat with you.'

'Please do. It is important that we all eat together like a family. The children want to get to know you, and we do too.'

'Ok, next week I promise I will get here in time for lunch. Thank you sir, I better head off to my class now.'

'Yes, good luck Mr. Don. Remember if you have any trouble send the children down to me. I know that they aren't too easy to manage so just remember the minute you mention my name they will be scared. They are terrified of this stick you know. It's an old fashioned rattan about three inches thick. You can imagine their faces can't you, Mr. Don?'

'Um yes, I can. I remember my high school principal had one of those in his office as well. We call it the cane where I am from. I still shudder at the thought when I remember Mr. Fisher and his big stick. So you don't need to remind me.'

'In Korea we will use the cane no matter what people think. Here our parents don't mind.'

'But should we put fear in our kids all the time?'

'Our old leader Park in the 1970s enforced an army-like manner to better us. He believed it was the only way we could survive against our neighbors,' he explains.

'Yes I have heard of this man Park,' I reply, remembering the wall hangings of him at the restaurant my work colleagues took me to a few weeks back.

'And what do you think of our great leader. Do you agree with what he stood for?'

'Well, I have only just heard about him. I would have been a kid when he was around. For me though, it's really a thing of the past. Teachers can't hit their students like they used to and in some countries like New Zealand for example, there are even moves to ban parents from smacking their own children.'

'That is the problem with you people from the west Mr. Don. I think sometimes you are too soft. I don't mean to be rude in anyway, but that is why a lot of your children lose their self respect. Our students' parents are mostly farmers and their kids need discipline.'

'Ok, I will remember what you say.'

'You're a good man Mr. Don, now go and teach your students and love them like you would your own children.'

'Thanks Mr. Zhang.'

When I arrive at the classroom upstairs I am welcomed by a loud chorus of 'Hello, how are you?' then followed by 'Thank you and I am fine' and 'And you?'

'Thank you everyone. How are you all?' I shout above their voices.

'I am fine thank you and you?' shouts Kil-hun a chubby boy at the back.

'Thank you Kil-hun. Remember you don't need to say I am fine thank you and you all the time.'

The students then all shout, 'We love you Mr. Don.'

'Aw, and I love you all too. Now let's start today's lesson. Can anyone tell me what today is?'

There's a hushed silence before Gil-kee, one of the girls at the front shouts out, 'It's Tuesday!'

'Everyone together, what day is it?'

'It's Tuesday!'

Grabbing the class textbook I attempt to start today's lesson, showing them what page to go to. I ask them if they remember what country I am from, but it falls on deaf ears. Again I start to draw a map of Australia on the board.

'Can you remember what country this is?' I ask.

Kil-hun then annoyingly parrots me.

'Can anyone remember? Where is this? What is the name of this place?' I patiently ask.

Do-hee, one of the shy students in the front row politely replies, 'It is your country Mr. Don. I remember because you told us last week. It is Australia Kil-hun. Don't you remember anything?' she snaps.

The class laughs and claps while Kil-hun drops his head to the desk.

'Thank you, Do-hee. Now let's practice it once more. Everyone say together – Australia'

'Au-stray-li,' they all reply.

I continue with some individual drilling checking each of their pronunciation. When I get around to Kil-hun I encourage him to take part by asking, 'Where am I from Kil-hun?'

'*Hoju*. You are from *Hoju* Mr. Teacher,' he reluctantly replies.

'*Hoju*? Where is that?'

'In Korean we say *Hoju* teacher because that is what Australia is,' explains Do-hee.

'I know that Do-hee. I am from Australia. *Na nin hoju saram imnida*,' I reply in Korean.

The class all give me a loud clap, shocked by my language skills.

'Your Korean is very good teacher,' exclaims Do-hee.

'I am just a student like you Do-hee. I have just started learning to read and speak.'

'That's great teacher. I hope that one day we can talk in Korean. By the way, can you teach us about your country? We want to know about Australia.'

'Ok I will. If you turn to page 85 I can tell you about our animals.'

Some are familiar with kangaroos and koalas, and not long before the lesson finishes, I have them pronouncing and mimicking the sounds that each animal makes. Kil-hun and his mates sit up the back looking bored and restless.

'Ok you three up the back. I want you to tell us what these animals are and what they do.'

'Fuck you,' replies Jin-heong who is sitting to Kil-hun's left.

'I beg your pardon? What did you say?'

'I said fuck you mother-fucker. Fuck you!'

The class is silenced except for the three boys who are now laughing at me. I am enraged by their comments and bang my fist on the desk shouting, 'I will have none of that language in here and I am sure Principal Mr. Park or Teacher Zhang won't either.'

The rest of the class turn around and face the three boys, shouting some words at them in Korean, warning them not to do such things or Mr. Zhang will be called in. Silencing them, I continue to teach but soon Kilhun and his mates start testing my patience again.

Whilst preparing something on the board, the three make their way quietly to the front with their hands clasped and second fingers pointed vertically. In Korean, this is known as a *dong-jip*, when a student comes up behind you and jabs their fingers between your cheek buttocks.

At the age of nine or ten it's considered by kids to be the most hilarious and funniest thing, but for a teacher, and particularly a foreign one it's a huge insult. The three boys take turns on me before I chase them around the classroom. With the help of some of the other students, we manage to corner them.

'Ok, you guys you are going downstairs. Come with me now.'

'No, no, no!' they shout, kicking and screaming.

'Yes, yes, yes.' I reply.

Downstairs, Mr. Zhang shouts at them in Korean grabbing his rattan, 'I am so sorry Mr. Don. These three will be punished for such actions. Please go back to your classroom. I will now deal with them and I promise they won't upset you ever again.'

The three boys are scared shitless, regretting their actions. I return to a hushed class knowing that I probably won't have any more misbehavior. Just as the bell rings to signal the end of the class, Mr. Zhang brings the three culprits upstairs to use them as an example. All three are crying and the very fear in their eyes has hushed everyone, including me.

I quietly tell the class, 'It's been nice to see you today and see you next week. Make sure you do your homework for me.'

23

TO THE BAR

By the end of the week I am ready for some fun. It's Daphne's farewell and I know I'm going to miss her.

'How are you feeling Daphne? Getting ready to say goodbye?'

'You bet. I am tired of all this crap Don. Mate, it starts to wear on you. I've got twice the amount of wrinkles as before, so you better not stay here too long or you'll go bald!'

'I'm thinning already but you have a few years on me. You could always get some surgery for those you know,' I reply, pointing to her wrinkles.

'Watch it kid,' she warns.

'Can't you take a joke? I am kidding you know.'

'Sorry Don, I am a little antsy at the moment. It's my last night and I've got such mixed emotions.'

'Daphne, you have been great to me. I won't forget you.'

'Just remember don't let these bastards get away with anything. It's our job to complain. Tonight I want you to meet Captain Cliff from America. He's a likeable guy and because he's an ex-Marine and business person he knows his shit,' she tells. 'He has been involved in some business with an English school here so he knows how these academies tick.'

'Thanks Daphne I'd really appreciate it if you could introduce me,' I reply. 'And don't forget I'll be keeping you in the loop as well with Global World after you go. We'll miss you and I want to say thanks for making my welcome here a warm one.'

'I don't know if it has been particularly warm Don. It is a fucking shame that we had to meet under such circumstances. No one, in their right mind, should have sent you to a shithole like this.'

'I wouldn't have got this far without your help you know.'

'Don, I just did what is expected for any new teacher. Will you really miss me?'

'Of course, why wouldn't I? You have been great.'

'Don, I am just like any teacher that comes and goes. Essentially my time is over now. This is no place for someone in their mid-fifties to be ripped off. Anyway, enough of this crap. We need to get out of here.'

'One more thing I need to tell you. My business guy hasn't shown since I wrote him an email to say I didn't want to join him in the Philippines.'

'That's because he's lost face. He probably thought that by offering you the moon he couldn't be refused, but you did it Don. And good on, you I reckon.'

'Jason told me it was the best thing to do and you're always going on about how you shouldn't get too close to your students.'

'Yes, always remember that. Keep it close to your chest, as you need to stay tight with your foreign friends. Have a few local friends, but remember you have to trust your intuition. Be wary of anyone, particularly your boss and even those sweet innocent students.'

'Thanks Daphne. Ok, let's get out of here and head to the pub.'

Jacks is looking tired. The ceiling is grimy with cigarette smoke and the carpet has an old worn look about it. Eminem is being pumped out on the stereo again, whilst a dozen or so university waitresses shine beer trays and cart large trays of fried chicken to different tables. Again, the two Mikes are the only teachers out; both trying to make use of their minimal Korean while failing to chat up some of the waitresses.

Noticing Daphne and I, Manitoba Mike welcomes us with his trademark boom, 'Hey, what's up? Good to see you Global guys out again. It's been ages.'

'Yeah, it has. We don't get out much, as you know,' I reply.

'I take it you're a little under-funded,' adds the other Mike.

'We haven't been as privileged as you guys let's say,' says Daphne.

'We both read you. I mean, just as well our boss pays us because there is no way we'd take the shit you guys get down there.'

'Down there? Now that's a good analogy Mike,' Daphne responds sarcastically, which goes over their heads.

'We're hanging on as well as we can,' I reply. 'At least Daphne doesn't have to worry anymore. She is out of here this weekend.'

'Is that so? I didn't know your time had finished Daphne? Shit, where are you off to?'

'I'm heading back home to New Zealand. You ever heard of that place you two?'

'Yeah of course we have. It's the home of the Lord of the Rings right?' asks Arizona Mike.

'Well done, you're smarter than you seem boys. I always thought you were military for some reason. Sorry for my sarcasm by the way but we're waiting for some friends. You guys should head back and practice your shit Korean on those prissy waitresses!'

Stunned by Daphne's sharp tongue, the two Mikes stay in the front bar area whilst we arrange a table in a private room out of the back. Not long later, Jack, Carol, David and Justin all appear and the table is soon cluttered with drinks and side dishes. The room is function-friendly, in that it is usually hired out for birthdays or farewells. They've even got an electronic *yeo gi yo* service button should we need assistance.

Soon Captain Cliff joins us with his own entourage of fellow teaching staff and a couple of students, 'Hey, what's up? Good to see you dudes, Jack and Carol, David and Justin. I haven't seen you guys in ages. And Miss Daphne, I brought a Kiwi friend along with me tonight. He said he wanted to see you before you leave. He is usually in Seoul chasing skirt.'

'That's lovely Cliff, isn't it? I mean we wouldn't want those girls in Seoul getting their skirts chased now would we?'

'I guess not. Anyway, do you remember Bruce? After all he is one of the few Kiwis in this town?'

'Ah I think we may have met once before though I am not sure. So where is he then?' she adds.

'That's him over at the bar with those two Mike guys. Of course he's trying to chat up the waitresses.'

'Aren't they all? And yes I remember him now.'

'He'll be over in a second so be nice to him. And please enough of that sharp tone young lady,' comments Cliff.

Bruce is short and stocky, and looks like he spends more of his time at a gym than in a classroom. He has a slight cockiness about him.

'Good to see you, Bruce,' she says as she shakes his hand. 'Please sit down and enjoy a drink and help yourself to the food before it goes cold.'

'Thanks bro. It's good to be here and not in Seoul for a change eh.'

'And why's that Bruce?' asks Daphne.

'I always get into trouble there bro eh. Cliff told me it was your last night so I thought I'd better make an appearance eh.'

She replies with cheek, 'Thanks bro. I am delighted.'

'I guess the only one who isn't here is Gordon. Is he going to make it? Does anyone know?' asks David.

'I doubt he will be out tonight. He wasn't too bright on it last night. He's had yet another fight with his girl,' says Justin.

'Here's to our Kiwi bro and here's to another round of beers!' shouts Jack.

'Fuck that!' Carol interrupts. 'Not another round here. C'mon guys, it's Daphne's last night so I reckon we should head to Hells Bells and have some tequila shots and listen to some decent tunes. This place is shit so let's finish our food and beers and then fuck off. What do you reckon?'

'Well I won't be out too late tonight guys. I've got to pack tomorrow morning,' says Daphne.

'You're staying out tonight miss whether you like it or not,' replies Captain Cliff.

Hells Bells is jumping with army GI's, most who know Cliff from his Marine days, including Hooch and Frank. Cliff was based in Okinawa two years ago before he took a payout because he damaged his knees on one-too-many patrols.

'Hey, it's good to see you guys. This place is rocking tonight and it's a shame we have to cut out of here before midnight, but that's the military - as you know,' mentions Hooch.

'Yeah, I don't miss that,' says Cliff. 'I'm a free man fighting no war over here and it's good.'

'Well the military has been good to us bud and we think what we do is kind of worthwhile,' replies Hooch.

Cliff can understand that for some Americans the military is a far better place than jail, but since leaving the Marines his attitude to war has taken a reverse status. For one he can't understand why his own people had to attack a country on the grounds of weapons of mass destruction that hadn't been proven.

'The fact that we are supposed to be Christians does not add up.'

'George Bush knows what he is doing man,' says Frank. 'It's an axis of evil like he said and we've got to smoke these guys out before they take real control.'

Shaking his head, Cliff whispers into Frank's ear telling him that President Bush is clueless and has no idea what he is doing. This draws a response from Chester, the very same man who challenged Justin for wearing an 'I am not an American' t-shirt a few weeks back. He tells Cliff to check his audience and to be aware that he is surrounded by military personnel, who by this stage are potentially up for a fight.

'Look old man, I have a democratic right to make this statement wherever the fuck I am. After all that's what a democratic country is, isn't it?' Cliff questions.

Suddenly the whole bar is hushed as both Chester and Cliff are standing over a table shouting verbal obscenities at each other. John tries stop them but the two aren't listening.

'You have no right to say what we are doing is wrong and that our leader has no idea,' informs Chester. 'Do you hear me punk? You have no fucking right.'

'Well, we had no right to invade Iraq unasked. Would you like me to come and bomb your family and children?'

Chester takes a swing at Cliff and thankfully misses while the rest of the GI's shout and motion to them both to square off but Cliff will have none of it. By this stage John is on the phone to the military cops.

'Stop it guys. Please no fighting in our bar,' shouts David the co-owner.

Cliff walks away from Chester and on his way out of the bar first apologizes to us for ruining the evening. However us teachers are pretty happy with what we have seen, praising him if anything, particularly Justin.

'They are so conceited some of these people. That guy Chester gives Korea a bad name.'

'It's not all of them,' interrupts Jack.

'Maybe not,' adds Carol. 'But they are a problem. This need to fight other people's wars is crazy I reckon.'

Meanwhile, Bruce is busy at the far end of the bar with a young local who is fawning over him.

He brings her over and says, 'These are all my friends but let me introduce you to one of my people first. Ji-yeon, this is my mate Daphne and it's her farewell party.'

'*Annyong hashimnikka*, hello. *Ban gap sim nida*, very nice to meet you.'

'How nice is this?' Daphne turns to Bruce, 'A nice looking local girl as well. You have surprised me.'

'I have more luck here than I'll ever have in Auckland.'

'So what are you doing here tonight Ji-yeon?' asks Daphne.

'Just playing with my friends,' she replies looking directly into Bruce's eyes.

Bruce soon realises that Ji-yeon is looking a little uncomfortable and wants to go somewhere else.

Remembering that there is a rugby game on tonight between the All Blacks and Scotland he says, 'Hey guys, I am not sure how interesting this is for you all but I am thinking of showing Ji-yeon some of the rugby. We're playing Scotland tonight and it is on at Bo M just down the road, so feel free to join us?'

'Count me out bro,' replies Daphne with a roaring laugh.

'Yeah, sorry Bruce but we're going to stick around here tonight and farewell Daphne.

'Remember it's her leaving party after all and we don't want to watch a stupid game of rugby,' adds Carol. 'We are here to party.'

'Yeah, sorry mate, but I can watch the rugby when I am at home, know what I mean?' I reply.

'Ok, as you can see I better go then,' he replies, knowing that Ji-yeon is becoming more uncomfortable.

'Man, sorry but he's a jerk!' says David after he leaves. 'I just can't get my head around why chicks would dig him?'

'Don't worry David your time will come,' replies Justin. 'It took me eight months to get anything and it was a long eight months let me tell you.'

'My girl is too young I think. We just text each other but the problem is I don't know how I should make the next move.'

'No offence mate, but she probably just wants to practice her English,' I add.

'Look, all you boys just need a bit of Dutch courage,' adds Daphne, sipping on her tequila sunrise.

'Be forward mate,' says Jack. 'After all in this culture they are not the ones who are going to make the first move. That's how you got me, wasn't it Carol? I was this useless shy bloke at college, and then one day she popped up at a Primal Scream show. She rammed her tongue down my throat. That was one Primal Scream you made, pardon the pun.'

'Ha-ha you're so funny Jack Peters, and you're also a filthy liar. I promise I did nothing of the sort,' adds Carol.

'Well, all I remember is we knew each other for a year, and that it wasn't me who made the first move. You have to be forward David.'

'So what are you trying to say?'

'What I am trying to say is to be more American for fuck sake would you,' suggests Jack. 'Take off your Cheltenham clothes and think of yourself as an LA Laker boy. The kids here love basketball and the players. Look at the African American soldiers here. They're the ones you mostly see armed with Korean girlfriends. Just go to the base or any of the fast food joints in the centre of town, hang out and talk the lingo mate.'

'Well, I'm hardly Afro-American looking.'

'That's not the point. Courage is what you need. Dutch courage as Daphne said, and she ought to know as she's been around a lot longer than most of us.'

'Hah, true I guess,' replies Daphne.

'Ok, I get your point. Maybe tonight I can start being a little more forward. Can I practice on you now Carol?'

'Sod off!' she says laughing as she pushes him away.

John bumps up the evening with some cheesy familiar old 80s hits like 'Hungry Like the Wolf' and 'Karma Chameleon' and soon both Carol and Daphne are up dancing. David at the bar continues to ply us all with a few more tequila shots, so we can have more energy.

By now the GI's are being rounded up by the military police, and it seems that the only people left here are half a dozen of our original entourage, and a few civilians connected with the base.

One civilian is John a helicopter engineer who Daphne has a thing for. Noticing each other, they both sit down and catch up. Apparently the last time they saw each other a Canadian in her fifties called Ellen managed to nab John from her.

'I would have made a move last time you know but that Ellen got in first,' Daphne says.

Booming out in a loud voice for everyone to hear, John says, 'Yeah, Ellen was a cougar that's why. God man, she was bonking younger guys like there was no tomorrow.'

'Ok you're on tonight then soldier,' Daphne tells him straight up.

I join Jack outside who is having a cigarette.

'Man, what a night this is. Carol won't stop dancing to bad 80s shit and she never usually dances.'

'That's because she is having a good time. Aren't you happy for her?' I ask.

'Sure, I am. It's just that it's getting close to my bedtime that's all,' he replies.

'You won't leave her out on her own then?' I ask.

'Don, for fuck sake, Carol, can look after herself mate. Anyway you will stick around right?'

'Sure I will.'

'Ah, look what we have here. It's our Kiwi friend. How was the rugby bro?' Jack asks.

'We won of course, but it looks like Ji-yeon hasn't. She has literally passed out as you can see, so I have to get her back home.'

'Yes, that's probably a good move. I'll tell Daphne that you said your byes and good luck. Maybe it's time for me to leave as well. I can't do these nights much more,' replies Jack.

'More drinking mate means a bigger hangover tomorrow. Anyway bro I better go and take this one back. See you later Jack. Bye Don, and good to see you mate.'

Even though two of the bigger personalities Jack and Bruce have left, the night is nowhere near over. Most of us are either dancing in a small area by the side exit or drinking.

An hour or so after leaving, Bruce returns looking out of breath and somewhat scared.

'God, you were quick. What happened bro? Too drunk to fuck I take it?' Justin cheekily asks.

'Nah, it never got to that mate,' Bruce replies. 'We bumped into two of her friends on the street didn't we? One of them was pissed off and told me to get my hands off her. She told him not to worry and asked me to help her back home. However the two friends kept following us. I turned around and noticed them and told her to run but she pushed me flat on my face and I hit the ground.'

'And then what?' Justin asks.

'Well, I just scarpered as fast as I could to Jack and Carol's place and luckily the old bastard let me in.'

'That'd be Jack,' I reply.

'It's not over yet Don. I was hiding in their study room and then I heard the door. Luckily Jack opened it and gave them a real tongue-lashing for knocking on his door so late. One of them was a student of his.'

'Jack the professor hey,' adds David.

Slamming down a shot at the bar, Bruce walks up to Carol and tries to talk to her, but she isn't that interested in what he has to say. Daphne on the other hand, is with John at the table, and they are now openly pashing.

'Hey, sorry to interrupt sis, but I thought I'd better tell you that I have arrived safely back,' Bruce tells her.

'You got a problem mate?' asks John.

'Look mate I am not looking for any. I just wanted to tell Daphne here that New Zealand won the rugby and I'm happy about that, that's all.'

'That's great Bruce,' says Daphne. 'I am happy for you and for my country. Anyway we better go now. I have to pack tomorrow and my lovely man is coming back to mine to help me, aren't you John?'

'Yes, lady, I can certainly do that,' John replies in his southern drawl.

We then all give her a rousing farewell and have one more shot before they both leave.

'Wasn't that the guy who started that big catfight at Brain last year?' Justin asks Carol. 'There was even blood on the footpath?'

'Yeah, that's him. Daphne had a thing for him but Ellen that cougar, as we called her, got in first. Daphne started telling her off about it but she didn't care. It started to get heavy and soon there was fighting on the stairs of Brain, before it spilled out onto the street. There was a bit of blood. It was awesome. Sadly Daphne came off second best though.'

'Well I am glad she got some back tonight. She deserves to have some fun.' I add.

'We all do, we all do,' replies David.

'Hey guys on that note I better go as well. Don, could you walk me back?' asks Carol. 'I know your place isn't too far from mine.'

'Sure, I can do that. The bar is going to close in five minutes anyway and I can't be bothered going on to Brain unless you really want to?' I ask.

'No, I am definitely not going there,' replies Carol.

Walking her home, Carol decides to confide in me again.

'Please don't tell anyone, but things are worse than before. Like I said Jack and I aren't what we were, and I am still bored shitless with my job. I don't know how much longer I can take it Don, know what I mean? I am just hanging out for the next semester break which is in summer. What can I do? Aside from the comfort women stuff, I am bored out of my mind.'

'God, don't ask me. I have no idea,' I reply. 'It's not that I can't relate because I do know your conundrum. You need to remember that things will wear off Carol. I mean you just have to ask yourself what you want from your life and if it's worth it or not.'

'Thanks for understanding and hearing me out. At least you can see where I am coming from. I love Jack you know, but it all feels weird now, because when we married last year we'd already been together for over ten years.'

'But it's not just about how long you have been seeing each other. You shouldn't be thinking about time otherwise you wouldn't have got married.' I say. 'What I mean is that time should be the last thing on a couple's mind.'

'To be honest that is the quandary I'm in. In some ways I reckon we shouldn't have got married. I mean, what point does it really serve you after knowing someone for such a long period of time? It's like a noose around our necks. It's completely fucked us Don. We're not happy like we were before.'

'Carol, go and get some sleep. You're tired and the alcohol is speaking. We can talk about this some other time. Whatever you do, please don't make any rash decisions before telling me.'

Hugging me firmly, she adds, 'Don't worry Don, you are my confidante and I will always talk to you. You really are a great friend. In fact ...' she grabs me again, in the same way Helen did, aiming straight for my lips. For a brief second I am stunned, but as with Helen I don't say no. It's only the blinds of a nearby apartment opening that interrupt us.

'Carol, please go and rest. I don't think this was such a good idea. I mean do you?' I ask nervously.

She stands back and looks at me, 'Actually I think it is fine. Don, it's been boiling in the furnace for a while now. Ever since I saw you that time with my leaflets,' she says.

'But what about Jack,' I ask?

'Fuck Jack, he can go to hell really. You know the last time he kissed me was on our wedding day. And he only did that because he was asked to. Know what I mean?'

I breathe in deeply, 'Yes, yes, I can understand. Anyway it is light now so best I walk you to your gate Carol, and we talk another time. Ok?'

'Stop saying ok Don, would you? Take my hand and walk me to the gate. Best we meet during the week or something?'

'We'll see. Get some sleep for now.'

I take Carol's hand and I walk her to her apartment gate. She knows that Jack will be sound asleep by now, and that she'll end up on the couch.

On my way home, I drop into my favorite Buy the Way convenience store for some late night munchies. I grab a few micro-waved buns and some potato chips. However just as pay for them, I'm confronted by an ageing suited man with slicked back hair, armed with bottles of beer and *soju*.

'Sorry young man, but it seems you also have a handful of things there. Why don't you ask for a bag from the young cashier here?'

'Um, it's ok. I'm close to home.'

'I can see that. So you live near here?'

'Yeah, it's not too far.'

'Get a bag or I will take the load off and help you to carry them.'

'Old man, I am ok. Trust me.'

I ignore him only to nearly fall head over tit outside the store. The cashier and the man quickly race out to help me.

'Are you ok, sir?' asks the cashier.

'Turn him over and check for any cuts or bruising,' the old man says in Korean.

'I am ok. For crying out loud, can you please let me go home? I'm tired and I have been out all night.'

'You're not going anywhere yet buddy. In fact, that ankle of yours looks a little sprained. Please take a seat first and I'll grab some necessities for you.'

The man demands the cashier's attention, barking to her in Korean for some cold ice and a drink. She brings some supplies whilst he prepares some *soju*.

'Don't worry sir. It's medicine and it works for pain, trust me.'

'You don't get it do you? I have to go home because I need to rest.'

'We all need to rest. What's your name by the way? Where are you from? Are you married? Do you have children? How old are you?'

'None of your fucking business mate! I said I have to go home.'

'Excuse me sir. You will not use expletives with me. I am an eighty-three year old man and I have fought for my nation. You will not use such words, not in this country or anywhere. Where is your respect young man? Where is your filial piety?'

'Filial piety?'

'It means respect for those older than you.'

Realizing that I might have to spend some time with him I introduce myself, 'I am Don from Australia. It's a pleasure to meet you. The rest I refuse to answer because it is culturally inappropriate for me to do so.'

'So where exactly is your hometown then? It's a big land my friend.'

'Yeah, it is. I'm from Sydney which is located on the east coast of Australia.'

'It's not an English lesson Don. I know where Sydney is. In fact, I have been there about five or six times and I have family in Sydney in a place called ...'

'Let me see is it Eastwood? Or is it Strathfield? Or what about Burwood?' I ask.

'The first one I think, I am not exactly sure. Anyway, they have a lot of Korean churches there and my church here is connected to one. It's a Baptist church, do you know it?'

'Can't say I do. Sorry, but I don't even know your name?'

'You can call me Mr. Kim. By the way Don, I am enjoying talking to you. As you can probably guess I was on my way to church this morning, but thank the lord I have met an Australian friend so who needs to pray? Now Don, I'd like you to pour some soju for me and once you have done that you can you have some yourself. That is how we do things in Korea. Old people are always first.'

'I know, I am not that stupid. We're not going to drink that now are we?'

'You are stupid Mr. Don. Of course we are going to have some, and the more we talk and drink the better your spirits will be. Then we can help you to your apartment.'

'What do you mean by we are going to? Do you mean that you and the little thing over there will carry me?' I ask with a hint of sarcasm.

'Let's say I have some friends who can help if we need. Now let me tell you a little about myself. I have lived here all my life and I was a decorated soldier in the Korean War.'

'Some Australians came here. Did you know any?'

'Yes, in fact I did. Some of our best friends were from there and they helped us to fight those communist chinks from the North.'

'So cheers to Australia then. Aussie fucking Aussie I say.'

'Don, how can you say that about your country?'

'It isn't my country that's why.'

'You need to be more proud of your country Mr. Don.'

For the next twenty minutes or so he bores me with endless war rhetoric. Finally, I stand up and shout that I have to go home, asking anyone to help me. A group of suited men notice my pain and help me to my apartment. By this stage Mr. Kim is staggering behind us drowned in a sea of breakfast shots. Relieved at getting home, I thank the men by giving them a 10,000 won note for their trouble.

24

JOINT SECURITY AREA

Bleary eyed the next morning I notice that Daphne has left me a note under the front door.

Well, it worked out to be an interesting night didn't it? Sorry to leave you this note but I didn't want to bother you so early knowing that you probably only got in. Well my good friend, I have no choice but to go now. I am happy to be leaving. I care nothing for the gangsters that work in this country. I have left my email address so make sure you come and see me some day and we will have a cup of tea and a laugh about all this mess we were once in. You just never know our money may come back to us one of these days - Daphne xxx'

Reading her note I instantly feel a pang of sadness and regret that I didn't get to say goodbye properly. In a short space of time, she had become a strong female figure in my life. It was as if she had temporarily filled a void left by the loss of Mum, and the separation from my ex. Knowing that the likelihood of seeing her again is pretty minor, I kick myself. I mean how on earth could some suited man going to church manage to hijack me in the early hours of the morning? And why am I hobbling around my apartment late in the afternoon with a sprained ankle, and yet again another ridiculous hangover.

My phone rings and I check to make sure it isn't an unidentified caller.

'Gidday mate, how's things? This is Gordy here, you know, Gordon from the bar? I was calling to see if you felt like going to see a movie?'

'Um, yeah I guess so. When Gordon?'

'Well, we go can go anytime Don. That's the beauty of a DVD room isn't it?'

'What? You want to go and see a film in a DVD room with me? Are you kidding you Scottish rogue you.'

'I'm not kidding Aussie, in fact I am asking.'

'Where were you last night? You didn't get to Daphne's farewell? You know, we were miffed that you didn't show, and that your phone was off when we tried to call you?'

'I was otherwise engaged last night but I can't tell anyone yet as it's a secret.

'C'mon. You can trust me. I can keep a secret.'

'No I can't tell anyone right now. So what will it be - a DVD and some dinner, or another boring night with your hand?'

'I'll join you mate but you do know I'm going to have to ask you where you were last night. You can't get away with things that easily.'

'Meet me at 6 p.m. at the central square in town and bring your phone just in case.'

The buzz in the centre of town is quite loud and happening for a Sunday evening. It's the anniversary of the incident that last year when an American tank ran over two school girls. There's a vigil, almost a mile long, leading down to the US army base front gate. I notice Carol with her supporters huddled in a circle singing protest songs, but I let her be and continue walking to the square. I pass angry locals who are chanting for the closure of the base and for all American military to be evacuated from South Korea.

In the crowd I spot Justin, sticking out again with his 'I am not an American t-shirt' so I shout out, 'Hey mate, maintain the rage eh. Peace and solidarity, right?'

'What the fuck are you doing here mate? Shouldn't you be in bed nursing that ankle of yours?'

'It's much better now. How did you know anyway?'

'I was the last person that Daphne talked to before she boarded her plane today mate. She said that she heard you coming up the stairs this morning and that she didn't want to wake you from your beauty sleep. Up to no good again were you?'

'Yeah I was mate and I'm kicking myself for it now. Anyway, you seem to know more about my life than I do. Good that you're wearing that shirt mate, otherwise you'd be mauled on an evening like this. I'd join you but I have to meet Gordon.'

'Just bring him with you. We're planning to descend upon the base.'

'Nah, we're off to see a DVD. Plus, you guys are a little too gung-ho political for my liking.'

'What do you mean? I didn't pick you for a conservative?'

'I'm not mate. Look you cannot be too staunch about this kind of stuff. The Americans have their place here remember. Sure people should be pissed off about the tank incident, but throwing the guys out of town and demanding that they be shut out is probably taking it a little far don't you think?'

'They don't need them here. Can't you see what we are about?'

'So then, who is going to help them if the North Koreans do decide to invade? Don't forget China help the north as well. Think about it... I'm not into war my friend but maybe this part of the world needs more security than we believe.'

'No way mate I don't agree with you. The less Americans pointing their noses into other's business the better the world is.'

'I better go and see Gordon.'

As I leave, hordes of people including Justin, and Carol who's now right at the front, march towards the main gate of the US military base. When Gordon arrives he's happy to keep his distance from the masses. If anything, for all his cockiness, he is a little conservative and is happy that the army has a supportive base like America.

'George Bush is ok. He's not as bad as people think. I mean it's those worshippers that the world needs to worry about. Its fuckin' great that the south has an ally 'because they'd be fucked if they didn't. People need to realise that incidents like the tank were unfortunate, but in the bigger picture they are isolated incidents.'

We walk away from the protestors before finding an alleyway cluttered with DVD rooms that rent out movies for 5,000 won (5 USD) a pop. Notices advertise a spacious room with reclining sofas and free popcorn, so it's a bonus deal that's very popular particularly with university kids who are mostly on dates and wanting some much sought after privacy. It's the cheapest anti-copyright experience in town, and while places like this don't exist in the west, here they are allowed to operate freely, much to the liking of those who can't afford the cinematic experience of the big screen.

'How about we get this one? It's called JSA, which stands for Joint Security Area, which is between the north and the south,' asks Gordon showing me a pile of Korean films.

'You mean the DMZ? It's also known as the demilitarized zone - the 38th parallel right?'

'Correct. It came out in 2000 and won a few awards. I have been dying to see it. It's a little long and a little bloodthirsty but we can stave off our hunger with unlimited free popcorn.'

The film is quite good, dealing with some interesting issues about the drawing up of the border and US intervention. Afterwards we head to a restaurant to grab some barbequed meat and to talk about the film.

'So what did I tell you?' says Gordon. 'There is a lot more to it than tanks and school girls. You need to know a little bit about history first before you start trying to close down a base. I know Justin and Carol wouldn't agree with me but you have to look at both sides.'

'Yeah I guess you do. In fact I think you really need to. Anyway, it was a powerful film mate and thanks for choosing it.'

'So Don when are you going to take a girl to one then? You know it's the first step mate.'

'Who knows? It's not the only thing on my mind. By the way I am starving. All this communal cooking can take forever.'

'It's Korea. That's how they eat here.'

'We do have barbeques in Australia you dumb ass.'

'At least we can have some more *kimchi*. Nothing like some stinky breath for the students tomorrow,' Gordy responds.

'Yeah, it's kind of rank but I am getting the hang of it. What befuddles me though is this: what other country on the planet would endorse eating garlic raw with fresh chilled radish? And then who would swig a bottle of rice wine to wash down the taste? What's it all about?' I ask.

'And people say we're fuckin' mad for having haggis,' laughs Gordy.

'So no real plans to go back to Scotland then? You sound happy here. The place kind of agrees with you. Am I right?'

'Yeah you could say that Don. But you know I am only twenty-two, much younger than you, and I have to say I am here to have a good time not really a long one. It's weird though because when I say that I kind of feel that I have the license to be all reckless you know, but in fact I have met a good girl in Mi-ra, and maybe it's now time.'

'Time for what, what do you mean?' I prod.

'Well, let's have a few swigs of this green bottle Don, and I might tell you.'

'Ah, you're a cheeky Scot aren't you? I will indulge a little, but remember my friend we both have classes tomorrow.'

'Well, the reason I didn't come to Daphne's last night was that I was with Mi-ra proposing to her.'

'What? Proposing? What do you mean?' I ask.

'You seem shocked Don?' he asks.

'I am mate. You just said you were twenty-two. That's young don't you think?'

'Sure I know I am young but Don the crazy thing is I love her and the way things are going, her parents will never recognize me if we don't marry,' he explains. 'You know she's a German major so we thought if we got married she'll have a real chance to get her EU passport, and we could maybe work over there and build a life for ourselves. It makes sense don't you think?'

'I don't grudge it as an idea mate, but you should really think this over. I only care because after all you are so young. You said you're here for a short time not a long time.'

'You seem testy about this Don. It's not the end of the world mate.'

'It's because I am, Gordon. Anyway what would I know about marriage? I married my best friend at university and she was ten years younger and some of my best mates thought we were both nuts. In hindsight, we might have been better off just staying together without doing the marriage thing but that's it, you never quite know do you?'

'That's life isn't it Don. It's a gamble sometimes and you know what, I want to take this chance.'

'Mate, go for it,' I reply.

25

GUESS WHO?

Bad Mr. Lee has returned. That chain-smoking *soju*-swiveling-excuse-of-a-boss has somehow made his way back to Chuncheon. Sitting proudly in his office, he is up to his old tricks by either demanding his secretary So-Hee to write out new business plans, or making sure someone like Jason has bought him a cup of coffee. On top of that he's driving the rest of his employees up the wall with his cheeky morning grins and fake mannerisms.

'Fuck, can you believe it?' Jason says with amazement. 'The clown has shown up and he's now telling me how the Chuncheon franchise of Global World is going to take over the whole of Kangwon Province, meaning the north eastern part of South Korea!'

'What the fuck?' I respond.' How can he expect this school to move up in the world? I mean we're barely getting students to our classes plus word is already out that we're on a slippery slope of demise. We'll be fucked once the company is blacklisted.'

'Yeah, but you watch how things go this week Don. Today, I assure you that we'll have a stream of students coming through the doors. But like you said, it won't last.'

'So why would they come this week and not the next? Is he the son of God or something?' I ask. 'After all he has been away for ages and nobody has been coming.'

'I have no idea Don. He's the kind of guy that holds a lot of power in the community for reasons people like us will never know. Quick, we better get back to our classrooms and prepare. Like I said he's here, so expect droves of students; some you may have never seen before.'

'You really don't like him do you - just like Kevin here.'

'We don't believe in him Don. He's taken that away from us. Trust me, he is a gangster; you can see it on his face.'

'He is more than a gangster. In fact, words defy me in his case,' adds Kevin.

Noticing that Mr. Lee is behind Kevin, I wink so he has enough time to display his cultural mores.

'My dear great boss it is good to see you today,' Kevin says, bowing deeply.

I do the same. I shake his hand firmly, welcoming his return and smiling almost naively into his deep set eyes. The two then mutter something in Korean before we all head to his office for a meeting. Kevin is busy translating for us and it seems that I will have a job teaching for a newly opened business on the other side of town.

'He wants you to help some church friends of his,' explains Kevin.

'What, as a volunteer?' I cheekily ask. 'Look, I don't want to do it for nicks as you can imagine.'

'I cannot really ask that question directly, because as you're aware culturally it isn't right to talk money straight away when you're being offered a job,' Kevin explains. 'In this case it is best to ask the people that you are working for. After all you can bribe them if you like.'

Meanwhile, the boss keeps smiling at me, making it known that I'm doing the right thing by taking this job. He lights another cigarette, awaiting my approval.

'So what will it be? He wants to take you there this afternoon after lunch to meet the children and his friends. Are you keen? I don't think you really have any option Don.'

'Ok I will do it.'

The business is located in the same wealthy area of apartments I visited a week or so ago when I had my fateful encounter with Helen. On arrival, I ask the *wang jung nim* manager if she or her husband can speak any English.

'Of course I can, but my English is a little poor so please excuse me. By the way, it's very nice to meet you Mr. Don. Welcome to our new academy. My name is Mi Na but you can call me Mary after the good virgin, while this is my husband Hyun Soo, however he doesn't speak much English. His English name is Kevin.'

'Nice to meet you both,' I reply extending a half-bow to both of them. 'I must say your business is looking very nice. This area is in a booming part of town and I think you guys can do well here.'

'We hope so Mr. Don. With the help of God and you being our new native English teacher, we believe anything is possible. Please have some coffee and biscuits and we can work out your schedule.'

Looking around it's obvious that this is a family run show. The couple has just married and like many new business people in town, they have decided to take a punt with an English academy. They have their own text books ranging from kindergarten to senior high school.

'We'll expect you to teach from all of these books,' Mary explains. 'Don't worry Mr. Don because our students are the children of God here. You will feel always welcome at our Chant academy.'

'Thank you Mary. I really hope we can have a successful time.'

'Ok, it is nearly 2 p.m. so I'd like you to start with this book today. Remember these children are very young and they are only learning their ABC's. Sing them a song and teach them some words,' suggests Mary.

Soon I am busy welcoming a small group of four and five year olds into my classroom who have little idea what I am saying. Mary watches through an open window, and when realizing I need help, she explains to the kids in Korean my name and that I come from Australia. I try the Hokey Pokey and Simon Says but again nothing seems to be working. The lesson seems to last forever, and after thirty minutes I'm exhausted.

'Thank you Don, you were very good and I know our students will like you,' says Mary. 'Please don't mind me watching you from the window. I think it is a good way for me to practice my oral English too, don't you think Don?'

'I guess so Mary. I take it we have another class now?' I ask.

'Yes, just one more today, but you'll be expected to teach up to four in an afternoon once you begin at our academy.'

'But didn't I just begin?' I ask.

'Today is a trial Don. You can start as soon as we decide.'

'But you can't do that?'

'Don, let's talk business later. That is how we do things here,' she explains. 'Now first I would like you to be back at 3 p.m. but before then I'd like you to go with my husband to the nearby supermarket. We'd like to buy you a cake.'

'Oh, fair enough,' I reply a little confused.

'You look like you enjoy the odd cake Mr. Don, am I right?' she remarks cheekily.

'Yeah of course, just like you and old Jesus huh?' I reply back with a hint of sarcasm. 'Ok, I will go and get some fresh air with your husband.'

'He'd like to practice his oral English with you Mr. Don. I better say now that I am sorry for that.'

'Sorry for what?' I ask, confused by her statement.

'Our English, our English! It is so poor Mr. Don because we get no chance to practice it,' replies Mary.

'Ok, whatever Mary. Let's go then.'

Like two kids on candy, Mary and Kevin skip and dance whilst opening the door for me. On the way to the Wal-Mart store, her husband asks me the usual barrage of questions - Are you married? How much money are you earning at Global World? Do you have any children? How old are you? I cheekily reply that these things aren't any of his business, but the answer falls on deaf ears, as he has no idea what I have said.

'I said no to the first three questions and the fourth meant fuck off,' I scowl.

'Fuck off? What does that mean? Fuck off?'

'It means none of your business,' I reply laughing.

'Fuck off? Means none of your business? Huh? Mr. Don I feel confused.'

'Kevin let's walk. You show me supermarket, ok?' I reply, now feeling a little guilty for having a bit of a go at him as he is totally oblivious to my intentions.

'Here is supermarket Mr. Don. This is supermarket. Can't you see? You don't know supermarket?'

It's another LG like place, a nauseating monster mall that's jammed with the wealthiest nouveau riche of Chuncheon. Brand names like Prada and Louis Vuitton are all on show and it stinks of cleansing detergent. It's almost the modern day equivalent of Dynasty opulence. The toilets even have assistants who are happy to spit-polish your shoes as you exit. Middle class ladies show off their brands and accessories, while some people have purple and red -dyed pooches attached to their trolleys. In this haze of almost a hundred *ajumas* Korean housewives I notice a particularly attractive woman who is looking nervously at the condom selection. She smiles at me, noticing my curiosity, but I immediately look away from her.

'Don't I know you from somewhere?' she asks.

I stutter, 'I think we might have seen each other before. I, I mean seen each other.'

It's Helen, A-reum's mother. She is dressed to the nines wearing dark shades and a visor. I can hardly recognise her. I'm doubly embarrassed because I also have Kevin who is hanging off me like an overactive dog trying to work out how I know her.

In Korean he asks her how we met, and from what I can understand she tells him that I taught her daughter. I notice that she is concealing a bruise on both her left eye and forehead.

'Helen, what has happened to you? Are you ok? That's one mean bruise.'

'What do you mean?' Helen asks.

'Your black eye Helen. I don't want to embarrass you in front of my new boss but I am concerned. Who did this to you?'

'Who else do you think? It wasn't my daughter so there's only one other person in the family.'

'Your husband did this?'

'Yes Don, he did.'

'I can't believe it. I mean why would he want to hit you?'

'He was jealous of me,' she explains. 'God, Don you are so naïve sometimes. Isn't that what some husbands do when they have a reason to be angry with their wife? You know, some of us can never do anything right once we are married, Don.'

'You poor thing, I mean how could you have upset him so much that he would do something so bad. It isn't fair.'

In Korean, Helen and Kevin talk a little more before exchanging business cards. They soon realise that they attend the same church.

Before Kevin and I leave, Helen taps me on the shoulder, 'Don, I will always call you my lovely man, but it is better we don't talk too much. My husband has a bad temper and I don't want to get you into any trouble.'

'So I take it the condoms are going to make you happy with that brute of a husband?' I ask.

'The condoms are none of your business, unless of course you are a good boy Don. Who knows I might save one or two for you.'

'You're kidding aren't you? He'd beat me to a pulp if that happened' I reply.

'Pulp? What do you mean by that?'

'Helen, forget it ok.'

'Ok I will Don. You better go with your boss. I have his card from Chant Academy. Maybe I can send A-reum to that school some day and who knows we can come and see you again. Bye Don, I have to go now.'

'Helen, one more thing. Can you please send my best wishes to your daughter? I miss her and do tell her to come to class when she gets the chance.'

'Bye Don, I have to go now. Goodbye my good Australian man.'

When we get back to Chant, Mary shouts at her husband for being late. The mothers of the children for the next class have been waiting for ten minutes to meet me and aren't happy. Mary quickly grabs my arm and leads me to the classroom, introducing me to the parents and about half a dozen eight to ten year old students.

'Hello all!' I shout, smiling at the mothers at the back of the room. 'I am Don and I am from Australia. I will be the teacher of this class. It's nice to meet you guys.'

The mothers bow in unison, before they leave the room and watch from the window. Mary then re-introduces me in Korean so that the kids can remember my name before joining the mothers for some chit-chat.

Not long later mayhem ensues when one of the students becomes so excited that he starts harassing the other kids around him. He pulls their ears and jumps up and down on the bolted down desks. Despite my pleas, the kid refuses to stop, so I call Mary and straightaway he is scared shitless by her presence.

'So one of our students has been a naughty boy,' she says pointing her finger at the boy who at this stage has his head down in fear of being punished. 'Just as well your mother isn't here!'

'Mother no more,' the boy replies.

'Mother with Jesus, Mother with Jesus,' Mary says repeatedly to the child.

Soon the boy starts sobbing uncontrollably as Kevin walks into the room slamming a stick down on one of the tables. Screaming in Korean, he warns him that such behavior is banned. Four of the girls then start balling, and rush to their mothers for comfort, whilst the culprit hides his face.

Mary shouts, 'You cannot do this here.'

She then grabs him by the ears taking him out to the main office while Kevin begs me to keep teaching. I won't have a bar of it and I leave the room so the class is put on hold. A few minutes later, Mary brings the sobbing child to me. He's red from head to toe with embarrassment and fear.

'I am sorry Teacher,' the boy says.

'He has been warned and his father will be told about this. Please Mr. Don can you come back to the classroom, pretty please?' Mary begs. 'We have only twenty minutes of class left then my husband will drive you back to your academy.'

For the rest of the class the students are pretty stunned. Judging by the red marks on the back of the boy's legs, he has been subjected to a rattan. He turns his head when I try to console him but he won't have a bar of it. At the end of the class I tell Mary that next time will be different.

'You cannot be sure of that. He has an attention problem – ADD they call it in your world. I need to talk to his Dad and then hopefully the Lord can help him as well.'

'Ok you know what to do. You just call me when you need me next Mary. I am busy as you know but I should be able to come back.'

'Thank you Mr. Don. We really appreciate what you have done today with your teaching and I am so sorry that you had to experience. Please do not worry. I'll make sure that it will never happen again.'

She then hands me my second white envelope which I happily accept as any money right now is a bonus.

Back at Global I bump into my flat mate Kevin and he asks, 'How was the church gig? Did they make you say grace to the kids?'

'It was ok. I know what you mean though. They are quite religious,' I reply. 'How are you anyway? Classes are full here like you said. Do you think we will see our money now that the head honcho is back on deck?'

'I don't think so,' he says. 'Look, I don't want to make you feel depressed because you are new, but seriously this week is another bullshit one. I mean you watch the prick. I swear we'll have classrooms full and then once he's gone it'll all turn to shit again.'

26

BACK AT THE RANCH

Kevin was right. Global World had returned to the halcyon days of a few years ago when they employed a dozen native English teachers, and ran half a dozen shuttle buses between shifts. I was not complaining. For the first time in nearly two months, my life was starting to show some semblance of stability. Sure, most of the foreigners at the bars were still a little skeptical about why I'd stayed on, but by now I believed that the faith I had invested in this town would pay off. With good Mr. Lee's money and the cash in hand from Chant, I was starting to believe that I could financially survive.

By the time the last classes are over on Friday evening, Global World boss Mr. Lee is ready for some social time and has invited us all out. Standing with Zac downstairs I start asking some questions about what to expect tonight.

'What are we going to eat?' I ask.

'Don't worry about what you eat Don. There'll be enough to feed an army of pigs, I am sure of it,' Zac replies.

'Is it true that we are really expected to have sex with these hostesses?'

'That is up to you my friend but remember it isn't so easy to say no.'

Yuri is running late and Kevin insists that we leave without her, 'Look, she can meet us there. There is no time to wait - trust me as I know what he's like. It's alright for him to fuck off, but if one of us is late or not there, then that's another story.'

'Ok *kaja* - let's go then,' replies Jason.

I am intrigued by the restaurant. Outside, the word Sydney is lit up in bold neon lights and stuck above it is a shiny image of the Opera House. What I do find funny is the image of two kangaroos – not boxing, but fucking.

'Only in Korea,' laughs Kevin.

'Well, it's pretty funny I guess. I mean I can see the humour in it but I'm not sure my Dad or family would approve. Who did this I wonder?' I ask.

'Some Korean who had absolutely no idea what they were doing. There's a funny sense of Asian humor here Don,' Jason replies.

Mr. Lee notices the four of us standing at the front of the restaurant gazing at the image. He laughs and smiles at us before he invites us all to come inside. I wait for Yuri who finally arrives puffing and short of breath. Upon seeing the image of the two kangaroos, she places her hand over her mouth.

'*Kawaii*, how cute, excuse me what are they doing Mr. Don?' she asks.

'They're having sex Yuri,' I reply.

'*E-eto e-eto* um um' she says. 'You mean fuck Mr. Don?'

'Yes, Yuri they are fucking.'

'That's very strange,' she says with a giggle.

'Ok we all better go inside now. We need to follow the boss. He wants us to hurry.'

Inside the surrounds are quite lavish. The decorations are adorned with two-dollar purchases of Australian images; coasters of Aboriginals with spears, boomerangs on the walls, a large painted didgeridoo in one corner, and some stuffed kangaroos and koalas in another. There are slogans that read OUTBACK STEAK IS AVAILABLE HERE as well as WE HAVE FOSTERS LAGER.

'So Don what do you think of this kind of place? I guess you feel at home?' asks Zac.

'Kind of, though I have to say that it's full of every cliché you can imagine. To be honest Zac, I'm not that patriotic. I guess you remember my feelings about Iraq and the war.'

'Yeah, but aside from that, don't you think it's a good representation of your country?' bellows Jason in his booming Chicago voice. 'The only thing missing is an Akubra hat right? I remember Greg Norman, the big White Shark who used to wear one whenever he played golf. I interviewed him once and he said his hat was the thing he really loved about Australia.'

'Ah you're talking about the Great White Shark I presume. Well, he's the kind of person who Australians these days love to hate. He's that successful golf journeyman, a bit like Pat Rafter the tennis guy that is now living overseas; away from sunny Queensland, yet is still dreaming because he cannot get his slimy hands on a US major. I can imagine Norman or someone like Rafter saying something like that.'

'That's a little rough don't you think Don?'

'Not really. I mean why do you think I am overseas? I kind of want to get away from the image that a lot of people have about us Australians. Sure it's true to some degree, but the people I hang out with aren't like Greg Norman or Kylie Minogue - those people represent the mainstream.'

'Kylie Minogue? She is wonderful. We love her in Japan,' adds Yuri.

'Fair enough but I don't associate myself with either of them.'

'Ooh, we seem to have hit a sensitive chord with you Don. Anyway, let's think about some food and drink because I am starving,' says Jason.

'We have to wait for the boss to say so?' I check. 'That's protocol isn't it?'

'Don you are learning fast. Well done - you'll be Korean in no time.'

The table is decked out in fake bark and paper serviettes, while waitresses have managed to find some Akubra hats to wear. At the head of the table, Lee has already ordered some *soju* for his staff. An array of steak and salads arrive and after a few cheers and several pre-dinner shots, we tuck into our steaks. Yuri is the only one not drinking, whilst Zac, Jason, Kevin and I are well on our way. Noticing this, the boss is more than happy to give us some more *soju*.

So what do we do next? I mean after the food?' I ask.

'You can't ask questions like that mate,' replies Kevin. 'We wait for him to tell us. He's paying the bill so I reckon we should all go up behind him and sock him one. What do you think guys?'

'You wish,' I reply. 'There's no way we can do that to him. He's being super nice tonight to all of us.'

'He's a cunt. A thief, a liar and a con and I think we have every right to.'

'Good idea in theory but not in practice,' booms Jason, knowing that the boss won't understand him.

Mr. Lee motions to me by singing and smiling at the same time. It is time for all of us, Yuri excluded, to now go upstairs. Most singing rooms in Korea are like one big comfortable lounge room. They have a mini bar, a few sofas, and a small PA attached to a large TV screen. This one however is a little different to those around the universities. The fact that Yuri hasn't been invited means that it's more of a brothel where the men rule the roost, and women are pretty much paid slaves. A hostess is assigned to each of us.

'They will follow you around the joint like leeches, so if you're up for it Don you'll be guaranteed some loving fun at a price,' Kevin explains.

'It's all a bit creepy don't you think?' I ask Jason.

'Don't think of it like that Don. Man, you're too serious sometimes. Just chill mate.'

Tonight Mr. Lee has all the cash and Korean tradition tells that he who offers once offers all night. By this stage the five of us are all liquored up on countless bottles of *soju* so our limbs are all over the place.

'What's he doing? 'I ask Jason, noticing Mr. Lee speaking to the chief hostess.

'He's telling her what he wants for us. He's probably spending all of our hard earnings, but this is his way of showing that he's sorry.'

'I'd rather the money. This is wrong,' I implore.

'The fucking cunt he is! We don't need to buy into this. Now's a great chance for us to fuck off here and now so he will lose face,' exclaims Kevin.

'Yeah, but if we leave then we'll never see any of our money,' replies Jason.

'Maybe we should just bite the bullet. I mean, we don't have to have sex with them. Nobody is forcing us so Don's there's no need to feel compelled mate. You never know what you might catch off these whores,' laughs Zac.

An entourage of ten women all wearing numbers, just like in an American Vietnam war movie, parade in the foyer, shaking their butts and rubbing themselves up against us. I can't control myself from laughing at the tackiness of it all, while the other three are doing their best to keep a straight face in the presence of Lee.

'Come on Don, you've got to choose someone or our boss will lose face,' Jason booms.

'I cannot bring myself to do it mate. I don't want to Jason. Look I'm sorry but man this is stupid, don't you think?'

'You have to. Stop thinking about it. If you don't play the game, there'll be no chance in hell of you ever getting your money back - trust me.'

'What fucking money? We are doomed like I said,' Kevin interrupts.

'Shut up Kevin. Just let Don point for fuck sake,' whispers an agitated Jason.

'Ok, I'll blindly choose someone then.'

I point aimlessly. The boss hangs his head in shame knowing that foreigners like me don't have a lot of experience when it comes to this kind of establishment. I choose someone who resembles one of my students - about twenty-two years old with that long black hair, gleaming white teeth, a likely nose job and double eyelids. She is the archetypal princess waiting for her prince. The only thing is that I am most reluctant.

'Inside my prince,' she says dragging me into her singing fuck palace.

'You don't need to hold me so tight,' I reply. 'Look I don't want to touch you. So how about we sing some songs then I leave you?'

'Me have little English. You sing and then we fuck. You not leave until we fuck,' she replies.

'You like Nirvana? Radiohead? What about Elvis Presley? I will sing these songs but we no fuck ok? I am married like a good man so me not fuck.'

'Good man? All man married and they are not good man. They are business man and they always fuck after work.'

In the songbook I notice that they have my three favorites. It seems 'Creep', 'Come as You Are' and 'Suspicious Minds' are all popular songs. I launch into them, first singing Elvis as I impress the hostess, who by now is sprawled across a mattress waiting for me to jump her. Ignoring her, I play the animated performer, punching my arm into the air, while doing the chicken dance and making faces. She doesn't get the irony though, and instead in a very playful sissy way punches me, as she tries to get my attention. But I don't want any part of this. I am almost dreading the end of these three songs so she can have her turn.

'Ok now my turn. I will sing Rain and Mayday. K-pop and Chinese pop. You like?'

'I have no idea,' I reply.

She cranks up the decibels and in an over the top soppy way, begins her woeful song and dance. I try hard to not laugh at her tackiness, while she points her legs up and down at my crotch.

'Ok fuck. You now fuck, Ok?'

'No, I don't fuck. We sing more, ok?'

'No we fuck.'

'Hwa jang shil oddi, where is the toilet? I need the toilet or I piss on you,' I tell her. 'You like me to piss all over you, my blessed whore?'

She has no idea what I have just said and reluctantly points to the toilet which is outside the room. I open the door but inside there's a janitor who's been hired to open doors and spit polish clients shoes. Seeing a window in the cubicle I try to open it but it's bolted down. I point to it, hoping that he can work out what I mean but he just looks at me blankly. I then shove some money in front of him, a crisp 10,000 *won* note which he happily accepts. Grabbing me by my lower half, the janitor manages to squeeze me through a half-opened window which fortunately spills out onto a ladder so I can lower myself onto the street.

I head for home and am busily preparing a hot Milo when Kevin arrives.

'You weren't long mate? Ten seconds and you are over? I ask him jokingly.

'Watch it Aussie. My girl was smoking man. She couldn't keep her hands off me.

'That's good mate I am happy for you.'

'You got home before me. What happened with your girl? She looked like a dead ringer for a chick from your Global night class.'

'What, she studies at our academy?'

'Well it is close to her place of work, so why not.'

'I left after three of my songs and two of hers. I managed to give the janitor some cash and he got me out.'

'What? You mean you didn't even lay a hand on her?'

'Not one hand.'

'Well done champ! You said you wouldn't. You're a clever man. Just don't tell any of the others what happened, particularly Mr. Lee.'

'I doubt he is going to understand anyway.'

'Yeah you are right. He'll just laugh and smile, the two-faced prick.'

'Kevin mate I have to go to bed. It's been good talking and I am glad you got your root. Well done buddy!'

Just as I am getting ready for bed I receive a text. It's Helen:

> Mr. Donald, I am very sorry to interrupt you but
> I need your help. I am outside your apartment.
> The reason is I can't go home tonight. My husband
> will kill me. He has given me another black eye
> Mr. Don. Can you please help me?

I loosen the shutters on my blinds and notice her van across the road. What can I do? It's late and I don't want her to come over, particularly with Kevin here. I message her back telling her that I will come to her car.

'Mr. Don thanks for reading my text. I am so worried. I don't know what to do,' she says, her voice shaking whilst trying to hold back tears.

'Oh you poor thing. You must go to the police. This is a domestic assault - it is serious and it cannot happen again.'

'I can't go to the police. They won't listen to most women. Trust me Don, my husband knows them all and he will make sure that there is no shame brought to his name.'

'Ok, Helen so what are you going to do? Are you going to let it happen again and again? Or will you leave the bastard?' I ask.

'All I know is I can't go home tonight. So, can I stay with you my Australian friend?' she asks politely.

'You can't stay with me in my room. You could stay on the couch but then there's my flat mate and that's another story.'

'Well, I am not staying on the couch sorry Mr. Don. I can stay with you only.'

'I know, I'll put you into a hotel. Surely there is one nearby?' I ask.

'Yes there is one close to here but please Mr. Don I need you to come with me as it isn't safe for a woman to be there on her own.'

I take her hand to let her know that I will support her, 'Ok, let's go to the hotel and I will make sure you can get some rest.'

'Thanks my dear Donald,' she says grabbing my hand tightly before trying to kiss my forehead.

'Helen, remember we are friends ok. I am here to help you just as friends do.'

I soon notice that it's a sex hotel but at this time of night we don't really have any choice. After all it is affordable, around 35 USD for a night. There is a car park, which is located under the building to protect clients. As we park, I notice that there are a countless amount of cars here with black-tinted windows. When we check in we are lead through an area which is all very secretive. We go up some back stairs to a room that is colourful to say the least. It has a large heart-shaped bed with endless cushions, piped music, and a television that's showing non-stop X rated porn.

'Isn't this great Don?' she says. 'As you may recall, I have some of those plastic things from the supermarket for us. I will take shower my lovely man?'

'Helen you are free to do what you want, but like I said I can't stay long,' I reply.

'You know what it means when Korean woman take a shower, don't you my kind Australian?'

'Yes I get it, but we are friends and I will not go there.'

She refuses to listen, taking a swan dive at me and almost nailing me to the bed. As the place is adorned in sexual items, she quickly finds a mask and some rope, almost suffocating me before tying me to the bed. I try valiantly to resist her but she tells me not to fear anything bad and to just hold on.

'Don't worry my lovely Don you will love being here with me. Trust me, Korean women make you feel good.'

'Take the mask off for fucks sake and the rope. Please untie it. You can't force me to do this,' I shout.

She ties me firmly to the bed before taking a shower. Upon her return she plants her naked body on top of me forcing me deeper into the bed. I struggle a little but at the same time I start to enjoy it.

'That's good Mr. Don. Now how does that feel? You like Korean women don't you Mr. Don. I can tell.'

She's right I do as I slowly stop resisting her advances.

Soon after, we both fall into a deep sleep.

Early the next morning she says, 'you see Donald, that wasn't too bad was it my friend?'

'Look it was a one-off Helen and I can't let it happen again. You need to go back to your husband and family.'

'Yes, Mr. Don, you are right. Now I must go and pick A-reum up from her friend's place. Please forgive me. We can meet another time but not straightaway. Thanks again.'

27

OLD BOY

Gordon calls again. I think it's for a drink, but I am wrong.

'Why is it just because I call you that you have to assume I want to go to a bar?' he asks.

'It's not entirely true Gordon. It's just that I am not up for drinking that's all.'

'I am thinking we should check out 'Old Boy'. It's a new Korean release and everyone's raving about it. Plus I have some news for you.'

'So you're going to get hitched mate?' I ask.

Gordon replies, 'I'll tell you after the movie is over.'

When it ends, I am somewhat shocked by the movie's brutality, asking questions about its ambiguity as we leave the DVD room. Around the corner we bump into Jack outside a CD store. It's the first time I have seen him since I kissed Carol and fortunately both Gordon and I are miles away, in another world.

'You guys look a little shell-shocked? What have you been up to?' Jack asks.

'We just went and saw 'Old Boy'. Do you know it Jack? It's by far the best cinema Korea has ever produced.'

'The best cinema Korea has ever produced?' I ask. 'What drugs are you on? You are joking aren't you Gordon?'

'It's different, it's hard hitting. You can see why Tarantino loved it so much,' he replies excitedly.

'How is Carol? I haven't seen her for a bit. Is she ok Jack?' I ask.

'Well, my friend, you probably won't be seeing her for a while now.'

'What do you mean?' I prod.

'She upped and left that's why. She went mate.'

'Shit, man that's got to be hard,' says Gordon.

'Actually that is why I'm here - to celebrate. Look, I've got the new Morrisey album.'

'What? I don't get it,' asks Gordon. 'You're happy, yet your wife has just left you?'

'Listen up you guys. You didn't have to be Einstein to realise that we were having our issues,' he explains. 'She wasn't happy here. She needed to head home to sort her life out. Sometimes you need to get out of your surroundings to get some perspective on things. I didn't want to force her to stay here and be miserable.'

'Does that mean it is the end for you two?' I ask.

'She did say she may come back here after Christmas. I will be off to see my folks then so she may well come back with me to Korea after that. She still wants to finish her work on the comfort women.'

'Good for her. I reckon she is a mint person that Carol. Anyway how about we meet up for a drink sometime the three of us?' Gordon asks.

'Sure we can do that next week. We could do a few beers at Hells Bells and listen to some tunes. But for now, I have to go guys,' Jack replies before heading off.

'Are you thinking what I am thinking?' I ask Gordon.

'I don't trust him to be honest. Can you believe that he'd be celebrating with Morrissey? That's kind of weird isn't it?' asks Gordon.

'It's probably his way that's all. I mean, he knew that she wasn't happy. You know I kissed her one night? Well, we kissed each other really. She initiated it.'

'You lucky dog Don. Carol, like I said she is perfect. Good on you I say. Don't worry mate, the old codger will never find out.'

'Best not to shit in other people's yards so to speak,' I say.

'What do you mean?' Gordon asks.

'Look it was brief – a kiss and that was it.'

Feeling a little choked up, I tell him I need to go home to rest. On the way I visit the lake to catch some silence. When I arrive there I light up a cigarette and enjoy the quietness. The stillness of the lake at night; the hush and the isolation is far away from the busy life and drama of modern day South Korea. What is it about people and their dramas? And I too have managed to create some of my own – the stab in the dark with Helen, and the drunken fumble with Carol.

The moment Gordon reminded me that Carol is a mint chick I knew he was dead right. But what am I going to do about that? Try and fly to London and track her down? Maybe it would be cool to have a rendezvous with her and then relocate to a place where no one knew us in, say, Europe?

I try to think clearly and I have to say that Helen, for one, seems to be the least of my worries for now, though there is still the potential that she won't go away. The good thing is I may not see her for a bit. To be honest, I am more absorbed in Carol's whereabouts and how fickle her husband Jack seemed earlier.

I find time to practice skimming some stones against the surface of the lake which is mostly frozen. Not long later a pissed-off bunch of ducks appear with one letting out a loud anxious screech. This is soon echoed by a frightening yet comical cacophony.

'What are you so pissed off with then?' I ask them. 'Can't a man in this godforsaken country have a moment to himself, some peace and quiet?'

The look on the duck's face indicates that he could well be saying in duck language, 'Fuck off, you hit me, you ugly cunt.'

'Aw, I am so sorry. I promise I will be more careful next time,' I reply.

'There won't be a fucking next time. You need to get out of our city and go back to where you come from. You're just a visitor you white cunt.'

I am lip reading their thoughts now. It's obvious that my stone skimming skills have interrupted one of them. Unfortunately this one is the leader of the pack, the oldest and the most vicious. They continue to scowl at me like an angry pack of wolves. When they start to eyeball me I start to literally shit myself. They firmly shake their wings with determined gusto, screeching one more time before pissing off. Not long later I leave for home, somewhat frightened and disturbed by this encounter with nature.

28

MOVIES AND FIGHTS

The next day Ji-hyun knocks on my door at around 10 a.m. unannounced.

'My poor teacher, I know that you aren't busy today so I thought I'd make your day a little brighter.'

'I'm the poor teacher with lots of spare time am I? I don't get what you mean? I was sleeping. You realise that don't you?'

'I'm sure you were. It's just that I worry about you Mr. Don. It's Sunday morning and you're only just getting out of bed. The whole street has been at church since 6 a.m. It really isn't good for your health dear teacher.'

'Look, I teach five days a week, morning and night, so I don't really care what the street has to say.'

'It's just that...'

'Look, come inside would you and get out of the wind. By the way, what are you holding in your hand?'

'Some tickets. It's my surprise for you dear teacher. I want you to accompany me to a movie today. Would you please Mr. Don? I have nobody else to go with and I have been dying to see this. Please come with me,' she says almost pleadingly.

'Slow down a little would you. What movie? When does it start?' I ask.

'The move is 'Chicago' and it will show at 11 a.m. So, please Mr. Don, take a shower now and we'll go and see it together.'

'Ok, you win then. I'll come with you. It'll be my first real cinema experience in Korea, so that's a good enough reason isn't it? It's better than seeing a DVD with my Scottish friend.'

'Scottish friend, what do you mean? You didn't tell me you had a girlfriend here in Chuncheon?' she asks.

'I don't and by the way he is a boy.'

'Well this time you are going with me, so even better dear teacher.'

'Well, we don't want people to get the wrong idea would we?'

'Don't worry my teacher. You are like family to me - we have an old saying in Korea that the teacher is like a parent to their students. We all love you Mr. Don.'

'Aw, now I'm blushing. Let me grab a shower then and I'll meet you outside in fifteen minutes.'

The cinema has that look as if time has stopped. It seems it hasn't had a clean since it was first opened back in the 80's. A grumpy, heavily set woman groans at us as she checks over the two tickets Ji-hyun is holding. She takes my hand, and this invokes some disapproving looks from a group of locals. They aren't too happy to see a foreigner with one of their own.

'You know what? I don't feel that comfortable here,' I say, nudging her.

'Don't worry teacher, they are just old fashioned people. This is a pretty conservative place you realise. You know I come from a village which is even more backwards.'

'We're only at a movie. It's not like we're going out or anything? Maybe you should stop holding onto my hand?'

'You're my teacher and that's what we do here. Remember when we went to Seoul? Well I held your hand then right? Don't worry – they'll get over it.'

'I know, but I do remember that working girl in Seoul' I comment.

'Yes, so do I but she deserved what she got. Trust me teacher please don't worry.'

'Ok then, how about this for a plan? Let's really annoy them and get super close,' I suggest.

'Better we don't Mr. Don. Things can get a little hot sometimes with these people. Please don't shame me in public.'

'Ok, I was only half joking. I guess I'm just a little pissed off with these stares.'

'*Annyong, annyong*, hello hello,' I shout almost mockingly, managing to annoy one of the older men outside.

He responds by letting out a loud hoik of phlegm.

'Such a pig, how does he get away with making such a noise? You'd be hung if you did that where I come from. Why doesn't he just go to a bathroom? It's disgusting. I just don't get it Ji-hyun.'

'I agree with you dear teacher, but for us Koreans it's just one of those things. Maybe there's a cultural difference? I don't know what to say Mr.

Don. I mean, you blow your nose with your white tissues and then you carry them around in your pockets all day. You have to understand that it's different for us. We express ourselves in other ways.'

The movie takes two hours, long enough for me to sit still and relax after an intense few days.

'What did you think of it then?' I ask after it's over.

'I loved it but I guess it's more of a movie for girls because we really love shopping and fashion. I loved the fashion of that time although you would never have seen anything like that here in our country back then. We were very poor Mr. Don.'

'Yes I have heard this all before,' I reply.

'Anyway, Mr. Don I am tired so I need to go now. Can you walk me home?'

For the rest of the following week the boss doesn't show to work. The amount of students dwindles and we start to expect the worse again.

By the time Friday comes around, Jason tells us that it is now likely the business will fold, 'He hasn't been answering any calls. He has not only bailed on his business and the town, but he is now ignoring his family. His wife hasn't even heard from him. You know the Chant people who you work for Don? Well I spoke to the owner there, and word has it that Lee left Saturday some time and hasn't been seen since. Nobody knows where he has got to. It's fucking annoying mate and I must say that it isn't good.'

'I guess there isn't a lot we can do but wait. I mean, he might still show up - you just never know. He came back before,' I respond.

'Yes he did but Don I have got to say that it was probably a smoke signal,' replies Jason. 'Our accounts are completely down and he has been embezzling money from the till. We are unlikely to get any of our pay. Just as well you have Chant. I only have this, and if we do go broke, I'm more likely to be the first person on the way home, back to Chicago to golf journalism.'

'That's not the worse place my friend,' I reply.

My head is spinning with ideas about my next move and when I get to Jacks the only person in sight is Daniel, one of the young Kiwi guys that I met when I first arrived.

'Hey mate, I haven't seen you in ages. Pull up a pew. How have you been?' he asks eagerly, starving for some conversation.

'Yeah, I'm ok I guess. What about you? I haven't seen you since I first got here.'

'It's because I went home bro. I needed to see the family and sort a few things out. Six weeks in total with my *whanau* mate.'

'*Whanau*? What the fuck do you mean by that?'

'You douche bag - typical Australian eh? *Whanau* my friend means family in Maori,' he replies.

'Geez mate don't get too precious,' I reply.

'That's right you're a skip aren't you? God, it must be six weeks since I last saw you, nearly two months eh? But, you're still here. What's that shit about?' he asks.

'Yeah Daniel, shit it has been and yeah I am still here, at least I think I am,' I reply.

'What's wrong mate? Work got you down has it? Please don't let it fuck you around eh, because you can always get by somehow in this town. Trust me mate we are like royals here bro.'

'Actually the work is ok. I've got three jobs at the moment. It's just the future that I'm worried about.'

'If you're going to be living here mate you can't think too much about your future. Just enjoy the moment, save some money, explore the country, the neighboring countries, then come back here and make some dough. Know what I mean? That's a better life than any cunt back home. Reckon we're the smart ones bro.'

'Who can really say? All I know is that I'm a little older than you Daniel. I have to think about other stuff, particularly now that it looks as if my company is going to the shitter. I'll probably be without a place to live by the end of the month.'

'Shit, that's no good bro. Look I have a few friends that might be able to sort you out. I've been living here on and off for four years and there's always someone around to help. If you give me a few days we can work something out for you. Are you hanging around with Gordon and the boys tonight?'

'Yeah, we're going to go out celebrating, but to be honest I don't feel up to it.'

'Brother I'll let you in on one thing. Like I said, you have to remember that things can go to the shit here - companies do go bust but you're always employable and there are always some good people about. C'mon mate you just have to remember that this country is English mad. They want to learn and we are here providing a service for them. We can name our price. We're like English whores, remember? Money for jam, or is it cash cows on a holiday?'

'Ok, I'll take your word for it Daniel,' I reply.

Out of the corner of my eye I notice Gordon in the distance talking to someone, 'That's Gordon over there.'

'Yeah, that's him. Best we leave him alone mate for now. He's going through a lot at the moment.'

When Justin, Jack and David turn up they're ready to eat, so we arrange a room out the back that's out of view from the rowdy university crowd. It's the second time I have seen Jack since I kissed his wife, and I have to say that this time I'm feeling nervy and awkward.

'What's wrong mate? Cat got your tongue has it?' Jack asks me.

'No, no I'm ok. I just had a shitty day at work. Nothing new you know. I'm kind of over it to be honest,' I reply nervously.

'So is it over or not?' Justin asks.

'Pretty much mate. As good as I can see,' I reply.

'That calls for a toast,' shouts Jack.

'Does that mean shots?' asks Gordon, who has just snuck into the room, armed with one of my evening students, who is busy covering her mouth with embarrassment.

'Yes, a toast for Don, one for you the drunken Scot, and another for Daniel who has just got back from home. Also let's not forget Carol who is no longer with us!'

'Aren't you going to introduce us to your lady friend Gordon?' asks David.

'Her name is Hae-yong and she also studies German with Mi-ra at university.'

'You can call me Hannah if you like. I must say gents that it's nice to meet you,' she says before giving us a deep bow.

Jack asks whether Mi-ra will be joining us but Gordon is quick to deflect his question. We leave them alone and go to a quieter part of the bar where we eat, before it's time hit Hells Bells. When we arrive I notice Mi-ra is sitting at the bar waiting, looking bored and a little worried. She asks David if he has seen Gordon tonight.

'No, not really,' he replies.

'What do you mean, not really?' she replies, surprising us with her English.

'Well, to be honest with you, Don and I just saw him at Jacks.'

'Ok I will go there then. Can one of you come with me?' she asks.

'I can go with you,' I reply.

She takes my hand and we head over to Jacks where she notices her best friend with Gordon in a booth holding hands and giggling.

'You are a bastard Gordon. I don't like you and I will never marry you.'
'Settle down Mi-ra. There are a lot of people here.'
'I don't give a fuck about who's here.'
'Just settle, would you,' he warns.
'You two need to talk. But you can't do it here,' I advise them both.
'Let's go outside darling and we can talk properly,' Gordon taps Mi-ra on her shoulder trying to settle her down.

'Take your fucking hands off me. Look everyone at this evil foreigner. He is a bastard and I recommend that all you girls should not trust any foreign guy. Sure, they act kind at first, but most of them just think with their dicks and how many locals they can score. They are rubbish!'

Hannah stays calm which only makes Mi-ra more furious, 'And here is my best friend who I have grown up with all my life with and now she is also cheating on me. Who can I trust?'

Gordon tries to settle Mi-ra but there seems to be no point. She is enraged and sobbing so hard that she grabs me by the hand again and we go back to Hells Bells. I try my best to console her but nothing is working. After a while I leave her with Frank and Hooch and some army guys. When Gordon arrives at Hells Bells he tries to console her again but it's too late because by now she is wrapped in the arms of an army guy twice his size.

'Fuck off Gordon. Don't talk to me ever again,' she shouts.
'But you cannot say that Mi-ra. We are going to get married, remember?'
'There is no way am I getting married to you buddy, no fucking way.'

29

I CAN PROMISE YOU THE WORLD

A few days later on our way back from the elementary school Mr. Lee tells me of his new plans.

'I have been thinking Mr. Don that maybe you can come and work for me. Broderick my teacher and his girlfriend will leave soon so I think I can provide you with all the things you need.'

'And what do you mean by that?'

'Well, I have a wife and she will cook and clean for you. I can also drive you to school once a week.

'How kind of you but...'

'No buts Don Laridis. I will get you more work and you can have a bigger salary; more than most teachers ever earn.'

'Let me think about it first as I need to consider a few things. I mean it is nice of you to offer this to me but I'm worried I will be little far from my friends. I have some good mates around me now.'

'Are they really your good mates? And it is only half an hour Don.'

'What are you trying to say? Of course they are,' I reply.

'They are the people you drink and smoke with. I can introduce you to some lovely people in our church and they will become your true friends.'

'Mr. Lee, please hear me out. As you know I am not religious like you. My Dad is always saying I can meet friends through the church, but it's not for me. I have tried it before and trust me I like who I am and I don't need to do that kind of thing. I respect you and I appreciate what you're telling me, but we're all different.'

Lee is a strict Sunday Adventist and as a way of deflecting the matter, I say to him, 'My Dad is getting older and I do worry about his health so this may influence my length of time here Mr. Lee.'

As we drive through the centre of town we hit a bottleneck of peak hour traffic. Mr. Lee stops the engine for a moment whilst other motorists busily honk their horns. Tired, he puts his hand on my leg and tells me that he hopes I can consider his offer.

'I really think we can become good friends. I don't want to see you hurt anymore.'

'Thanks. I appreciate your kind thoughts - but can you move your hand please? In fact I'd like to get out here if that's ok with you.'

'Don't be silly Mr. Don. I can take you home. It's not far now.'

Luckily, I spy Daniel on the other side of the road on his skateboard. I tell Lee that I'd like to get out of the car so I can join my friend. Shouting, I manage to get his attention, but Lee is still determined to keep me with him. He locks all the electric doors.

'Sorry, Mr. Lee but I have to go. I need to talk to my friend.'

'He's your friend? I know him from before. He has been in Chuncheon for a few years now. She's a New Zealander right? I mean he is?'

'Yes, you are right. Now let me out and I'll talk to you later. I promise I will strongly consider your offer.'

'Ok, you win, but I want you to tell me as soon as possible ok?'

'I will I promise,' I say leaping nervously out of the van.

'Hey, brother I thought I could hear you calling my name. What's up?'

'See that van just there? The driver seems to know you.'

'Ah, I know that van. Have you been working for Mr. Lee from Hongcheon?'

'Yeah mate, he got me this mad gig at an elementary school in the countryside. He's ok I reckon, just a little religious for my liking. He wants me to come and live with him and has even offered me a new job at his own school.'

'He did the same with me once bro. I'd be careful of what he has to say. After all, the guy nabs people off the street. He's dodgy and he is making money out of you. I bet he isn't paying you insurance is he?

'Not that I am aware of.'

'Well, that's what got me in the end - the whole security thing. He doesn't give a rat's arse about it. Sure he can promise you casual privates, which pay well, but then when he tries to offer you more work, your salary is suddenly slashed because he can't pay you what you expect to earn. Be careful mate. The guy has a reputation around town.'

'That's interesting. Well, at the moment he and these other religious freaks at Chant are the only ones paying me so I need to take what I can get.'

'Yeah, but that's no reason to live with him. Look, he's a Sunday Adventist guy and like Mormons they have a cunning way of recruiting people. It's worse than the Catholic Church bro.'

'So, what about those leads you were telling me about?' I ask

'Good timing mate. I was just catching up with one and I reckon I may have something for you. There's a woman Jacey, and she has a small school on the other side of the lake. She seems interested in building her business. At the moment she's got a Korean American working for her. She's interested in meeting you tomorrow.'

'Sweet as bro,' I reply mimicking a NZ stereotype.

'No worries cobber,' he replies in his best Australian slang. 'All you have to remember is that you are the one that's always in the box seat. The exciting thing is that there's always going to be work for us, no matter what pans out.'

'But sometimes when you're in shit, those words mean nothing.'

'Just be patient and tolerant, a bit like some of the locals here. That's how some of them work bro. I mean there are the exceptions in a traffic jam or a crowded subway. They're impatient on the inside but when it comes to face they are masters at not showing it.'

By the time I get back to Global World I can sense that my student Mari can notice a change in me, 'You seem preoccupied tonight teacher. Are you ok?' she asks.

'Yeah, I'm fine. Of course there are a few pressing things, but there's no need to worry,' I confirm.

Changing the subject I ask her about the wedding, 'No comment,' she replies.

'Be honest Mari you can tell me. Is it the parents - your future in-laws?'

'You are right Mr. Don. I can't handle those people.'

'That's kind of normal Mari. After all they don't really know who you are deep down, do they?' I reply.

'No they don't know and I have to say that if they keep interfering in everything I do or say I will lose my head. You know the guy I am marrying is the first and only son, so in traditional Korean culture that means he is spoilt rotten already. The wife he marries is expected to do everything for him and his parents. We even have to live with them once we are in wedlock. It is crazy Mr. Don, not like your country.'

'I guess you could be right, but just remember we can't make such grand statements,' I reply.

'What do you mean teacher?' she asks.

'It's not so black and white Mari. Where I come from we also have family pressures. It isn't just what you imagine it to be, Hang in there Mari for the moment. You will know whether it will work or not.'

'Don't worry I will Mr. Don. You make me stronger every day,' she replies.

Before the last class an older lady appears, 'I'd like to join your class tonight. I'm new around here so if you don't mind I will watch you. Ok?' she asks.

'Have you informed our boss? I mean it is polite to ask me, but you also need to ask the manager of our academy.'

'Well, I can't really ask him now can I? I did ask the man in there, so there's no need to worry,' she replies pointing to the office.

Jason soon gives a thumbs up to acknowledge our guest.

I also notice that Hae-yong has arrived, Gordon's friend from Jacks the other night. She is busy covering her mouth in embarrassment after what happened with Gordon and Mi-ra. I walk over to her to make her feel comfortable.

'Yes I had a good time,' she says nervously. She then adds, 'Sorry, Mr. Don but my English not very good and I feel bad for Mi-ra. She not like me anymore and she not want to talk at me.'

'I'm sorry to hear that. Don't worry about it. We can talk another time.'

The guest introduces herself and the rest of the students are soon embarrassed by her high level of English. When the class finishes she is eager to talk more to me.

'That was great work Don. You seemed really organized. A real teacher for once,' she says.

'I don't know about that. I'm doing it for my students.'

'Look, here is my card if you want. I can't really talk too much now but I'd like you to contact me if you want.'

'Thanks I might just do that,' I reply confidently. 'By the way I don't even know your name?'

'It's Lee, but you can call me Jacey as in the letter JC.'

'I know that name from somewhere.'

'I doubt it,' she replies. 'There are thousands of Lee's here in Korea. Anyway, I have to go now so please go gently into the night Mr. Don, and who knows I may see you sooner than you think.'

Mari and Ji-hyun give JC the up and down look as she leaves the room. Noticing something is amiss, I ask them if everything is ok.

'No problem Mr. Don I promise,' replies Mari enthusiastically.

'So why were your faces red then?' I ask.

'It's a Korean thing Mr. Don,' Ji-hyun replies. 'Whenever there's a dominant student in the class it is normal for most of us to be quiet and to be a little embarrassed. For us, it is kind of rude for someone to stand out in a class.'

'But, surely she wasn't that bad, was she?'

'No, she was great,' Ji-hyun replies cheekily. 'It's just that we like to see ourselves as being all the same. It's a cultural thing.'

'Ok, I can see your point,' I reply.

'Yes teacher, we like to see ourselves more as a group. Most of us believe that no one should stand out, that's all.'

'Ok I get it.'

On my way out Jason says, 'To be honest, things are at an end here Don. I had to send both Kevin and Zac home early tonight because none of their students showed,' he explains. 'Lee has still not been found, so it's kind of serious. It won't be long before our students will hear about this but for now I urge you to keep coming to class.'

Before I leave I ask him if he knew about the lady that came to my class tonight.

'All I know is that she's new to the area and that she has lived abroad for some time. I take it you were impressed by her English?'

'Her English was excellent Jason. I also thought she was sincere as well.'

'I am glad you liked her. Sweet dreams then Don. Have a good sleep mate.'

30

A MEETING OF MINDS

When Daniel notices me in my trusty suit he's shocked by my formalness and says, 'Mate, we're not going to a wedding or funeral. What are you imagining bro?'

'Well, aren't these Koreans big on appearance and looks mate?' I ask. 'After all, this woman could well be the best opportunity I have now. I mean Global is fucked and it won't be long before the cops shut the place down.'

'That's why you have to find ways to get out. Trust me Alberta could be a winner Don,' he replies.

'Alberta is the academy name? That's in Canada somewhere isn't it?'

'Yeah it is. The boss lived there for some time. You'll notice it when you hear her English.' The Alberta academy is on the fourth floor of a modern building on the new side of town.

'We're on the death floor mate so be careful won't you?'

'You believe that shit? Where are we by the way? This place looks familiar,' I reply.

'That's because we're on the other side of the lake - the new rich part of town.'

'I get it. I have been here before. One of my student's parents place is here and so is Chant Academy. Now I am feeling like the true whore like you said the other day.'

'Sure after all, we are all English prostitutes! Don't worry Don, just go with it,' he replies.

A young girl greets us at the door, 'My mum said you have to tell me who you are or she won't let you inside.'

'Tell her it's the police and we have come knocking about a problem,' jokes Daniel.

'Mum, the police are here about a problem,' relays the girl to her mother who is out the back making tea.

'I'm coming Sandy,' the mother says before realising the joke. She sees us and then invites us both inside, 'Please, please come in you two. I have just put the kettle on.'

'How are you JC? Are we all good?' Daniel asks.

'JC? Your name is Jacey Lee? Don't I know you?' I ask. 'Weren't you the woman who came to my class last night?'

'Yes that was me Don. We have met and I must say what a pleasure it is now to have you here in our academy,' she replies, before telling Daniel that he can now leave us to talk.

'Don, I am not sure what Daniel has told you about me but I like to cut corners to ensure that I'm hiring the right teacher. Remember this business is new and we want to make it as successful as possible. And that means having a standard,' she explains.

'So can you fill me in more JC?' I tentatively ask.

'Well Don, our aim is to let mothers in the area know who we are. We believe that we can succeed but we need a foreign face. Tell me, do you like teaching kids?'

'Sure, I can teach any age,' I reply, knowing that kids are probably the hardest.

'You are sure aren't you, Mr. Laridis? You seemed quite at home teaching the university students last night, but just remember teaching these children is a different kettle of fish. You can't always have their attention and I have to warn you that a lot of the kids around here are well-heeled because they come from decent money. That means some are a little spoilt and you don't really want to rile them, so to speak.'

'Look, I like a challenge and I can guarantee that my teaching will work.'

'Good Don that is exactly what I want to hear. I'm about quality as you can tell.'

'I was told you like to set a standard. That's important I think,' I reply.

'Another thing though is that you are from Australia. You do know that the kids here aren't used to your kind of English.'

'What do you mean my kind of English? It's what I have been brought up on. It won't be a problem. After all, the English language does originate from the UK which is where the bulk of Australian and North American ancestors come from.'

'Yes, I know but it is 2003 now Don and things are changing. Korea has strong ties with America so I'd like you to take this tape home for me and practice your pronunciation,' she replies forcefully.

'I am not sure I can.'

'Look, this might be the only drawback hiring you. I just want you to speak more American or Canadian.'

'But this is the way I talk.'

'It's my academy and you will do what I require if you want to work here.'

'It has to be two-way,' I reply.

'Look, I can promise you accommodation in the next week, cable television, a comfortable bed, and a return flight home. With your new visa I can ensure that you won't have to go back to Japan again. You'll also be paid two million won a month which is very good salary. It's only a tape Don.'

I pause, 'Can I think about it? After all, I need to find out what is happening to Global World.'

'What, you haven't heard yet? It was all over the news this morning. Mr. Lee, a forty-four year old Korean man and manager of Global World in Chuncheon has been arrested for laundering business clients' money,' she confirms. 'He'll be lucky to see the outside world for ten years at least.'

I'm shocked and can't speak. Finally I splutter, 'He'll go to jail for that long?'

'Probably, but this is Korea remember?'

'It's a good thing that he's finally been caught,' I respond before adding, 'Shit! Excuse my French but this isn't good. Last night I still thought there could be some hope, but to be honest I don't care anymore. I will take your job on your conditions.'

'Deal then. I'd like to have you start ASAP and we'll do all the paperwork for you straight away.'

'Thanks Mrs. Lee. I really appreciate it. I'll work on my pronunciation but to be honest I can't be an overnight American or Canadian success as they say. It will take time and practice.'

'I'll help you, and if you succeed there will be bonuses.'

When I get back to the apartment Kevin is pacing about waiting to tell me the news, 'Man, where have you been? I've been searching high and low for you. I even hit up one of the bars thinking you were on the sauce again.'

'Well, you were wrong Kevin. I was out looking for my third job and guess what, I got one.'

You little prick. Here's me hanging out here all morning wanting to give you this news and you're out already getting a head start on us.'

'I reckon I've landed something pretty neat as well.'

'Good for you. So, I guess you know what has happened to our cunt of a boss then?'

'All I heard was that he's been on the news all morning and that he will go to jail?'

'Who the fuck knows Don? I don't that's for sure,' he replies.

Sensing his confusion I ask, 'What are you trying to say Kevin?'

Look, I reckon he'll spend some time in the slammer, however I wouldn't speak too soon because it's these very people who have a habit of getting away with murder. Word has it he will be trialed in six months time, but if he has financial support, he could be out on bail anytime. All I have to say is what a cunt.'

'Jason must be well peeved. What's going to happen now? Any ideas of where he is going to take this?'

'Well if we want to see our money then that is another story. There is the Labor Office but it takes forever and to be honest I don't have the time. I want to get a new job and get out of this town as quickly as possible.'

When we both go to Global World for a meeting, Jason is busy fielding phone calls from anxious clients wanting to know what will happen to their paid fees. With Mr. Lee arrested and in custody, the business will be frozen which means all tuition fees for classes as well as electricity will be under lock and key. Within forty-eight hours all accommodation linked to the company will be shut down.

'I'm sorry guys but as you are all probably aware, we cannot operate under the given circumstances,' Jason announces. 'I have had a call from our head franchise in Seoul and they have told me that the company will go into liquidation. We have lost so much frigging money. Lee has taken us to lunch so to speak.'

'He's a cunt. I have no time for these uneducated business people. I hope he rots in his cell,' remarks Kevin.

'Thanks Kevin but this is a formal meeting and I'd like you to calm down.'

'How can I calm down? How can any of us? We have all been taken to the cleaners by this imbecile and some of us are worse off than others. Yuri hasn't seen a cent of her money and neither have I. We were here for months before Don or you two clowns were hired.'

'Watch your words Kevin,' warns Jason.

'At least Don is going ok. He's got three jobs now.'

'Congratulations Don,' offers Jason. 'See we can all get work if we try.'

'I think Don is right you know,' says Zac. 'We all have to move on and get new jobs. We have the Labor Office, but essentially the most pressing question for us is where we are all going to live now?' offers Zac.

'Well you're lucky, given that your family is here mate,' says Kevin.

'Look can you stop talking bullshit,' replies Zac. 'We can't afford to be to be competitive about what one has or doesn't have.'

'Zac is right. Don't forget if you are stuck, there are affordable hotels around,' Jason replies.

'Fuck it. I'm planning to go to Seoul. I have a couch to stay on,' barks Kevin.

'I'm not sure what I have yet,' says Yuri. 'I might get a possible job teaching Japanese in a university in Bucheon, just out of Seoul. But first I will see my sister in Kobe.'

'Ah Yuri, can you take me?' I reply, half-kidding.

'Yes of course you can come with me Mr. Don. I'm going tomorrow though.'

'Ah, I was joking. Maybe another time would be fine.'

'Any time Don. You are always welcome.'

'What about you Zac?' asks Jason.

'I will stay here with my family. I think I can pick up some tutoring. And you?'

'Well guys I will head back to the States, maybe Miami and forget this place as quickly as possible. It'll be back to golf freelancing.'

For a moment we all realise the enormity of the change, before Jason breaks out with, 'Ok guys, it's now time to get pissed!'

'Sure where's the *soju*?' asks Kevin.

Standing around Jason's office for around an hour we all enjoy a few shots and some side dishes from across the road. In the evening, upon hearing the news Mr. Lee from Hongcheon drops over and we decide to get some noodles from my favorite ajuma Korean aunt down the road.

'I take it you have had a few drinks again today Don?'

'Yeah I did with work friends and I must say that it was great. It will probably be the last time some of us see each other. It's a pity that our boss wasn't there to participate in the last rites.'

'Yes, he was a bad man. I knew it when I saw him the first time. He wouldn't look straight into my eye. I'm very sorry Don for your news.'

'And me too.'

'So, what will do you now? I take it you have considered my offer? Hongcheon isn't that far away you know, and I did promise I will look after you.'

'Yes, I know you did and I appreciate it but I have found my own job Mr. Lee.'

'And what is it?'

'I will work for a lady on the new side of town.'

'It's an academy? There are only two on that side of town. Chant and Alberta and you're already working at Chant.'

'Yes that's right. I almost forgot the name Alberta. You are correct Mr. Lee.'

'Yes Don you're right. I have to say that this is a good choice,' he replies enviously. 'I mean, we'd like to have you at our little school, but I think Mrs. Lee could be your calling. Just make sure you're better with the kids.'

'Better?'

'You need to show more energy and you can't get flustered,' he warns. 'Female bosses will really push you because they too are mothers. Don't piss her off ok? Just do everything she tells you and the money will come. I will also have a talk to her.'

'No, I've been warned not to mention other jobs,' I reply emphatically. 'Daniel said so.'

'What would Daniel know? You need to be upfront with her. You now have two people looking after your interests. We will draw out a plan for you Don. Please don't worry.'

'I look forward to seeing it.'

'Ok then just trust me. When is she planning to accommodate you?'

'She told me as soon as possible.'

'Good. One more thing I like to do you a favour. As you can't speak Korean I can help you lodge a complaint with the Labour Office for the money you never received.'

'Wow, that'd be great. Would you be able to help my Japanese colleague too? She is leaving tomorrow for Japan,' I reply.

'Well, we better go first thing tomorrow morning then before she leaves,' he says.

At the Labor Office the next day the queue is frighteningly long for opening time but luckily Mr. Lee uses his connections to barge through the waiting customers.

'Don't worry! Just follow me you two,' Mr. Lee says to both of us as we make our way to the front of the line.

'But we're pushing in and people are getting angry, Mr. Lee,' says Yuri frantically.

'This is not Japan girl. Sometimes you have to be assertive, isn't that right Don?'

'That's not the right word. You mean impolite don't you?'

'Assertive in an impolite way is what I mean. Now how much money are we talking, you two?'

'I haven't been paid for two months, plus I was promised a month's severance when my contract finished,' I confirm.

'I haven't been paid for five months, but I wasn't promised a month's payment on leaving,' replies Yuri in a softer polite tone.

'Ok then, that is six million won for you Laridis, and about the same for you my Japanese friend.'

'How come we get the same amount when Yuri was here longer than I have been?' I ask. 'It doesn't add up?'

'Laridis don't ask questions - just sign,' barks Mr. Lee. 'Look, I cannot promise when you two will get paid but I can say that the final result will be a good one. Like I said you just need to be patient.'

Turning to Yuri, I ask her if there's been any discrepancy but she doesn't seem too perturbed if there is.

'You have been a really good friend to me Don. More than you can probably imagine. I won't forget our early morning talks and you were always kind about my English. This means a lot to me. I hope you can come to Japan one day and I can show you around. I think you will love it.'

'Thanks Yuri. Remember the feeling is mutual and that also means if you are in Australia I will do the same for you.'

'Don, I better go now. I have to get to the bus station.'

We hug and wish each other well.

Lee, who's been busy chatting to an acquaintance, tells me that it won't be necessary to go to Sangcheon this week, 'They know what you are going through and that you need time,' he explains.

'That's really nice Mr. Lee and good of you to allow it. I hope we can both share our gratitude somehow when this is all over,' I reply.

'It doesn't matter. It is my job and I won't accept any money or gifts. We can have lunch or something.'

'I'd love to give you something more than that. Surely we can negotiate.'

'Like I said Don, I am doing this for my country. Any money is not necessary. We need to stop this rot from happening. Now, best you go home and get organized.'

When I get back to my apartment Kevin has his bags on the lounge floor and is ready to go. Boxes are piled in one corner of the living room, whilst all the cupboards are empty. The only thing left in the fridge is some stale *kimchi* that has nearly rotted.

'I guess you're off then?' I ask.

'Yeah it looks like it doesn't it? I'm fucking off to Seoul as you probably guessed. Anyway life will be good for you, I am sure.'

'Look Kevin, life isn't a competition. I'm just another teacher, like Daphne, and I'm here doing what I do because I chose to. Good luck in Seoul.'

We both hug, knowing that it will probably be some time before we see each other.

31

A NEW START

When JC knocks on my door her mission is simple and that is to get me out of this old cold apartment and into a new one by the end of the day.

I welcome her by saying, 'You look like you have a plan. I take it you have found something?'

'Let's just say, I hope you can do for me what I have done for you, young man.'

'I'm not sure what you mean. I like the young man reference, but there seems to be a hidden message there, boss.'

'Grab your bags. We're leaving. I cannot believe that you have lived in a dump like this. The smell is rotten. You do know you can't leave *kimchi* in the fridge forever? Particularly, if it's uncovered - it's revolting! You do this at your new place and I will hang you.'

'That was the person I shared with. He was bad on the house front that's all. Like they say JC, it's time to close the door to the past, and open another to the future.'

'Well get a move on then,' she replies.

I slam the door behind me, armed with my backpack from Australia and a day bag - the only two things I arrived with two months ago. Luckily where I am going is fully furnished with the necessary table, wardrobe, bed, washing machine and stove. My new apartment is located in a flash new area close to the national university on a hill overlooking town. The apartment is only a few years old, and it's about a twenty to thirty minute walk or cheap cab fare to Alberta, my new workplace.

'I hope it isn't too far for your legs young man. Anyway, you look like you could do with some exercise,' she tells me.

'Oh, do I now?' I question. 'Can I ask why in the world are some of you so obsessed with weight here? I thought better of you at least JC.'

'I'm just joking. I saw far larger people when I was in Canada. We have our own here as well,' she replies. 'All I was saying was that I hope you will leg it over to my academy. If it's chilly you can always take a cab. Whatever you do Don, just make sure you aren't late for my classes. As you can tell I run a pretty tight ship.'

'You don't need to worry.'

The first thing I do notice is that I will be living above a church, 'I take it Sundays are going to be busy then?'

'They have services in the morning on Sundays, and some activities during the week. Let me introduce you to the pastor. I know he is looking forward to meeting you.'

A tall angular man in his late fifties smiles and greets me with a warm handshake. He doesn't speak a lick of English, so we have little to converse about, but we manage to somehow share a few laughs.

'Ok, it seems that you need to learn some simple survival Korean Don. I take it you have learnt to read?'

'Yes, I can read, so I can now order most food. Maybe you can set me up with a lesson or two?'

'We can find someone here to do that for you. There are also a lot of mothers who are in touch with our academy. I'm sure they would be more than happy to exchange some Korean with some English.'

My apartment is a shoebox but the one godsend is that the shower has good hot water pressure and it's also equipped with a few other handy things, such as a microwave and a large television that takes up most of the floor space.

'I hope you like cable TV Don. You have over fifty channels to watch, so you shouldn't be too bored at night. Trust me the last thing you'll probably want to do around here is go out, so just remember you have CNN, BBC, HBO, and Star Sports on this network.'

I almost feel like giving her a hug for the kindness she is showing. Although she seems a little hard in her approach, I can sense that underneath she is a good sport.

'Now tomorrow I will need you to come and start at my place, but firstly we need to sign some documents which shouldn't take too long.'

'What do you mean by we need to?'

'Your friend Mr. Lee and I have spoken. We are going to work together to manage you and your finances. Don't worry we have it all under control.'

'I'm a bit worried about two of you managing my finances. What do you mean?'

'You'll get paid I can assure you. The money he is paying you for the elementary school will be factored into your hours with me. It won't change too much. In fact you will be winning because you will not lose the other school. On top of that you will have the security of Alberta and my classes to back you up.'

'Ok, so how much am I expected to get from the hours I work?'

'I'll be upfront with you Don because I know foreign culture and how you work with regards to wages. Frankly speaking, you will work five hours per day with me and four hours at the school over one week. I don't want you doing any other classes so let me know now if you have any.'

'I do have a few classes at Chant.'

'Sorry but you'll have to say goodbye to those,' she replies sternly.

'But I like them.'

'Well you are going to have to stop. In fact I'd like you to go and see them tomorrow morning and tell them before we sign the contracts.'

'So again JC, I need you to reconfirm how much I will get each month.'

'Like I said, a total of two million won all up, which is pretty good I think. You can check it out with the other teachers you know. Just remember to go and see Chant tomorrow before coming to see me at 11 a.m.'

Approaching Chant was always going to be a difficult task knowing that Mary and Kevin would be persistent and would not want to let me go. Arriving the next morning to tell them, I notice on a table that there is a stack of pamphlets, each with a photo of me.

'What are these? What have you done?' I ask.

'My husband is going to send these to the community. We will be rich Don and it's all because of you,' Mary exclaims.

'But you can't do this without my permission?'

'But Don you look so handsome again. Our Photoshop program has made you lovely and slim. You aren't fat anymore Mr. Don.'

'Jesus fucking Christ,' I curse under my breath before saying out loud. 'Look, it is too late. I cannot teach here anymore.'

'Who can't? What? We got you through our church, and we will not let you go so easily. Not in God's name.'

'My new boss told me I cannot work here. I am working for Alberta now. Yes, I met you through your god forsaken church, but my boss back then is now in prison. Global World is now no longer so because of that Mary, I cannot work for your academy anymore.'

'Yes, you will. I can talk to your boss. I know her quite well and we can work something out.'

'To be honest Mary I'd rather you didn't.'

'Ok you won't tell her then. Let me know your schedule now and we can have you in here anytime.'

'I'm not some white teaching monkey you can use at your own will. I apologize, but that's life. It's a big enough town for you to find someone else,' I explain.

'But we want you. We need you. Please Mr. Don, just two classes. The kids love you and don't want to see you go.'

'The kids don't love me. C'mon, you just want me for your reputation,' I reply.

'Don, I can make it up to you,' Mary begs.

'Make it up to you? What do you mean make it up?' I ask.

'Look, Don, my husband told me about the woman in the supermarket. In fact I know her,' Mary explains.

'So...?'

'Well she has told me everything. You know that we Korean women like to share our secrets.'

I feel a slight sense of unease, as if there is nowhere to hide in this small provincial city, but then Mary says, 'Look Don, I will pray for you and between us, the good Lord will look after all of us. And I think you definitely need some looking after.'

'But now I have other work and that means that I can't work for you anymore. Mary, it's just not going to happen.' I patiently explain to her again.

Mary is finding this particularly hard to take and she can't hide the rage that is now showing in her face, 'You can't leave. You just can't!' she says, her voice getting louder and louder.

'Look, I was never tied to this place. It was a favor through your church. There were no contracts, so you are just going to have to accept it.'

Mary can't take it anymore and yells, 'Get out of our place. Get out!'

32

ALBERTA

At Alberta, the students are well behaved and easy to teach. For once I feel like I am working for an academy that cares. Like their neighbor Chant, this school is also heavily endorsed with 'good Lord' references of Jesus and his disciples on the walls. There's a copy of the Lord's Prayer posted on every classroom door.

'You are doing well Don. Our students seem to like you and as long as you keep it simple there shouldn't be any problems,' JC tells me.

'The accent is ok?'

'Look, I was only half joking about that. I just wanted to put some pressure on you. What I really want you to remember is that this is not some travel job on the side.'

'It's ok I am with you. I can see that it is essentially a business that has to survive and good for you. All I can say is that as long as you treat me like you'd want to be treated overseas, then I will serve you no end.'

'Don't you worry, Don. You have to remember that the people running Chant and Global have never been overseas and they may not have that special insight. You're working with me now and I would like to say that I am about being ethical.'

'How about we start an adult class in the evening as well then?' I suggest.

'That's exactly what I was thinking. You could maybe recruit some of your old Global World students?' she asks.

'I reckon I could. I'll speak to Zac and ask him for their records. I have a few numbers of my own but it's probably best to ask a local. I'll call him now and we'll work something out.'

'Hey what's up Aussie?' bellows Zac into the phone receiver.

'I've been busy but I need to talk to you now about some stuff.'

'Am all ears, Aussie.'

'I need to see you, and the sooner the better.'

'Yeah sure, I can meet up with you. How about we go for a few shooters at Hells Bells, say tonight at 7? Are you in?'

'Ok, I can do that. Not sure about the shooters though but we'll see hey.'

'By the way, what's it about?' he asks.

'Well, you know that I've got a new job. It's just that the boss wants me to get in contact with a few of our old customers from Global World to see whether they'd be ...'

'Interested in coming to learn from you?'

'Yeah, you got it in one.'

'Ok. I can see where she is coming from. After all she needs to drum up business in these hard times. Every man and his dog has the same idea, let me tell you that. Let's talk about it tonight.'

At Hells Bells there is a huge military presence and I can see Frank, Hooch, John and Chester drinking in one corner.

Zac is closer to the entrance enjoying the mood, 'Hey dude! What's up?' Zac shouts, slapping my back as if he's trying to fit in with his military counterparts.

'I'm fine mate. How about yourself? How are you doing?'

'Me? I'm better than ever. It's great to be here listening to these tunes, and hanging out with our saviors. God Bless America I will always say.'

I look down at the carpet, slightly embarrassed by his comments.

'By the way I have brought one of my students with me. He's in the washroom at the moment. Wait and you can meet him.'

'He is your student?' I ask.

'Yeah, mate you are on the money. I have to get some brass from somewhere as you know.'

'That's true we all do.'

'Here he is. Don this is Min-seok. You might have met before?'

'Min-seok! What are you doing in here? You're too young to be in a bar.'

'Don, he is too young to be anywhere, but he's with me now, so it's ok. You know him don't you?' Zac asks.

'Yes, we have met a few times. He was in my evening class, but he didn't always come.'

'I'm sorry teacher, but I'm not addicted anymore to computer games I promise. Mr. Zac here is going to help me to go to America,' he replies excitedly.

'That's great news. By the way Zac, did you get the lists?'

Leaning over towards me Zac whispers into my ear, 'Not in front of

Min-seok mate. We better not say anything about that. He wants to practice his oral English with you and we can only stay for an hour max.'

'But...'

'Yeah I know, but it will have to be another time. I'm also trying to get myself started with some students, and as you know it isn't easy. Anyway, I might need your help later on down the track with some teaching.'

'What from me? I've got a job mate.'

'I know but I can also help you, I promise,' he says, winking at me at the same time.

I can see an obvious element of shiftiness or opportunism in his eyes and am quick to realise that maybe Min-seok is also not the only ex-Global World student he plans to teach. I start feeling a little annoyed that maybe I am being used here.

'So, what is our topic tonight, Min-seok?' Zac asks.

'I'd like to know what my old teachers are doing now. It makes me so sad that our academy has closed. Can you both tell me where they have all gone?'

'Well Min-seok. I am now teaching at an academy called Alberta?'

'Isn't that a city or state in Canada?'

'Yeah you are right.'

'Actually I know that academy. It's new and quite close to A-reum's house. You should go and visit her Don teacher.'

'I haven't seen her in weeks. Do you know if she is ok?'

'I don't know. Her mum is a cow and she won't let me talk to her.'

'Min-seok, please don't use that language. It's not polite to speak like that,' warns Zac, who then steers the conversation towards the other teachers.

'I can also tell you that Jason flew back to the States yesterday. We had to clean up all the garbage that was left behind. It took us forever mate. By the way, what happened to Kevin? He didn't offer to do anything at the end.' Zac continues.

'He hurried out as soon as he could. He went to Seoul on a bus the day before yesterday.' I reply.

'That'd be right. How about Yuri? What was her plan?'

'She went to Japan but she will probably return and take a job in Incheon teaching Japanese at a university.'

'Well, that'd be a good job for her. In Korea, a university is the best kind of job for any teacher. You won't get ripped off like us. I hate sharks.'

'Sharks? You mean sea creatures?' asks Min-seok.

'Not quite that kind. Anyway, your new teacher can tell you what a shark is, can't you?'

'What's wrong Mr. Don? You don't seem very happy?' asks Min-seok.

'I'm not happy Min-seok! In fact, I have to leave right now. I need to go.'

'But what about our lesson Mr. Don?' the boy pleads, not wanting me to leave.

'Min-seok, I am no longer your teacher. Zac is your teacher now and he shouldn't be bringing you, a high school student into bars like these. I have to go now.'

Standing close to Zac I whisper into his ear, 'You're full of shit mate. I don't ever want to see you here again.' As I exit I turn to Min-seok and sarcastically say, 'Good luck with your English young boy. I hope you can get to the States some day. Just avoid those PC rooms.'

33

FRESH OFF THE BAT
Summer 2003

By the summer I am sitting pretty. I have an apartment to myself, a new job, and both Mr. Lee and JC are now my established guardians. The only thing that I regret is that I hadn't been able to see people like Mari or Ji-hyun. It seemed as if they had completely disappeared.

'Don't worry Don. We Koreans can be ruthless sometimes. Out of sight out of mind, if you know what I mean,' offers JC as a piece of advice.

'But I had established a friendship with them both. One of them even invited me to watch a DVD while the other invited me to her wedding. It doesn't add up.'

'Look Don, you have to remember that as a teacher in times of change, you lose and you gain students. Once they are out of the classroom they aren't really your business anymore. But there will always be new ones. I notice that you get along with Emily? I know she likes your class Don.'

'Ah yes Emily, she is what we call a mature age student. That's probably why we get on,' I explain. 'She is a single mother I believe, and she's lived in the States.'

'Why don't you ask her out?' JC asks.

'JC, I am not here for that. Like you said, our relationship with students should belong in the classroom.'

Tonight when Emily arrives at my class she takes me aside to ask me a question, 'Teacher, I've been thinking that I'd like to ask you to come and join my daughter and me on a picnic this weekend. It's not a date I promise.'

'Sorry Emily but my time here is separate to what I do outside class. I hope you can understand that.'

'I understand. I know you foreigners need your distance. Don't get me wrong. I have experienced this before in the States. It's just that the weather is warmer now so it'd be an honor to have you join us at Lake Nami. It really is quite beautiful there you know.'

'But...'

'What, you'll be too busy nursing yet another hangover? I'm not stupid Mr. Don. You often look like you spend all your spare time in bars. I would've thought you were smarter than that?'

'Emily, I'm not sure what you mean?'

'What I'm trying to say is you need to soak up where you are and not just hang out in bars like those in your home. After all, this is the country that you have chosen to work in right?'

'But I need my time with foreign friends. You can understand that, can't you?'

'C'mon Mr. Don, I know what it was like when I went to the States with my husband. I'd go to these English classes and I'd be forever making excuses to people who would ask me out. "Stop hiding and stop being an island," I would often say to myself, but I'd continue to be one because I was too content. But you know what Mr. Don?'

'What Emily?'

'I was really lonely. It was my excuse to cover up all the pain that was going on inside me.'

'Maybe you have a point, but I don't see myself as an island. I don't always hide alone I promise. It's just that this kind of job is a little taxing at times so I need time to be either alone or with my friends. Does that sound harsh?' I ask.

'No, I can understand you but I also think you have to stop making excuses. God, do you foreigners have to analyze everything? All I want to know is whether you will come or not?'

'Oh, ok then, why not. I will join you and your child. After all, I have heard about Nami Island from that Korean drama series. Am I right?'

'Yes, Don you are. It's our most famous one too.'

'It's called 'Winter Sonata' yeah?'

'Yes, Don teacher, you are right again!'

Much in the same way that Ji-hyun chaperoned me, Emily does the same, turning up to my apartment, 'You look great today Emily and I guess this is your daughter?'

'Yes, this is Suzie. She's seven years old.'

'Hello Suzie. How are you?'

'Fine thank you and you?'

'And?'

'And what do you want me to say?'

'Not fine thank you and you.'

'Don't laugh at my English. You're not my Daddy,' she pouts.

'Suzie, please don't be mean to Don. He is our friend,' Emily warns.

When we arrive at the lake it is jam packed with mostly rich tourists from Japan who are familiar with the TV series.

'Japanese, hate Japanese,' shouts Suzie.

'Helen, you can't say that. All Japanese aren't bad people,' Emily hastily explains to her daughter. 'Remember our good Japanese friends in America?'

'Yes mum I really miss them.'

'Yeah, I do too,' she says and then says to Don. 'We liked America so much.'

'So, what brought you back?

'Well, my husband got busted so he's now in a prison in LA and we are both here,' she explains quietly.

'Oh no, that's terrible. How long will he be there?'

'Well he has to serve some of his time in LA. The judge gave him seven years which he has only just begun. The worse thing was that Suzie and I were deported so we can't see him until he gets out which could be up to five years.'

'Oh, Emily I am so sorry.'

'It's ok Don, I think we are strong enough to endure this. My mother helps me a lot. It will be alright in the end. Don't worry about Suzie. I am sorry she is a little moody today.'

'I understand, but if there is anything I can do please ask me. And by the way, thanks for bringing me here today. You managed to get me out of my own rut as well. I needed to get out. You're right – bars really are boring.'

'In moderation they can be fun.'

'Yes, in moderation. Maybe you can come and watch me play music sometime in the future. My friend Justin and I are planning to do a show one day. I will let you know if you like?'

'That would be good. Maybe we could bring the whole class?'

'I'll mention it to them.'

'Wow, it would be amazing to see a concert. You know most of us Koreans don't see live performances unless they are really famous acts. What do you and your friend Justin play?'

'It's just the two of us. I sing and he plays guitar. Nothing special – it is two skips from Australia singing songs from yesteryear.'

'Skips? Oh, I get it you are both Australian like the kangaroo. Where will you play?

'At a bar called Hells Bells near the university.'

'Ah, I know it well. I used to go there years ago.'

'What a coincidence. Are you a spy? Is that how you knew about me and bars?' Don says jokingly.

'Like I said I'm not stupid. My husband was in the Marines you know. That's why we went to the States. He grew up there, you know, he's a *kyopo*.'

'Yeah, I see.'

'In my opinion I believe that the military is a bad place. If you get busted with drugs your whole life can be destroyed, and being Korean was always going to make it harder, particularly with the way our society views dope.'

'What do you mean?'

'I mean, a lot of us Koreans are not very open to drugs. That's why we will often go overseas to have our first dope experience. It is better that he was busted there because he could have got hanged if it was here.'

'It must be hard for you guys?'

'Don, that's the second time you have mentioned the word hard. It's alright I promise, because we cope. After all we are now divorced. Suzie is the one who finds it harder because she loves him so much, whereas my love for him dried up some time back. I can never forgive him for this you know.'

'I understand.'

'Anyway best we not talk about him anymore. Suzie can pick up on more than you and I think. Anyway I have to go to the supermarket after here so I'll drop you home ok?'

'That'd be great.' I reply, admiring the view of the lake.

At the supermarket, Suzie is running around the aisles with ice cream dripping off her face, and she starts to beg Emily to buy her something. Infuriated, Emily ties a leash on her so she can't get away.

'That's a bit weird don't you think? I mean having your kid on a leash. Aren't those things for dogs?' I ask.

'You obviously haven't had kids have you?' she replies scornfully.

'Oh, I'm sorry Emily. I don't want to make you angry, and you're right I haven't had kids so there are a lot of things I don't really know.'

'It's ok. I need to attach it to her sometimes otherwise she goes crazy, trust me. She has ADD, you know, Attention Deficit Disorder. I shouldn't give her too many ice creams.'

'That can't be easy.' I say.

'Is anything easy?' she says with anger in her voice.

I try to easy the situation by asking her if she'd like to go hiking sometime. I tell her that because it's summer now it's a perfect idea. Also I could do with the exercise.

'Teacher, we can talk about it some other time. I'm a mother you realise and I'm committed to my daughter first. You're my teacher so I will see you again for my English class and that concert.'

Moving closer I thank her by touching her on the shoulder. However this draws a loud response from a person a few meters behind us. I turn around to see what the commotion is - and I am aghast. It's Helen and A-reum. I motion to Helen to shut it by covering my mouth as a warning, but it doesn't stop her from becoming hysterical. A-reum tries to calm her down but she doesn't respond. I leave the line quickly only to be followed out by Helen who is now in a manic and aggressive state.

'You bastard, I don't want to see you ever again you hear me?' Helen shouts punching my shoulder.

'I didn't do anything Helen. You are the crazy one,' I reply.

'How can you touch that lady? How can you dare to touch her? I am better than her. I am the best Korean lady you will ever have,' she screams repeatedly.

'You're married!' I reply.

'So the hotel meant nothing to you then?' she asks.

'Look, you almost forced me. We need to move on from that. After all it was months ago.'

Noticing A-reum behind me I turn around and try to explain what's happened but she won't have a bar of me, 'Mr. Don I cannot talk to you,' she replies.

'What do you mean? How are you?' I say trying to keep her attention.' Look, I'm really sorry about this mess. I don't even know what I've done.'

'You have upset my mother. Why did you do this?'

'I didn't mean to. Anyway, I haven't seen either of you for a long time, so what does it matter? By the way how did your exams go?'

'I can't talk to you. You are not my teacher anymore. I have Zac now and he's really cool. He's teaching me so much. It is better that you stay away from us Mr. Don.'

Emily and her daughter are both shocked and embarrassed. Apologizing profusely as if she has done something wrong, Emily speaks to Helen in Korean.

'Why are you talking to him like that?' she asks, gaining little response.

'Don't worry Emily. She's an old friend. Let's just go.'

'I never want to see you again Don. You hear me? I never ever want to see you,' shouts Helen.

'You know what Helen? I don't want to see you either,' I respond relieved before we leave the parking lot.

34

A WAY OUT

Justin is over life. The longer he stays here the more he resents it, 'It is shitting me to bits man. I've had enough of the whole bar scene, and just about every single prick here,' he says. 'I even saw Jack the other day and I reckon he got what he deserved with Carol. I just hope she has the balls to tell him she will never see him again.'

'Yes well there was a lot more to it than we knew that's for sure,' I reply.

'He even had a young girl on his arm. Typical, don't you think?'

'What do you mean?' I ask.

'A lot of the guys here are like that. He is just another foreigner sucking up the marrow of this place. I mean the guy is a designated loser let's face it. Who's to say he wasn't fucking someone else when he was with Carol?'

'We can't really say that can we?'

'Look mate, she was very unhappy,' Justin says fuming.

'That's what I was trying to tell you,' I reply.

'So what do you know then?' he asks.

'I kissed her. We had a moment together on the way home from Daphne's farewell.'

'What happened then?'

'I was walking her home and she confided in me for the second time. She lunged at me mate and I just stood there and melted.'

'Well there you go. Good on you I say. Just make sure Jack never finds out about this or you are Harry history!' he warns.

'I won't be going out of my way to tell him that's for sure. But you're right, their differences weren't always easy to detect.'

'What got me was that friendly façade that they always put on. You know, the two bohemian Brits who got together at university? What a load of crock I reckon. And now I hear your news! Ah, life is interesting, isn't it?'

'How about you?' I ask. 'Are you ok? What about your job? I heard on the grapevine that you were trying to get a job at the university here. Is there a chance of getting that gig? You could take Carol's position if you want.'

'Fuck no. My boss has told me that I am not allowed to. She will make sure that I sign on for another term.'

'She can't make you. Anyway you could always do a midnight runner? You know, just fuck off without telling anyone?' I ask.

'I can't,' replies Justin.

'I don't get it.'

'It would make things twice as worse. For one, I'd lose a shitload of money which I don't have – especially now that I have had these crowns put on my teeth.'

'So what will you do then?'

'Hang around till Christmas I reckon.'

'Whatever works mate. At least we have the band.'

'That's right. It's the music that keeps me going. It's not as if we have to pay to play. What about Sydney these days – some bands are really struggling. It hasn't been the same since before the fucking Olympics. Essentially I'm a nomad Laridis. I've driven cabs and worked on boats. I don't like regularity. That's who I am mate.'

'Anyway we better get rehearsing now as we have a set of songs to bash out.'

'Yeah I talked to John earlier when I was at Hells Bells and he said he may even pay us.'

'He doesn't need to do that. Free drinks would be enough, don't you think?'

'Look, I'm not expecting too much. He is pretty generous but he's also a businessman, so bring as many people as you can.'

'What about students? ' I ask.

'Well, mine are all ankle biters so they won't be anywhere near a bar, plus I don't think any of the mums are worth inviting.'

'No one worth looking at?' I ask with interest.

'No definitely not. That's a road not worth going down. You don't want to be stupid, and then get caught out. Guaranteed you will be pummeled - and that isn't pretty.'

'So it's best to keep away then?' I ask.

'Yes like I said mate. Why are you asking?'

'I went to Nami Island the other day with a student and her daughter. She's really nice but I know it probably isn't worth pursuing.'

'Bring her to our gig by all means, but be careful, I mean real careful. Don't get with a student or someone who has been married for that matter, regardless of whether they are divorced or not.'

'Her ex is in jail in the States. What's the problem?'

'Even worse and trust me on this one. He probably has friends here – and do remember one thing, people talk you know.'

'Ok first song then?' I ask.

'Waiting for a Friend' says Justin.

At our first show the bar is overflowing with teachers and military. JC, Emily and some of my other students have also arrived. They are excited and curious as they will be watching a gig in their second language.

'You will be great tonight Don. I just know it,' says JC.

'Thanks, I will give it a go, just for you,' I reply.

'Why are you so nervous dear teacher?' questions Emily. 'You're here with friends, so there is nothing to worry about.'

'No, you're right Emily. Sure, I don't need to be nervous but I can't help it. You know, it's kind of normal to feel this way before a gig. It doesn't have to be a bad thing.'

'Ok, whatever,' Emily replies.

'C'mon mate he wants us to start now,' interrupts Justin.

'Ok, I am ready. Emily, this is Justin.'

'Lovely to meet you Justin and I must say you're very handsome,' says Emily in a confident yet shy manner.

'Thanks Emily and likewise, I mean you're very beautiful,' replies Justin.

'That's a bit rich don't you think mate?' I interrupt, thinking back how he'd advised me against making any moves on students.

'Maybe it is, but I like to compliment when it's necessary. Ok, it's time we start playing.'

'C'mon hurry up sweet Jesus. We have to go soon. We have a curfew after all,' shouts Hooch.

'And remember no gay shit. Play some Metallica and Led Zepplin,' shouts Frank.

Starting with the Stones, some ACDC, then Oasis, the crowd gets louder. The army guys in particular are revved up over our rendition of 'The Passenger' from Iggy Pop. The place settles down not long after the military police arrive and the soldiers have to leave.

Justin and I are feeling hyped after the performance and we go to join some of our friends to wind down.

Daniel tells us, 'Frank and Hooch said to say thanks guys. They've left these tequila shots, beer and side dishes for all of us to enjoy.'

'Wow, that's cool,' Justin says before noticing Emily alone at another table, 'Come on over and join us Emily,' he asks.

'You don't mind me sitting down with you both?'

'Not at all,' replies an enthusiastic Justin.

I leave them alone for a bit, noticing that they have taken a shine to each other. I'm kind of shocked by it, but fielding the slaps on the back from friends and strangers becomes a nice focus. Everyone has turned up except for Jack. There's Gordon, David, both the Kiwis Bruce and Daniel, and even the two Mikes.

'Man if we could only have live music here more often. It makes a lot of sense don't you think Don?' asks Gordon.

'Yeah for sure it does. Maybe we could start something - but who really knows what would come of it?' I ask. 'I mean, what with everyone coming and going. Did you know that there are about five people leaving at the start of the fall semester? It's only really ever going to be a floating concept.'

'It's better than nothing aye. If you think of it, in places like London, Glasgow, and Dundee, some musicians are paying to play, but here you have an instant crowd.'

By four in the morning, there's still a lot of booze and scraps on the tables. Emily and Justin have been talking for a few good hours and are looking very comfortable with each other. I go over to say hello to them but my heart races a little when I notice them holding hands and getting a little close.

'Emily, should I walk you home? I mean shouldn't you be home now?' I ask. 'It's four in the morning for god's sake. What about your daughter Suzie? Is she ok with Mummy being out at a bar at this time of the morning?'

'She is ok and that is none of your business Don. If you really want to know, she's with her grandmother fast asleep,' she explains. 'I am here having a good time with your cute music friend Justin. He is a very nice person Teacher Don.'

'Is he? Oh, that's good. And of course I'm just your Teacher Don aren't I. Oh, I forgot that!'

'There's no need to be angry Teacher Don.'

'Stop calling me fucking Teacher Don.'

Emily smiles, covering her mouth in embarrassment.

'Go on then. Smile for fuck sakes and then cover your mouth' I reply.

'Look it was nice meeting you Justin. Goodbye Don.'

Walking out, Emily slams the door behind her, forgetting to pay her bill. When David comes up to ask me about the money, I slam down a few 10, 000 *won* notes to cover her.

'No need to get pissed off mate,' adds Justin.

'No mate, no fucking need is there? I've got to go. Talk to you some other time,' I reply angrily.

'You need to cool down a bit and chill out.' he responds.

'Justin, do not ever tell me to chill out. I hate that fucking word,' I reply. 'I just need to... get away, um, fuck, I don't know what I need.'

'Call me in a week or so when you're feeling better. You need to take it easy alright? You did well tonight,' adds Justin.

'Did I? I'm not sure about that now.'

The next day I am feeling considerably hungover and a little guilty. Emily chooses not to answer my calls, but it is Justin that I really want to talk to.

'I need to apologize for last night. I shouldn't shit on your bush . That was wrong of me,' Justin answers.

'No you didn't do anything wrong. It's ok. If anything I should be the one apologizing.'

'No, I shouldn't have been hitting on your student. That was bad form.'

'Let's forget it, it's alright really,' I respond.

'I know what it's like,' continues Justin.

'What do you mean? What what's like?' I question.

'How it is to be lonely sometimes. I totally understand it.'

'I gather you would. Sometimes I don't know how to act and I get jealous. I don't have a lot of confidence. I mean I can get up and sing and I can teach a class, but essentially I'm still reeling inside from what went on back in Sydney.'

'You're allowed to be reeling man. You're allowed to feel that pain. Life bowls us some curve balls sometimes and it is hard. You have to grieve and when you're ready you will let go I promise. Don't be hard on yourself,' says Justin with some empathy.

'Thanks, I appreciate it. I know it isn't easy for you either. Weird isn't it, how we both ended up here in similar circumstances.'

'This place has been good for me but it won't be a forever thing. It's hard you know, because you can get involved with people here, but most of them just want marriage. But for us, we are trying to get over the ones that broke us. It's really nuts. Your time will come Don. Don't ever doubt it.'

'There's no rush. Anyway there's more fun to be had.'

'I know. You're not like the others Don,' he replies. 'Actually there's a bit of an exodus happening this weekend. From what I hear Padraigh the Irish guy who works at the university is leaving, whilst Arizona Mike and two of the Canadian girls are heading back home. Another rumor from Gordon is that Jack is finally leaving town. That's five people in one weekend.'

'I did hear something. That's pretty dramatic!'

'Not really. People seem to come and go either in the summer or the winter, so this is going to be one big farewell this weekend.'

'So what's in store?'

'We're having a pub Olympics and it's being organized by Captain Cliff and Brit David. Are you in? It'll involve some table tennis, pool, a quiz on the final night, as well as some softball and an Amazing Race.'

'Sounds good to me. Do I look busy? How many people are going to be coming?'

'Over forty at least from what I have been told. Enough to make it a real competition - and we can sing on the final night if it all works out. It'll be cool man. Just like the Beatles but we'll be on top of a bowling alley just up the road from Jacks.'

'Great, let's do it. I just hope Jack can lower his ego a little.'

'Yeah we can definitely do without that,' Justin says with some intensity.

'And it's a long weekend I hear?' I ask.

'Yeah it is Liberation Day so there'll be shitloads of Koreans celebrating.'

'Which means a lot of people drinking including us foreigners I take it?'

'When don't we drink?' asks Justin.

'Every second night it seems.'

35

ROLLING BOWLING

The venue above the bowling alley is fairly upmarket offering a full 360 degree deck view of the city, as well as cocktails and food. It is the perfect place for the quiz event on the final night of the pub Olympics.

Justin groans, 'You know, Jack has been a real competitive cunt this weekend as expected. Is there anyway we can give him some comeuppance? Shut the guy up for once.'

'Well, you cannot blatantly do it can you? I think it's more of a case of niggling and then getting a reaction and seeing what comes of it. He's a big guy after all,' I respond.

'A big guy with a small dick I am sure. What really annoys me is how academic he thinks he is. Can you imagine, mate, what he will be like once this quiz starts?'

'I can Justin, and I think we have to show some patience.'

'You're probably right. By the way have you met Linda? She's over there sitting next to some guys I play cricket with. I reckon you should meet her. She's one of us after all – even if she is a Kiwi.'

'You didn't tell me you played cricket? You never told me about that mate. I fucking love the game.'

'Those guys over there take it pretty seriously. There is a South African guy and he's created a pitch at the university where he works. That's why we rarely see them over this way. They're also cricket nuts and most of them have families as well.'

'Well are you going to introduce me to them? I've met just about everyone else here. Plus, I reckon Linda may have been on my bowling team on the first day. We were terrible.'

'Hey Linda, Warren, and Colin, this is Don, a good mate of mine who's also out here from Australia.'

'Good to meet you Don. I've always got time for another Aussie. I hope you can play cricket,' replies Colin, a graying early thirties Literature Professor from South Africa, who has been teaching here for the last four years.

'Thanks Colin. Yes I can play a bit of cricket, although it has been some time.'

'I'm Warren. It's good to meet you Don.'

'Linda is my name.'

'Linda, now I have a question, weren't we on the same bowling team on Friday?'

'Yeah I think we were.'

Linda tells me that she comes from a small town in the north island of New Zealand which is almost beyond pronouncing. She also tells me that she has been teaching overseas for nearly seven years.

'That's some time don't you think? I mean, do you ever get the seven year itch and want to go back home and start all over again?' I ask.

'What? You have to be joking. I don't plan to go back. I probably never will. Waking up one day with a lawn mower was enough for me.'

'What do you mean? I don't get it?'

'It was enough to get me out of NZ - as simple as that. It was all far too grown-up when I was there. I couldn't play the responsible card.'

'Fair enough I suppose. We all have our stories.'

'True, we do Don. Of course for me it was more than that, but I would like to say that it was a pivot, a catalyst for some kind of change,' she explains. 'I had a mortgage, a job I hated, a backyard that needed cleaning all the time and a relationship that was dying. One day I went fuck it and I took a plane to a place I knew nothing about. I came over here and the rest is history.'

'I can relate to that,' I reply. 'Where do you normally hang out anyway?'

'Don, I don't live here. I used to, but right now I'm just visiting. I'm here in Korea because I am doing a summer camp at a university south of Seoul.'

'What's the story with the camp?' I ask.

'It's an intensive summer thingy for kids, so I've managed to use it as part of my holidays from China.'

'China! Ah I get it.'

'Yeah, I needed something new. I was here for nearly four years Don, and I also spent three years near Seoul.'

'Fuck, you get around don't you then?'

'I like to stay in a place for a few years and get to know the lay of the land, then move on when it's time.'

'Itchy feet some people call it.'

'Not really. I guess life is short, right? After all we have the perfect job for new beginnings.'

I am curious about Linda's life, and can already tell that she's around the same age as me - most likely mid to late-thirties and that she's someone who's ended up in Asia taking a different route in life. We talk for a while before David the Brit starts the quiz. Jack meanwhile is excited and ready to pounce on any answers.

'You know that guy?' I ask Linda.

'Yeah of course I do. I'm a good mate of Carol's. She's back in the UK now, the poor thing. I wish it was the other way round.'

'Yes! There sure is six degrees of separation in this town,' I add.

'Call it two. He's not my favorite person as you can tell. Colin also feels the same way. You watch – I reckon these two will probably have a verbal blue before the night is out.'

Colin and Jack have known each other for some time and both hold prestigious jobs (at least in their minds) at the two universities here. Both are well-read and seem slightly opinionated. Soon Colin challenges Jack, as they scream hyperboles at each other.

'Again your history is all fucked up my friend,' shouts Colin.

'I'm not your fucking friend,' retorts Jack. 'You know absolutely shit all about anything. I am surprised they even gave you your first gown you Irish-South African-no-idea-what-you-are cunt!'

Soon, they are in a headlock and it takes the help of the local security to calm them down before they are both removed from the premises.

As they leave, Jack turns back to everyone and says, 'That's why I'm leaving this dead end town. I'm sick of you teachers – you are all so clueless and opinionated.'

'That's a bit rich,' remarks Brit David.

Jack ignores the comment and walks off in a huff.

Much to my dismay, Linda gets up to leave too.

'Sorry but I have to go and help Colin. Like I said it was always going to get a little heated tonight with those two around.'

'You were dead right,' I reply.

'Anyway it was nice meeting you. Here is my number. I'll be here for another day or so. I've got a bit to do but hey, don't be a stranger. We could have a coffee or something?'

'That sounds great Linda. Take care and see you soon then.'

'It was nice to meet you Don, so do give me a call.'

'That I will,' I add.

After the quiz, Justin and I play a short half hour set. A few people continue to drink but by this stage I'm pretty tired. I head home happy to have met Linda and knowing that I might meet up with her again in the next day or so.

Later the next day we meet in a café near the back gate of the university.

'Well, we were robbed weren't we? Thanks to good old Colin and Jack,' says Linda.

'Yes they did get carried away. I was really worried for a moment.'

'They always fight those two. It's like this annual arm wrestle. You can't stop them.'

'He's leaving for Seoul didn't you know?'

'No, I didn't. Shit I better tell Colin, he will be ecstatic. But then again it doesn't really matter because they will both hang around Korea forever I'd say.'

'Colin has kids doesn't he?'

'Yeah he has two and a wife who we are all fond of.'

'I like Colin. I might even can catch up with him some time and have that game of cricket.'

'For sure you should. He's a bit erratic from time to time, but he has a really good heart trust me. After all he isn't as precocious as Jack can be. He doesn't need to be. I think that maybe having two kids has mellowed him somewhat.'

'Yeah I guess it would.'

'How about you Don? Any kids?'

'None at all thank god. I was married once but we didn't go down that road, which was probably a good thing.'

'I know what you mean. It's a pretty big commitment.

'It sure is.'

'Anyway, I have to head off now so here's my email if you want to get in touch again.'

'Ok Linda, that sounds good. Thanks for coming and see you around soon, maybe on the cricket field.'

'Yep, no under arm bowling from me that's for sure.'

'Ha ha! It's an eternal joke eh? Have a fun week.'

36

CRICKET

On the phone Linda tells me that she is an avid hiker, and that she's going on a hike near Chuncheon this weekend. Coincidentally, Colin has planned a cricket match for the same day. He's arranged for people to meet up after for drinks at Heaven, a swanky bar on a hill that overlooks town.

'What's this place Colin? You sure like grand establishments, don't you?' I ask.

'I only go for quality these days because there's little point in any of us adults drinking cheap beer and what are probably fake shots at Hells Bells and Jacks,' he explains. 'They're dives if you ask me and full of dumb military and dodgy teachers I reckon.'

'Yeah, Linda told me that you preferred these kinds of places. Her hiking crew will be here soon to join us,' I say.

'Yes I know, my Australian pal,' he replies. He then asks, 'Hey Don, you like her don't you? I mean she's pretty nice don't you think? She's definitely a lot more down to earth and reliable than some girls you'll meet at Jacks or Hells Bells.'

'I wouldn't know, would I Colin. I've only just met her, but we've been in touch quite a bit of late via a few emails and the odd phone call. I'm not expecting anything to be honest.'

'I definitely wasn't expecting to get married and have a kid straight away either.'

'Haven't you heard of condoms mate?' I ask sheepishly. 'I am kidding of course. Don't take me seriously.'

'If you weren't Linda's new friend, I would deck you here and now,' Colin replies.

'Like I said, I was having you on.'

'You're all right for an Australian. Good luck with Linda and if you do anything to hurt her I will eat you alive,' warns Colin.

By the time Linda and her group arrive we are all tucking into dinner.

'You guys look absolutely buggered,' says Colin.

'How can you say that? We've only been walking since 7 a.m! Of course we're tired,' replies Linda. 'Tired and in need of a beer and a feed thank you, young Colin.'

'When are you off girl? Is this the last weekend then?'

'Yeah you could say that. I'm heading on Monday in fact. The camp is over so it's back to lovely China, isn't it?'

'Lovely China you say?' Justin questions. 'I've never heard someone use that expression before. Most people on ESL sites call it a dump and that you don't get paid very well.'

'Look it's better than some places, aside from the blooming SARS,' Linda adds.

'So why stay then?' adds Justin.

'Because I needed a break from here is why. Anyway, you're aware of that so why ask?'

'Well you deserve to go out a winner every time you come here my dear, so I say cheers to you and let's have some fun tonight,' shouts Colin.

At Heaven we have enough food and alcohol to stay for a few hours and later there's some talk of singing.

'Sorry but I can't do the *noraebang* singing room bit tonight,' says Linda.' Please don't mind me though. You guys go off while Don and I stay here for a few more.'

'C'mon you two, let's go and sing. I thought you guys liked to get stuck in?' goads Colin.

'We don't want to so you'll have to go with the others,' replies Linda.

'What is this? A fucking mass exodus?' asks Colin.

'No, it's just two people saying no, that's all. Something you can't handle? Look, there's still half a dozen people saying yes,' I add.

Eventually Colin and company head off for the singing room and Linda and I venture off to my place to have some quality private time.

The next day Colin meets us for lunch smiling and joking about last night, 'So Linda, now that you and Don have obviously become good mates does that mean you will come back to Korea soon?'

'Sure I'd be interested, especially as I have now been offered a job in a university in Suwon. But it would involve me breaking my contract with my university. The SARS stuff has really got to me too; it's really fucked up. If I do decide to leave the biggest problem I guess is how to tell them.'

'You could do a midnight runner?' I ask.

'It'd be more than a midnight run. Remember it's a communist country that we are talking about,' Linda replies.

'Maybe you could help her Don?' Colin suggests. 'C'mon you're a big guy. If you went there with Linda mate those Chinese would buckle when they see you.'

'That's not a bad idea Colin. Could you help me Don?' Linda asks. 'I would really appreciate it if someone could be my partner in crime as it might get a little hairy. I'll even shout the ticket for you.'

'You're kidding me? When are we going? You said Monday, right?'

'On Monday the plan is to go to Shanghai first, then to Yichang where my stuff is. And if we can, we will then go to Beijing at the end for a couple of days.'

'Wow that sounds amazing. I have always wanted to hike the Great Wall. Man, I'd be honored to.'

37

AUTUMN'S CLOSE

Since our trip to China, Linda and I have become almost inseparable, spending every weekend with each other and making daily contact. Work-wise, Linda has pretty much the perfect situation – a twenty-hour week, great students while her accommodation is in a luxury five star resort off campus. She's also able to save extra money teaching private classes.

When I visit her on the weekends, the two of us often go hiking and find temples in the hills. Her knowledge of the country is extensive and she introduces me to a life outside of bars and DVD rooms.

So when I get a call from Justin it does seem worlds away, 'Hey it's Justin here. Remember me?'

'Don't be stupid mate. What's up?'

'The sky I guess. What do you reckon?'

'We haven't spoken in months. Not since my trip to China.'

'That's right. You've been avoiding me haven't you?'

'Hardly. I don't avoid people unless I need to. What's up with you?'

'Well it has been nearly three months and we haven't played a gig since the pub Olympics. It's about time we did one don't you reckon?'

'Nah, I'm not going to bars. I'm tired of them. I mean, have you ever checked your clothes after a night at Hells Bells?' I question. 'They reek, plus I'm over all the bullshit, the military, and all their crap. You know how it is. We've talked about this before.'

'That's why I'm leaving. It is time for me to do a runner.'

'But you told me you'd be here to the end of your contract? You said you would make it to at least till Christmas?'

'Nah fuck that. My boss is being such a bitch of late. I can't handle it anymore. This weekend I want to play one more gig. Are you into it?'

'Of course I'd be into it mate. Shit, sorry to hear that you're going.'

'I'm not sorry mate. Seriously, after two years I have had it. Being here, it's as if you're watching time pass in front of you - you know paint when it dries? It's that bad I swear,' he explains.

'It's time then.'

'Fuck yeah. I need to get home and seriously make some applications for some post-graduate degrees,' he replies. 'I have arranged a soft-style landing. I reckon if I can get admitted into a university then at least I can go back to being a student and live off my savings. I can still have great holidays and create a good life for the future. Time is up for me here I reckon.'

'Since when did the future become a priority for you? Do you think you can have one, I mean a good life in Australia these days?'

'Of course you can. I don't want to be like those others who can't get a job in their home countries because they've stayed here for too long. Remember, I'm a little younger.'

'I understand mate.'

'It's different for you. You have Linda now, and you're a little older, so in some ways you have been there, done that. I'm really happy for you and her.'

'Thanks Justin. She has made a big difference I reckon. Ok, let's get in touch with a few of the guys who are still here, and arrange a small shindig this Saturday night. Linda will be up for it and I'm sure she'd love to see you as well before you fuck off.'

'Listen Laridis this is no joke. I don't want all the guys to know about it. You can tell Linda if you want, but she can't tell anyone at least until I am gone. You got it?' he asks. 'The last thing I need is some cunt knowing and I get stopped at customs. It has to be kept under your hat, ok?'

'Mate, you can trust me.'

Justin has purchased a ticket online and will take the 2:30 a.m. bus to Incheon Airport straight after the gig on Saturday. Sure, I will miss him as we have become close confidantes, but I know that we'll look each other up at home one day.

On Saturday everyone is out so Justin and I are lapping up the company. There's Gordon, Bruce, Daniel, David, Captain Cliff, Manitoba Mike, and Matt the military engineer.

'Man, I haven't seen you in ages? How have you been? What's up?' asks Matt.

'I'm good mate. Just been having a real life for a change,' I reply.

'Fuck, how so?' he asks.

'You know. My job has finally worked out and my boss is ok,' I explain. 'And I now have a good friend down in Suwon and we often go hiking.'

'You've got it made now brother.'

'Yeah Linda is mint I reckon,' adds Manitoba Mike.

'That's cool Don you have her and you have your band. What else do you need? You see, I told you life would work itself out. It always does,' adds Captain Cliff.

'Good on you Don. We're all happy for you,' says David.

'Yeah dude fuck mate. We're really happy for you. You know, when Arizona Mike and I first met you I have to say we felt sorry for you,' Mike explains. 'We thought you were nuts for sticking it out at Global. All that shit with those cunts not paying you. Fuck man, I would have been on the first flight out. But you stuck around buddy and you're still here to tell the story. That took a lot of guts you know. Let me buy you a shot.'

'I better not Mike. I have to play after all.'

'Don't be a wimp Aussie. I thought all you guys can drink down there?'

'Ok just the one, and then we have to play,' I concede.

Mike orders a tray of OP 151 rum shots for everyone.

'Just remember I saw a bro shitfaced on this once. Take caution,' advises Daniel.

Liquored up we can barely play but it doesn't seem to matter as the majority of the audience is also off its face. When we finish I look around at Justin and say, 'Mate, on the quiet I'm going to miss you but I'm glad you're doing this. You're stepping out of the circle and trying something new. Good on you.'

'I know. It took a lot of guts coming here in the first place and I stuck it out for two years. You're doing the same. I reckon it'd be great if you too can get out of here and at least try a new place. Why don't you ask Linda to invite you to her university?' he asks. 'That's the shit here in Korea. You don't want to be working for these private academies. There are too many dodgy sharks as you know.'

'That's good advice, thanks mate.'

'This kind of life isn't for everyone,' Justin adds.

'No, it isn't but I have to say when things finally do gel you realise that you can have more options than back at home. That's not to say that you won't have a good time in Australia.' I explain. 'You've planned a soft landing and I wish you well. One more shot?'

'Is that your second or third? Remember Daniel told us to watch this shit,' he warns. 'My Australian friend Glen got totally legless on these a year or two ago. We were all really worried about him. Military boneheads drink it without any problem, but for us teacher wimps we aren't used to it.'

'I'll have one more if you do.'

We each skull one back, washing the taste down with some beer, before Justin quietly leaves. Realizing that he's finally going, I follow and walk him halfway down the road before he takes a cab back to his apartment to get his stuff.

'See you in Sydney mate in the summer,' I shout, as the cab pulls away.

'For sure mate. It's not goodbye yet. See you back in Sydney!' he shouts out the window.

When I get back to the bar, Linda knows that I have just seen Justin off and she senses my sadness.

I say to her, 'He is such a good guy. I wouldn't have lasted this long if it wasn't for him you know.'

'I know,' replies Linda. 'It hurts when people leave. Just remember you will see him again.'

After one last beer, I can feel myself swaying and I know that it is time to go home. Linda helps me into the cab, but when we arrive downstairs at my apartment, I am well out to it and talking gibberish in the back of the car.

'Don Laridis wake up we have to go. C'mon my friend, we can't hang around in the cab all night. This man wants to go home and he's getting a little pissed off so let's go.'

Delirious and oblivious to Linda's wishes I reply in a slurred tone, 'I can't walk sorry. Where are we? I have no idea where I am.'

'Well, if you hadn't drunk those shots you wouldn't be asking, would you? Now wake up so we can get you inside.'

I ignore her wishes and continue to make little sense. She tries to lift me but my body won't respond and finally the driver has to help carry me to my apartment door. By the time we're there, they virtually have to push and drag me to my bed fully clothed.

During the night I get up to visit the toilet, but instead of heading back to the bed, I stumble aimlessly into the kitchen. Blind and naked, I try to find my way back but I end up taking the wrong door, instead heading up to the top of the church where there's an attic and a vacant bed. Totally out to it I crash there for the next few hours. Noticing the sound of the street late in the morning I realise what I have actually done and return downstairs much to Linda's relief.

'Don, what the fuck happened to you? I have been looking for you since 6 a.m. I was calling Gordon and even David. I had to call the police and I nearly had to make a report.'

'I must have been sleepwalking. I'm not sure what went on. I guess I couldn't find the way back to my bed. I was out to it upstairs. How did I get there? It doesn't add up. Luckily no one was around. Damn, I shouldn't have had so many shots.'

'You're an idiot Laridis,' she replies, half serious and half in jest. 'Like I said, some of the boys and the cops know about this. What will you do, hey? I mean, you don't want your boss finding out after all the things she has done for you?'

'She won't find out. We better call and let everyone know that it was a false alarm.'

COLD AND STARK
December 2003

When I arrived in South Korea in February, winter was ending but now being the end of year the worst is yet to hit. There are absolutely no leaves on the trees, and everything seems so lifeless. The only way to escape is to hang out indoors which at times can be unbearably hot because of the heating. From my observation Koreans seem to like these extremes - their food is either salty or spicy, their weather moist and soggy in the summer or cold and hard in the winter. To escape the big freeze, it is welcoming to know that there is a healthy supply of *on-dol* heating; this is a traditional system that transfers smoke from cooking fires under the floor. It's also Christmas time and with the rise of Christianity in South Korea, it's become particularly important for teenagers and adults to secure dates on Christmas Eve. Linda and I plan to celebrate it at her place in Suwon with a few of her colleagues, yet unbeknownst to me, she has a Christmas gift or two of her own.

'Hey, do you want to go to North Korea?'

'Your kidding aren't you? North Korea? How the fuck will we ever get into there?'

'We'll catch a bus, you idiot. They are running tours from Seoul.'

'Who is?'

'Hyundai is. They are loaded with money and because of this Sunshine Policy both governments are arranging reunions for families, plus some of us foreigners who are on work visas can also go. It's exciting times don't you think?' she says. 'C'mon Don, they are taking people up there every weekend. It's a chance of a lifetime. Do you want to die regretting that you never went?'

'No I don't. You can count me in. I'd love to go'.

'Cool.'

'What's the cost then?'

'Don't worry about the cost. Consider it my Christmas gift to you, but first you can't go unless you consider hitting up my bosses at Suwon for a job. They need new teachers and I reckon I can get you in if you are keen.'

'Man you are the shit Linda aren't you?' I say eagerly. 'I can't believe what I am hearing. A university job and a trip to North Korea would be the fucking icing on the cake after the kind of year I've had. Oh, and of course meeting you was pretty damn good as well.'

Pecking me on my receding hairline, she whispers, 'I'll set the job interview up for the middle of next week. Just be ready. And remember to wear your Sunday best.'

Suwon is one of Korea's oldest cities, with a walled fortress dating back to the 18th century. It was designed to honor Prince Sado who was locked alive in a rice chest after failing to obey his father's command to commit suicide. Apart from the town's old history, it's simply yet another Korean satellite city caught in the throes of modernization. The university is out of town in a place called Hwaesong, somewhat trapped in an oasis of new construction and freeways.

When I finally arrive, there is a line of other job candidates in front of me, 'But I was told 11:30 and it is now 11:25?' I ask.

'Yes we appreciate that you are on time Mr. Laridis but our staff isn't ready yet. Please sit down, drink some water and we will try and make some room for you,' replies a young student.

'Ok,' I respond reluctantly. I then text Linda.

```
Finally arrived and they're behind schedule.
It's making me more nervous.
```

Linda replies:

```
Breathe will you. Just enjoy it Don, it'll be ok
I promise.
```

My turn has nearly arrived, and I can hear someone in front of me being asked some whacky interview questions like 'Are you single?' and 'Do you like to drink?'

The foreigner asks, 'Look we don't have much time. I'd like to know more about the job please. Can you tell me more about the pay? What kind of hours will I be working?'

His accent sounds a little hard to decipher. It could well be Irish or east coast Canada but the fact that he's asking about salary means he may have made a bit of a faux pas.

'Excuse me sir. What country are you from again?' one of them asks.

'I am from Ireland. The Republic of Ireland don't you remember?'

'Where's that? I have never heard of it.'

'What do you mean where's that? You should know surely? Like Korea, we're a country who is technically still at war.'

The more I listen the more I realise that it's Padraigh, the non-alcoholic Irishman who I met when I first arrived in Chuncheon. This is confirmed when I hear the staff asking him to leave.

'We think it is best that you don't live here Mr. Pad? Sorry I can't pronounce your name.' says one of the interviewers.

'My name is Padraigh Finnegan and I am proudly from the Republic of Ireland. I don't want your job anyway!' he shouts furiously.

Slamming the door behind him, the staff members break into laughter, partially through embarrassment.

Padraigh then notices me waiting, 'You're not fuckin' going for a job here are you? These guys, mate, could not arrange a root in a brothel. They are fuckin' gangsters I am telling you. They didn't even know where Ireland was!'

'Padraigh it's nice to see you my friend. I heard that you were looking for jobs in Seoul?'

'I have no idea what I am doing Don. All I know is that I'm not going back home that's for sure. The economy has dried up and the IT days are over.'

'Yes, I read about. It sounds awful. Anyway, I better go inside. I hope it all works out for you.'

As I nervously wait, another assistant arrives and says to me, 'Welcome Mr. Laridis to our interview today. Please get ready, you are next. Also before you enter I need to see your passport sir.'

'My passport?' I reply in a surprised manner. 'I wasn't told to bring it.'

'You need your passport sir. Do you have any photo ID?'

'This is my Korean alien card. Will that suffice?'

'Suffice? What do you mean? Sorry but my English is so poor,' she replies, covering her mouth.

'Will it be enough for now?' I reply somewhat sternly.

'Yes it will be.'

'Thank you. Wish me luck then.'

'Good luck Teacher.'

Inside is a huge office space with three interviewers; one has a mushroom-shaped hairstyle that resembles a perfect combed over wig, while the other two are slightly younger and well groomed.

'So Mr. Don isn't it?' asks the older Professor Kim, flashing his gold teeth.

'Yes that's me!' I reply which manages to set them off into raucous laughter, more a form of embarrassment or nervousness if anything.

'Good to see you Mr. Don. My name is Doctor Noh, which means I am a doctor so you can trust me.' He leans forward and shakes my hand. His hands are tiny and he possesses a particular cockiness about him. Next to him is his colleague Kevin who does the same greeting but more in a rapid rote learnt manner.

'Hello Mr. Don. Welcome to our university. My name is Kevin. You are from Australia I believe?'

'Yes Sydney. Are you familiar with it?'

'Absolutely I am Mr. Don! My family and I spent three years there. I worked in Macquarie. Do you know that place?'

'You mean Macquarie University? You were a professor there were you?'

'Yes. No, I wasn't. I worked there in the cafeteria sir and I studied there at night.'

'That's great. I hope you had a fantastic time there.'

A huge warm smile lights Kevin's face, knowing that he has won some respect.

'So you are keen to teach at our university Mr. Don? Why do you want to do that?' asks Dr. Noh.

'I have been in Korea for nearly a year and I think my skills are best suited to university students.'

'What do you mean by that?' asks Dr. Kim.

'I have spent a good portion of my life in universities. I like the atmosphere of learning and I believe that I can be a good teacher here.'

'Ok Mr. Don that will be enough. Thanks for coming to see us today and good luck,' replies Kevin.

'Yes good luck,' affirms Dr. Noh.

'That's all?' I ask.

'Yes, you can go now. Enjoy your trip back to Chuncheon. It is so beautiful there. My wife and I like to go there very much. Maybe we will see you there one day.' says Kim.

'Sure. Linda has my contact details.'

'Yes we know about Linda,' winks Kevin.

The interview has taken under five minutes, which seems weird as it took me nearly five hours to get here. Hurriedly I call Linda.

'I'm outside,' she says. 'Come and see me and we can have some lunch if you like?'

'Good idea I can meet you now,' I reply.

When we meet outside, not far behind us are the very three staff members who interviewed me. They are also making their way to lunch.

'Hello Linda! Hello again Mr. Don. Have a nice lunch won't you,' shouts Dr. Kim.

'Thank you. Nice to meet you too Dr. Kim. Nice to meet all of you,' I reply.

'Nice to meet you too,' Kevin winks.

'Did you see that? 'I whisper to Linda. 'He keeps winking at me. He did it during the interview as well.'

'Yes he's a bit of character is our Kevin.'

'I was only in that room for five minutes Linda?'

'It probably means they want you. Don't you worry about it hon as I am sure you made a good impression. Let's grab some lunch.'

'Do you have any news yet on North Korea?' I ask.

'No North Korea until you get the job, remember?'

39

SIZEABLE CONTRASTS

Within a few days of the interview the job is mine and we are both on our way to North Korea. At the border we are suddenly at the beck and call of a different way of thinking.

'Give me phone now and no photos. No photos of our great people,' shouts one of the patrol guards.

We are now entering the DMZ - the 38th parallel, which was drawn up in the early 1950s to divide the Korean peninsula. I must say I feel quite overwhelmed, even intimidated. The officer looks as though he is in his mid-twenties and yells like a Nazi.

He makes a command through his loudspeaker, 'You must do what we and our great leader say.'

Grabbing Linda's hand tightly, I ask her how a place could ever come to this.

'Are you naïve or something? Think of Ireland and its borders. I mean it's no big deal Don. Most of all just be a good ambassador and don't judge. This isn't middle class suburbia silly. They are only protecting what they consider theirs.'

'Middle class suburbia doesn't talk to people like that though. Plus they're so skinny. Take a look at his shoulders. You couldn't compare him to say Hooch or Frank our GI soldier mates in Chuncheon now, could you? They'd have him for breakfast.'

'You'll be in a gulag soon Don Laridis if you don't shut the fuck up. You need to be patient.'

'Linda you are the coolest. Thanks for giving me this chance. I really appreciate it,' I say as I kiss her softly on the cheek.

The morning bus ride has been a slow amble from the south. We are part of a thirty-person group tour, mostly made up of South Koreans, but

229

including an Australian mother and her daughter, and some Japanese students who are studying Korean in Seoul. We have been divided into two vans (Hyundai of course) with one tour guide to each bus. Word has it that the company has been successfully operating tours since the late 90s.

'Where are you two from?' I ask the mother and daughter.

'We're from Maitland mate. Good to meet you both. I'm Sandra and this is my daughter Emma.'

'Don, and this is Linda. By the way she is a Kiwi but we won't begrudge her that.'

'Anyway, it looks as if we are the only white fellas here,' replies Emma.

'Passport! Show me ID card now!' shouts the same stern young officer.

'Shit he has some gumption doesn't he? Not even a please. If my son spoke to me like that I would give him a good whack over the head,' remarks Sandra.

We all show our passports and are then asked to leave our cell phones at a designated area at the checkpoint.

'Also no photos of people absolutely none ok? If you do you will be in trouble straight away. Our guards will hold a red flag up in the air and you will be punished. Do you hear me?' says another guard looking straight into my eyes.

'Yes, yes I do,' I nervously reply.

Entering the DMZ, the bus passes through land which is only occupied by soldiers and wildlife.

'It's beautiful here,' I remark. 'You'd never think that this was all fortified would you?'

'We've got Aboriginal land like this in the Pinta region. You need to get out more,' offers Sandra.

'Did you know that some birds from here migrate all the way to New Zealand in the winter months, and come back here for summer?' says Linda.

'Why do they do that?' I ask.

'Because it is potentially one of the quietest zones on the planet for bird life, plus it's one of the most natural. Sounds weird I know but it's true,' she adds.

'Makes sense though doesn't it. I can see why,' replies Sandra.

'A bit like Raymond Terrace isn't it Mum without the undesirables?'

'Yes Emma it's a bit like that.'

'Who is Raymond Terrace?' asks Linda.

We three Australians all have a laugh at her expense before I quietly explain that it's a town in New South Wales. Sandra is based in Busan in the south doing some research on the division between the Koreas and Emma is fresh out of high school, spending time with her mum until she works out what she wants to do.

The tour guide stands and addresses the group. A graduate of Pyongyang University, he is in his mid to late-twenties and is relatively soft spoken compared to the guards.

'Welcome my friends from Seoul and other countries. We are happy to have you here. Now we are travelling through the DMZ before we get to our destination. Please ask me if you have any questions and I will try my best to answer what I can.

'Notice how he says 'what I can?' I bet he is being monitored for sure,' suggests Sandra.

'Whatever. We cannot assume. Plus we have to remember we are visitors to their country,' replies Linda.

'What's your fucking problem?' mutters Sandra under her breath.

'Look, I'm here like you to observe and enjoy so please no more North Korea comments,' says Linda. 'One thing I can't handle is people who bash other countries without even visiting them. You might as well work for that Sydney paper the Daily Terror, I mean Telegraph!'

'I am visiting here now aren't I? In fact I did once work for that paper,' replies Sandra.

'No way, you couldn't have! Don also worked there, didn't you?'

Somewhat embarrassed, I mutter under my breath, 'Yes, I think I did once but I'd prefer not to go there.'

'You think you did? What do you mean by that?' asks Sandra.

'Look can you sock it please? It's obvious he doesn't want to talk about it,' Linda replies.

When the thirteen kilometer stretch of the demilitarized zone ends, we enter what can be best construed as another planet – North Korea. Shocked by the poverty that we see, we are immediately voyeurs to this strange land. It's as if time has stopped. The locals look down to avoid eye contact. Some are pushing carts of fruit and vegetables, as others cycle on pot-holed roads.

'They don't look that healthy do they?' comments Sandra.

'What do you expect? Linda replies. 'They're not fed like us that's why.'

'God, I was only commenting. Emma please darling no taking photos here babe. Remember what the man said. We don't want to embarrass ourselves again now dear.'

'Who said you embarrassed yourself?" asks Linda.

'Well, we obviously did with you lot now didn't we? No more questions. I'm finished talking here.'

'So middle class,' retorts Linda under her breath.

Up ahead we take the entrance to Mount Geumgang which is otherwise known as Diamond Mountain and is in one of Korea's most stunning ranges.

'It reminds me of back home,' says Linda.

'What do you mean? How can this be anything like New Zealand?' I ask.

'Check out the air and the pines. It hasn't been tampered with by human idiocy. You know what I mean?'

'I get you. Clean and green eh. Just like that 100 percent pure New Zealand ad on television,' I reply wryly.

Inside the resort we are lead to our accommodation. Most of the hostesses speak immaculate English. They seem somewhat less manicured and cosmetic than their southern neighbors.

'It's refreshing not see so many broken faces if you know what I'm saying,' I comment.

'They haven't got the money to be so cosmetic here. It'll happen one day,' adds Linda.

As we are taken to our room one of the young attendants asks, 'May I ask where you are both from?'

'I come from Australia and she is from New Zealand.'

'Such beautiful places I have heard.'

'This is beautiful here as well. How about you? Where do you come from?' I ask.

'I'm from China, but my family is Korean,' she politely replies.

Most of the customer service staff are of Chinese ethnic Korean origin. They are working in cahoots with universities to supply the best English spoken people for hotel resort jobs.

After settling in, we are all welcomed with a large banquet and some North Korean alcohol. Within an hour or two, the groups start to get a little rowdy, and not long later Linda and I are targeted for some karaoke, which we politely refuse.

'How about *soju*? You try? C'mon! Where you from?' a South Korean man asks.

'Hoju saram imnida,' I reply.

'Ah, hoju saram. Ah, you're Korean is very good. Please some *soju*.'

In a very obliging manner I accept the man's offer taking one shot before I am asked to have another. Linda carefully avoids being his attention, knowing that the North Korean variety, just like the beer is far stronger than the one in the south.

'No more for him please. *Ah-ni ah ni!* No more! He doesn't want anymore,' she tells the man in her broken Korean English. By this stage I am on the cusp of losing my limbs again.

Trying to avoid another case of sleepwalking, Linda does a great job to get me off my seat, and we make a beeline towards the lift and our room. On our way we notice Sandra and Emma, who are getting a lot of attention from two men who have taken a shine to them.

'Excuse me,' Sandra shouts trying to get Linda's attention. 'Is he ok? I mean your friend?'

'He's a little bit drunk that's all. What's going on with you?'

'These men are starting to hassle us a little.'

'Kick them in the balls and head to your room as fast as you can,' advises Linda.

'That's not good form in this part of the world. You should know that. We're not in the sticks back home girl.'

Linda's annoyed and says, 'More politely, you could do what I just did. Tell them you're feeling sick and that you have to go to bed.'

Finding the lift we manage to escape from the hounding men and get back to our rooms for the night. When we wake up the next day, the four of us gravitate towards each other. We watch the early morning sunrise at breakfast before we take part in a hike. The trail is through some ranges that lead past a frozen waterfall, up to peaks that are far colder than the minus twenty-five degrees we'd experienced on the lake last night. On our way, some vendors try to sell us herbs, cigarettes and souvenirs promoting their country as a proud historic place. It's when I take a toilet break that I meet two curious vendors who ask me in Korean where I am from.

I reply, 'Hoju. Chon nin hoju saram imnida.'

They both have no idea what I am talking about so they ask me again. The third time round I have to imitate a kangaroo but they still have no idea. In the end I show them my passport, which they study for what seems to be an eternity. Feeling vulnerable, I grab it from them before running back to the others.

'You took a while there Don? Last night's drinking giving you some grief then?' asks Emma.

'No, it's ok. Just a word of advice that some of the people here are um...'

'What Don? Linda asks.

'Don't show them your passport that's all.'

'What are you talking about?' asks Sandra.

'I mean, don't be too friendly is what I mean,' I reply, quickly changing the topic before we start the ascent.

For lunch, we are welcomed by North Korean waitresses who I notice are wearing badges of their leader Kim Jong Il. There are even inscriptions of Kim and his father engraved on cliffs. By the afternoon we reach a bath house that has hot springs. However, it is the acrobatics show in the evening that illustrates the most significant difference between the two divided lands. Well-trained trapeze artists from the North perform brilliantly, receiving huge praise from their southern neighbors, the most touching part being when the latter are asked to join them on stage at the end. One can only imagine what it must be like for these people who speak the same language, eat the same food, but are hopelessly divided by political ideals.

'It's got to be so fucking hard for them. I mean, did you see the look on their faces?' I ask.

'Yes it's been more than fifty years. I can't imagine what it would be like to know that some of your family is a few hours away and you aren't allowed to see them,' adds Linda.

'It is so different here; such an insight. I mean look at the staff here. They aren't bothered by the modern day traps that we set ourselves up in.'

'They have no choice,' Sandra adds.

I reply almost shouting, 'What I am trying to say is that those trapeze artists mean something and so do the people serving us. Yet, they don't care about an MP3, a busy department store downtown, or some new cosmetic arrangement. Sure her breakfast might be rice and kimchi and the pipes in her room may not always be warm, but she is ok, isn't she?'

'It's two different societies Don and I agree we don't have to judge. This has been the way for some sixty years now and it appears that maybe it is ambling on ok – better than we thought or are told,' Linda replies.

Sandra interrupts, 'You guys are living in a bubble. If we were in Pyongyang, or even some more remote areas, I bet we'd be seeing a completely different world. Anyway enough of this as Emma and I are both going to bed.'

On the final day, Linda and Sandra decided to go hiking while Emma and I choose to go on an ocean tour. By the sea, we meet a painter originally from the capital Pyongyang who tells us about a great teacher he once had. It's obvious that he wants to talk to us more but he can't as there are some restrictions. It seems that these locals have been warned not to indulge in dialogue. The surrounds are beautiful and quiet. By the end of the day it will be a ghost town here, and the man will have gone back to his patch, silenced in a fishing village that has little power and light.

'That's what Chinese people can see from the border of the Yalu River further north. They see pitch black, and that isn't a bash - it's a fact,' remarks Sandra on our long trawl back to Seoul.

As the bus passes the DMZ heading south we forge ahead on a different path that will take us back to neon lights, cosmetics, Christmas decorations and other forms of hustle and bustle.

40

THE NEW

Now that the job at the university is official it is time to let people know that I'm leaving Chuncheon. The first person I need to see is JC and to my surprise she handles the news quite well.

'It's ok, really. In fact I'm aware that you need to do this,' she says. 'After all you haven't had an easy year. Thanks for your hard-work and I hope you succeed down there.'

'Thanks JC. I will never forget you. You have been so supportive – a bit like a mother. In fact I'd like to call you my *omma* here - my Korean mother.'

'Forget that crap and just be strong Laridis. That's what they teach us in the army here. Whenever there is change, you have to be tough ok, and you have to stand up to anything. Fighting Laridis!' she responds pragmatically.

For my mates, guys like Gordon, David, and more recently Daniel, it is not so straightforward. After all in the last year we'd all become a bit of a fixture at Hells Bells and Jacks. I would also miss the guys behind the bars, the little shops and even the hole in the wall restaurants here. I will be leaving a lot behind, but the security of a university job and being closer to Linda makes a lot more sense.

'It's the right thing mate. Good on you I say,' says Daniel. 'Not many people can leave saying that, and I reckon you're the right age to keep travelling, working and experiencing. It's cunts like me that get to our early thirties who end up in a mess because we get tired of the work, and then we find it difficult to settle in back home.'

'Like I have said before, you're at the right age. You've done all that shit back home. Just look after Linda or we'll wring your bloody neck,' laughs Gordon. 'She's a good bonny girl that one, and remember a university job is mint here. You best hold onto it.'

'Cheers Gordon and Daniel. You two are my real mates here. I won't forget you and I will be up to visit you some time.'

'Some time? What a load of bullshit! They all say that Don,' adds Daniel.

'Yeah, but we have email and cell phones these days. It's much easier than before when you had to go through poste restante to keep in touch.'

'Email has its perks for sure. Good luck with the university. I hope I can do the same someday in Japan of course,' adds David.

'Listen to him would you Don. Japan! Just stop dreaming would you David,' says Gordon.

'You have to have dreams otherwise what's the point?' asks David.

'Yeah, but you have been fucking talking about it for years,' adds Daniel.

'Ok guys I have to go and see one more person. Bye for now. Take care and remember to keep in touch,' I reply before setting off to see my other boss.

Mr. Lee isn't so backslapping when he hears my news.

I politely explain, 'That's just the way it goes. Look, you have been great to me but I have to do this.'

'Sorry, but I can't accept your news. You just can't walk out on us Laridis,' he replies.

'Yes I can. JC said she understood. I am moving to Suwon because I now have a university job.'

'Of course you say that, but remember I have helped you so much. I don't get it. You do have a heart don't you?'

'Of course I do but I need to get a real job and some integrity.'

'You can't just take off now.'

'Look, you have been great to me Mr. Lee but to be honest, how can you stop me? After all, you found me outside a supermarket. That's the kind of risk you have to take.'

'Look, I can't release you just like that. We have a contract, an agreement.'

'JC has given permission for me to go.'

'Don't forget the money from the Labor Office. I promised I would get that for you and I will. C'mon, just stay with us here and enjoy your life.'

'I appreciate what you have done for me. I am really thankful for everything. However it isn't as simple as that. I also have a Linda now to consider. Look, you can find another Don outside the supermarket. Mr. Lee, as you are aware, there are always teachers coming and going.'

'I will talk to JC about this,' he replies slamming his fist against the car dashboard.

'Don't be angry. Like I said she has released me. She said it is ok.'

'Ok Don you win again. But you have to come and see me from time to time. I want you to introduce someone to me. And I need to say that you're also my friend. We have gone through a lot together.'

'I know Mr. Lee, I know. Please don't fret as it isn't easy for me to do this either. And thanks for saying what you said. It means a lot to me. Anyway, I better go. I have to catch the bus.'

'I'll run you there if you like.'

'It's ok. I'll grab a cab.'

Looking him in the eye while shaking his hand, I know that it will be a while before I will see him again. I assume that I will be back, not just for the money, but also to see him and my other mates. Without his help I probably wouldn't have stayed on here, and the last thing I want is for him to resent me.

COUNTING COIN
Late February 2004

'Is that you Don Laridis?'

'Yeah, it's me. Who's this?'

'Out of sight out of mind are we? You have forgotten us friendly country folk I take it? It's your old boss, remember me?'

'Of course I remember you Mr. Lee. What's up? It's so good to hear from you.'

'At the end of the week I will have you and the Japanese girl's money. If you want it, you better get your ass up here on Friday. First, we will treat our friend to lunch then you will both get your money. We need to thank Mr. Park from the Labor Office. It was he who made it all possible.'

'Of course we must. I'll see you Friday for sure.'

Hanging up the phone, I feel a huge sense of relief. To be honest amidst all the time and changes, getting reimbursed had meant less to me. But the fact that Yuri and I had been wronged and we were being compensated, would at least prove to both of us that this country wasn't so messed up after all.

On the bus the following day, I am well aware that it's been a year since I left Australia to teach English here. And nothing had really changed – I'm travelling north east along a freeway, and the starkness of mid-winter had killed most forms of life. It seems that the only living things are the birds and the people ice fishing.

When I arrive at the bus station Mr. Lee is there to collect both Yuri and I. As we travel in his trusty van, I notice Daniel skateboarding to one side of us.

'Can you pull over for a minute, please Mr. Lee?' I ask.

'No, I am not supposed to do that Don. I can't just stop. After all we are on a mission to get your money. You can see your friend later at a bar can't you?' he replies, with a hint of sarcasm.

'But I only want to talk for a minute. Please Mr. Lee,' I beg.

'Ok, but only a minute.'

'Hello mate. Long time no see. How are you?' Daniel asks.

'Well it might seem like a while but it's only been a month or so.'

'What brings you here?'

'A special visit - you know how it is. I have that shit from last year to sort out,' I reply. 'By the way how is everyone man? How are the dudes at Hells Bells and Jacks? What about Gordy and David? Is everyone ok?'

'They have cleared off bro. They've have both left for good.'

'Fuck, they could have texted and told me. Or emailed?'

'It all happened so suddenly. Gordy actually got back with Mi-ra. They are in Scotland sorting stuff out for their wedding and future life in Germany.'

'What about David? Did he finally go to Japan?'

'Yeah he did. He finally got his dream gig.'

'Anyone heard from Jack,' I ask.

'No word. He is probably still in Seoul the old bugger.'

'Good riddance. And what about the military guys, Hooch, Frank, and Matt the engineer. What happened to them?'

'No idea, though I did hear from David at Hells Bells that the base will be closing down soon so they'll all leave as well.'

'That has to be hard for the bar. They provided a lot of business. Please say hello to David and John from Hells Bells from me. Man, that's one exodus. Is anyone left?'

'Look people come and go. Shit happens remember? You left as well.'

'Yeah, I did.'

'Look, I might pop in for one tonight. Are you going to stay for old time's sake?'

'I can't mate. I have to get back straight after lunch. I have classes tomorrow.'

'How's it all going there?' he asks.

'The students are great. They are so giving and you can tell they really want to learn. It's like they help me to take my mind off any dramas. And get this; our holidays are like five months off a year – three in the winter and two in the summer.'

'That's great. You will be able to do some travelling as well as go home and see your mates.'

'Look, I better go.'

'Yeah same, I have to go and teach your old classes at Alberta.'

'Tell JC that I will call her soon. And how about we arrange a beer sometime? We can meet halfway in Seoul.' I say.

'Sure, that's a great idea.'

As we speed off Yuri is curious about Daniel and how anyone would ride a skateboard at this time of the year.

'Ah, that's the kind of person he is. The weather doesn't stop him.'

'He must be a strong boy,' she says.

'He is an idiot,' adds Mr. Lee. 'He is always dodging cars being Mr. Tough! When is he ever going to learn?'

'Don't worry Mr. Lee. How's the supermarket? Been treating you well has it?'

'Don't be so funny Laridis! After all I wasn't talking about finding teachers. I was telling her about his road behavior. Do you think I always care about getting you foreigners a job?'

'I was only joking. You seem a little edgy today. Are you ok?'

'We're dealing with money Laridis and yes it is a big deal for me and both of you. Also, Mr. Park has some urgent news for me which I am kind of nervous about.'

'We are going to get the money aren't we? I mean you didn't drag us here for nothing did you?'

'Laridis, could you please hold your horses?' Lee replies.

'Hold your horses? Wow such great English Mr. Lee. You seem to know your idioms.'

'The same as before. Nothing has changed. I practice for three hours every day. What about your Korean young man?'

'I learn enough to get by. I can order food and introduce myself.'

Yuri then interrupts us saying, 'Mr. Lee, we really want to thank you for your hard efforts.'

'Don't thank me. Thank the Labor Office and our good country Korea. Your bad Mr. Lee will never be forgotten of course. I hope he is rotting in hell in a prison. You know that the money you are getting has been paid by his family.'

'Well I am sure they aren't happy,' I reply.

'No, they aren't Laridis. He will forever be a shame to his family.'

'Are we here now?' I ask.

'I think that is the man over there?' asks Yuri. 'I remember him from the office.'

'Yeah, that is him. His name is Mr. Park and don't forget he doesn't speak English. Please be on your best behavior. Please smile and look grateful.'

We get out of the van and make our way into the restaurant for lunch. It is the very same place that we went to last year after bad Mr. Lee had first disappeared. I remember the pictures of Park Chung Hee, the infamous late President and the doting service of the waitresses.

Mr. Park is dressed in an immaculate pin-striped suit with slicked back hair and polished black shoes. He smiles as we bow and beckon to his calls. Once we finally get over all the formalities, we are lead to a large conference room full of waitresses.

'This place is a little over the top don't you think?' I comment.

'Laridis you need to be quiet,' replies Mr. Lee.

'I was just saying something. I cannot stand all this quietness and pandering.'

'Laridis, I warn you. Please be quiet and just be grateful.'

Once seated, we are immediately plied with a huge banquet of food. The dialogue is all in Korean and luckily Yuri can understand some of it. She whispers to me that Mr. Park is speaking as if he is a little angry.

'What's he saying then?' I ask.

'I think, though I am not exactly sure, that he is saying that our old boss never went to prison. That he has a new business south of Seoul!'

'Shit, you are kidding me? Are we going to get our money back?'

'Yes, the money is here but it's not as simple as that.'

'We need to ask our good Mr. Lee what is going on.'

'He may not tell us everything Don. Remember this is a different culture, which is probably why he didn't want any English.'

After we finish, we all stand and shake hands, and white envelopes are exchanged. After a few more pleasantries, we then bid our last farewells to Mr. Park. On the way back to the bus station I ask Mr. Lee if everything is ok. First I ask if there were any complications. Then I ask him about the money we have been compensated. I am a little concerned as the figures on the envelope seem different to what we'd expected.

'Sorry to ask you these things but we couldn't help noticing that something was wrong?'

'What do you want to know?'

'First, forgive me for my not-so-good Korean, but I overheard something about bad Lee never going prison,' says Yuri.

'Correct. He didn't go to prison. The bastard paid the police some money. He was never actually punished. And you know what, it doesn't surprise me one bit. I am incredibly angry about this as you can tell,' Lee replies, again slamming his fist against the car dashboard.

'What do you mean?' I ask tentatively.

'This is South Korea remember. The country I come from. Some call it the hermit kingdom but it is people like him who lower our reputation. I mean all the money he stole from not just you two, but other teachers and parents. And now he is free. How fucked up is this?'

'That sucks. I know what,' I say.

'What?' responds Mr. Lee.

'You should take him out,' I say sarcastically. 'I am joking, but man this is so off.'

'It won't be the end of this. I am tired of this kind of thing,' adds Mr. Lee. 'At least you two have some money.'

'That's our other question. Um, there seems to be a discrepancy. The amounts aren't right.'

'Yes, I know. You got three million won and Yuri received two million.'

'It doesn't make sense. Yuri is totally out of pocket. Daphne told me that Yuri was owed much more. She was at Global for a long time. It was something like four months by the time I had even started, wasn't it Yuri?'

Yuri quickly interjects by saying, 'Don, please it doesn't really matter. You know what, I am happy with what I have, and you should be as well. After all we Don are the lucky ones - at least we are getting some money. What about Daphne, Mona, Kevin, Jason, and Zac? The people before them and the office staff as well. How would they all feel right now knowing that we got something and they didn't?'

'You say that we are lucky?' I interrupt. 'We have been fucked over Yuri, don't you get it?'

'Look, I don't think it's a good time to be talking about money we might have lost. A lot of people suffered more than us and they are getting nothing. What about those poor families who paid for their kid's lessons?' Yuri adds.

'It is the principle though and it's still not fair. My pay was 2,000,000 a month so my calculations say 4,000,000. We are owed much more Mr. Lee.'

'Look kid, I remember you telling me that you'd be thankful for what I could get you. I did a lot of hard work. It wasn't that easy you know.'

'We appreciate it Mr. Lee, don't worry about anything Don says,' adds Yuri.

'Look you can't change it Don. This is all I have for you.'

'This is not the end. I will fight for my remaining part,' I add.

'Again, you will get nowhere kid. This is not your home country. Or have you forgotten? I have done my best for you both and there is nothing more we can do. Just get out of my van and stay away. Go to Suwon and stay there.'

'It's not the last you'll hear about this,' I scream back. 'Let's go now Yuri. I am not so sure this is the great man I once believed in. Before I left this town he said he was sad to see me go – that I was his friend. Now look at what's happened.'

'Think what you like Laridis. Maybe you will wake up one day and remember what I have done for you both and all the horrible stuff that your boss did in the first place.'

I can't bare to look at him while we're waiting for our bus and he knows it. On the way back Yuri and I talk at lengths about what happened. She does her best to calm me down, mostly to save public embarrassment on a packed bus bound for Seoul. Listening to me rant she somehow reminds me of the good things that I actually have as well as the year ahead.

By the time we arrive I can't stop thanking her, 'You were so cool and calm with Mr. Lee. And you are dead right. There are a lot of people who got nothing. I only wish some of us could share it, know what I mean?'

'I do as well. Look Don, you need go home to talk to Linda about this. After all, I know she will understand.'

EPILOGUE
Late March 2004

For the next few weeks, all I can think about is how I had really lost it with Mr. Lee. Linda tells me to put it all behind me and move on but my guilt is too strong. On my way back from classes one afternoon I pass a small temple and notice a monk putting the garbage out so I stop to talk to him and ask if it is ok to come inside. He welcomes me with open arms.

'English ok?' I ask.

'A little,' the elderly monk replies. 'Trouble my friend? Are you ok?'

'I have been angry.'

'Don't be angry. It doesn't solve anything. Listen to your body and your mind my friend and please don't feel any guilt. There is enough of that in society today.'

After meditating for a bit, I leave the temple intent on calling good Mr. Lee to apologize for my behavior the last time I saw him, however I can't get through. The message redirects me to what looks like his home number.

Mrs. Lee answers but she can speak very little English, 'My husband gone. He now jail.'

'What do you mean? He is in prison?'

'Yes, he is in prison. Goodbye teacher Mr. Don.'

In shock, I call JC, hoping that she may shed some light on this news, 'Don, I thought you would have heard by now. It's been on the news for the last few days. The police discovered body parts belonging to bad Mr. Lee in the Han River last week. It looked like some ducks had a real go at him.'

'What do you mean some ducks? Or was it that good Lee actually murdered bad Lee and now he is in jail?' I ask, unable to comprehend the enormity of it all.

'Look, it's too early at this stage to work out what exactly happened, but it seems like something bad went on between the two of them. Something about how good Lee received a tip-off that bad Lee was working in Ilsan near Seoul under a new guise at some English academy.'

'Oh my god JC, can you believe this? You mean he actually did it? Shit, fuck, damn! We talked about this but I wanted to say that I was only joking. Can you believe it? Fuck, our good Mr. Lee he has...'

'Look, I have to go now as I have a class. Take care Don and again I'm sorry that this has happened.'

'Sorry, what does that mean? The wrong man is in prison JC. Fuck it! How can you just say sorry?'

'Like I said I have to go. It doesn't concern you Don. Please don't worry. Just enjoy your life with Linda.'

Furious and confused I try reaching Daniel to get some more news but his answering machine is on:

```
You have reached Daniel and I can't come to the
phone at the moment because I am not in Korea
right now. Please leave a message and one day I
will get back to you.
```

By now I am freaking out swearing obscenities at the unbelievable news I have just heard. It feels as if I have nowhere to run and no one to talk to about what's happened. Yuri is probably in class as she isn't answering her phone whilst Linda is out and won't be back for at least an hour. But I can't wait. I am totally shell shocked. I mean how on earth could things have come to this? How ironic is it that a guy who was only trying to do good by me is now in a prison cell? Surely I could visit him and at least comfort him and let him know that he is not a bad man.

I call the Australian embassy for advice and ask them to explain the protocol for visiting people in prison. However, I am firmly told that only families have the right to do so, particularly in a murder case like this.

Walking around the nearby lake I ponder the kind of year that I have had. For one how did I even end up here? How did this all eventuate? Why was I ripped off? How was it that only two of us were compensated and the rest received jack shit? But there are no answers, not even ducks to talk to.

When I get to the end of my walk I see Linda on her motor bike about to go up the hill to home. I shout out to her frantically and she rides towards me noticing how distraught I am.

She gives me a big hug and offers the words that I need to hear, 'Look Don, I know this is tough and I know this seems all wrong. I know you can't believe that it has come to this, but you have to move on. Put your energy into your students. Out with the old and in with the new I reckon. Trust me, I know it is hard but what can you do?' she asks.

'I could go and see him and apologize. I could tell him how much of a great person he is. After all the last time I saw him I was screaming at him telling him how bad he was and how we had been cheated.'

'They are not going to let you visit him. You will have to write to him and hope someone can pass it on for you. After all it is different here and it could be ages before we know the ruling on this. At least we have each other.'

'True.'

— — —

Biography

Originally from Sydney, in 2003 Bob ventured on a journey of work and travel abroad, finding employment in the education field. Since then he has managed to find a suitable balance between teaching, dabbling in writing, live bands and languages.

As an avid music fan and editor of *Blunt fanzine* (started in 1986) in 2000 he released a book *Blunt: A Biased History of Australian Rock* which was published by Prowling Tiger Press. The tome documented twenty years (80s and 90s) of a burgeoning independent music scene in Sydney and Melbourne.

This new work, *The Year My Hair Fell Out* is loosely based on his first year teaching and living abroad in 2003. He has since spent the last 11 years in different parts of Asia, including South Korea, Japan, and now China.

Bob Blunt departing Incheon Airport, South Korea, 2006